Adèle Hugo

Victor Hugo: A life related by one who has witnessed it

Including a drama in three acts

Adèle Hugo

Victor Hugo: A life related by one who has witnessed it
Including a drama in three acts

ISBN/EAN: 9783744723077

Printed in Europe, USA, Canada, Australia, Japan

Cover: Foto ©Raphael Reischuk / pixelio.de

More available books at **www.hansebooks.com**

CONTENTS.

THE

LIFE OF VICTOR HUGO.

XXXII.

NEWS OF GENERAL HUGO.

Victor suffered, but did not give up his point. Of the
two obstacles against his union, one, that of his age,
would disappear of its own accord; the other, that of
poverty, depended on his own efforts. He therefore set
to work with indefatigable assiduity. During the year
1820, he sent to the Academy of Toulouse "Moses on
the Nile," which gained him another prize. Three prizes
constituted him Master of the Floral Games, and at the
age of eighteen he became a provincial academician.

Abel was not a printer's friend for nothing. Gilé printed
the "Ode to La Vendée" that Victor had just written,
and then a satire. They sold pretty well. Abel then
conceived the idea of a review, which should appear twice
a month; he founded, with his two brothers and several
friends, the *Conservateur Littéraire* to which Victor

contributed largely.   He published "Bug Jargal" in it,
and wrote for it both poetry and prose.   Everything was
quite Royalist in its tendencies, for he associated with no
one but his mother.   His father he saw less than ever, for
it was only twice or thrice a-year at most that he paid a
brief visit of a day or two to Paris.   On these hurried
visits, the General did not even stay at his wife's house.
Their perpetual separations had, as one may easily imagine,
greatly weakened the domestic ties.   Husband and wife
had got used to living apart, and at last their own will
as much as necessity kept them asunder.   The children
had naturally fallen to her share; they had never left
her, she had constrained them in nothing, she had brought
them up in the greatest freedom, she had allowed them
to select their own walk in life, she was to them liberty
and poetry personified.   Their father, on the contrary, was
almost a stranger, who had only made their acquaintance
at Madrid to shut them up in the College of Nobles, and
again in Paris in order to imprison them in M. Cordier's
school, where they were condemned to mathematics in
perpetuity.   For all these reasons, the father's opinions
were not much respected by his sons.   He himself understood the uselessness of combating a few hours in each
year against daily and hourly influence.   He resigned
himself to his fate, and left the result to his children's
after-reflections and natural good sense.   On one occasion,
during one of these journeys, always so few and far between, he saw Eugène and Victor at General Lucotte's.
Victor having expressed himself warmly in favour of the
Vendeans, his father, who had listened to him without

interruption, turning towards General Lucotte, observed
to him,—

"Let us leave all to time.   The child shares his
mother's views; the man will have the opinions of his
father."

XXXIII.

A WORD ABOUT CHATEAUBRIAND.

I HAVE already mentioned that Victor, although quite submissive to his mother in all the daily routine of life, and in his political opinions, had his own opinions in all matters in which nature and art were concerned, and in these was utterly uncontrolled by her. Like everything that smacks of originality, *Atala* had been much ridiculed when it first appeared. The bursts of laughter were still to be heard so lately as in 1819, and a parody, entitled *Ah! là! là!* was supposed to have annihilated the descriptions of Meschacébé and the virgin forests, by occupying twenty pages with the description of a potato-field. Madame Hugo approved of the parody. Victor was energetic in behalf of *Atala*.

The study of Chateaubriand, in whose writings he delighted, very materially modified his ideas on one subject. The "*Génie du Christianisme*," by pourtraying the poetry of Catholicism, had taken the best means of making converts of the poets. Victor, by degrees, adopted this belief, which, in his case, was mixed up with the architecture of cathedrals and the vivid colouring of the Bible, and he abandoned the Voltairian Royalism of his mother, in order to adopt the Christian Royalism of Chateaubriand.

The death of the Duke de Berry inspired Victor to write an ode, which had great success in the Royalist circles. Louis XVIII. recited several times, in the presence of his intimate friends, the strophe that begins—

" Monarque en cheveux blancs, hâte-toi! le temps presse ;
    Un Bourbon," &c.

M. de Chateaubriand, whilst conversing with a Deputy of the Right, M. Agier, alluded to this ode in enthusiastic terms, and informed him that the author was *un enfant sublime,* a wonderful child.

M. Agier, in his *Drapeau blanc,* wrote an article on this ode, and mentioned M. de Chateaubriand's remark. These words of the great writers were repeated everywhere, and Victor became a real celebrity.

He went to M. Agier, in order to thank him for his article, but he durst not face the formidable Chateaubriand, who was astonished at not seeing him, and said so to M. Agier. The Deputy called on Madame Hugo, and mentioned the circumstance to her. She no longer sneered at *Atala,* since its author patronized her son, and she desired Victor to prepare to pay this dreaded visit. He himself felt that as M. de Chateaubriand wished to see him, he could not refuse to go, and he submitted to the honour inflicted on him.

At seven o'clock the next evening, M. Agier came for him. He did not reach No. 27, Rue Saint Dominique, without emotion. He followed his guide across a court-yard, at the far end of which they ascended a flight of stairs. M. Agier rang the bell. A man-servant in a white apron answered the summons, and led the way into the antechamber, and from thence into a large, simply-furnished drawing-room, the chairs of which had grey covers.

Madame de Chateaubriand, who was seated on a sofa, did not stir. M. de Chateaubriand, who was standing leaning against the chimney-piece, did not come forward, but accosted Victor thus :—

" M. Victor Hugo, I am charmed to see you. I have read your verses, those you wrote on ' La Vendée,' and those which you have just written on ' The Death of the Duke de Berry.' Amongst them, in the last especially, there are passages to be found that no poet of the present day could have written. My age and experience give me the painful privilege of boldly speaking the truth, and I honestly confess to you that there are also to be found in your writings passages less pleasing to me. But what is fine in your odes is in reality very fine."

There was no damning with faint praise in anything he had said; nevertheless, there was, in his manner, in his tone of voice, and in his way of picking out passages, something so haughty that Victor felt rather humbled than exalted. He stammered out a confused answer, and longed to be safe at home again.

Two friends of the family, the Marquises of Talaru and of Herbouville, arrived opportunely, and turned the conversation. Victor felt somewhat at his ease again, and

was able to have a good look at the glorious writer, whom
he had only hitherto known by his writings.

M. de Chateaubriand affected a military style; the man
of the pen could not forget the man of the sword. His
neck was imprisoned in a black cravat, which hid the
collar of his shirt: a black greatcoat, buttoned all the
way up, confined his little stooping body. His head was
the finest part of him; it was disproportioned to his
height, but it was a noble-looking, serious head. His
nose was long and straight, his eye keen, his smile bewitching, but it came and went with the rapidity of
lightning, and his mouth would quickly resume its
haughty, severe expression.

It grew dark. No lights were brought in. The
master of the house allowed the conversation to drop.
Victor, who had begun by being nervous when spoken to,
finished by being equally nervous at not being spoken to.
He was delighted when M. Agier rose to go.

M. de Chateaubriand, seeing them about to leave,
invited Victor to come back and see him, telling him he
was always to be found between seven and nine in the
morning.

Victor recrossed the antechamber and courtyard
without stopping to look back. Once in the street, he
breathed again freely.

"Well," said M. Agier, "I hope you are satisfied."

"Yes, at having got safely out of the house."

"What do you mean?" exclaimed the Deputy; "M.
de Chateaubriand was most affable towards you. He
spoke very much to you. You don't know him: some-

times he will be four or five hours without uttering a syllable.   He makes an exception to his general rule, in consenting to receive you so readily, both on state and on private occasions.   If you are not pleased, it is a hard matter to satisfy you."

Victor remained unconvinced.   He liked the author of "Les Martyrs" better in his works than in his drawing-room; and, had it not been for Madame Hugo, whose wishes were all-powerful with her son, he would have taken no further steps to encourage this intimacy.

To gratify his mother, Victor one morning retraced his steps towards the Rue Saint Dominique.   The same servant answered the door.   On this occasion M. de Chateaubriand received him in his private room.   Whilst passing through the drawing-room, he came across Madame de Chateaubriand, who, notwithstanding the earliness of the hour, was going out, and wore one of those bonnets with narrow fronts, then the fashion in the Faubourg Saint Germain.   Victor, who on the occasion of his first visit had hardly noticed her, because she was seated with her back to the light and the evening was advancing, then perceived a tall, thin woman, with a dry expression of countenance, much marked with the small-pox.   She did not stop to notice so young a man.   She condescended, however, to give him a slight bow.

When Victor entered the room, M. de Chateaubriand was in his shirt-sleeves, and had a handkerchief tied over his head; he was seated at a table, with his back to the door, sorting some papers.   He turned round hurriedly.

"Ah, good morning, M. Victor Hugo! I was expecting

you. Sit down. Well, have you been hard at work since we last met? Yes? Have you composed many verses?"

Victor replied that he was always doing something of the kind.

"You are right. Verses—write verses! It is the literature of the skies. You are on a higher platform than I am. The poet is the real author. I, too, have written verses, and am sorry I did not do more. My poetry was better worth reading than my prose. Do you know I once wrote a tragedy? Come, I must read you a scene from it. Pilorge, come here : I want you."

A red-haired, red-whiskered, red-faced individual made his appearance.

"Go and fetch me the manuscript of *Moïse*."

Pilorge was M. de Chateaubriand's secretary, which situation was no sinecure. Not taking into consideration the arranging and keeping in order the manuscripts, the correspondence alone which devolved upon him took up an enormous deal of his time. Besides the original letters that he wrote, and which were signed by M. de Chateaubriand, he had to keep a duplicate of each for a register, in which the illustrious writer, with an eye to posterity, carefully preserved the most unimportant notes. It was Pilorge's business, too, to classify and number every letter which came to the house.

The secretary brought the required manuscript.

The author of "Réne" then read aloud, in a pompous and confident manner, a certain dialogue, then a chorus, in imitation of the chorus in *Athalie* and *Esther*, which

poetry did not impress his listener with the idea that his
verses were superior to his prose. Victor tried hard to
think it all very fine, and positively did succeed in
admiring this verse of the chorus,—

" Et souvent la douleur s'appaise par des chants ; "

and he stuck to it as a drowning man does to a plank.

The servant who had opened the door to him brought
in an enormous bucket filled with water. M. de Chateaubriand untied his handkerchief, and began taking off his
green morocco slippers. Victor rose to take leave, but the
great man would not let him go, but went on undressing
regardless of his presence; he removed his grey swan-
skin pantaloons, his shirt, and his flannel-waistcoat, and
at last got into his tub, allowing the servant to wash and
rub him. Once dried and dressed up again, he cleaned
his teeth, which were very beautiful, and for the use of
which he kept a whole case of dentist's instruments.
Greatly revived by his dabble in the water, he began
to chat in a most animated manner, all the time working
hard at his jaws. This quite charmed Victor. He discussed the censorship.

"What a Government! They are wretched fools.
Thought is freer than they are, and they will hurt
themselves whilst attacking it. If they only compromised themselves it would not matter, but they will anni-
hilate the monarchy at that rate."

Victor carried away a better impression after this
second interview, than after his first. He wrote on M.
de Chateaubriand an ode, entitled " *Le Génie.*" He often

went to see him, but very seldom found him in so happy and cheerful a mood as on the occasion of his second visit. The great author generally had the same coldness of manner that he had exhibited on Victor Hugo's first interview with him. Nothing could be gained by opposing a character of which it was impossible to bend the stiffness or diminish the hauteur. One felt more respect than sympathy for such a man, and one never lost the consciousness of being in company with a genius, instead of a man.

Victor experienced much secret joy on hearing that M. de Chateaubriand was appointed Ambassador to Berlin. He went in person to offer him his congratulations, and bid him good bye.

"What! good bye!" said the Ambassador. "You are to go with me."

Victor stared wildly.

"Yes," replied this lord and master; "I have had you attached to the embassy without asking your consent; and I shall take you with me."

Victor cordially thanked him for his kind intentions on his behalf, but told him that he could not leave his mother.

"Is your mother the only obstacle?" said M. de Chateaubriand, smiling. "Go, you are free. But I regret that you cannot accept my proposal. It would have been an honour for both of us."

Madame de Chateaubriand came into her husband's room. She had never spoken to Victor, and hardly appeared to know him. He was therefore much surprised to see her coming towards him with a smile on her countenance.

"Monsieur Hugo," said she to him, "I've caught you now, and you must help me to do a kind action. I have an infirmary for poor old sick priests. This infirmary costs me more money than I possess, so I have a chocolate manufactory. I sell it rather dear, but it is excellent. Will you buy a pound?"

"Madame," said Victor, who took Madame Chateaubriand's haughty demeanour towards him rather to heart, and who wished to dazzle her, "I will take three pounds of it."

Madame de Chateaubriand was dazzled, but Victor was left penniless.

Madame de Chateaubriand was not the only charitable person of the family. M. de Chateaubriand always had on the mantelpiece in his dining-room piles of five-franc pieces; every minute his servant would appear and present him with begging letters, sometimes from real or pretended emigrants, or from Vendeans and Knights of the Order of St. Louis, just as the case might be. He would approach the pile of money grumblingly, would wrap up the money in the letter, and send it out by the servant.

Madame Sand in the history of her life speaks of the shoals of beggars who pounce upon celebrated authors. It would soon become a systematic expoliation if steps were not taken to prevent it. Every one takes advantage of such characters, the real poor, swindlers, wretched creatures clothed in rags, and decayed ladies with lace to

sell. And these do not always request you to purchase
with so winning a smile as Madame de Chateaubriand did.
On one occasion, a lady beggar of the Faubourg St. Germain, attacked M. Victor Hugo in such terms, that she
drew upon herself the following reply,—

> Voici vos vingt francs, comtesse,
> Quoiqu'on puisse, en verité,
> Manquer à la chárité.
> Qui manque à la politesse.

M. de Chateaubriand gave indiscriminately, and spent
his money in the same manner. Money flowed from his
hands like water. When visiting Charles X. in exile at
Prague, the ex-King questioned him as to his fortune.

"I am as poor as a rat," said he, "and am hail-fellow-
well-met with all Madame de Chateaubriand's pro-
tégés."

"Oh, that won't do," said the King. "Come, Chateaubriand, how much money would it take to make a
rich man of you?"

"Sire, it would be a loss of time. Were you to give
me four millions this morning, I should not have a
farthing left by to-night."

The worst of all this noble contempt of money was,
that it placed the great author at the mercy of money-
lenders. Economy helps to render a man independent
and consequently dignified. Those who opened their
purse-strings to him, assumed to themselves the right of
interfering in his political opinions, and sometimes
the day after a discussion at the Houses of Parliament,

or a newspaper article, they would come to him and threateningly remonstrate with him, and he was obliged to put his pride into his pocket, and listen to them. His advancing years were embittered by monetary embarrassments, and he was obliged to sell his *"Memoirs d'Outre Tombe,"* and to mortgage his very corpse. A pension was accorded him of 20,000 francs a-year, but as he did not die so soon as was expected, they got tired of paying him so much, and reduced the amount to 12,000 francs. He owned that he was in the wrong, for living to such an unconscionable age, and accepted the reduction.

XXXIV.

DEATH OF THE MOTHER.

EVER since her attack on the chest, Madame Hugo had
not enjoyed very good health. She attributed this to
her present apartments. She was accustomed to breathe
the fresh air, and could not get used to four walls. She
could not bear it any longer, and at the commencement
of the year 1821, she left her third storey and established
herself in the Rue Mézières, No. 10, where she had the
benefit of a garden. She was in such a hurry to remove
thither, that she did not allow sufficient time for repair-
ing and repainting the rooms she was about to inhabit.
Once settled down there, in order to hasten matters,
and also, perhaps, through economy, she set to work
herself, and made her two sons work too. One of her
views was, that a man should know how to do everything
for himself on any emergency. She had already accustomed them to help her in the dyeing of cloth, a thing
she particularly excelled in, and they were such adepts
at it, that they could have given lessons to dyers themselves in the art of colouring woollen and silken goods.

From being dyers they easily became white-washers and paper-hangers. They also became gardeners once more: the garden was in a bad state, and it was necessary to set it to rights. It was just the proper season for this work, for spring was drawing near. The earth had to be turned up, and it required digging, sowing, planting, and grafting. Their mother would dig just as hard as they did, and even harder; her love of flowers was so great that it prevented her from feeling fatigued. One day, when she was determined to finish one of the beds, she got heated, and drank a glass of cold water. Almost immediately she began to shiver, and then became feverish.

A second attack of inflammation of the chest set in. Her sons once more watched by her all night; the much-loved invalid recovered from the acute attack, but the lungs were affected; she dragged on for some weeks apparently improving, and took to her bed again towards the close of the month of May. Notwithstanding this relapse, the doctor continued sanguine. Towards the middle of June, she was to all appearance decidedly better, and the two brothers quite expected she would soon be well.

On the 27th June, towards midday, they happened to be both alone with their mother.

"See," said Eugène to Victor, "how nicely mamma is going on. She has not awoke since midnight."

"Yes," said Victor, "she'll soon be well."

He drew near to look at her and to kiss her brow. It was icy cold. She was dead.

Abel was immediately summoned, and undertook the

mournful details. The next day but one, the three
brothers, a few intimate friends, and some people
attracted by Victor's youthful renown, accompanied the
corpse to the Church of St. Sulpice, and from thence to
the Cemetery of Mont Parnasse.

Kind friends led away the three brothers, and tried
to distract their thoughts, but Victor preferred the
indulgence of his grief, and returned alone to the empty
house. He could not bring himself to remain in it, so
he left it once more, and retraced his steps towards the
cemetery. When the gates were closed, he wandered on
to the boulevards, overwhelmed with grief and tired of
life. The ardent desire of having something still to
hope for caused him to wend his way towards the
Rue du Cherche-Midi. It was eleven o'clock at night,
and he expected to find the people at the War Office asleep
and the lights put out; but he perceived that the door
stood wide open, and that the courtyard and the windows
were brilliantly lighted up. He was pushed about by a
group who entered there, indulging in shouts of laughter.
He wished to make his way out, but it was impossible to
take a step in advance. He paused for an instant, and
then, impelled by a strong desire to suffer, he hastened
towards the courtyard, rapidly ascended the great staircase, and entered into a large deserted room, where a play
had just been acted, the stage of which reminded him of
another tomb. He saw his face reflected in a mirror and
noticed that it was deadly pale, and he also saw the crape
round his hat, which he had not removed from his head.
The sight of this brought him to his senses. He fled

precipitately and lost himself in a dark passage, whilst overhead he heard the sounds of music and dancing. He could not resist ascending one flight of stairs, and then another; knowing the plan of the house he directed his course towards a sort of skylight, which lighted the ball-room from above. There, alone, and in darkness, his eyes glued to the window pane, he gazed despairingly on the gay multitude. He soon saw her for whom he sought. She was dressed in white, crowned with flowers, and was dancing with a smile on her countenance.

Mademoiselle Foucher had suffered quite as much as Victor did at the separation that had occurred between the two families. Her father and mother sought to cheer her by taking her to every kind of entertainment. The 29th June was M. Foucher's *fête* day; they had solemnized it to the best of their ability; they had organized a ball, and had got up some private theatricals. *Monsieur Guillaume* was the title of the piece they acted, and Mademoiselle Adèle took the principal female character.

On the eve of that important day M. Foucher heard of the death of his old friend, whom he had not seen for so long, and whose illness he had scarcely heard of. He thought of his daughter, who would be deprived of an entertainment, had she known of it, and he kept the sad intelligence to himself.

The next day Mademoiselle Foucher, dizzy and tired with the gaiety of the preceding evening, was sauntering in the gardens belonging to the War Office. She perceived Victor coming in, at the sight of whom and of his pale face she knew immediately that some misfortune had happened.

She ran up to him. " What is the matter ? "

" My mother is dead ! I buried her yesterday."

" And I was dancing at the time ! "

He saw at once that she had known nothing about it. They began to sob together, and thus were they betrothed.

XXXV.

LA ROCHE-GUYON.

THE mourners at Madame Hugo's funeral had noticed at the entrance to the Chapel of the Virgin a young priest, who had listened to the service, and who had also visited the cemetery and thrown his shovelful of earth on the coffin. This priest was about thirty years of age: his silky hair formed a complete ring round his tonsure; his linen and the cloth of his cassock were wonderfully fine for a priest. His personal appearance displayed an air of distinction and high breeding.

It was the Duke de Rohan. He had but just married when his wife died—burnt to death. In despair, he had taken orders, and he was sub-deacon at the Seminary of Saint Sulpice.

Some years after, he requested, through a mutual friend, permission to visit Victor. Victor replied that he should rather take the initiative, and thank M. de Rohan for having followed his mother to the grave. He went to the Seminary: the Abbé was engaged in the chapel at the time. He was shown into his cell, the only furniture of which consisted in a wooden table, a wooden bed, and a wooden crucifix. He was touched by this indifference to worldly matters in the person of a man of the world, boasting so noble a name.

The Abbé hastened to meet him, and treated him with cordial simplicity. He began by mentioning the dead, with real emotion. This went to the heart of the son at once. He then led the conversation to less sad matters, complimented Victor on his verses, all of which were known to him; foretold that his future career would be a glorious one; informed him that as for himself he had given up everything; that he wished for no clerical honours; and that had it not been for his delicate health, he would have become a Trappist, and added that his ambition was now centred in becoming the curate of his native village.

Victor took to him greatly, and frequently called on him until the vacation season at the Seminary. He spent this time in his native village, and tried hard to persuade Victor to accompany him thither, rather than to remain in the house where his mother had died. Victor did not do so, however, but promised to follow him there.

One morning, therefore, in the month of August, he seated himself in the diligence with the mutual friend who had brought them together, and who was M. Rocher. The village was La Roche-Guyon. When they reached the banks of the Seine, M. Rocher hailed the ferry-boat. When half-way across, the two guests perceived their friend waving his handkerchief from the balcony of the country-house. When they reached the principal court the young seminarist received them on the flight of steps, and behind him were standing a dozen juvenile majordomo-abbés and valets, which rather unsettled Victor's mind as to the Duke's humility.

The castellan of La Roche-Guyon was nevertheless as kind and demonstrative in manner as he had been when seminarist of Saint Sulpice. Dinner awaited the visitors: there were about a dozen guests, almost all of them priests. The Duke placed Victor on his right-hand side, and was charming, but a princely etiquette characterized the dinner. The guests treated the master of the house with ceremonious respect; they called him by no other name than *monseigneur*, with the exception of one abbot who was afterwards almoner to the Duchess de Berry, and who called him *altesse*. Behind His Highness stood a tall, ill-made man, with a sword by his side and a table napkin under his arm. Victor was much surprised, in answer to his inquiries as to who he was, to receive the following answer from the Duke:—

" It's the Mayor of La Roche-Guyon."

Victor no longer placed such implicit belief in the Duke's assertion that he only desired the position of curate at La Roche-Guyon.

After dinner they were shown over the château, which was very magnificent and manorial. Victor much admired some very fine pictures, amongst which were the duel of Jarnac and La Rochefoucault. The Duke de Rohan claimed to be a descendant of Jarnac, and rather boasted of it. The subject of the picture was Jarnac hamstringing his adversary with his dirk.

One of the greatest curiosities in the castle was a bed

ten feet wide in carved oak, hung with alternate stripes of garnet-coloured velvet and tapestry worked in gold and silk, and celebrated as a bed in which Henry IV. had slept.

The Duke's bedchamber bore no resemblance to his cell : it was furnished with every luxury. It opened on a kind of boudoir drawing-room : the table and piano were covered with volumes of sacred music, richly bound, and all bearing the following inscriptions in letters of gold :— " Sa Seigneurie le Duc de Rohan Chabot, Duc de Monbazon, Duc de Beaumont, Prince de Léon, Pair de France."

In front of the piano hung the Duke's portrait, painted by Gerard, in the full uniform of a red musketeer. These words were inlaid in the wood :—" S. A. le Prince de Léon."

It was too late to visit the park. Conversation ensued, after which the Duke led Victor into a large and rich Gothic chamber, the windows of which overlooked the Seine. This room was still further distinguished by the fact of its having been once occupied by the Duke of Larochefoucault, the author of the " Maxims."

The next morning, Victor, who rose at dawn, went out alone into the park, which extended over the hill behind the house. The house itself stood on the slope of the hill, half-way up. The remains of the Tour de Guy, the original castle, which gave its name to the village (*La Roche à Guy*, afterwards *La Roche-Guyarde*, and finally *La Roche-Guyon*), first attracted his attention. " Nothing remained of it but a circular wall, which was very thick, and covered with ivy and moss. The ceiling of its four floors had all crumbled away to the ground one after the other, and there formed an enormous pile of rubbish. A narrow staircase, without a balustrade, and broken in many places, led up spirally through the inside of the wall to the summit." The ruin was accurately described in these words by our hero, under the name of the Tower of Vermund the Outlaw, in his " Hans of Iceland," the tale that he was hard at work upon at that time.

The sound of a bell brought him back to the house: he thought it might be for breakfast, but it was for mass. The chapel was an underground one, and built in the rock. In wandering through the crypt he heard the sound of an harmonicon. He pushed open a door and saw a chapel splendidly illuminated. A full-sized figure of Christ rendered the scene almost life-like : a jet of vermilion gushed from his wounds; the woodwork as well as the linen which enveloped the figure, was painted white, the body was flesh-coloured, the eyes were made of enamel, and the crown was of real thorns. Behind this figure of Christ, a cloud of seraphim in high relief, similar to those at St. Roch, stood out from amongst gilt rays. All the abbés of the establishment were present. The curate of La Roche-Guyon was repeating mass, and was aided by the Duke, who wore the dress of a deacon ; but it was easy to see that the deacon was not the subordinate.

Victor had intended remaining there two months, but he had had enough of it after four days had elapsed. The next day but one after his arrival he wrote to a friend at Paris:—" These enormous gilded drawing-rooms, these broad terraces, and above all, these tall obsequious

footmen, fatigue me. I like nothing here but the wooded
hill, the old towers, and above all, the captivating society
of this amiable Duke of Rohan, one of my dearest
friends, and one most worthy of being dearly loved.
I am leaving him directly, but he is happy. What need
has he of me, who am unhappy? The Duchess of Berry,
who is at Rosny, is to visit the Castle in a few days.
M. de Rohan would like to detain me here, at least
until she arrives, but I am on my guard against his
kindness. I do not choose that my singular position
should expose me to become the client of a man, whom
my social position places in the light of friend. I love
the Duke de Rohan for himself alone, for his noble
nature, but not for the material services he is likely to
render me."

He left, leaving behind him the friend who had accompanied him thither, and who vainly tried to detain him,
saying that by thus hurrying his departure, he would vex
the Duke, who liked him very much.

"I, too, like him very much," said Victor, "but I
like him best in his cell or at my own house."

Between Rolleboise and Mantes there is a hill, which
he ascended on foot. He there fell in with a young lady,
who had descended from her carriage, and in order to see
the scenery better had clambered on a steep hillock. She
appeared to find it difficult to get down, and was only
accompanied by an old man, who had to take every care
not to slip himself. Victor drew near and offered her his
hand, which was cordially accepted. At Rosny, where
he stopped to visit the Castle, he was told that the

Duchess of Berry had just started from thence for La Roche-Guyon with M. de Meynard, and that they must have passed each other on the road. The Duchess of Berry little knew that she was touching the hand which had written the ode on her husband's death.

It is pleasant to recall old memories. · In 1835, M. Victor Hugo, when again travelling on this same road, wished to revisit La Roche-Guyon. The Castle no longer belonged to the Duke: he had sold it to Madame de Liancourt. The Duchess was very hospitable towards strangers. A servant good-naturedly showed them over all the rooms, and amongst other apartments introduced them into one which he said had been occupied by Victor Hugo, and which happened not to be the right one. He then begged the visitor to inscribe his name in a book kept for the purpose. M. Victor Hugo was just going to do so, when in turning over the registry to find a blank page he saw his name at the end of some verses written in a little round-hand. Fearing that he should not be able to imitate well enough this signature, so as not to be suspected of forgery, he wrote: *In se magna ruunt,* and signed it *Lucain.*

XXXVI.

FRAGMENTS FROM LETTERS.

GENERAL Hugo offered to find means to support his sons if they would adopt a more regular and less speculative profession than that of literature. Victor declined, and found himself dependent on his own exertions. All his worldly goods consisted in eight hundred francs, which he had gained by his pen. With this small capital he launched into the unknown world.

His public life commenced with a considerable amount of notoriety, and the world in general sought him out. He was asked everywhere, and I perceive, amongst others, the following invitation :—

"The Count of Chabrol, Préfet of the Seine, and the Countess of Chabrol, request the pleasure of the company of M. Victor Hugo, Member of the Academy of Floral Games, to dinner on Saturday, the 29th December, at half-past five." But whenever he entered the house and remembered that his mother was no longer there to welcome him, he felt that he stood alone in the world. He could not live thus, and demanding an interview with M. Foucher, requested the hand of his daughter.

He had no property, nothing but a stout heart and the affections of the young girl for whom he petitioned. M. and Madame Foucher, out of love for their daughter, and deeply sympathizing with the poor young man who was struggling to get on in life, unaided, and who so boldly confronted his fate, consented to the marriage, only postponing it for a while till Victor's circumstances should appear a little brighter.

Armed with this promise, he set to work again with renewed vigour. He undertook all kinds of work— journalism, odes, novels, and plays. For two long years he led an active, though feverish and excited existence, full of dreams, hopes, and anxieties. He had obtained the consent of one of the parties interested in the matter, but he needed also another. His father must be asked— would he agree? He delayed asking until the necessary time came. The following extracts from some of his letters will give an idea of his occupations and of his state of mind during these two years:—

" Nothing is to be despaired of, and a little check does not damp great courage. I neither conceal from myself the uncertainties, nor even the gloomy prospects, of the future; but I have learnt from a strong-minded mother that one may, to a certain extent, command events. Many walk with trembling steps on firm ground; but when one enjoys a quiet conscience, and possesses a legitimate object, one must walk with a firm step on ground that sinks and trembles.

"I am now engaged on purely literary work, work which, at all events, gives me moral liberty whilst I look forward to social independence. Literature, considered as a source of private satisfaction, affords a real happiness when all goes well, and a resource and consolation in time of trouble. Even now, I find it able to snatch me from the turmoil of the small society of a little town, and procure for me an isolation in which I can indulge to my heart's content in sad and sweet ideas. In my solitude, it seems to me that I am near the two beings who constitute my whole life, although the one lives far from me, and the other, alas! lives no more. My material existence is too unimportant and neglected to interfere with or prevent my seeking to create for myself an ideal existence, peopled with those most dear to me. Thanks to literature, I am able to do so."

Unfortunately, literature was not always a consolation to him. His rising reputation exposed him to attacks already somewhat violent. He was not yet inured to attacks and ill-feeling, and he was not so indifferent to them as long habit ultimately causes us to be. His usual melancholy rendered him more sensible to everything of the kind, and made him exaggerate the importance of these stings.

". . . You little know either how much or how often I am annoyed. Putting my private sorrows and my domestic anxieties quite out of the question, I still have to resign myself to all the unpleasantnesses attendant on literary jealousies. I know not what demon could have urged me to choose a career, where every step is tram-

melled by some secret opposition or some base rivalry. It
is pitiable, and I blush for literature.   It is tiresome to
awake every morning the butt of stinging little attacks
from a herd of enemies whom one has never injured, and
whom, for the most part, one has never seen.   I would willingly inspire you with a feeling of esteem for this noble
and great profession of letters; but I am obliged to own
that, in following it, one makes strange discoveries of
human baseness.   It is, so to speak, a deep swamp, in
which those must plunge who are not provided with wings
to keep them above the mire and dirt.   I, who do not
possess the wings of genius, but who have become isolated
owing to my peculiar disposition, am sometimes inclined
to laugh at all the little injuries people seek to do me;
but oftener, I must admit, to the shame of my philosophy, I am ready to get angry with them.   You will perhaps think, with some show of reason, that as I am occupied with so many important interests, I ought to be
indifferent to such annoyances; but it is precisely the state
of irritation I suffer which renders them insupportable to
me: that which would only teaze me if I were happy, is
now odious to me.   I suffer when wretched flies come and
settle on my wounds.   Let us drop the subject—it is not
worth notice: they are not worthy the pen I am using,
nor the paper on which I write. . ."

But soon he began to treat the matter with more firm-
ness and self-respect :—

"I find on my return a little literary annoyance—just
enough to teach me patience.   But I am as indifferent to
malice as I am grateful for good advice.   Scattered about

the world are abortions, who are not satisfied with being despised, and demand my hatred; they will not obtain it."

Very soon he began to reflect, and there grew up in him that idea of universal toleration, under the influence of which was written his poem, *La Prière pour Tous*, and all his plays.

" . . . You cannot imagine the warmth of fellow-feeling with which I regard all the human race. I early accustomed myself to look for the motive when anyone desired to do me harm, and from that time my anger has almost always changed into a profound feeling of compassion. It happens, not unfrequently, that I actually find a good and praiseworthy principle at the root of a bad action. Thus, you will allow that there is but small merit in forgiving others and comforting oneself when wronged."

He explained to his future wife in what light he regarded poetry, and how it affected him :—

" In the word poetry is the expression of virtue. An intellect capable of high aspirations and a great poetic talent generally go together. Poetry proceeds only from the higher faculties of the mind, and may be indicated as clearly by a good action as by fine verses."

Then, in another letter, he says :—

" . . . Verses alone do not constitute poetry. The poetry lies in the ideas, and they proceed from the soul. Verses are but as fine clothing on a handsome body. Poetry may express itself in prose, but is most perfect when embellished by the gracefulness and majesty of verse. It is the poetry of the soul that inspires men to noble sentiments and noble actions, as well as to noble writings. A bad man who is a poet, is a degraded being, sunk lower and more blameable than a bad man who is not a poet . . ."

His idea of love was not inferior to that of poetry.

"Within us dwells an immaterial existence, living as if in exile whilst confined in our bodies, which it must eternally survive. This existence, possessing more refined feelings and a better nature than the body, we call the soul. The soul originates every high aspiration and every best affection. By it we obtain our conception of God Himself, and of heaven. The soul, which is raised so far above the body to which it is united, would live on earth in hopeless isolation, if it were not permitted to choose from amongst all other souls a companion to share with it in the sorrows of life, and the hopes of eternity. When two souls which have thus, for a longer or shorter time, recognized each other amongst the crowd; when they discover that they agree in their ideas, and understand one another; in a word, when they perceive that they are one; from that moment there is established between them a union as warm and as pure as they are—a union which is begun on earth, only to finish in heaven.

"This union is *love*, true love, such as, indeed, few men understand; such a love is a kind of religion, which renders the beloved object a divinity, which lives on devotion and enthusiasm, and for which the greatest sacrifices are in reality the sweetest pleasures. . . ."

" . . . Love, in its divine and real meaning, elevates every sentiment far above this miserable human sphere; it unites us to an angel who exalts us continually towards heaven."

His affairs did not advance as he could have wished. Promises on which he had relied were never performed, unforeseen obstacles were separating him from the goal which he imagined he was about to reach, and he felt discouraged. He wrote thus to Monsieur Foucher:—

" . . . All my future career is veiled once more in obscurity. There is nothing positive, nothing certain about it. I would fain rest assured of something, were it even misfortune: at any rate, if I could only be advancing, knowing whither progress would tend. As it is, I am obliged to wait. My only qualities, which consisted in activity and energy for work, are now paralyzed; and circumstances require of me *patience*, a virtue I have not, and probably never shall possess. . . . It is impossible that this state of stagnation should last: I shall do all in my power to put a stop to it. I would rather die carried away by the stream, than drown myself in a ditch."

M. Foucher tried to comfort him.

" . . . I can understand how you feel. Louis XIV. once said, alluding to a poor officer who preferred the cross of the order of Saint Louis to a pension, "He is not yet crushed!" I could say the same of a certain young man, who prefers misfortune to the paralysing uncertainty which circumstances place between his present and his future career. Nevertheless, matters do not appear to me to be getting worse. Let us wait and see.

Obstacles will not always prove insurmountable, and until we can conquer, let us occupy our impatience by working steadily in the field that no one can take away from us. Let us work. Literature is a vast field; you have sown it, and now we must await the harvest. Whether the fruit be sweet or bitter, ripe or unripe, we are bound to accept it, and it matters but little."

Whilst harassed by so many cares and impediments, by so many hopes and uncertainties, one thing in him never varied: this was the firm determination only to succeed by legitimate means, which should never cost him a disturbed conscience. His determination to deserve happiness was never less powerful than his efforts to obtain it.

". . . If, in order to advance the period of my happiness, I do not act in opposition to my nature, it will be a great thing in my favour. It is a cruel position, that of a young man, independent in his principles, affections, and desires, and yet dependent on account of his age and his fortune. Yes, if I escape from this trial as pure as I was when I entered upon it, I shall consider that I deserve to be esteemed for myself alone. I must trample many cares under foot, for I must go through much tribulation. . ."

". . . Every path is suited to me, provided one can walk in it firmly and uprightly, without grovelling on one's belly, or lowering one's dignity. These were my sentiments, when I told you that I infinitely preferred to earn my livelihood by working for it, rather than expect fortune from the haughty benevolence of men in high position. There are many ways of making one's fortune, and I should have already made mine if I had condescended to buy favours with flattering words. This is not my way. What remains to a young man, who disdains advancement under such circumstances? Nothing except the reward of a quiet conscience, and the preservation of self-respect. It is necessary to make one's way nobly and openly, and to get on as well as one can without rubbing against or upsetting others, leaving the issue to God's justice."

I add a few more lines, in order to show how much he desired to stand alone, and not to place a blind confidence in the opinions and ideas he had imbibed from others.

". . . I acknowledge that I think but little of what is conventional in the matter of popular beliefs or traditions. I consider that a man ought to examine everything by the light of reason, before he accepts it. If, after all, he is mistaken, it is not then his fault."

LAMENNAIS BECOMES VICTOR HUGO'S CONFESSOR.

HE began about that time to write the "*Han d'Islande.*" In one of his letters he says:—

"Last May, feeling anxious to promulgate certain ideas which had taken hold of me, and that our French verse cannot express, I undertook to write a novel in prose. My soul was full to overflowing with love, melancholy, and youth. I dared not confide in any human being, so I chose a dumb confidant—the paper on which I wrote. I knew, also, that this piece of work might bring me in a little money; but this was only a secondary consideration when I commenced my book. I sought some place wherein to deposit the agitating feelings which oppressed my young and bleeding heart, something to still the bitterness of my regrets and the uncertainty of my hopes. I wished to portray a young girl who realized in her person the ideal of every fresh and poetic image, and thus console myself sadly by retracing the image of her who was lost to me, or at least who only appeared to me in the far-off future.

I wished to place by the side of this young girl a youth, not such as I really was, but such as I desired to be. These two characters governed the development of a plot, partly historical, partly imaginative, and brought out a great moral lesson, which formed the foundation of the tale.   Besides the two principal characters, I introduced several others, to give variety and effect, and to set the wheels in motion.   These were grouped in various plots, according to the importance of the parts they were to play.   The whole novel was a long drama, the scenes of which were pictures, where the want of decorations and costume were made up for by descriptive writing.   In addition to this, every person spoke for himself.   Walter Scott first gave me the idea, and I wished to attempt it in order to improve our French literature.   I spent much time in collecting historical and geographical material for this tale, and still more time in ripening the plot, in disposing of the groups, and combining the details.   I employed all my poor faculties in this composition, so that when I wrote the first line of it I knew what the last would be.   I had hardly began it, however, when terrible misfortune dispersed all my ideas and annihilated all my projects.   I forgot all about my undertaking. . . . . "

M. de Chateaubriand was nominated Master of the Floral Games.   The announcement was to be made to him by an academician.   Six were then in Paris, one of whom was the colleague of the newly-made head of the *Chambre des Pairs;* but Victor, who was the youngest, was the one selected.

Our hero had kept up a correspondence with M. Alexandre Soumet. One day he received a visit from a man who was about forty years of age, handsome, of pleasant manners, and who, when he smiled, displayed a very fine set of teeth. This was M. Soumet, who had come to settle in Paris. He was a ready-made friend. M. Soumet exactly realized the vulgar ideal of a poetical countenance. Long black eyelashes shaded his eyes, which he was in the habit of raising to heaven when he spoke. His mouth had a seraphic expression : his want of hair was supplied by a tuft, into which he contrived to throw the wildness of inspiration. He was an odd mixture of the knight and the bard, rather provincial, not unacquainted with Parnassus, and beneath his superficial insipidity lay concealed much uprightness of purpose, a very uncommon amount of generosity, and steadfastness equal to any emergency.

During the same week, Victor was called upon by the Duke de Rohan, who had returned to winter in Paris, and who was about to become a plain seminarist once more. One evening, when Victor was paying him a visit in his cell, an old, decrepit priest entered. His head, which he could no longer hold up, drooped on his breast. He walked with trembling steps, leaning on a stick which reached two feet above his bald head. A shabby great-coat and a pair of trousers almost threadbare completed his attire. The old man was radiant. " You appear very joyous," said the Duke. " Some good luck has befallen you ? "

"Yes," said the old man. " My income as Vicar of St. Nicholas du Chardonnet amounted to four hundred

and fifty francs a-year : my salary has just been reduced
to three hundred and fifty. I thank God for it. I feared
that, being so near death, there would be no time left for
my faith to be tried."

Victor gazed on the man to see if he was talking
seriously; but the dying man would not have joked about
the grave, and Victor read in his countenance that he
spoke the truth.

Some days after this, the Duke, when calling on him,
found him pre-occupied and silent, and led the conversation to the old priest.

"See," said he, "he is old, he is infirm, he is wretched,
he has but a mouthful of bread, and half of that is taken
from him, and yet he is happiness itself. Such is religion.
Suppose you only looked on it in a philosophical light, is
not the highest philosophy that which turns our sorrows
into joys?"

"But I am religious."

"Have you a confessor?"

"No."

"You must have one.   I will see to that."

Victor was passing through one of those moments of
despair when a man cares not what becomes of him, and
when he allows things to happen without attempting to
interfere. He was, therefore, quite willing to confess the
sins of a life concerning which he had nothing to conceal. The Duke had but little difficulty in persuading
him to do as he wished, and, in order that he might not
change his mind, called for him the following morning.

Victor was just going to sit down to breakfast, and was

about to partake of a couple of eggs and a glass of water
when the Duke made his appearance.

"Don't eat your breakfast," said he, "we will go and
breakfast together with the Abbé Frayssinous."

The Abbé Frayssinous was that year the fashionable
preacher. He denominated his sermons *conferences*, and
called his hearers *gentlemen*, instead of *brethren*, in consequence of which the Church of St. Sulpice could not
contain the crowds who came to hear him.

He lived at the Abbaye-aux-Bois, where he owned a
single room, which served him for bed-room, drawing and
dining-room. He was expecting his two guests, and gave
them a breakfast very similar to the one Victor had left
untouched at home. The want of victuals was amply
made up for by his flow of words.

The preacher began his career as future director of
Victor's conscience by tracing out for him the line of
conduct he was bound to adopt. Religion did not require
her followers to shut themselves up in the cloister, or to cut
themselves off from all terrestrial interests. God did not
confer talents on a man in order that he should hide them
under a bushel, but that he should employ them in the
cause of truth. One of the best ways of propagating the
faith was to live in the world and offer a bright example
by word and deed. Success was strength. It was necessary, therefore, to do everything in one's power to succeed.
Victor must not devote himself to literature alone; he
must aspire to political power. The clergy relied on him
and would help him.

This worldly and convenient religion did not suit Victor

at all.   The Abbé settled the matter by speaking well
of the Jesuits, and evil of M. de Chateaubriand, whom
he treated as a disguised Jacobin, all the more dangerous
because he wore a mask.

As he was leaving, Victor told the Duke of Rohan that
the Abbé Frayssinous was very unlike the old vicar, and
that he should never be his director.

"But it won't do to take the first who comes.   If you
select some common priest, you will direct him instead
of he you.   You must have an intelligent man.   Come:
will you have an austere one?   Will you accept Lamennais?"

"Lamennais, and welcome."

It was agreed upon that they should start the next
day.

As Victor was returning, he met M. Soumet on the
stairs.

"My friend," said M. de Soumet, "I beg to inform
you that you are invited to dine to-day with Mademoiselle
Duchesnois.   This astonishes you!   You do not know
her, but she knows you.   Her head is full of your
verses."

Victor wished to refuse, and said that he was not in the
humour to be a very agreeable guest.

"All the more reason that you should have some
amusement; beside which, I promised for you, and if I
do not bring you with me, Mademoiselle Duchesnois has
threatened to refuse her part in my play."

They were rehearsing his *Clytemnestre*, at the Théâtre
Français, and his Orestes was Talma.

Victor allowed himself to be persuaded. The two friends set out, and soon reached a little house situated in the Rue de la Tour des Dames. A winding staircase, lighted by au alabaster lamp, conducted them to a room whose furniture was in the style of the Empire, and which made up for want of taste by having cost an enormous price. They passed through one drawing-room and reached a second, when M. Soumet exclaimed, " Here he is ! "

A door opened, and a woman appeared. Her neck and shoulders were frightfully bare. She thanked Victor very much, and, whilst conversing with him about his odes, led the way into a boudoir, where another actress was seated, who was stout and handsome, although pitted with the small-pox ; her neck and shoulders were as bare as those of her hostess : this was Mademoiselle Leverd.

There was a third female guest Madame Sophie Gay, whose comic opera, *Le Maître de Chapelle*, was that very evening to be performed for the first time. She complimented Victor, but was not astonished at seeing him such a mere school-boy, as her own daughter Delphine, who was scarcely grown up, also composed exquisite odes ; and she suggested that they should give a soirée, at which each of the young people should repeat verses in turn.

The dinner was first-rate. Victor sat between Mademoiselle Duchesnois and Mademoiselle Leverd, and every now and then his thoughts would revert to the singular day he had spent. It had begun by a breakfast, at which he was placed between two curates, and terminated by a dinner, where he was seated between two actresses.

M. Soumet, who was from the south of France, and was very quick at making friends, addressed the two actresses with the utmost familiarity, and called them at once by their own names. "I say, Leverd!" . . . "Duchesnois, have you heard?" . . . These manners shocked Victor, who had never in his life spoken thus to any actress whatever, nor called her anything but madame.

Madame Gay presented them with a private box for the first representation of her play. They therefore set off to witness the performance of the *Maître de Chapelle*. The box was in the centre of the house, and had three front seats in it. The tragedian and the comedian placed Victor between them. His youthful celebrity, and above all, his grave and bashful mien, attracted them, and they played him a thousand tricks, which annoyed rather than pleased him. He thought the piece would never come to an end, and cared for no part of it but the last scene.

"Well," said M. de Soumet, whilst accompanying him home, "I hope you are pleased with your evening? The greatest tragedian of the day, the wittiest comedian, and the most literary of women, have thought of no one but you. Good heavens! how anxiously Duchesnois and Leverd inquired, when you were bidding them good-by, what day you would come to see them again! Come, now, which of the two shall you go and see to-morrow?"

"To-morrow," said Victor, "I shall call on the Abbé Lamennais."

These half-naked women, addressing him and each other with so much familiarity, belonged to a sphere very different from that of which his mourning youthfulness had dreamed. He rose the next day more than ever predisposed to a severe and religious life, and was glad to see the Duke of Rohan coming towards the house. They got into a carriage together, and drove off towards the Faubourg Saint Jacques.

Victor caught sight of a tall tree overhanging the courtyard of the Deaf and Dumb Asylum.

" That tree is an old acquaintance of mine," said he to the Duke. " I lived in this neighbourhood the greater part of my childhood. Does the Abbé de Lamennais live near here ? "

" Close by."

The carriage drove into the cul-de-sac of the Feuillantines. He stopped in front of the gate.

" What ! " exclaimed Victor, " does the Abbé de Lamennais lodge at the Feuillantines ? "

" Yes; but what is there so astonishing in this ? "

Victor told him that he had spent his childhood at this identical house, Les Feuillantines. They entered the apartment formerly occupied by Madame Hugo. Nothing was changed in it, except that for the moment everything was in disorder : the dining-room and the drawing-room were crowded with trunks and parcels, and amongst them moved about a weakly little man, with a bilious-looking face, and large and beautiful but restless eyes ; his nose all but touched his chin. His childish-looking mouth formed a wonderful contrast to his other features, which were harassed and nervous-looking.

This little man was but poorly clothed. He wore an old great-coat of grey cloth, which displayed a shirt of brownish linen, and a cravat originally of black silk, but now reduced to a mere rag: the shortened trousers scarcely reached his lean ankles, and permitted a pair of stockings of a faded blue colour to be seen.   At every step he took, the treble row of nails with which his coarse shoes were fastened clanged against the ground.

"Dear Abbé," said the Duke, "I bring you a penitent."

He introduced Victor to him, and M. Lamennais offered him his hand.

Victor came at the wrong moment to the confessional, in the middle of a move.   The Abbé Caron, with whom M. de Lamennais resided, was quitting the Feuillantines, and M. de Lamennais was to leave that very night.   He gave Victor his new address, and made an appointment with him.

Victor attended, and confessed himself very seriously and with scrupulous and conscientious minuteness.   His greatest sin consisted of the temptations to which he had been subjected by the demoiselles Duchesnois and Leverd. M. de Lamennais, perceiving that these really were his greatest crimes, substituted in future a quiet chat for confession.

XXXVIII.

A WEDDING.

WE now find our hero installed in the Rue du Dragon, No. 30. He kept house with a young cousin of his, a son of Madame Hugo's brother, who had come from Nantes to study the law. They had hired together a garret, in two compartments. One of these they turned into a drawing-room : its beauty consisted in a marble chimney-piece, above. which hung the golden lily of the Floral Games. The other compartment was an ill-lighted, narrow alcove, which held the two beds with some difficulty.

Victor had seven hundred francs of his own, and on this he existed for a year. Those who wished to know how he managed it, must read the budget of Marius, in the "Misérables." He never borrowed a farthing, and yet would often lend his friend five francs. He, nevertheless, contrived to buy a superb blue coat, with gold buttons, and to return by a *déjeuner*, that cost him two louis, the hospitality of M. Henri Delatouche, who, after inviting him to his pretty and comfortable apartment, decorated with tripods and statues, had treated him to a banquet of plain boiled potatoes and a cup of tea.

The cousins had one cupboard between them. Some will think that was a good deal. It was a good deal for Victor, who boasted but three shirts. But the Nantes man possessed a provincial's stock of linen. The shelves were weighed down with the enormous weight of his shirts, of which he took great care, and which he sent to Nantes to be washed. He was a very orderly youth, and very careful to wear each article in the exact order in which it came from the wash. He was so rich in linen that the shirts that had been longest washed had time to grow yellow before they were worn, and thus formed a striking contrast with Victor's, who, as he only owned three, and was obliged to put them on the moment they were returned to him, was always to be seen in dazzling white linen.

Victor and his cousin were fast friends: the latter was kind-hearted and hard-working. Once a-week, Victor would call at the War Office. M. Foucher would not allow of his coming oftener, whilst his marriage was so unlikely to take place. But Madame Foucher rather tempered the paternal severity by often promenading with her daughter in the gardens of the Luxembourg, and sanctioning their meetings in that place. On the other hand, Victor often received visitors in his garret. M. Soumet brought several of his friends to call, amongst others, M. Alexandre Guiraud, M. Pichat, M. Jules Lefèvre, &c. M. Soumet, M. Guiraud, and M. Pichat were engaged in theatrical affairs; and perceiving that a new style was coming into fashion, although they had no power to influence it, they revived tragedy. They desired, rather than determined, to induce this change, and were too timid to venture on anything. M. Soumet, one day, confided to Victor the dilemma he was in. Hugo had written the following line in his *Clytemnestre* :—

Quelle hospitalité funeste je te rends !

"Well, what of that?" said Victor.

"I don't much like to allow this line to be recited on the occasion of the performance."

"Why not?"

"Are you not afraid of this epithet, that seems to stride over the hemistich?"

"Oh," said Victor, "I will make them take longer strides than that!"

M. Soumet went away somewhat reassured, but he soon took fright again, and insisted on Talma's saying,—

Quelle hospitalité, Pylade, je te rends !

Talma also acted in the *Macchabées* of M. Guiraud. M. Pichat's *Léonidas* had but a partial success, and its author lasted not much longer than his composition. M. Pichat, who was very broad-shouldered, with thick black hair, and the manners of a drum-major, died very young.

M. Jules Lefèvre, although he did not write tragedies, was, nevertheless, very tragical himself. He assumed the Byronic style, his hair floating in the wind, and having a deep-set eye and hollow voice. He wrote wonderful but incomprehensible verses, he spoke little, he was mysterious, a fatalist, and gloomy. He lost all these tendencies by a rich marriage, and a happy home, and " Lara" found out, in this way, that he was really a very good fellow.

M. Emile Deschamps, with his easy-going manner and good-nature, made one of this group. Wherever he visited he induced people to put faith in rising merit. His own verses, which were of a tolerant and conciliating originality, helped to convert the timid portion of the public. His misfortune consisted in his having been too well received: he was inundated with invitations to parties, and with requests to write in albums; and from impulse, rather than from want of power, he too often brought his poetry down to their level. He was a deep thinker coined into a man of the world.

The Pleiades were increased in number by Alfred de Vigny, who was then a captain in the Fourth Regiment of the Guards. He came one morning to fetch Emile Deschamps and Victor Hugo, and took them in a phaeton to breakfast at Courbevoie, where his regiment was stationed; the three poets agreed to talk in rhyme only during the whole of the drive, and engaged in an absurd conversation, and in extemporaneous bursts, which made the driver think that they were three idiots.

M. Soumet introduced Victor to Madame Gay, whose daughter, Delphine, welcomed him quite fraternally. Madame Gay informed them that her daughter's talent for poetry came quite of its own accord, when she was fourteen years of age. It burst upon her one autumn evening while she was walking alone through an avenue of large trees. Madame Gay, who was a writer herself, had not thrown any obstacles in the way of her daughter's

writing; she had only given her two pieces of advice.
Knowing, from experience, that people are only too easily
inclined to treat female literature with contempt, she had
said to her :—" If you wish to be considered in earnest,
set an example ; thoroughly study the language, do not do
so by halves, and teach those who have learnt Latin and
Greek." The other excellent piece of advice was "not
to adopt, in her style of dress, any of the eccentricities of
the blue-stocking tribe; to dress as others did, and only
to be distinguished for her talents." She would frequently say to her :—" Be a woman in your dress, and a
man in your knowledge of prosody."

Mademoiselle Delphine Gay often went into society.
She was always very simply dressed, generally in a plain
white muslin, with a blue gauze scarf covering her
shoulders and her slender waist. She wore no flowers in
her pretty fair curls. There was nothing odd or in-
fatuated about her. When she was asked to repeat some
verses, she would comply, but she soon relapsed into the
young girl, like others of her age. One evening, when
a fashionable lady was complimenting her, she replied :—
" It would better become me, madame, to compliment
you : it is better for a woman to know how to inspire
verses than to be able to write them."

Up to that time Victor had published his odes one by
one, either in the *Conservateur Littéraire* or as pamphlets,
through a bookseller in the Palais Royal, whose name
was Delaunay. Abel advised him to make a complete
book of them. But not a single publisher was to be
found willing to undertake the risk of printing a book of

poetry; and Victor had no money to spend on it.
He dared not indulge so lofty an ambition, and was
much surprised to receive one day a proof-sheet of his
verses, with the signature B at the bottom of the page,
which seemed to promise that others were to follow.
Abel, without letting him know anything about it, had
robbed him of his manuscript, and carried it off to a
printer's office.

He still required some one who would undertake the
sale of it. Booksellers in general disliked the idea of
putting poetry in their shop-window, as it occupied the
place of a book. The uncle of one of Abel's friends,
however, out of good-nature towards his nephew, consented to give the " Odes " a place in his establishment.

The volume, entitled "Odes et Poésies diverses," had
not been a quarter of an hour exposed in the window
before a passer-by entered the shop and bought it.
This was M. Mennechet, reader to Louis XVIII.

Louis XVIII. took the volume, looked at it, opened it,
and remarked, " It is very badly got up." The book in
reality was not fit for admirers of typography. It was
an octavo, on dirty grey paper, printed with old type,
thought to be quite good enough for that sort of work.
The cover, which was too small for the book, was ornamented with a drawing representing a vase surrounded
by serpents, which no doubt were meant to do duty for
the serpents of envy, but which much more resembled
some adders escaping from a bottle in an apothecary's
shop.

Its unfortunate appearance did not prevent the King's

insisting that the "Odes" should be read to him : he even read them over again himself, and made notes on them with his own hand. His notes were in general puritanical, offended at any innovations, and more frequently finding fault than praising. The ode he thought the finest was the one in which he himself was mentioned: he had written on the margin of *his* strophe, " *Superbe !* "

Victor sent the book to M. de Lamennais, who replied thus :—

"Chenaie, 9th June.

" I have read your collection of poetry, my dear Victor, and beg you to accept a thousand thanks for the pleasure you have given me. Fine verses resemble the sunshine of the South, which gives all objects a more vivid colouring, and spreads around them more varied and harmonious tints.

" You are right in thinking of your future career. No one is better acquainted than I am with the troubles from which I would fain see you freed. I, too, hope to come out from them, some day ; but in order to accomplish this I need a few more years of hard work. I feel, nevertheless, quite contented to resign everything to Providence. Providence, indeed, is ever kind to us. Yet, we, on the other hand, are as anxious as if we had none to look after us. One of my friends, an *emigré*, had spent all he possessed ; had absolutely nothing left but a small coin. He looked at it for a few moments, and read on it the inscription " *Deus providebit.* " From that moment his confidence was renewed, and, although in after years he experienced many reverses, he was never in real need.

" You ask me, my dear friend, how far I am advanced
in my third volume. That is finished; but the work itself
is not nearly finished. My intention at first was only to
illustrate results; but these results, though incontestable, have been questioned because of the feelings people
entertain towards me. I have, therefore, decided upon
bringing forward proofs of everything—in other words, I
mean to represent human tradition as illustrating the
great truths of religion. I quite feel that these long
illustrations will make the third part of my essay very
heavy; but what is to be done? The author will lose
by it, perhaps; but I think truth will gain; and I ask
for nothing more; for all the rest is too childish to occupy
one's mind about. Therefore, in addition to the volume
I have completed, I still have two to bring out, and they
will take me eighteen good months of hard work. That
which grieves me most is the long separation from my
friends. I have to remind myself continually that God
requires it of me; and in truth this idea answers every
murmur, and consoles me for everything. Pray for me,
dear Victor. I never forget you at the altar, and the remembrance of you is one of the sweetest souvenirs of my
heart.

" Your friend,

" F. M."

Victor, during the publication of his book, was at
Chantilly, where Madame Foucher had taken up her
quarters that year. He had obtained permission to spend
the summer near his betrothed. Madame Foucher was

inhabiting one story of an old presbytery, where there was no apartment that he could hire, but the house, which had been entirely rebuilt and quite modernized, had left untouched an old turret belonging to the former building, and in it was a room—a real nest for a poet. Four windows, admitting the light from the four points of the compass, ensured the admission of sun-light at all hours of the day.

The lodgers had the advantage of a large piece of ground, bordered to the right and left by two avenues of poplars, remarkable for their height and large size. Part of this piece of ground, which was cultivated, had all the cheerfulness of the open country; the rest was a flower garden. One of the plantations was bordered by the Bièvre, which separated the old presbytery from the church. From the other the valley was discerned, smiling, and covered with verdure.

The owner was an old woman, active, neat, and rosy-cheeked, very economical, and utilizing everything, even her neighbours the mad people of Bicêtre. Some of these who were harmlessly mad were allowed to go out, and would split her wood or weed her garden for her. Amongst them was one man, who stammered and squinted, whose teeth were falling out, and who was of a lively disposition. The old woman called him Coco. There was another of a gloomy tendency, who seldom spoke.

The two lovers were walking in the garden, and talking of their future life together, now so near at hand, whilst watching the sun disappear behind the hill. Another couple were enjoying themselves in the same

way; these were the grandson of the proprietor, and
Doctor Pariset's daughter, who were also going to be
married in a few weeks; they stopped at every garden-
bed, and the enamoured youth would present his lady-
love with enormous bouquets, too heavy for her to carry.
The four lovers walked up and down, beaming with joy,
and every now and then fell in with the melancholy madman, who, with his head bent down, was employing himself in digging, or with Coco, who was indulging in
shrieks of laughter, yet more melancholy than the silence
of his companion.

One day Victor brought his betrothed a paper carefully
folded and pinned. She thought it contained some
precious flower, and opened it cautiously; while she was
opening it, a bat made its escape. She was much alarmed,
and only forgave him for causing so disagreeable a surprise when she read the verses written on the paper, and
called *La Chauve-souris*.

I do not think I have yet mentioned a second son of
Madame Foucher's, called Paul, who was then twelve
years of age. He was being educated at the College of
Henri IV. On Sundays he came down to Gentilly, and
was sometimes accompanied by a companion of his own
age, a gentlemanly boy, of tender build, with flaxen hair,
of a clear and decided expression of countenance, expanded nostrils, and half-open lips of a beautiful vermillion
colour. His name was Alfred de Musset. One afternoon he entertained them all by imitating a comic scene,
in which he personified a tipsy man, with the most extraordinary ease and truth.

Notwithstanding the bad paper on which it was printed, Victor's book sold. The first edition, which consisted of 1500 copies, was exhausted in four months. The price was three francs fifty centimes, of which the printer and publisher took three francs. Victor, therefore, received 750 francs, less a certain deduction, owing to the habit of the bookseller to pay him in six-franc pieces, which involved a loss of four sous. But when he once realized this great sum, he became rich; the King had given him a pension of a thousand francs out of his own privy purse.

It is possible to marry on a thousand francs per annum. The happy couple therefore returned to Paris to make preparations for the all-important day of their wedding. They first required the General's consent. Victor did not venture to ask it without a sense of discomfort and even alarm. Since the death of his first wife, the General had married again, which had not strengthened the affection his children bore him; for they still worshipped their mother's memory. Would not his new wife persuade him to refuse his consent? But the General's kindness of heart was stronger than any outward influence. He was not satisfied with merely giving his own consent, but he requested the consent of the parents of the young lady. I copy from the letter he wrote to M. and Madame Foucher the following passages :—

" . . . The military duties which engrossed me in my long career have prevented my having so thorough a knowledge of my own children as you have. I know that

Victor is exquisitely sensitive and has an excellent heart, and I am fully persuaded that his other moral qualities in no way fall short of these. That heart, those good qualities, I venture to lay at the feet of your daughter. . . . Victor begs that I will demand from you in marriage the hand of this young lady whose happiness is bound up in his, and with whom he anticipates the greatest felicity. Already, in order to do away with all preliminary difficulties, he has, with rare distinction, opened out for himself a brilliant career; he has in some measure secured a dowry in order to be able to offer your daughter a fitting establishment, reasonable hopes, and excellent prospects. You know what he is, and what he possesses. Should brighter days ever dawn and the treaty of May, 1814, be ratified,—if the mixed commission of sequestrations and indemnities should ever arrive at conclusions which would be adopted by the Government,—Victor would receive from his father the means of decently furnishing his house. As soon as I have received your answer, if it is what I hope it will be, I shall enclose Victor the formal consent required by article 76 in the Civil Code. . . . "

I also copy these few lines from M. Foucher's answer :—

" Your Victor has just delivered us the letter you have done us the honour of writing to us. Victor is all you suppose him to be. He possesses, besides, that gravity which in young people so well takes the place of experience, and, what is rarer still, disinterestedness and the spirit of order are united in him. . . . The union you propose to us is, we are sure, quite as advantageous for our

Adèle as it is flattering to all the members of our family. We therefore very willingly give our consent, and I, for my part, feel still greater pleasure in doing so owing to the hopes I entertain that this marriage will revive an old friendship which has always had an extreme value in my eyes, and which you, General, so kindly remind us of. I am sorry not to be able to do for our young people all they so richly deserve. Adèle will contribute towards the housekeeping two thousand francs' worth of furniture, clothes, and other matters, and they will live with us and be cared for by us, until they have got on sufficiently to set up housekeeping for themselves. This arrangement will, no doubt, agree with their views, and it will be doubly gratifying to us, as we shall thus continue to enjoy the society of all our children. . . ."

When he heard of the approaching wedding, M. de Lamennais wrote thus to Victor :—

" Chenaie, October 6th.

" Any event relating to your path in life interests me, my dear Victor. You are about to become the husband of the person you have loved from infancy, and who is as worthy of you as you are of her. I trust, with all my heart, that God will bless this happy union, which He appears Himself to have prepared by implanting in you a long and unchanged affection and a mutual love as pure as it is sweet. But whilst tasting the happiness of being thus united to the chosen one of your heart, who has ever been so faithful to you, remember to sanctify your happiness by serious reflections on the duties which devolve upon you. You must no longer act merely as an ardent lover, but you must cultivate more lasting and deeper, though perhaps less impetuous, feelings. You are a husband and may become a father; reflect then, reflect frequently, on all that is required of you by these two positions. You will never forget it if you remember that you are a Christian, if you seek in the paths of religion the necessary rules to direct your future life, and help you to bear those evils from which none are exempt. You must also seek strength to bear prosperity properly. The joy you now experience is legitimate; it is according to God's will, if only you recognize his hand, and I am sure that you do so from your touching and artless letter. But understand well that this is a happiness belonging to time, and that there is another kind to be sought for in eternity. You ought, with all your heart and soul, to seek for the latter. May Heaven, dear friend, confer on you and on her whose lot is for ever linked with yours every best blessing that a young married couple could desire! May it avert from your path in life anything and everything likely to affect your happiness or to disturb your peace! These are the wishes entertained on your behalf by the sincerest and most affectionate of your friends, "F. M."

Soon after writing this letter, M. de Lamennais returned to Paris and he granted Victor the certificate of confession required before he could get married.

The seven hundred francs which Victor had earned by his "Odes" did not now keep him a year: he spent the whole sum in buying a magnificent French cashmere shawl, which was the gem of the trousseau.

The General was not present at the wedding. Victor's witnesses were M. Soumet and M. Ancelot. The religious ceremony was performed at Saint-Sulpice in that very Chapel where, eighteen months before, Victor's mother's corpse had been interred. Another Madame Hugo now knelt where the bier had rested, and her white veil took the place of the funereal drapery.

Madame Foucher's dining-room being too small, the wedding breakfast was spread in one of the rooms in the War Office, separated merely by a thin partition from the one in which Lahorie had been tried and found guilty. After his mother's death, Victor had to mourn that of his godfather.

The next day a sadder event even than a death occurred. Biscarrat, the kind usher at M. Cordier's school, had been, as a matter of course, asked to the wedding. At the breakfast he had been struck by some incoherent expressions of Eugène's, who, for some time, had been rather singular in his behaviour. He warned Abel of the state of the case, and when they rose to leave the table they had led him away without troubling any one else about it. In the middle of the night madness declared itself. The next day Biscarrat made his appearance quite upset. Victor followed him quickly and found the poor companion of his childhood quite out of his mind. He monopolized all their thoughts. The General, who would not take part in the rejoicings, came up to Paris when he heard of this misfortune. He got better,

and they entertained hopes of him : they tried to watch
over the dear invalid themselves, but they soon discovered
that he would be better cared for in a private asylum.
But reason had fled to return no more, and only death
put an end to his sufferings.

M. ALPHONSE RABBE.

Victor Hugo now set to work again on the "*Han d'Islande;*" he finished it a few months after his marriage, and sold the first edition, for a thousand francs, to a ruined marquis who had become a bookseller. This marquis (M. Persan) purchased from him, at the same time, the second edition of his "Odes," which then appeared more suitably got up, and the bottle of adders on the back was now replaced by a lyre.

I take it for granted that this noble bookseller preferred poetry to prose, for he cared but little for "Hans" in comparison to the "Odes." Perhaps it was that he fancied poetry required to be well bound in order to attract purchasers, and that prose would fight its own battle. Whatever may have been his ideas on the subject, he merely had "Han d'Islande" printed on coarse grey paper, with wretched type, and it came out in four small volumes, without the author's name, thus imitating the example set him by *Réne, Werther, Adolphe,* the *Voyage autour de ma Chambre,* &c., the first edi-

tions of which did not bear the names, afterwards so
great, of Chateaubriand, Gœthe, Benjamin Constant, and
Xavier de Maistre.

The newspapers, which had almost all mentioned the
" Odes " favourably, were less inclined to praise the
" Hans of Iceland." Two parties were forming, the
classical and the romantic; and the latter was not, at
present, the most numerous, at least in the journals.
The book excited equal anger and astonishment. I find
in an old copy of the *Quotidienne* an article by M.
Charles Nodier, well illustrating the literary feeling of
the moment, and the kind of restless and excited pleasure
that literary novelties produced on those who were not
determined beforehand to find fault.

" . . . . Classical literature still maintains supremacy
in Europe in the name of Aristotle, but the classics, after
all, are now like dethroned monarchs, who only preserve a
shadow of power by an unrecognized sovereignty, and an
empty title without authority. Their domain now is only
a vast desert, whose productions, drooping and fading from
their earliest growth, strongly attest the poverty of an
exhausted soil, and of a decrepit nature. If the arts desire to raise a monument worthy of posterity, they select
another soil. Should some talent appear prodigal in rich
hopes, it must enlist under another banner. Classics are
always in the ascendant in the journals, the academies,
and the literary circles. The romantic, on the other
hand, bears the palm in the theatres, among the booksellers, and in general society. The world talks about
the former, but reads the latter, so that the finest work

that could now be produced by a member of the correct school, would not have a chance against the irresistible attraction of those reveries, often extravagant enough, which issue from the press every day from the opposition. What conclusion must we draw from this but that the state of society has changed; that its wants have also changed; that this state of things is inevitable; and that if we do not accept literature as it is, we run the risk of having none at all? One of the characteristics of this new state of literature, and one which will not diminish its attraction in the minds of a patriotic people, is the scrupulous observance of habits and localities which lend to works of fiction something of the usefulness of history. Mathurin has made himself remarkable in this school by the monstrous fables, *Melmoth* and *Montorio;* and one might have thought that the author had exhausted in these atrocious combinations all the horrors with which this poetry of Newgate and Pandemonium can terrify the imagination.

"This style has been appropriately enough called the 'sensational,' and it will probably keep the name because it has *not* been given by any authority. But there has arisen among this new generation of poets, which in France has made the fortune of romance, a rival to the melancholy English novelist, unfortunate enough to surpass him in the horrible exaggeration of incident. This writer, anxious, as is natural to his age, to exhaust every resource of the imagination, has shown himself more desirous of displaying at one stroke all the faculties which nature and education have bestowed on him, than to manage them skilfully and with advantage to his permanent reputation. There are men of a certain organization, to whom glory and distinction are temptations, just as happiness and pleasure tempt other men. Precocious intellects and deep sensibility do not take the future into consideration—they devour their future. The passions of a young and powerful mind know no to-morrow; they hope to satiate their ambition and their hopes with the reputation and excitement of the present moment. 'Hans of Iceland' has been the result of this kind of combination, if indeed one can describe as a combination that which is only the thoughtless instinct of an original genius, who obeys, without being aware of it, an impulse at variance with his true interests, but whose fine and wide career may not improbably justify the promise of excellence, and may hereafter redeem all the anxiety he has caused by the excusable error he has committed when he first launched into the world. Very few men commence by erring in this way, and leaving to the critic only the opportunity of reprimanding them for those faults they willingly own to. I shall not make an analysis of 'Hans of Iceland,' but I will give a much truer idea of it than any analysis, however correct, could convey, by remarking that 'Hans of Iceland' is one of those works in which one cannot separate the plot from the style without falling into caricature as unjust as it would be easy. Imagine an author condemned of his own free will to undertake a painful search for every moral infirmity of life; for every horror in society; for every monstrosity; for every degradation; for every hideous exception to the natural state of man, and to the condition of civilized society. And all this in order to select from the hideous heap some disgusting anomalies to which language has hardly given a name, the Morgue, the scaffold, the gibbet, cannibalism, the executioner, and I know not what other nameless horrors; and attaching to these, a series of execrable ambitions and incomprehensible joys. Why should one with such an amount of talent think itself obliged to have recourse to such means? It was so easy to have found others. A minute acquaintance with the places he mentions or a wonderfully careful study of the accounts of them, have given the author of 'Hans of Iceland,' to some extent, that extreme accuracy of local colouring, for which the author of 'Waverley' is so distinguished. *To some extent*, I say, because, being perhaps more familiar than he is with the sky in the latitudes he describes, I sought in vain in his descriptions for some of those effects which it would have been easy to portray when the shortness of the days and the singularity of the polar seasons is taken into consideration. In 'Hans of Iceland' a good account of the Edda and of the island history is given. There is much learning, and much wit, even of that kind which springs from happiness, and that may be called fun. There is also much that is generally derived from experience, but which the author has not had time to learn from association with the world or from observation. We find in it a lively, picturesque style, full of *verve*, and what is yet more surprising, that delicate tact and that refinement of feeling which are among life's choicest's gifts;

and which here contrast in the most surprising manner with the wild extravagances of a diseased imagination. Nevertheless, these are not the qualities that will make ' Hans of Iceland' the fashion, nor will it be these that will oblige the inflexible and learned Minos of the bookseller's shop to acknowledge the sale of some 12,000 copies of this novel, which everyone will certainly be anxious to read. It is its defects that will cause this result."

Victor Hugo only knew M. Charles Nodier by name. He called on him in order to thank him: he ascended three flights of stair in the Rue de Provence, and rang a bell. A smiling young girl answered it.

" Is M. Charles Nodier at home ? "

" Papa is out, sir."

" Might I write him a little note ? "

Whilst the young girl was gone to fetch writing materials, Victor Hugo examined the antechamber, which served as a dining-room, and the furniture of which consisted of straw-bottomed chairs, a table, and a sideboard of walnut wood, the homely appearance of which were relieved by a degree of cleanliness worthy of Holland.

The next day, M. Nodier hastened to call on Victor, who no longer resided at the War Office. The King had of his own accord given him a second pension of 2000 francs, which he was to receive from the Minister of the Interior. Already a rich man, he had wished for a home of his own, and he had just established himself in the Rue de Vaugiraud, No. 90. The novelist and his critic became friends at first sight. It was agreed upon that M. Nodier should come to the house-warming, and should bring with him his wife and his daughter. Madame Nodier, who had never seen Madame Hugo, accepted the invitation with that intelligent simplicity which distinguished her in everything. She came with her daughter Marie, without further invitation; and this was the commencement of a friendship which has known no interruption.

Amongst the few supporters of "Hans of Iceland," M. Mery may be mentioned as one of the most courageous. The *Tablettes Universelles* of which he was the principal editor, encouraged the novel by the double force of energy and talents. M. Mery's coadjutator was M. Alphonse Rabbe, who, like himself, was a Marseillais. M. Rabbe had once been a very handsome man, but a bad illness had disfigured him : his eyelashes, nostrils, and lips were eaten away ; he had no beard left, and his teeth were as black as a coal. He had only his hair left, the fair curls of which floated over his shoulders. Only one eye was left, but his firm glance and frank and genuine smile still lighted up this hideous mask. He had started at Marseilles an opposition journal, *Le Phocéen,* and he had afterwards come to Paris, where he was engaged upon the *Courier Français* and the *Tablettes Universelles.* An article, in which he courageously upheld "Hans of Iceland," led to a correspondence with its author, for whom he immediately began to entertain an affection almost paternal, as he was twenty years his senior. Victor Hugo, on his side, took to him very much, on account of his strong and resolute nature.

They often met, especially at the house of M. Rabbe; for this gentleman avoided going out because of his looks. Victor Hugo, however, occasionally persuaded him to come to his house.

Once he even accepted an invitation to dinner, as he was anxious to meet M. de Lamennais.

" Well," said Victor Hugo, " I will ask him to dinner, and you shall come and dine with us."

" So be it," said M. Rabbe.

But something in the conversation made him acquainted with the fact that Madame Hugo was with child; he said nothing at the time, but when the day of the dinner party arrived, he wrote word that he was ill, and during several months he did not make his appearance in the Rue de Vaugirard. Victor Hugo, one day, was reproaching him for never coming to see him, and insisted on knowing the cause.

" Your wife is with child," answered the poor disfigured man.

He was very moody, and fancied everywhere that he met with allusions to his ugliness. He was all but angry with Victor Hugo, on account of an ode that he wrote on Ramon de Benavente, his old schoolfellow at the College of Nobles. This ode appeared at first with the initial : " To my friend R—." As the verses mentioned a mysterious malady, he thought that " R—" meant Rabbe, and in order to appease him, it was necessary to republish the ode with the name Ramon in full.

M. Rabbe was a fatalist. One day, when he was defending his opinions on the subject against Victor

Hugo, who had unexpectedly met him in the gardens of the Luxembourg, he said :—

"Listen, this is a fact, which I defy you to contradict. A few months ago, during the winter, there was a thick fog passing into a fine rain, and the Luxembourg was nearly deserted. Five men were walking in the avenue in which we are now. Four were conspirators, and the fifth was their confidant. They were discussing means of action, and the chances of an opportunity. Three of the number were for immediate action, the fourth recommended a little delay. The three first, impatient to bring matters to a crisis, informed the fourth that if he would not join them, they would act without his assistance. A playing card, lying with its face to the ground and soiled with mud, happened to lie at their feet. "Well," said he, "if this card is the queen of hearts, I will join you." There were one-and-fifty chances against its being so. He picked up the card. It was the queen of hearts.

The four conspirators were the sergeants of La Rochelle. The confidant was M. Rabbe himself. Some time after he related the anecdote in the *Tablettes Universelles*. "He had seen the head of the doomed one fall," he would remark.

One day, when Victor Hugo was calling on M. Rabbe, they began disputing about M. de Chateaubriand, whom M. Rabbe disliked. The conversation, which had been carried on amicably enough between the two friends, became more excited by the intervention of a person whom Victor Hugo had not seen enter, and who was concealed by a desk at which he wrote. This person in an

imperious and determined tone, declared that Chateaubriand was an affected and puffed-up writer, whose
reputation would not last twenty years, and that all his
writings put together were not equal to a single page of
Bossuet. Victor Hugo, replied rather sharply to this
unknown speaker, who came out with his opinions as if
they were commands, and M. Rabbe had some trouble
to bring back the conversation to the usual tone.

When Victor Hugo had left, the man at the desk inquired of M. Rabbe, who that little gentleman was who
had contradicted him so boldly.

"It is Victor Hugo," replied Rabbe.

"He who writes royalist verses?"

"Yes, I was only waiting for you to finish writing, in
order to introduce you to each other. But you rushed
into the conversation so rapidly, that I was unable to do
so. I must, however, make you known to one another.
I must look for an opportunity."

"It is already found," said the questioner.

He wrote a few words on a sheet of letter paper, and
offered it to M. Alphonse Rabbe.

"Will you take this to M. Victor Hugo, from me?"

It was a challenge, signed Armand Carrel.

"Are you mad?" said M. Rabbe "Fight a duel, because people differ with you in opinion, as to a page
from Bossuet! As it happens that all this occurred at
my house, and it is my fault, I ought to have mentioned
to you both with whom you were in company : you would
then have shown the caution when discussing matters
which sensible people always do on such occasions. If

there is any harm done, the fault is mine, and it is with me you must quarrel. Let us fight it out if you wish it"

M. Carrel, who had returned from Spain after the French expedition, against which he had fought, and being ruined in his military career, had taken to newspaper writing, was grateful to M. Alphonse Rabbe, who had introduced him to the *Courier Français.* He was subdued by the decided tone of his friend, and tore up his letter.

On one occasion, Victor Hugo breakfasted with M. Rabbe with several friends. There was no servant, but on entering the dining-room, everything was ready laid on the table ; clean plates were conveniently placed near the guests. Suddenly the door opened, and a young and pretty girl, dressed as a servant, entered; she wore a smart little frilled cap. M. Rabbe rose angrily, and asked her harshly why she came without being called. The poor child left the room, and was not seen again. The guests, embarrassed at this occurrence, did not recover their spirits for some time.

Another time, at M. Rabbe's house, Victor Hugo once more perceived through a door, which was left ajar, this same little girl, in the pretty cap. M. Rabbe rushed to the door and shut it violently.

It was found out at last that he was the lover of the young girl and that he adored her. Was it through jealousy that he hid her from everybody? or through shame at having consented to be loved by this pretty creature, so disfigured as he was?

His unsociableness suddenly became misanthropy, and his melancholy became despair: the young servant was dead. She was buried in the cemetery of the Mont Parnasse, and he used every day to go and weep over her tomb. The porter was often obliged to turn him out when the hour arrived for closing the cemetery.

I read as follows in a letter that he wrote to Victor Hugo :—

" I passed in front of your door just now, my dear friend, and, notwithstanding the temptation, I did not enter. I had just placed some flowers on a tomb where I had also so completely left all my thoughts that you would have taken me for a madman. However, as you well know, the heart is sometimes so crushed that it cannot even keep its troubles to itself. My tears are already dried, but my grief will be everlasting. She who has just left me possessed, under a common appearance, a soul of which I alone knew the secret: in her utter simplicity and candour she remained ignorant even of herself, and I was all the world to her. Her most anxious wish was fulfilled, and she breathed her last in my arms. I remain in lonely bitterness."

M. Rabbe died suddenly on the night of the 1st January, 1830. His death was attributed to his own imprudence. He had mixed too much laudanum in a poultice which he had applied to his face. When looking over his papers, after his death, these words in his own handwriting were found : " When a man has arrived at a certain stage of suffering, he may put an end to his life without remorse."

XL

A VISIT TO BLOIS.

M. SOUMET and his friends Guiraud and Emile Deschamps took it into their heads to establish a review, and asked Victor to unite with them in the undertaking. He held back, as he had work of his own to finish, but the capitalist made his assistance an absolute condition, and he consented out of friendship. Thus began the *Revue Française.* He soon found out that it could not live. The temperate and peaceful style of criticism assumed by its contributors had none of the harshness and passionate audacity necessary in times of literary revolution. Its polemics were timid and moderate. Public questions, instead of being attacked boldly and met face to face, were evaded, and no conclusion was arrived at. But, harmless as it was, the review alarmed the Academy. M. Soumet was a candidate, and was informed that he would not be elected whilst the *Revue Française* was in existence. He therefore entreated them to give up. M. Guiraud and Emile Deschamps consented, but Victor Hugo said that though the others might retire from it he should keep it up alone. This was not what the Academy required : they would have gained nothing by having open war instead of a mere drawing-room quarrel. M. Soumet returned to the charge and entreated Victor Hugo, as a personal favour, to abandon his idea. The *Revue Française*, therefore; ceased to exist.

The editor of the review, M. Ambroise Tardieu, was publishing a selection of celebrated letters. He begged Victor Hugo to undertake to sort and annotate those of Voltaire and Madame de Sevigné. Victor Hugo consented at first, but had hardly commenced when he got disgusted with this work of amputation : he therefore gave it up, and only wrote that notice on Voltaire which is to be found in the "Littérature et Philosophies Mêlées."

At the theatre of the Odéon they were acting that year with great success *Der Freyschutz*. Everybody who belonged to what was then called the romantic school came to support with enthusiastic cheers Weber's grand music. Victor Hugo and his wife, whilst waiting the opening of the office, found themselves side by side with a tall young man, with a firm and cordial expression of countenance. Between poets and painters acquaintance is soon made. This young man was M. Achille Deveria, who for the twelfth time had come to applaud Weber and to encore the drinking song. He asked Madame Victor Hugo if she had an album.

" I shall have one to-morrow," said she.

He came the next day and extemporized a charming drawing. He united a singular facility of touch and rapidity of execution to his great talent. His sketch was

so much admired that he promised to come and make
some more, and the album was the excuse for repeated
visits.

M. Achille Deveria had two pupils, his brother Eugène
and Louis Boulanger.   All three, on quitting the studio,
would often come and dine with Victor Hugo without
waiting for a formal invitation.   The dinner, which was
generally mediocre, was enriched by the providential omelette, which they would soak in rum and try to set fire
to, but in this lay the difficulty.   They would use for the
purpose fag ends of matches : everyone would set to work,
and only succeeded in blackening the spoons or in covering the refractory liquid with odds and ends of burnt
wood.   The omelette always grew cold under the process,
but the bursts of laughter it occasioned warmed it up
again.

The young couple in the Rue de Vaugirard would sometimes call on M. Achille Deveria.   It was only a few steps
from their house; he lived in the Rue Nôtre Dame des
Champs.   The house, hidden by gardens, was a quiet
retreat, but very cheerful.   He there lived as a family
man.   His grandmother, who was still robust and active,
was in fact as young in heart and mind as her grandchildren themselves, and was almost their playfellow.
His mother, on the contrary, was a sleepy, indolent
person ; sometimes two years would pass before anyone
ever saw her ; one might have set off for China, and on
returning, she would have been found precisely as she
had been at starting, occupying her large armchair of
crimson velvet.   She would look as if she had never

taken her clothes off during the whole time. Winter and summer, she was always clothed in a short nightdress and petticoat of white piqué, and on her head she wore a white muslin handkerchief arranged à la Creole. Being very stout, she thus looked like a snow ball. She never did anything but embroider, and never came to an end of that, but she nibbled incessantly at bonbons. She had five children : Achille, Eugène, another son in India, and two daughters. The younger of the two girls, Laura, was loved and admired by all. She was fêted, dressed up, and waited upon like an idol. Her sister was deformed though active and devoted, kept house, and economized the money gained by Achille. This brave youth was the main support of his family ; his ready talent was of use to him in multiplying his productions : he would rapidly strike off clever and spirited lithographs, for each of which he received one hundred francs : he acknowledged that he rather wasted his talents, which were superior to work of this kind, but he consoled himself with the idea that what he thus lost in reputation his mother and sisters gained in substantial comforts. Eugène could not yet assist him in this pious undertaking : he was then only a student ; and announced only by his broad-brimmed hat, large Castilian cloak, and beard which resembled a mane, that originality which in 1827 ensured the success of his fine picture of the birth of Henry IV.

Nothing could be more hospitable, more lively, and more pleasant than this home of the fine arts and family affection. There was always an open table. In summer, the garden was at any one's disposal, filled with fine fruits and green almonds. On winter evenings, Laura would seat herself at the piano, and sing airs she had herself composed; the conversation was lively and cheerful, and when their numbers amounted to a dozen, they would have a dance. Time, age, and death have put an end to these homely pleasures.

Eugène Hugo's sad illness kept the General in Paris. Victor had but to see his father to know him at once. As the hoarfrost melts in the heat of the sun, so did the bitterness the son entertained towards his father melt away before the genial kindness of this excellent man. He now understood the real greatness of those soldiers who had carried the flag of France into all the capitals of Europe; and without ceasing to detest the man who had led them to battle, for the sake of his own personal aggrandisement, he could distinguish between their heroism and his ambition. This improvement is manifest in his " Ode à mon Père : "—

" Courbés sous un tyran, vous étiez grands encore !

. . . .

Reprenez, ô Français, votre gloire usurpeé,
Assez dans tant d'exploits on n'a vu qu'une épée !
Assez de la louange, il fatigua la voix !
Mesurez la hauteur de géant sur le poudre !
Quel aigle ne vaincrait, armé de votre foudre ?
Et qui ne serait grand, monté sur vos pavois ?"

[*Translation.*]
Beneath the tyrant's sway you still were great !

. . . .

Take back, O Frenchmen, all your usurped glory;
Too long a single sword has shown supreme !

Enough of praise—it but fatigues the voice!
Measure the height of this giant in the dust!
What eagle would not conquer, armed with your thunder?
And who would not be great, defended by your shields?

Some months after this, he celebrated the "Arc de Triomphe de l'Etoile." In June, 1824, he warmly espoused the cause of M. de Chateaubriand, who had been dismissed from the Ministry. General Hugo's predictions to General Lucotte were gradually being realized, for the opinions inculcated by his mother were disappearing one by one from the intelligent man.

The General would not return to Blois without a promise from his son and daughter-in-law that they would pay him a visit there. This promise could not be performed till the spring of 1825.

They set off, a party of three, for a little girl had been born, and their mother was nursing it, and could not be parted from it. The best conveyance was the *malle poste*, but this went on as far as Bordeaux, and it was necessary to pay for the whole distance to secure a place, which was rather a serious matter for people of limited income. Victor Hugo was advised to call on the post-master-general, who perhaps might help him to obtain places only as far as Blois.

This official was Roger, the academician, who was said to have much influence in the academical elections; so that it used to be said at the time that he ruled equally over letters and literature.

He received Victor Hugo very graciously, and granted his request at once. After settling this little matter of business, they proceeded to chat together.

"Apropos," said the postmaster, "I am certain you have not an idea why your first pension was given you. You believe, don't you, that it was owing to the verses you had written?"

"Why, what else should it have been?"

"I will tell you. You were once acquainted with a man called Edward Delon."

"Yes."

"This friend became a captain in the army, he conspired, and was condemned to death for contumacy."

"Well."

"You then wrote to his mother."

"How do you know that?"

"I both know that you did write to her, and also what you said to her. Wait a minute."

He rang the bell, and a bundle of papers was brought to him. He selected from amongst them a certain paper which he held out to Victor Hugo, who read as follows :—

"MADAME,

"I am not aware whether your unfortunate Delon is arrested. I am ignorant of the penalty which would be inflicted on the person who should be found to have concealed him. I do not pause to consider whether his opinions are or are not diametrically in opposition to my own. When he is in danger, I only know that I am his friend, and that we met as friends not a month ago. If he is not arrested, I offer him shelter at my own home, where I am living with a young cousin, who is not acquainted with Delon. My strong attachment to the Bourbons is known, but this circumstance is an additional security for you, for it will avert from me all suspicion of having concealed a man taken in the act of conspiracy, a crime of which I cannot help thinking Delon to be innocent. Whatever may be the state of the case, be so kind, madame, as to make him acquainted with my offer, if you can find means of doing so. Be he innocent or guilty, I shall expect him. He may rely on the loyalty of a Royalist, and on the devotion of the friend of his childhood.

"Whilst making you this offer, I do but carry out the last wishes of my mother, who always preserved the warmest affection for you. In this melancholy affair, it is very pleasant to me to be able to give you a proof of the respectful attachment with which I have the honour to remain," &c.

"This is an exact copy of my letter," said Victor, "but how comes it here?"

"Innocent youth!" said the functionary. "You write to the mother of a conspirator whom everyone is looking for, and you send the letter by post!"

"So my letter was withheld?"

"Oh, no! It was copied, and due care was taken to seal it up again in such a manner that nothing should be noticed, and Madame Delon duly received it."

"So that, in fact, my letter became a kind of ambush, and Delon might have considered me an accomplice in it. But what you are now relating to me is literally abominable."

"Come, come, be quiet! Delon had quitted France, so he could not pay you a visit, and your letter was the cause of a happy result : the King, to whom it was read, said, "That is a good youth; I shall confer on him the first vacant pension."

Nevertheless, this was a fresh attack on the Royalism of Victor Hugo. He had, until that time, contented himself with shrugging his shoulders when the opposition newspapers abused the *Cabinet Noir;* he was disenchanted when he found out that kings allowed themselves to break the seals of letters.

But this was just in the style of Louis XVIII. At that time the King had been dead six months. The usual hopes entertained by all at the commencement of a new reign, and some fortunate expressions dropped by Charles X., brought together for a short time those who were gradually dropping off from the Bourbons. It was thought that, as Charles X. had said, "No more censorship, no more halberds!" he might perhaps add, "Away with the Cabinet Noir!"

A few days after this interview with the Postmaster-General, Victor Hugo was about to step into the coupé of the *malle poste,* in which his wife and little daughter were already seated, when a commissionaire ran up quite out of breath, and presented him with a huge letter, sealed with red, which had just come for him, and which his father-in-law sent him in the greatest haste. It was the official announcement that he had been created Chevalier of the Legion of Honour.

At Blois, the General met them at the coach-office. Victor Hugo, knowing how pleased his father would be, held out to him the letter he had received, and said,—

"Here, this is for you!"

The General, who was delighted, as he had anticipated, kept the letter, and in exchange, unfastened the red ribbon which decorated his button-hole, and fixed it on his son's coat.

The next day but one, he received the new Chevalier with the customary ceremonials.

The young couple perceived, for the first time, the "square white house, standing amongst orchards," which is afterwards mentioned in the "Feuilles d' Automne." The General also possessed, in Sologne, a country seat, with about eighteen acres of land, to which they made an excursion. The small house, which was only a story high, was only remarkable for its stone balcony, under which was a pond filled with fish and surrounded by yew-trees and oaks. Beyond, nothing was visible but sand, marsh, and heather, here and there interspersed with. oaks and poplars.

XLI

THE CORONATION OF CHARLES X.

THE son's acquaintance with the father ripened into affection. He was forced to leave him in order to be present at the coronation of Charles X., to which he had been invited, but he left his wife and infant daughter as hostages.

In passing through Paris, Victor Hugo found a note from M. Chas. Nodier awaiting him, and he hastened to the Library at the Arsenal, where M. Nodier had recently gone to reside. The Librarian was at breakfast with two friends, M. de Cailleux, and the artist, M. Alaux, who was nicknamed the Roman, because he had obtained the prize at Rome. All the three had been invited to the coronation, and were discussing the means of going there. There was no hope of seats in any of the diligences, for every place had been engaged for the last three months. M. Nodier suggested a livery stable keeper, whom he had employed in his excursions, and who offered the use of a large carriage, at the rate of one hundred francs a day. There were four places in it. Victor Hugo would take one; they would travel by easy stages, stop when and where they liked, sleep comfortably at night in their beds, and make the whole affair a pleasant excursion.

The thing was thus arranged, and they set out on their journey. The road from Paris to Rheims was gravelled and raked just like the avenues of a park. At intervals, grassy seats had been erected, shaded by extemporised plantations. Diligences, coaches covered with armorial bearings, cabs, carts, every kind of vehicle, were hurrying along, and gave to the road all the noisy animation of a street.

Victor Hugo admired the woods, the plains, and the villages, and quarrelled with the Roman, whose tastes lay in a more severe and simple style of landscape, and who declared that the windmills only prevented people from having a good view of the country, by the movements of their sails. When Nodier was asked his opinion as to windmills, he replied that, as for him, what he loved was the king of trumps: he had made a capital card-table of his hat, which he held between his knees, and during the whole time the journey lasted, he and M. de Cailleux played at écarté.

They had to break off the game when they came to a steep ascent, as it was necessary to walk up the hills in order to save the horses. Whilst doing so, M. Nodier found a five-franc piece on the ground.

"Ah!" said he, "the first poor person we meet will be rendered happy!"

"And what will the second feel?" said Victor Hugo, who perceived on the ground another coin of the same value.

"And how will the third feel?" said M. Alaux almost directly afterwards.

Soon M. Cailleux had his turn. Every minute the sum increased.

"I wonder," said one of the party, "who the fool is who thus amuses himself in scattering his treasures about?"

"He is no fool," said Victor Hugo; "he is much more likely to be a generous millionaire, who, in order to enhance the pleasures of this festive occasion, keeps an open purse."

"For my part," said M. Nodier, "I think it must be the King, who has commanded that at the entrance to Rheims the road should be paved with money."

"It is like a fairy tale," they all exclaimed; "let us keep aloof from the carriage. Only pedestrians have such good luck, and by this evening we shall all be rich men."

Unfortunately, they shortly after picked up, together with some more five-franc pieces, a cross of the Legion of Honour, and this shower of money was explained. Victor Hugo's portmanteau had a hole in it, and at every jerk the money fell out.

On the fourth day they arrived. It was the evening before the coronation. They alighted at the first hotel they came to, and asked for four rooms. They did not even obtain an answer to their request. They tried another hotel, then another, and everywhere the only reply was a significant shrugging of shoulders. They were so often repulsed that they had begun to comfort themselves with the idea that they had at least the carriage at their disposal, in which they might sleep and dress themselves for want of anything better, when they were suddenly accosted by the manager of the Rheims Theatre. M. Nodier, who was acquainted with him, had a few moments' conversation with him.

"Where are you staying?" asked the manager.

"We lodge in the street," said M. Nodier.

He related their awkward position. The manager was astonished that any sensible men should have come to the coronation without having previously engaged apartments. His house, he was sorry to say, was literally crammed, and he was himself reduced to a bed in a garret. But a lady who occupied apartments in his house, Mademoiselle Horville, had managed to reserve for herself two rooms, and perhaps when she heard who the travellers were, she might be induced to give up one of them.

The actress was good-nature itself. She had a drawing-room and a bed-room, and gave them up the use of the former. The sofa made an excellent bed, and three mattrasses on the floor formed a better bed-room than they could have hoped for.

The next day the actress's guests, in court-dress, with sword at their sides, and feeling rather uncomfortable in their fine clothes, presented themselves at the door of the Cathedral. An officer, who was one of the Body Guard, asked for their cards of invitation, and showed them their seats. The decorations concealed by painted cardboard the noble architecture of the building, and marked by paper arches three rows of galleries, which were crowded

to suffocation with spectators. From top to bottom of
the vast nave, it was one mass of men in uniform, and
ladies covered with lace and precious stones. Notwithstanding the cardboard and the bright colouring,
the ceremony was not without grandeur. The throne,
at the foot of which stood the princes of the blood royal,
and next them the ambassadors, was shut in on the left
by the Chamber of Deputies, and on the right by the
Chamber of Peers. The deputies, dressed soberly in cloth
coats buttoned to the chin, whose only decoration
consisted in being turned up with green silk embroidery,
formed a striking contrast to the peers, who wore sky-
blue coats of embroidered velvet, with velvet mantles
of the same colour, sprinkled with *fleurs de lis*. They had
on white silk stockings, and black velvet shoes with high
heels and rosettes. Their hats were in the style of
Henry IV., ornamented with white feathers, and having
the coif encircled by a twisted fringe of gold.

On his return from the Cathedral, Victor Hugo was
speaking of the impression made on him by the whole
affair. With the exception of the decorations, the
ceremony had struck him as imposing. One thing, however, had annoyed him, and this was to see the King
stretched at full length at the feet of the Archbishop.

"What are you talking about?" said M. Nodier;
"where did you see anything of that kind?"

They began to argue the subject. M. Charles Nodier
affirmed that it had not happened, and Victor Hugo persisted that he had seen it.

Victor Hugo quitted M. Nodier to go and call upon

M. de Chateaubriand. He found him about to re-enter his house, bursting with indignation both at the decorations of the Cathedral and at the ceremony itself.

"I should have suggested a coronation of a very different kind," said he. "An unadorned church, the King on horseback, two open books, the charter and the gospels, religion united to liberty. In lieu of that we have had a mountebank's stage and a ridiculous parade."

He went on with the subject, calling everything mean and wretched.

"They don't even know now how to spend their money. Do you know what has happened? There has been a contest between the King of France and the English Ambassador, and the King was beaten. Yes, the Ambassador came here with such a splendid carriage, that everyone flocked to see it; I even went myself, though I am not naturally curious. By the side of this carriage the King's looked like a hired chaise, and it was mentioned to the Ambassador, who, out of pity to the King of France, condescended to make use of a less magnificent coach.

Victor Hugo related his conversation with M. Charles Nodier.

"Here," said M. de Chateaubriand to him, "show him this!"

He took from the table the formal programme of the ceremony, on which it was written that, at a given moment, the King should lie at the feet of the Archbishop.

"Well, what do you say now?" said Victor Hugo to M. Nodier, showing him this sentence.

"Well," said M. Nodier, "I had looked well at the whole affair, and my eyes are as good as other people's. Thus it is that things we look at every day are never seen at all. Had I been in a court of justice I should have been prepared to assert, on oath, with the most perfect conviction that I was speaking the truth, that it did not happen."

"Yes," said Victor Hugo, "it often happens that a single witness suffices to cause the execution of a human being."

The four travelling companions stayed at Rheims, in order to be present at the admission of the Knights of the Holy Ghost, which was to take place the day but one after the coronation. Victor Hugo spent the intervening day in visiting the town, which was of use to him at a later period in his story of the Chante-fleurie in "Nôtre Dame de Paris."

The admission of the Knights took place in the Cathedral just as the coronation had done. Charles X. made his appearance with the crown on his head, followed by some of the princes of the blood, who stationed themselves, according to their rank, on the steps of the throne. The apse was occupied only by the members of the royal family and the knights.

One of the incidents which most attracted public attention was the meeting of M. de Chateaubriand and the Minister Villèle.

They had been mortal enemies. M. de Chateaubriand having been expelled from the Ministry by M. de Villèle, revenged himself by writing stinging articles in the

Journal des Débats. The most amusing part of it was that these adversaries had been the last two appointments, and consequently were placed close together. They thus awaited the moment of their admission, and the public had plenty of time to gaze at them.

M. de Villèle seemed to bear the meeting better than his companion. In the first place, the costume, very handsome in itself, did not suit M. de Chateaubriand. Its colour was nearly identical with that he had worn on the former occasion. Instead of the cloak of blue velvet, he wore one of black velvet, the lining of which was of flame-coloured watered silk, and the pantaloons, waistcoat, and rosettes on the shoes were the same. The hat retained its plumes, but the twisted fringe of gold was replaced by flame-coloured gold lace, and the ornaments were in imitation of flames and doves. This gorgeous dress seemed to crush his little body, and his plumed hat quite concealed his head, which was his most telling feature. He looked out of humour, and anxious to get the thing over.

M. de Villèle, on the contrary, was triumphant. He was President of the Council, and looked quite at his ease. No one would have said that he had the least acquaintance with his neighbour; he looked at him without noticing him, with that profound indifference so natural in a Minister of State towards a man of genius.

XLII.

A VISIT TO LAMARTINE.

M. DE LAMARTINE himself had also come to the coronation. Four years before this time, when the " Méditations Poetiques " had first appeared, Victor Hugo had
saluted the rising poet. He had written thus on the
subject in the *Conservateur Littéraire* :—

" At last we have poems from the pen of a poet;
poetry which deserves the name.

" I read the whole of this remarkable book; I read it
again, and, in spite of occasional careless treatment, a
fondness for introducing new words, abundant repetitions, and some obscurity, I was tempted to say to the
author, 'Take courage, young man ! You are one of
those whom Plato would have covered with honours, but
would afterwards have banished from his model republic.
You must expect to be banished also from our land of
anarchy and ignorance, and to you will be wanting the
triumph which Plato at least thought due to the poet,
namely, the palm branch, the flourish of trumpets, and
the crown of flowers.' "

Some time after, the Duke de Rohan introduced to Victor Hugo a young man, tall, with a noble and gentlemanly bearing. This was M. de Lamartine. A friendship was formed between the two poets which no absence could alter.

In the winter they frequently met, and when the summer heat drove M. de Lamartine to Saint-Point, they would correspond. They kept each other mutually informed as to what they were at work upon; they discussed matters relating to art; and they differed in opinion as to accurate writing, which De Lamartine despised.

"Grammar crushes poetry. Grammar was not meant for us. We must not know a language merely by rules; we must speak as we feel."

In another letter from the same author I read as follows:—

"I trust that the ills you suffer from are but troublesome rhymes, and that in your next letter you will tell me that you are all well in your little snuggery in the Rue de Vaugirard. I, for my part, am better, without being quite the thing. But I have been composing some verses the last few days, and that comforts me. Very shortly I will send you some hundreds of them. What I am doing is a serious badinage. But how pleasant it is to feel in the mood for it, and to give one's self up to it! The ode shall be dedicated to you; therefore, you must dedicate yours to me as soon as it is finished. May our united names teach posterity, should they ever reach so far, that there are such things to be found as poets who have loved one another!" . . .

On another occasion he was invited to Saint-Point, and to render the invitation irresistible, it was in verse:—

> " Oiseau chantant parmi les hommes,
> Ah ! reviens à l'ombre des bois ;
> Il n'est qu'au désert où nous sommes
> Des échos dignes de ta voix ! . . .
>
> Non loin de la rive embellie
> Où la Saône aux flots assoupis
> Retrouve sa pente et l'oublie
> Pour caresser les verts tapis
> Où son cours cent fois se replie . . .
> Au sommet d'un léger côteau,
> Qui seul interrompt ces vallées,
> S'élèvent deux tours accouplées,
> Par la teinte des ans voilées,
> Seul vestige d'un vieux château
> Dont les ruines mutilées
> Jettent de loin sur le hameau
> Quelques ombres démantelées ;
> Elles n'ont plus d'autres vassaux
> Que les nids des joyeux oiseaux,
> L'hirondelle et les passereaux
> Qui peuplent leurs nefs dépeuplées ;
> Le lierre au lieu des vieux drapeaux
> Fait sur leurs cimes crénelées
> Flotter ses touffes déroulées,
> Et tapisse de verts manteaux
> Les longues ogives moulées,
> Où les vautours et les corbeaux,

Abattant leurs noires volées,
Couvrent seuls sombres créneaux
De leurs sentinelles ailées.
Ce n'est plus qu'un débris des jours,
Une ombre, hélas ! qui s'evapore.
En vain à ces nobles séjours,
Comme le lierre aux vieilles tours,
Le souvenir s'attache encore ;
Miné par la vague des ans,
Sur le cours orageux du temps
Leur puissance s'en est allée ;
Ils font sourire les passants,
Et n'ont plus d'autres courtisans
Que les pauvres de la vallée.
Autour de l'antique manoir,
Tu n'entendras d'autre murmure
Que les soupirs du vent du soir
Glissant à travers la verdure,
Les airs des rustiques pipeaux,
Ou la clochette des troupeaux
Regagnant leur étable obscure,
Et quelquefois les doux concerts
D'une harpe mélancholique,
Dont une brise ossianique
Vient par moments ravir les airs
A travers l'ogive gothique,
A l'écho de ces murs déserts.
C'est là que l'amitié t'appelle.

. . . .

Victor Hugo promised to go. At Rheims, Lamartine

reminded him of his promise, and M. Nodier being present, he also was invited.

"We'll not only go ourselves," said M. Nodier, whose trip to Rheims had induced a love for gadding about, "but we'll take our wives and daughters with us; and I see how it may be done without costing us anything."

"How's that?" asked Victor Hugo.

"It is by taking advantage of the opportunity to pay a visit to the Alps."

"Well, what next?"

"Why, then we will write an account of our travels. If you don't like the idea of it, I'll carry it out; you shall merely contribute a few verses; Lamartine, too, if he will join us. We shall be sure to find somebody who will illustrate our book for us. And thus it will happen that that most praiseworthy publisher, Urbain Canel, will pay us for our journey."

"Agreed," said the two poets.

M. Urbain Canel accepted the proposal willingly. A treaty was signed immediately they returned to Paris, in which M. Lamartine, Victor Hugo, M. Charles Nodier, and M. Taylor united in engaging to prepare a work which was to be called, provisionally, "Voyage Poétique et Pittoresque au Mont-Blanc et à la Vallée de Chamonix" (A Poetical and Picturesque Trip to Mont Blanc and the Valley of Chamouny.) M. de Lamartine was to receive two thousand francs for four "Meditations," M. Victor Hugo two thousand for four odes, M. Taylor two thousand francs for eight drawings, which he engaged not to draw himself,

but to provide, and M. Charles Nodier two thousand two
hundred and fifty francs for all the text.

The copyright of the book was sold, but M. Hugo
wished to reserve for himself the right of reprinting his
four odes in a collection he was about to bring out.
The publisher consented, on condition that he would add
two or three prose sheets, which should be the sole copyright of the "Voyage."

M. Charles Nodier and M. Victor Hugo each immediately received seventeen hundred and fifty francs on
account. All they now had to do was to prepare for departure. They followed the same plan they had adopted
on their journey to the coronation, except that instead of
one coach they hired two. M. Nodier took a *caléche*, and
gave M. Gué, the gentleman who was to take the sketches,
a place in it. M. Victor Hugo, who, in order to accom-
modate his little girl, took with him a cradle and a nurse,
hired a *berlin*.

The two carriages started from the Barrière of Fontaine-
bleau, where they had arranged to meet. They drove on
abreast, and set off chatting to each other from one
carriage to the other.

At the entrance to Essonne, M. Nodier told them to
stop at the first inn on the right.

"Let us breakfast here," said he. "This inn shall be
mentioned in our book. It was here that Lesurques was
taken prisoner."

The assassination of the courier of the Lyons mail was
the subject of conversation during breakfast. M. Nodier,
who had known Lesurques, spoke about this victim to

the fallibility of judges with so much feeling that he brought tears to the eyes of the ladies who were present. He perceived that he had cast a gloom over the meal, and wished to restore cheerfulness.

"Bah!" said he, "this inn is full of gloomy recollections. They say, sometimes, 'It's a wise child that knows its own father.' Now, I assert that one can't always be certain of knowing who one's mother was, and here's a proof of it."

"How do you make that out?" asked every one.

"By this billiard table."

There was a billiard table in the adjoining room.

They asked him to explain himself, and he related that, two years before, a carriagefull of nurses was returning from fetching their nurslings from Paris, in order to convey them to Burgundy, and stopped for breakfast at this inn. In order to feed at their ease, the nurses had deposited the children on the billiard table. Whilst they were in the dining-room some waggoners had entered to play a game, and in removing the babies had placed them pell-mell on the benches. The nurses, on their return, were much puzzled how to recognize their nurslings; for we all know that newly-born children are exactly alike. So they merely exclaimed, "Well, it can't be helped," and took the children at random from the pile, merely making a point that the sex of the child was all right. Thus at the present day, probably not less than twenty mothers are tenderly lavishing on the children of others the endearing epithets of "my son," or "my daughter."

"That's too bad," said Madame Nodier, "as if the linen was not sure to be marked!"

"Ah, well," said her husband, "if you always look for probability you will never find out the truth."

M. Nodier was a first-rate talker. His lively and highly-coloured narratives formed a striking contrast to his sleepy and drawling manner. He possessed the rare faculty of combining the enlarged ideas of the philosopher with the naïve charm of the believer. The stories he told, which generally owed much more to his imagination than to the real facts, exhibited in the fiction every appearance of truth, and in what was true the appearance of being impossible.

M. Victor Hugo had left his passport behind him in Paris, and this forgetfulness was nearly the cause of a very unpleasant result. He had just stepped out of the carriage to mount the hill at Vermanton, and was running, the first of the party, up a steep ascent. He was fair and slight; his light-grey dress made him look even more juvenile than his twenty years warranted, and gave him all the appearance of a school-boy at home for the holidays. Some gendarmes, whom he met, asked him what he meant by wearing a ribbon in his button-hole? When he replied that it signified that he belonged to the Legion of Honour, they observed that the cross of that Order was never given to mere boys, and requested to see his passport, without which, he must prove his right to wear the ribbon. The non-appearance of the passport confirmed them in their suspicions, and they arrested this

usurper of the ribbon.   Happily, M. Nodier was forty
years of age.   He hastened to the spot, and said to the
dragoons,—

"This gentleman is the celebrated Victor Hugo."

The gendarmes, who, probably, knew nothing at all
about him, did not choose to appear ignorant, and allowed
their prisoner to depart, making him many apologies. The
passport, which was sent from Paris, reached the traveller
at Verdun, and M. Victor Hugo was allowed to be as
young as he pleased for the future, without running any
risk.

It will easily be believed that all they saw on their
journey, such as churches, ruins, towers, pointed arches,
and glass windows, were visited in detail. Thus they
reached Mâcon, where they had appointed to meet M. de
Lamartine, in an inn recommended by him. M. Nodier
asked for him as he alighted from the carriage.

"M. de Lamartine!" said the innkeeper; "you mean
M. Alphonse?"

They had not yet become accustomed to the poet's
new name at Mâcon, for he had not used it till after the
publication of "Les Méditations," and he was better
known by his Christian name.

M. de Lamartine was at Mâcon, but he did not live at
the inn, having a house where he used to stop when he
came to the town. M. Nodier went there, and brought
him.

"I am going to carry you all off to Saint-Point," said
the great poet, in the kindest manner.

"To-morrow," said M. Nodier. "Our wives must have time to shake off the dust after so long a journey, and we ourselves have to inspect the town."

They dined together. After dinner, they went to the theatre, where an actress from Paris was performing, Mademoiselle Léontine Fay. "The good people of Mâcon," said M. de Lamartine, "would never have forgiven me, if I had not brought Victor Hugo and Charles Nodier to be stared at." The ladies drew from their trunks their only silk dresses, and the gentlemen the only dress coats they possessed. M. de Lamartine, more familiar with the townspeople, kept on his hunting coat and his white trousers, which he had worn in travelling, and also his hat, which was torn in several places.

They were performing an opéra-comique and a vaudeville, one of which, written on purpose to include 'La Petite Fay,' was called *La Petite Sœur*. *La Petite Sœur* had, however, grown a good deal, for Mademoiselle Léontine Fay was now between sixteen and seventeen years of age, and was but ill concealed in an inordinately large *corbeille de marriage*. She was a great favourite on account of her beauty, and her thinness and dark complexion were lost sight of in the charms of a pair of large and splendid eyes.

The next day the two carriages set off for Saint-Point, and, after a three-hours' journey, they reached the poet's house. M. de Lamartine had preceded his guests, and, with his wife, was awaiting their arrival in the courtyard. Had he not been there to receive them, M. Victor Hugo would have thought the drivers had made a mistake.

The " embattled summits," which his host had described in his verses, consisted of flat tiles. Of the " bushy ivy," there was not a single leaf; and the " tone that had been given to it by years," was, in reality, a yellow wash.

" Where is the castle you mentioned in your verses ? " said M. Victor Hugo.

" You see it," answered M. de Lamartine. "I have but rendered it habitable. The thickness of the ivy kept the walls damp, and gave me the rheumatism, so I had it pulled down. I had the battlements destroyed, and I modernized the house, the grey stones of which made me feel melancholy. Ruins are nice things to describe, but not to inhabit."

M. Victor Hugo, who had already commenced his attack on the destroyers of the picturesque, was not of M. de Lamartine's opinion : he could only be comforted by looking at the scenery, which quite corresponded with the description.

They followed their hosts into a large drawing-room, with deep recesses, where were M. de Lamartine's two sisters. They were young, slim, fair, smiling, and elegant. His mother, a venerable and amiable woman, was also there. They walked about, they breakfasted, they returned to the house, and M. de Lamartine repeated some admirable lines. At dinner, the poet's daughter made her appearance, a little child, with a complexion of lilies and roses, whose face was buried in her golden hair. She was one of those angels that God only lends to mothers to give them a moment of happiness and a life of mourning.

Madame de Lamartine, who was an Englishwoman, dined, as is the custom in her country, in full dress. She and her sisters-in-law wore low dresses, and were decked out with ribbons. The unfortunate high silk dresses of the travellers were rather out of place amidst such grandeur.

Although Madame Nodier was under-dressed in comparison to her hostess, she was over-dressed so far as her own feelings were concerned. As she had worn a silk dress all day, she felt tired and unwell, and wished to return to Mâcon the same night. M. de Lamartine, who understood true hospitality, which consists in allowing guests to go as well as to come, had his own horse and carriage got ready for them, as the travellers had dismissed their conveyance on arriving.

There was only room for the ladies inside the carriage, and as Madame Victor Hugo had brought her ladies'-maid and her daughter with her, M. Victor Hugo and M. Nodier returned home on foot, accompanied by M. de Lamartine, who shortened the road to them by taking them across the mountain. The path was very steep, and at the highest point they stopped to take rest. M. de Lamartine alighted from his horse, and they sat down and began to chat. The rich plains of Burgundy lay at their feet, the setting sun gilded the horizon, the woods had all the soft and dying tenderness common to them on fine summer nights, everything seemed full to overflowing with the great beauties of nature, and the three friends poured out their hearts to one another.

M. de Lamartine conducted his guests as far as the

high road: they now had only to walk straight on, and
could not lose their way. He grasped their hands cordially, and returned home.

The unexpected return of M. Charles Nodier and M.
Victor Hugo astonished the innkeeper, who did not expect them for a few days.

"Why," said M. Nodier, "our wives must have told
you we were coming?"

"The ladies themselves have not come yet."

M. Nodier gave reins to his imagination. As they
were driving, it was hardly possible, in the natural course
of things, that they should reach home later than themselves, who had come all the way on foot and had taken
a long rest. Some accident must have occurred; doubtless, the coachman had got tipsy and upset them, and
probably his wife and daughter were at that moment
lying at the bottom of a precipice. He confided his
fears to Victor Hugo, and both set out immediately for
the high road leading to Saint-Point, only stopping to
question the passers-by, or to listen for the slightest noise.

In the course of half-an-hour they heard the noise
of wheels, and then perceived the carriage advancing at a
foot pace. The ladies had desired to enjoy the beautiful
evening, and had told the coachman to drive very slowly.

M. Nodier was vexed with his wife for having given
him such a fright, and declared that no one had a right
to drive at a foot pace. But as he was, at the bottom of
his heart, very much pleased, she laughed at his anger
and kissed him, and he allowed himself to be appeased,
scolding all the time, and in ecstasies.

XLIII

GENEVA.

THE next morning at five o'clock they left Mâcon. The drivers lost their way, and at noon, not perceiving the inn at which they intended to breakfast, they were obliged, though a party of seven, to be satisfied with an omelette made of four eggs, which was all that could be procured at a wretched lonely little inn. At Tournus they admired the beautiful romanesque abbey, with its three steeples; and at Bellegarde the Perte du Rhône. The river here sinks into the earth with a formidable bubbling which causes the bridge to tremble, and it reappears further on without ever returning anything which has been thrown into it. The travellers did as it was the custom to do on such occasions, and threw several things into the abyss, in order that they might never see them again.

On the morning after this, they left France in a thick fog, which the sun suddenly dispersed, permitting them to enjoy the dazzling apparition of Mont Blanc, of the Alps, and of Geneva.

M. Nodier, who had recently visited that part of the

country undertook to lead the party. M. Victor Hugo, enraptured with the Lake of Geneva, was outrageous when M. Nodier's carriage stopped in front of a hotel, from the windows of which there was a superb view of a high grey stone wall.   But M. Nodier, whose gastronomical ideas had sustained a severe blow on the appearance of the omelette made of four eggs, told them that he did not select inns on account of the view one might obtain from their windows, but for their good cookery, and he intended to go to the one where they excelled in that respect. They were obliged to give up to him, and almost owned that he had reason on his side when they had once tasted those excellent lake fish, the *féra* and the *ombre chevalier*, dressed in exquisite style.

The police regulations at Geneva were very annoying. Each hotel possessed a register in which every traveller was bound to write his name, his age, his profession, from whence he came, and his object in travelling. All this annoyed M. Nodier, who, in reply to the last inquiry wrote :—" *Come to upset your Government.*"

The Rue des Dômes was still the old street, with pointed roofs overhanging and supported by wooden posts; this constituted a long covered gallery, enlivened by the objects displayed by the shopkeepers and by swarms of purchasers.   This picturesque bazaar has been replaced by a straight, regular, and dull-looking street, a source of great pride to the citizens.

The promenades of the town were ornamented with fine grass plots, which would have been pleasant enough, had not the eye been frequently shocked by posts on which the following sentence was inscribed: "No one is allowed to walk on the grass slopes."

Those who desired to walk on grass certainly might find it in the country, but then, in order to quit the town, it was necessary to get one's passport visé, which turned a simple walk into a walk under the superintendence of the police.

The open carriage and the berlin were only used on one excursion, and that was to drive to Lausanne to be present at a public fête in honour of William Tell. They saw Coppet on their way thither. The lake was covered with boats decorated with gay flags, and its deep blue rivalled and reflected the azure tint of the sky. Lausanne was too small to contain all the joyous crowd who had hastened from every canton. Geneva, on their return, looked all the duller by the contrast, and they determined to leave it the next day.

The next day, however, when they desired to leave the town, the gates were shut; it was Sunday, and the bells were ringing for church. Whilst divine service is going on, Geneva is quite like a prison. To pass away the time, M. Victor Hugo wished to visit the Church of Saint Peter; but he had hardly set foot in it when they requested him to take his departure as he disturbed the congregation. He came back and shut himself up in the berlin, quite angry with the Protestants, who neither allowed people to go out nor to come in.

At length they came to an end of the last psalm and the town was thrown open again. The horses, urged to their full speed, flew along the road to Sallenches, and

there they breakfasted.   While seated at table, Victor
Hugo and M. Nodier began talking about Urbain Canel's
book.

"What a beautiful book it will be!" said Madame
Nodier.

"If it is ever written," said Madame Hugo.

"What do you mean by 'if it is ever written?'" called
out the two authors, quite offended at any doubts on the
subject.   "As if we could avoid writing it when we are
already half paid for it."

"You are at this moment eating a wing of it," said M.
Nodier, pointing out to Madame Hugo the white meat of
the chicken she had on her plate.

In order that there might be no further doubts raised
as to the book, M. Victor Hugo set to work the next day
on the two chapters which fell to his share, and in them
he described the journey from Sallenches to Chamounix.

The reader will prefer his own account to mine, and will
be grateful to me for bringing to light these notes, which
were not published as originally intended, owing to the
unforeseen insolvency of M. Urbain Canel, and which
M. Victor Hugo has nowhere included in his published
works.

XLIV

M. VICTOR HUGO'S RECITAL.

AT Sallenches we quitted the carriage. From this town to the Priory of Chamounix, the journey is made by *chars-à-bancs*, drawn by mules. This conveyance consists of a single bench, on which one sits sideways, under a kind of little leather canopy, which may be closed should a storm come on.

This new way of travelling warns you that you are passing from one kind of scenery to another. You now penetrate into the heart of the mountains. The round, flat shoes of the horses are no longer of any use in these rugged, steep, and slippery ascents. An ordinary kind of wheel would get injured at once in these narrow paths, broken at intervals by the jagged points of the rocks and worn away by torrents of rain. Light and yet strongly-built waggons are necessary, which can be taken to pieces when the difficult passes are reached, and which can be carried across on the shoulders of guides and muleteers, at the same time as the traveller. Until this point is reached, the Alps are only seen : they now begin to be felt.

As we advance, and rise higher, it is necessary to dismiss even these light equipages: the indomitable soil of the Alps will refuse to bear them. The sure-footed mules will still carry you for some time in these high regions, where there is no other road than the course of the torrent which rushes by the shortest way from the mountain top to the bottom of the abyss. You still advance, until dizziness or some unconquerable obstacle obliges you to descend from your steed and continue the perilous journey on foot. At length you reach those spots which man himself is obliged to shrink from, those solitudes of ice, of granite, and of mist, where the chamois, pursued by the hunter, boldly ventures for safety, and hides itself between gaping precipices and falling avalanches.

While pondering on the dangers which threaten the footsteps of the inquiring traveller, wandering amongst these scenes of savage nature, one is tempted to consider as mere fables, the accounts in ancient writers of Carthaginian implements of war, and in later days of the French artillery, being transported across the Alps. We ask ourselves, half in fear and half in doubt, how it was possible that the heavy military train of a great army could have been transported over paths which sometimes want sufficient space for the delicate foot of the chamois, and how it came to pass that men have twice succeeded in doubling those far-stretching promontories of rock which dip into the clouds and plunge deeply in the blue sky. It can only be explained by remembering the power that God has given to human intelligence. These marvellous things are accomplished in order to show how completely man can control physical nature. At sight of the Alps, it would seem to appear that nothing short of a complete army of giants could cross them. Is it not worthy of admiration that, in order to accomplish such a miracle, and to revive it in our time, it should have required for each army only one such giant, strong in will and of commanding genius—namely, Hannibal, in former days, and Napoleon, in this century?

I perceive that I am far outstripping in thought the pace of our conveyances. We have hardly lost sight of Sallenches, and already I am trying to distinguish on the glistening crests of the old Alps, traces, which indeed, the two great invaders of Italy have never left there. To say the truth, it is difficult not to feel some emotion, when, on a fine August morning, descending the slope on which Sallenches is built, we perceive gradually unrolling before our eyes that vast amphitheatre of mountains, different in colour, different in form, and different also in elevation and grouping. They are dazzling and sombre by turns, some green and some white, some distinct and some confused, reached occasionally by a bright sunbeam which falls obliquely upon them, and lights up every crevice; and above them, like the sacred stone in a druidical circle, Mont Blanc itself rises majestically, with its diadem of ice, and its mantle of snow.

On leaving Sallenches, the road to Chamounix lies across a vast plain, which gives one ample time to admire the grand and unchanging landscape. This plain, which is nearly two leagues in width, had been a complete lake on the preceding day. It had rained heavily, and the

Arve, which intersects it from one end to the other, had
converted the whole of it into its bed, as often happens
after heavy storms. But twenty-four hours had been sufficient for the torrent to re-enter the channel from which it
so often escapes, and the road, although still muddy when
we drove over it, was only at rare intervals interspersed
with pools of yellowish water, which served to refresh the
feet of the mules, and also to wash the low wheels of
the *chars-à-bancs*.

It would be very pleasant to travel across the rich
verdure which surrounds one on every side, if one did not
feel impatient to reach the mountains and to take leave
of the plain and its bright green covering. When, therefore, after several hours of monotonous travelling, the
guide pointed out, on the other side of the Arve, perched
up at a considerable elevation on the shoulder of the
mountain, the roofs of the houses belonging to the village
of Chède, nearly hidden in the trees, we were glad to
reach the red wooden bridge which conducts across to
the opposite bank of the river, from whence at last we
begin to ascend.

It is very delightful to pause a moment on this bridge,
whilst it is trembling under you, shaken both by the
movement of the *chars-à-bancs*, and also by the roaring
of the Arve, which is white with foam, and which is
tossed about under the single arch between blocks of
granite. Having the back turned towards Mont Blanc,
nothing meets the eye but smiling and tranquil scenery,
which is all the more welcome because of the turmoil
beneath. To the left there is a lovely amphitheatre of

woods, châlets, and cultivated fields; in the foreground, at the further extremity of the plain, lies Sallenches, with its white houses and its metal-covered steeple glittering in the sun, and situated at the foot of a lofty mountain, covered with verdure, and surmounted with huge fragments of rock, looking like some old fortress of the Titans. At length, and towards the right appears the magnificent waterfall of Chède, which bursts forth from a kind of natural shell, about half way down the mountain side, expanding as it falls, and encircled with a glorious halo—the rainbow which it has itself made.

After having climbed with difficulty up a road covered with rolling stones, rattling under the mules' feet, we cross the village of Chède, and leaving the waterfall behind us, enter the mountains. Here, for some time, the road is shaded by huge oaks, birch-trees, and tall larches, which intermingle their branches and shut in the view by this roof of green leaves. In one moment the wood ceases, and, as if so arranged by art, a new scene of a very different kind of beauty is presented to the eye. This is a little lake, called, I believe, the *Lac Vert*, or Green Lake, because of the thick carpet of grass which encloses it, and makes it appear like a glass mirror lying on green velvet. This lake, whose waters are exquisitely clear, is equally striking by its freshness and the graceful elegance of its position, contrasting very pleasantly with the gloomy severity of the mountains in the midst of which it lies. One would fancy one's self suddenly transported to another land and under other skies, were it not that Mont Blanc is at hand with its wide sweeps of snow, its vast

fields of ice, its needle-shaped and lofty peaks, commanding attention, and as if jealous of any softer impressions
which may arise by these more delicate beauties, it is
seen reflected in all its stern grandeur even from the
peaceful waters of the lake.

I know not by what invisible thread, by what electrical
communication, the things of nature are connected with
things of art; but, at the first glance of this fine contrast,
I thought of those grand creations of old Shakespeare, in
which a tall gloomy character dominates over the whole
play, and here and there, in some apparently unimportant
scene, is seen reflected in a soul clear, transparent, and
pure as the waters of this Lac Vert. Such works are
complete, like nature itself. An Ophelia is always at
hand when Hamlet appears. There is always a Des-
demona for Othello, and there is the Lac Vert for Mont
Blanc.

One must not bid farewell to this lake without dis-
tributing some small coins amongst the little children of
Chède and of Passy, who offer the traveller glasses of its
fresh and delicious water. I have often heard travellers
complain of the importunity of these people, who, if such
an expression may be allowed, sell you by retail the
beauties of the country they inhabit. We ought not to
grumble: these poor creatures have nothing but their
Alps to live upon.

The scene changes. The soil is barren, and the verdure
disappears. The road, which is constantly obstructed by
rocks, turns and coils like a long serpent all along the
sides of a steep mountain, which looks as if it had been

overthrown by some disturbance of nature. We reach *Nant Noir*.

In a deep ravine, where all vegetation seems dead, between red escarpments of ferruginous soil, amidst blocks of granite which might be taken for blocks of ebony, there rushes with a frightful sound a black torrent whose foam even is not white. This is the *Torrent Noir*, so called because of the dark colour communicated to its waters by the particles of slate with which it is loaded, or perhaps on account of its being extremely dangerous to cross when swollen by heavy rains. Everything here is gloomy and desolate. Naked ridges, overhanging rocks, echoes angrily repeating the furious roaring of the torrent. There is not a single tree, with the exception of the gloomy veil of pines, which the mountains display at the horizon. So far as thoughts and impressions are concerned, there is an interval of worlds between the Lac Vert and the Nant Noir.

The country abounds in traditions relating to this torrent. On its banks, they tell you, the spirits of the *montagnes maudites* hold a devil's sabbath on winter nights. It is these spirits who shake a whole mountain to hide their treasures within it. Their tumultuous flight has destroyed all the trees which formerly grew on the spot. It was whilst dancing there that the ground was burnt, and whilst bathing there that the water was blackened. There is also a demon of the Nant-Noir, who pushes travellers into the abyss and laughs at them as they fall in. His eyeballs are two fiery globes; and more than one hardy chamois-hunter has heard his hoarse and sonorous voice replying to the voice of the torrent from the bottom of the abyss.

I own to a certain weakness in matters of this kind. The terrible beauty and grandeur of this savage spot would have wanted something to complete its fascination, had there not been some popular tradition to lend it a colouring of the marvellous and supernatural. I have willingly dwelt on these details, because I am an admirer of superstitions : they are the daughters of religion, and the mothers of poetry.

The torrent once crossed, the *nants* become more frequent; the windings of the road are more sudden and steeper; the crown of the hill, over which the road passes, has been deeply scooped out by the heavy rains, by the falling down of the rocks, and by numerous avalanches. Notwithstanding all this, vegetation springs forth again as lively and fresh as ever on the roadsides, and hides from sight the river Arve, which is heard rushing along at the bottom of the ravine.

A gloomy and melancholy-looking valley next succeeds. In the midst of it rises a steeple, around which a few huts are grouped. This is Servoz. Enclosed on all sides by high mountains, the valley seems to be buried in a winding-sheet of snow, under a black shroud of fir trees. It adds to the singular impression of melancholy which it produces on the mind when we see it overtopped and threatened by the huge ruins of a mountain which fell, I believe, in the year 1741. It is said that the fall of this mountain, which destroyed forests, overwhelmed villages, and opened deep abysses, was accompanied by such a deluge, both of dust and ashes, that for three whole days it was dark as night in all the country round. The savants declared that it was a voleano. They were mistaken, and so were the ignorant, for they thought it was the end of the world. Of the two mistakes, I prefer that of the ignoramuses : theirs, at least, is the most original.

This mountain in ruins is both frightful to look at and to think of. I do not know, and no one can tell, what occurred to disturb the equilibrium of this vast mass, nor what cause undermined the foundations on which its immense terraces, its uplands, its slopes, and its peaks reposed. Was it an internal convulsion of the earth ? Was it a drop of water which had been slowly making its way for centuries ? . . . *Felix qui potuit.* . . .

But it is difficult to avoid giving one's self up to useless speculations concerning this great mystery, in presence of so tremendous a phenomenon. The soil, the snow, and the forests, whilst being suddenly precipitated into the surrounding valleys, have brought to light what may be called the skeleton of the mountain. These blocks of black marble veined with white, are its monstrous feet, still half hidden by pyramidal masses of fallen earth ; here are its bones of flint; its arms of granite are stretching out on high, towering above the clouds ; and that large zone of calcareous rock, which exhibits horizontal bedding, is the wrinkled brow of the giant.

How little the monuments of man appear by the side of these marvellous edifices, constructed on the earth by some more powerful hand, and suggesting themselves to the soul as fresh manifestations of the Deity ! In vain, as time rolls on, do they change their forms and aspects: their architecture, ever renewed, retains always its original type.

To these overhanging and precipitous rocks succeed others which pierce the clouds; fresh trees will grow without culture where these old dead trunks now lie; these torrents glide away, but other cataracts will succeed them. For centuries the aspect of the Alps has not varied: the details change, but the great whole remains.

Happy the people who, like the descendants of William Tell and Winkelried, possess monuments such as these to which they can confide all their memories of glory, religion, and liberty! How can these sacred traditions ever be forgotten, when nothing is perishable of that which recalls them to us? These sublime edifices need fear neither the ignoble discoloration which has affected our beautiful cathedrals, nor the scraper which has mutilated the front of the Louvre and other noble buildings, nor the hammer which has done and threatened so much mischief to our monuments. Very soon every monument in France will be a ruin; yet a little longer, and these ruins will be nothing but heaps of stones; and after a time, these stones will be reduced to dust. Here, on the contrary, in Switzerland, everything, it is true, is transformed, but nothing dies. A fallen mountain is still a mountain. The colossus has changed attitudes, that is all. In every part of creation there is an animating breath. God's works live, those of men only last for a time; and that time, how short is it!

We quit Servoz after taking some refreshment, as it

is the half-way between Sallenches and Chamounix. Now the road begins to follow the course of my reflections, and we pass from a mountain overturned to a castle in ruins. We have been coasting along for the last quarter of an hour close to the Arve, which flows on a level with the road. Suddenly the muleteer points out to us on the right a sort of high promontory, which the neighbouring mountain projects into the middle of the river, some fragments of dismantled wall, with the ruins of a tower, some narrow arches, made by the hand of man, and large fissures caused by time. It is Saint Michael's manor, an old fortress belonging to the days of the Counts of Geneva, celebrated in the country, like the Nant Noir, because of the demons who inhabit it and the magical treasures it contains.

This formidable palace, the ancient citadel of Aymon and of Gérold, is now solitary and gloomy, like the raven which croaks amongst its ruins. The black ramparts, broken by the hand of time, are hardly seen above the tufts of holly and broom, and the thorns which now fill up the ditch and obstruct the avenue. Curtains of ivy usurp the place of heavy drawbridges and portcullises of iron. Above, towering beyond the reach of human eye, rises a forest of larches and pines; underneath is the roaring torrent of the Arve, blocked up with fragments of granite, which have fallen from the rock on which the Castle of Saint Michael is built. One of these rocks, rounded by the force of the water, forms a more serious impediment, and stands up above the rest.

From time to time the Arve attacks this rock with angry

waves, rolling along and leaping up the smaller rocks till they hide it. The giant is thus concealed for a time by the foam, which covers it as with tresses of golden hair. Then the water retires, and the angry river recommences a new attack, while the rock is once more seen, bald and naked.

A bridge is now reached. We return to the left bank of the Arve, and whilst our *chars-à-bancs* have some difficulty in following us, we begin to climb the ascent on foot. It is a narrow and steep road, cut out with great labour, on the edge of a frightful precipice, to which nothing can be likened unless it be the mountain that borders the Arve on the other side.

This path, sometimes cut in the hard rock, sometimes suspended and projecting over an abyss, is the road from the Valley of Servoz to the Valley of Chamounix. We slip every minute as we walk along it over the granite flagstones, against which the iron shoes of the mules strike fire. To the right are perceived, suspended overhead, the roots of great larches laid bare by the rains : to the left you can touch with your foot their summits, which are as pointed as the extremity of a steeple. An aged woman, both infirm and idiotic, seated in a sort of movable niche, is stationed at the entrance of this perilous road, and solicits charity from the passers-by. I seemed to behold one of those begging fairies we read of in fairy tales, on the look-out for an adventurer by the roadside, and resolved either to destroy him if he refused, or to make his fortunes if he offered, an alms.

Hardly has one passed this beggar than a cross is

reached. It is erected at the extreme edge of the gulf. One must pass quickly in front of this cross, as its presence announces an accident and a danger.

A little further on, one stops to listen: an extraordinary echo is to be heard there. Formerly, before Dr. Pocock's discovery of the wonders of this Valley of Chamounix, which had been made over in the eleventh century, by Aymon, Count of Geneva, to "God and Saint Michael the Archangel,"—before man had traced any path whatever on the ridge of this mountain,—there was a legend attached to it. If the chamois-hunter, carried by the ardour of the chase into this formidable gorge, should by any chance reach this spot where we now are, he would put to his mouth with a shudder the horn suspended at his belt, and would sound three times the magic call, *Hi! ha! ho!* Three times from the distant horizon a voice would bring back to him the triple adjuration *Hi! ha! ho!* He would then rush away horror-struck, and would relate, when he had reached the valleys in safety, that a fairy chamois had enticed him beyond the limits of the Castle of Saint Michael, and that he had heard the voice of the Spirit of the Accursed Mountains.

Now, in this same spot, travellers may be seen, and well-dressed women alight from their *chars-à-bancs,* rolling over a decent road. Little ragged boys run up, armed with long speaking-trumpets. They bring forth from them shrill sounds, which still bear some resemblance to the adjuration of the hunter. A mountain voice repeats them still more distinctly, but in a more feeble and distant tone.   And then, should you inquire of these children what that sound is, they will reply, "*It is the echo*," and will hold out their hands for money.   Where has the poetry gone to ?

Leaving the young beggars, the speaking-trumpet, and the home of the echo behind us, we plunge further into the gorge, which becomes gradually narrower and yet more savage.   For some moments a grey, dull mist has concealed the sky from us.   We mount; it descends ; and we watch it, as it enwraps, one after another, the valleys between the opposite ridges.   Its extremities, which thin out and die away, if one may make use of such an expression, resemble the fringe of a net.   White shreds of vapour from the Arve rise slowly into view, and unite with this mist.   It reaches the pines and spreads rapidly from tree to tree, suddenly closing in upon us, and hiding from us the mountains at our feet, just as a curtain drops over the scenery of a theatre.

We were now on a spot the most terrible and beautiful of the road, at the most elevated point of these ascents.   The opposite escarpment could still be distinguished through the mist, its bristling pines almost parallel to the ground, so perpendicular is the slope.   The ranks of the trees are sometimes lighted up by tall dead trees, which must decay where they have fallen, and which could only have been destroyed by the thunder of heaven, or by the avalanche, that thunderbolt of the mountains.   Before us, at the bottom of the black precipice, the white Arve was seen, so far below us that its frightful roaring only sounded to us like a murmur.   At that moment, the clouds opened above us, and on looking up, we saw, instead of the sky, a châlet, a green field, and some almost imperceptible goats browsing far above the clouds. I never met with anything so singular. That which we saw below us, we might have described as the river of hell, while that which was over our heads, resembled an island in Paradise.

It is useless to describe the impression thus made upon us: while fancying it a dream it made us feel giddy from the reality.

*   *   *   *   *

The whole length of the Valley of Chamounix is seen by the traveller who arrives from Sallenches. The winding Arve traverses it from one end to the other. The steeples of the parish churches of its three little villages, Les Ouches, Chamounix, and Argentière, are seen in succession, glittering in the distance. To the left, sur-mounting an amphitheatre covered with gardens, châlets, and cultivated fields, the Bréven, rising almost perpendi-cularly, exhibits its forest of pines and its peaks, around and amongst which the wind circulates, dispersing the clouds as the thread is unwound from the spindle. To the right, Mont Blanc appears, the outline of its summit vividly brought out by the deep blue of the sky, rising above the high glacier of Taconay, and of the Aiguille du Midi, which rears its thousand peaks like a many-headed hydra. Lower down, at the extremity of one of the immense blue mantles of ice with which it is covered, and which the giant mountain allows to trail behind it, even into the midst of the green fields of Chamounix,

G 2

appears the sharp outline of the glacier of the Bossons
(Buissons). The marvellous construction of this glacier
seems at first to present to the eye something incredible
and almost impossible. It is an object certainly on a
grander scale, and perhaps more extraordinary, than that
strange Celtic monument of Karnac, whose 3000 stones,
arranged in fantastic fashion on the plain, are neither
mere rocks nor definite constructions. Let the reader
imagine enormous prisms of ice, white, green, violet, or
blue, according as the sun falls upon them, closely com-
pacted, affecting an infinite variety of position—some
curved, some upright—and their dazzling crests standing
out from a groundwork of sombre larch-trees. The
scene suggests the idea of a town constructed of obe-
lisks, columns, and pyramids; a city of temples and
sepulchres; a palace built by fairies for disembodied
spirits. I cannot wonder that the primitive inhabitants of
these countries often imagined that they perceived supernatural beings flitting amongst the spires of the glacier,
at that hour when the broad light of day sheds upon this
strange architectural medley of nature the pale monotone
of alabaster, or the iridescent colours of mother-of-
pearl.

Beyond the glacier of the Bossons, opposite the priory
of Chamounix, appears the round wooded mound of the
Montanvert, and higher up, in the same direction, are the
two peaks of the Pélerins and the Charmoz, which
resemble magnificent cathedrals of the Middle Ages,
covered with towers and turrets, lantern, spires, steeples,
and belfries. Between these, the glacier of the Pélerins

winds along, looking like a stream of white hair on the grey head of the mountain.

The foreground of the picture completes this magnificent landscape. The eye, which is never wearied with wandering over all parts of this vast edifice of mountains, meets everywhere fresh objects to admire. In one direction, a forest of gigantic larches is seen carpeting the opposite end of the valley. Above this forest the extremity of the Mer de Glace comes down surrounding the Montanvert, as with an embracing arm, and bearing along, to precipitate into the valley, blocks of marble, enormous fragments of gneiss, towers of crystal, monoliths of steel, and hills of adamant. Terminating with perpendicular walls of ice of silvery whiteness, this great glacier pours forth from its vast mouth the river Aveyron, which a mile beyond has become converted into a torrent.

Behind the Mer de Glace, towering over all the surrounding scenery, is the *Dru*, a pyramid of granite, consisting of a single block, 9000 feet high. The horizon, in which one can just discern the Col de Balme, and the rocks of the Tête-Noire, is broken by a multitude of snow-covered peaks, from which stands out, isolated and of a greyish hue, contrasting with their dead whiteness, this prodigious obelisk. When the sky is clear, one might mistake it for the lonely tower of some ruined cathedral, so delicate is its form and so sombre its tint; and the avalanches constantly falling down its sides, look like pigeons, which have paused to rest for a moment on its deserted ledges. When dimly seen through mist, it suggests the idea of a cyclops, as described by Virgil, seated on a mountain, the white patches on the Mer de Glace being the flocks which he is counting as they pass under his feet.

And all this glorious landscape is completed by the eternal presence of Mont Blanc, one of the great mountains of the globe, and by the character of grandeur, which every really great natural object communicates to all that surrounds it. On this summit, which one may speak of, in the exaggerated language of poets, as one of the extremities of the earth, one may contemplate with advantage the marvellous accumulation in so restricted a circle of a multitude of objects, each unique in its appearance. The result will be, that we shall feel ourselves, in Chamounix, to be entering—if I may use such an expression—into the great museum of nature, or into one of the workplaces of the Creator, where are preserved specimens of all created things, or perhaps, I should rather say, where the elements of the visible world are deposited in a mysterious sanctuary.

On the day of our arrival, the 15th August, it was the Feast of the Assumption. We quickly descended the mountain, our eyes meanwhile rivetted on the magnificent picture presented by the valley, which was now at length exposed to our gaze. On a sudden, a turn in the road offered us a new spectacle. Below us, in the green plains, and on the slope of the hill, which raises the church of Ouches above the level of the village to which it belongs, were to be seen in a winding line two rows of villagers, with clasped hands, young girls wearing veils, and children, preceded by several priests and a crucifix. It was a procession returning from the Priory to Ouches, and chanting as they went along. From time to time, the wind conveyed an echo, broken by the sound of their voices. It would be difficult to describe the deep impression thus produced, which sealed up and rendered permanent all the former impressions that had been made. At the moment I speak of, all the Alpine sounds were audible in the valley; the Arve was foaming on its bed of rocks, the torrents were raging, the waterfalls were trembling as they broke at the foot of the precipices they had leaped down, the hurricane was driving the clouds into a corner of the Bréven, the avalanche thundered from the solitudes of Mont Blanc; but to me none of these terrible mountain voices spoke so loudly as the voices of those poor shepherds, in chanting their litany to the Virgin.

How mighty is the power that draws forth, on the same day, at the same hour, the Pope and the College of Cardinals from the golden doors of St. Peter's, the royal *cortège* from the rich portals of Nôtre Dame, and the humble procession of a set of poor villagers from the mountain valleys of Chamounix! What an intelligence must that be, which can at the same moment suggest to a whole world the same thoughts !

The valleys of the Alps possess this peculiarity : they are all to a certain extent complete. Each of them affords frequently, in the most limited space, a kind of separate world. Each has its own aspects, forms, lights, and sounds. One might almost always recapitulate in one word the general effect of the physiognomy of each. The valley of Sallenches is a theatre ; the valley of Servoz is a tomb ; the valley of Chamounix is a temple.

XLV

A LETTER FROM LAMENNAIS.

As soon they reached Chamounix, M. Nodier busied himself in securing guides for the next day ; for an ascent of the Montanvert was in contemplation. He wished to take old Balmat with him, whom he had made acquaintance with on a former journey, and of whom, since the day before, he had been speaking in such enthusiastic terms, that M. Victor Hugo, when asked to write his autograph on the registry at the Inn of Chamounix, wrote thus :—

"Napoleon—Talma.
Chateaubriand—Balmat."

But old Balmat was ill, and M. Nodier had to content himself with one of his relations, whom he selected on account of his name. M. Victor Hugo took the first who came, a very young man.

They rose with the sun, and breakfasted on bread and milk, and on honey from the comb, which they thought excellent. They then started, the men on foot, and the ladies on mules. They were ascending, and every now and then turned round to admire the valley. The houses and their inhabitants gradually looked smaller and smaller, and they seemed to be travelling in Lilliput. The houses, which were almost all gaily coloured, looked like toys. The Aveyron resembled a silver thread flowing over green velvet. They continued to ascend, and when they turned round, nothing more was to be seen; the clouds were under the travellers' feet, and hid the earth from view.

At last they reached the summit. A building was erected on the plateau, and on it was inscribed " *Temple of Nature.*" They entered the temple, and found that the priests consisted of innkeepers, who retailed libations, consisting of a mixture of milk and kirsch.

They still had the Mer de Glace to visit, but the ladies, who were already quite satisfied with what they had done, allowed the gentlemen to proceed there alone. M. Victor Hugo, M. Nodier, and M. Gué, preceded by their guides, then started, assisting themselves with their pointed sticks, and with the hooks at the end of them laying hold every now and then of the rhododendrons, which grow plentifully and are very hardy in the mountains.

M. Victor Hugo's guide, who was new to the business, mistook the path, and ventured on a tongue of ice, situated between two cliffs, which became gradually narrower. Soon the neck of ice was so narrow that the guide became uneasy, but he would not own to his mistake, and he went on in front telling them that the road soon grew wider. On the contrary, it grew narrower still, and very soon was only a thin slice between the abysses.

The guide seized M. Victor Hugo's hand, and said to him, "Do not be afraid." But he was deadly pale himself. A little further on, one of the clefts closed up, and the little tongue of land was united to a plateau; but it was necessary to walk on till you reached it. There was not room for two abreast. The guide had but one foot on the level, and the other on the slippery slope of the precipice; the young mountaineer, however, did not stumble, and bore the pressure of the traveller with the calmness of a statue. After some moments of intense anxiety, they reached the plateau; but there the danger was not over. The plateau was five or six feet above the place where they were, and the step was quite perpendicular.

"We must leave hold," said the guide. "Remain where you are, leaning on your stick, and close your eyes, for fear of becoming giddy."

He climbed up the wall of ice, and after a few seconds, which seemed like quarters of an hour to Victor Hugo, he stooped down, stretched out his two hands to him, and quickly drew him up.

This plateau was well known to the guide, who at once saw where he was. They soon also perceived M. Nodier and M. Gué, who were looking for him, and rather alarmed. M. Nodier's guide, seeing from whence his fellow came out, guessed at the imprudence which he had committed, and harshly reprimanded him for it. He had imperilled the life of a stranger and the honour of his profession; he had cast a stain on the whole body of guides, &c. The young Swiss, who had been so bold in presence of the

abyss, was less so at these reproaches, and hot tears fell
from his eyes.

The ladies were rejoined at the Temple of Nature, and
shuddered at the recital of the danger. It made them
imagine precipices on every side; they dared not make
the descent on their mules, but their footsteps were less
sure than those of the animals, and they slipped more
quickly than was pleasant on the steep sides of the
mountain. They would slide, scat themselves on the
ground, and refuse to get up. They got angry with the
gentlemen for having brought them, became vexed, and
cried. When they were fairly back in the valley, they
laughed at their fears and their tears; the fears of the
guide, and the danger that M. Victor Hugo had incurred,
were all converted into joyful exclamations.

The guides of M. Nodier, and M. Gué, and the guide
who had attended to the ladies, offered their books for
remarks, for they are obliged to ask the traveller to say
how they have performed their duties. Victor Hugo's
guide was thus obliged to present his; but he was quite
out of countenance, and trembled greatly when M. Hugo
gave it him back. His countenance beamed with joy
when he read in it: "I recommend Michel Devonassous,
who saved my life."

M. Nodier and M. Victor Hugo now began to get to
the end of their seventeen hundred and fifty francs, and
were obliged to think of returning home. They turned
their backs sadly enough on this fascinating country, and
returned slowly, stopping at every place where there was
a ruin or a library to be found; for M. Nodier preferred

books to stones. At every spot where they alighted, the two friends would get hold of the innkeeper and question him both at a time, the one about the ruins of the old architecture, and the other on the stalls of the second-hand booksellers. The inkceper would get confused by this cross-examination, and would give contrary answers. M. Nodier would get angry.

"My friend," he would say to M. Victor Hugo, "you are possessed by the demon of the pointed arch!"

"And you by the devil Elzevir!"

They spent a day at Lyons, where Martin, the singer, was performing. Madame Nodier, who never missed any opportunity of going to a theatre, wished to go and hear him, and insisted on every one's going, too. Every one did, except M. Victor Hugo, who did not care for comic operas. At Satoris they were breakfasting at an open window on the ground floor, and the windows were open, admitting the brilliant August sun. Whilst they were enjoying their meal with the hunger and zest a journey gives, an unfortunate girl, of about fifteen years of age, who saw this excellent meal going on, advanced towards the window, and her ragged, thin, and degraded condition struck them the more seen in contrast to the brilliant sunshine. M. Nodier drew from his waistcoat-pocket the first coin which came to hand. Just as he was giving it to the beggar-girl, Madame Nodier told him it was a twenty-franc piece.

"Bah!" said he, "I shall be none the poorer for it in eternity!"

And he gave her the coin.

The two carriages re-entered Paris on the 2nd September, and it was quite time they were back. M. Charles Nodier had twenty-two francs left, and M. Victor Hugo eighteen. They shook hands at the barrière, the caléche driving off towards the Marais, and the berlin towards the Faubourg Saint Germain.

The following is a letter from M. de Lamennais to M. Victor Hugo on the subject of this journey :—

"La Chenaie, 4th November, 1825.

"I congratulate you, my dear friend, on the way in which you have spent this pleasant season. Were I rich and at leisure, I should enjoy travelling, for it is an inexhaustible source of instruction. We learn very little from books, and now less than ever. I had read many works, both on England and on Italy, before I journeyed thither. These two countries struck me in quite a different light, in many respects, to that in which they had been represented to me. One sees but little, it is true, when one only sees with one's eyes, for they are scarcely good for anything else than to make maps; it is the imagination and the intellect that do the rest. 1 have known people who could not bear the sight of the beautiful Campagna of Rome, which is a model of grandeur, and even of grace, in its apparent desolation. When in the evening one passes before the tombs of Metella, and the catacombs of Saint Sebastian, and when crossing among the shadows of the old Romans and the souvenirs of a score centuries, the only inhabitants of these solitudes, one arrives at the Sacred Mount, the feelings that are stirred up in the soul are inexpressible. Not a cottage, not a tree is there; a few eagles only hover over this deserted soil, where a multitude of small hills, like the waves of the sea, form great undulations, and where a soft and dreamy daylight gradually deepens into the gloom of night.   This is all, but it is still Rome, powerful, and imperial; and you are subjugated by this phantom.   Forgive me for this distant excursion, which I was not dreaming of two minutes ago.   It is for you and Nodier to describe the marvellous scenes you have witnessed; as for poor me, I can only feel them. Geneva, on the borders of its lake, sad, cold, and depressing, every now and then raising a discordant and piercing shriek, resembles a cormorant seated on a rock.   It would be doing it too much honour to offer it as a sacrifice to the Eternal City.   When industry shall have been converted into a divinity, one may, perhaps, be able to drag it to its altar.   The minister's words are remarkable and true: 'Those people have, then, sometimes the misery of being in the right.'

"You wish me to mention the state of my health.   It has been very ailing.   For four months I have been unable to work.   My affairs are not prospering; and I am annoyed at it because of my debts.   I must, however, get resigned to it all.   Good-bye, my friend; say everything respectful and kind from me to Madame Hugo, and kiss your dear little girl for me.   A thousand compliments to M. Nodier.   I beg to thank him for so kindly remembering me.   Others also recollect me, but not in the same way.   A little esteem and affection from people who honour me is of great service to me in helping me to fight in the amphitheatre.

"' *Vale et me ama.*'"

XLVI

THE ODE TO THE COLUMN.

MADAME HUGO little supposed that her remark at the breakfast-table at Sallenches would turn out to be a prophecy. The book never was finished. Her husband was the only one who completed his contribution. M. Nodier waited for the sketches before he began; these took months to prepare, and gave the editor time to become a bankrupt, so that M. Nodier's work was never called for.

In January, 1826, M. Victor Hugo published, after having altered and re-written it to a great extent, " Bug Jargal," which had first come out in the *Conservateur Littéraire*. In October there was a reprint of his first odes, with the addition of several others, and of some ballads, together with a preface, which openly supported the cause of literary liberty. The partizans of established institutions attacked both preface and verses violently; but they also had their partizans, less numerous, it is true, but equally energetic.

There was then a journal conducted by Guizot, M. Dubois, M. Jouffroy, and M. Cousin, men whose names ensured a certain degree of importance, especially in the salons. The *Globe*, an organ of the university, and sententious, extended towards innovators a kind of protecting benevolence. It stepped in between the combatants, advocating progress on the one hand, and moderation on the other. M. Dubois wrote an article with more spirit than the author had expected, and almost enthusiastic, on the ode entitled *Les Deux Iles*.

Victor Hugo never denied himself to any one, not even at meal-times. One morning as he was breakfasting, the servant announced M. Sainte-Beuve. A young man came in, who introduced himself as a neighbour, and as the editor of a friendly journal; he lived in the Rue Nôtre-Dame des Champs, and he was a writer in the *Globe*. The *Globe* would not be contented with a single article on Cromwell, and he was to write the rest. He had requested to have the management of it, dreading M. Dubois' return, who was not every day in such a good humour, and who was likely soon to fall back into the position of professor. The interview was a most agreeable one; and they arranged to see each other again. This would be facilitated, because M. Victor Hugo was about to reside very near his critic, and proposed to take up his quarters also in the Rue Nôtre-Dame des Champs.

A few weeks afterwards, he had established himself there, in a house divided from the street by an avenue of trees, at one end of which was a garden, whose laburnums reached up to the windows of his apartments. A lawn extended as far as a rustic bridge, which was hidden in the summer by the foliage.

M. Victor Hugo would sometimes go to read the newspapers under the arcades of the Odéon. One morning in February, 1827, he found the Liberal journals in a great state of excitement. A scandalous affair had taken place the day before at the Austrian Ambassador's. The Duke of Taranto, who had been asked to a ball at the embassy, had been astonished to hear the usher announce him as Marshal Macdonald. When the Duke of Dalmatia arrived, the fellow announced Marshal Soult. The two dukes were asking each other what all this could possibly mean, and whether it was a mistake of the usher's, when suddenly the Duke of Treviso arrived, and he was announced as Marshal Mortier. The same suppression of foreign titles had been made in the case of the Duke of Reggio. It was no longer possible to entertain any doubt on the subject. It was an intentional and pre-arranged act on the part of the ambassador. Austria, humiliated by titles which recalled its defeats, publicly denied them. The marshals had been invited in order to show contempt for their victories, and the Empire was insulted in their persons. They immediately quitted the embassy in a body.

The soldier's blood which flowed in M. Victor Hugo's veins rushed to his face: it seemed to him as if they were insulting his father, and he felt an irresistible desire to be revenged upon them. He therefore wrote the "Ode à la Colonne."

This ode, originally published in Paris by the *Débats*, and thence copied into several journals, made a great impression. The Opposition press, which until then had been hostile to the Royalist poet, was now in favour of him; but, on the other hand, the Ministerial press gave up praising him. To attack Austria was to attack the Bourbons, whom they had brought back into France. Glorifying the marshals was to glorify the Emperor. To the Royalists, the ode had all the effect of an abandonment of their cause.

This was the beginning of the rupture. Under this insult from Austria, Victor Hugo felt that he was no longer a Vendean, he was now a Frenchman.

" Contre une injure ici tout s'unit, tout se lève,
Tout s'arme, et la Vendée aiguisera son glaive
Sur la pierre de Waterloo ! "

[*Translation.*]
Against an insult all united rise,
All fly to arms: La Vendée whets her sword
Upon the stone of Waterloo !

He had foreseen for France something higher than mere party spirit, something which should obliterate no fact from its history, and which should say to the imperial column,—

" Au bronze de Henri mon orgueil te marie."

[*Translation.*]
My pride unites thee to great Henry's bronze.

It is now no longer the army whom he accepts, as in the ode to his father: he also includes the Emperor. "Buonaparte" is now "Napoleon;" the "tyrant" is forgotten; and "the spur of Napoleon" takes the place of "the sandal of Charlemagne."

XLVII.

CROMWELL.

M. Taylor was then Commissaire Royal at the Comédie Française. He asked M. Victor Hugo why he never wrote for the theatre.

" I was thinking of doing so," was the reply; "in fact, I have actually commenced a drama on the subject of Cromwell."

" Well, finish it and give it to me. A Cromwell of your writing should only be acted by Talma."

In order to settle the matter, he brought the poet and the tragedian together to dinner at the *Rocher de Cancale.*

It was a large dinner-party, but M. Victor Hugo and Talma, placed side by side, were able to converse at their ease.

Talma was then sixty-five years of age : he was worn and ill; he died a few months afterwards, and felt at the time of this meeting that he was going fast. He spoke of his profession with bitterness : actors were not men; he was not a man in spite of his success and reputation. Having been applauded and treated almost as a friend by the Emperor, he had requested that the cross of the Legion of Honour might be given him; but the Emperor had not ventured to accede to his request. Even in his own profession he had done nothing.

M. Victor Hugo exclaimed against this remark.

"No," said the tragedian, "the actor is nothing without his part, and I never acted a part quite suited to me. As for tragedy, it is fine, it is noble, it is grand. I should have desired as much grandeur and more reality. I should have liked a character possessing all the variety and movement of real life, who was not all of a piece, but on the contrary one who was tragic with something of the familiar, a king who was still a man. Did you ever see me in Charles VI. ? It produced some effect when I exclaimed, ' *Bread ! I want bread ! '* This was because the king was no longer undergoing a suffering peculiar to him as a royal person; but one affecting him as a mere human being. No doubt it was tragedy, but it was also truth; it was both sovereignty and misery, it was a king and a beggar at the same time. Truth ! I have sought for it all my life, but what would you have ? I ask for Shakespeare, and they give me Ducis. Truth being absent in the piece itself, I introduced it into the costume. I played Marius with bare legs. No one knows what I might have been, had I found the author for whom I was seeking. I shall die without having really acted once. You, M. Hugo, who are young and full of vigour, you should compose me a part. Taylor tells me that you were inventing a

Cromwell. I always longed to act Cromwell. I bought
his likeness in London. Were you to call on me you
would see it hanging up in my room. What is your play
like? It must be unlike other people's!"

"Your dream as to what acting should be," said M.
Victor Hugo, "exactly corresponds with my dream of
what should be written."

And he then explained to the tragedian some of the
ideas which he was going to embody in *La Préface de
Cromwell;* a drama substituted for a tragedy, a real
man for an ideal personage, reality for conventionalism;
the piece was at liberty to pass from the heroic to the
positive; the style was to include all varieties, epic, lyric,
satiric, grave, comic; there was to be no *tirade,* no " verses
for effect." Here Talma interrupted him hastily.

" Just so," said he; " I wear myself out in trying to
impress that upon them. Let's have no fine verses."

He listened very attentively to the poet's theories.

" And does your Cromwell carry out those ideas?"
said he.

" So much so, that, in order to mark from the very be·
ginning the determination to be natural, its very first line
is a date :—"

"Demain, vingt cinq juin mil six cent cinquante sept."

"You must know whole scenes of it by heart," said
Talma. " You would greatly oblige us by repeating
one."

The other guests added their entreaties to his. Victor
Hugo repeated the scene in which Milton adjures Crom-

well to give up all idea of making himself king. The
scene was ill-chosen; for it was only a long speech, which,
however much it may have been broken up by the expression of strong feeling and the style of wording, was not
quite an abnegation of the *tirade;* besides which, Milton
was speaking all the time, and Talma would have only
had to listen to him. He said the verses were " very
fine," which was rather a questionable eulogium, as he
had just been animadverting on such things. He asked,
however, for another specimen. M. Victor Hugo repeated
the scene where the Protector questions Davenant about
his journey. This time they were far enough removed
from tragedy. At every local detail, at every touch of
frank reality, Talma applauded.

" Logez vous toujours chez votre même hôtesse ?
A la Syrène ? . . .
Vous avez un chapeau de forme singulière !
Excusez ma façon peut-être familière ;
Vous plairit-il, monsieur, le changer pour le mien."

[Translation.]
With the same hostess do you still reside,
The house that's called the Syren ? . . .
You wear a hat of strange outlandish form !
Excuse me if my ways are too off-hand,
But would you, sir, with me a change effect ?

" Capital ! that's it, that's the way to speak ! " And
when the scene was finished he offered his hand to the
author, saying, " Be quick and finish your drama, for I
am in a hurry to act it."

Shortly after this Talma died. M. Victor Hugo, having

lost his actor, did not hurry about it, and was enabled to
develope his drama more than would have been consistent
with a piece intended for representation.

He often composed when he was taking a walk. He
had but a few steps to go in order to reach the Boulevard
of Mount Parnassus, and there he would stroll about
amongst the numerous crowd attracted by the *cabarets* in
the outskirts, by the shops in the open air, by the out-
door shows, and by the cemetery. In full view of the
cemetery there was, at that time, a booth of mountebanks.
This antithesis of Punch and the grave rather fell in with
his idea of a dramatic method that should combine ex-
tremes, and it was there he first conceived the plot of the
third act of *Marion de Lorme*, where the mourning garments of the Marquis de Nangis contrast with the gri-
maces of Gracieux.

It was customary in those days to go and partake of
galettes at the Moulin de Beurre (Butter Mill), so called
from the fact that its proprietor had made his fortune by
selling butter. The mill was in the country, on the road
to Vanvres. Once there, people did not return to dine at
Paris, they dispersed amongst the neighbouring public-
houses. One Sunday, M. Abel Hugo, whilst looking
about for a house where he could get something to eat,
heard music proceeding from under some trees. This
was—

"Les vagues violons de la mère Saguet."

He went in and found a little house, with a courtyard
in front full of flower-beds, and a shady garden behind.
He dined in an arbour, and was so well pleased with the

cookery that he recommended the place to all his friends.
He was warmly congratulated on his discovery, and in
future was only known by the title of Mother Saguet's
Columbus.   He was in duty bound to dine there frequently; sometimes he would call in the Rue Nôtre-
Dame des Champs, and carry off his brother. People
arranged to meet there; the reputation of the spot quickly
increased, and it attracted the painters and sculptors, who
were very numerous on that side of Paris. M. David,
M. Charlet, M. Louis Boulanger, the Deverias, and the
excellent artist, Robelin, often met in these arbours. The
cook's great merit consisted in her youth and in the good-
humour which pervaded the dinner-table. Almost the
only pantry belonging to Mother Saguet was her poultry-
yard. Her provisions were soon exhausted, but she would
pay her hen-house a visit, and bring back from it eggs
and chickens. People would be eating the omelettes whilst
she was wringing the necks of the chickens, cutting them
in half, putting them on the gridiron, and preparing a
highly-flavoured sauce for them. Besides this, what with
cheese and as much white wine as they could drink, there
was sufficient to keep the guests at table from six o'clock
to ten, and they would then disperse, delighted with their
entertainment.

One day, when Victor Hugo was on his way to Mother
Saguet's with M. David, they encountered in the Rue
Mont-Parnasse a girl of thirteen or fourteen years of age,
all in rags. M. David looked at her, stopped, spoke to
her, and wrote down her name and address. M. Victor
Hugo, when calling on M. David in his studio the fol-

lowing week, found there the little girl, quite naked. She was slender, emaciated, and withered by misery, but nevertheless beautiful. M. David was availing himself of her to represent the young girl in the "Tomb of Botzaris," which, in his conception of the subject, represented Greece, oppressed and suffering. She seemed pleased at the notion that her poor body was going to be immortalized in marble. Alas! the marble lasted no longer than the flesh. The French made a target of the tomb of the Cid; and the Greeks in like manner made a target of Botzaris' tomb. M. David, who left France in December, 1851, went to Greece. A ball had then struck the forehead of his statue, and another ball had broken one of the hands. This sorrow, in addition to that of his exile, rent the heart of the poor but great sculptor. He begged to have his wounded and mutilated statue restored to him, in order to heal and repair it. But he died before he had time to accomplish this.

At the close of the summer, M. Victor Hugo was one evening at the house of Madame Tastu. She begged him to recite a scene from *Cromwell*, which he had just finished. M. Tissot, who was present, considered it a very fine scene, and asked the author if he had made arrangements with any publisher. On his replying in the negative, Tissot offered to speak to his own publisher on the subject. Accordingly, the next day, M. Ambroise Dupont came to purchase the manuscript, and the author set to work on the preface.

The success achieved by *Der Freyschutz*, had given the Odéon a taste for dramatic novelties. After Weber came

Shakespeare. When the news was circulated that some English actors were about to perform one of the plays of their own great poet, the whole of the rising generation was excited on the subject. M. Eugène Delacroix wrote thus to Victor Hugo:—"There is a general invasion. *Hamlet* raises his hideous head. *Othello* prepares his pillow, for the express purpose of committing murder, to the utter subversion of the whole polity of the drama. Who knows where it will end? *King Lear* is about to tear out his eyes in the presence of a French audience. The Academy would show great dignity in declaring that any novelty of this kind was incompatible with public morals. Farewell to good taste. At any rate, provide a good cuirass under your coat, and avoid classical daggers."

In addition to the great poet there were great actors; and amongst others Miss Smithson, an actress of prodigious talent. Mademoiselle Taglioni would have been jealous of her dancing, Madame Pasta of her singing, and Mademoiselle Mars of her voice. She made painters rave by the admirable taste of her costumes. She succeeded in every possible way. M. Berlioz, who was then first violinist of the orchestra, made her an offer of marriage.

These admirable dramas, admirably played, strongly affected M. Victor Hugo, who was at that moment writing the preface to *Cromwell;* he filled it with his enthusiasm for "this theatrical deity, in whom seemed to be united, as in the Trinity, the three great geniuses characteristic of our drama, Corneille, Molière, and Beaumarchais."

The preface, like the piece itself, assumed vast proportions. The one volume, which would easily have made
two, was quickly printed, and came out in the early part
of December, 1827.

The effect of the drama was even exceeded by that of
the preface. It burst like a declaration of war on received
opinions, and provoked a paper war. It was attacked at
all points, both as to ideas and style. Here are some lines
from one of the important journals of the day, the *Gazette
de France* :—

" What is remarkable in the first lines of this preface
is the disdainful and haughty tone in which a young
writer, whose reputation has not yet extended beyond a
few friendly circles, speaks of all who differ with him.
There was a time when he contented himself with writing
odes like other people. . . He was then satisfied to gather
beforehand the laurels which the hope excited by his
early essays rendered it likely he would secure, and which
unfortunately, to use figurative language, are as yet un-
culled. To-day it is quite another thing. The young
and modest poet is become a professor, proudly distribut-
ing his instructions to his absent audience. . . . Who
dreams now for a moment of reproducing that old and
tiresome question of the classical and romantic, which the
whole world has settled long ago ? Only these two, M.
Hugo and M. Darlincourt, who have done it at the same
time, and often in the same words. If there is any difference between them it is wholly to the advantage of the
latter, whose prose appears to us very preferable, where
taste and simplicity are concerned, to that of the author

of *Cromwell* . . . His openly avowed aim is to break 'all those threads of spiders' web with which the army of Lilliput have undertaken to chain the drama whilst slumbering;' that is to say, in good French, to render themselves independent of the three unities. We might make the author of this phrase remark that in this Lilliputian army there are some dwarfs to be found not so very despicable after all, and amongst others stand out those men who have written for the stage from *The Cid* down to *Cromwell;* but what would these men be worth in the eyes of him who calls Shakespeare (whose name he cannot even spell) the god of the theatre? People who do not accept this idea—and we believe the number of them is tolerably large—will at any rate not deny its novelty. For the first time, doubtless, the idea has been entertained of placing the author of a few witty and libertine plays on the same level with Molière and Corneille (for it may be noticed that Racine is not even quoted, these gentlemen paying no more attention to him than if he did not exist). These whims, which are not worth serious consideration, have a ludicrous side, which would cause one some amusement if they were cleverly brought forward. It is necessary to possess some strength to venture to attack giants; and when one undertakes to dethrone writers whom whole generations have united in admiring, it would be advisable to fight them with weapons which, if not equal to theirs, are at least so constructed as to have some chance. The language should be elegant and pure enough to be comprehensible, to show that it is not from absolute impotence that they are attacked; but what harm can any one expect to do them who writes like the author of the preface to which we are alluding?" . . .

The defence was no less earnest than the attack: the young men especially energetically declared themselves in favour of theatrical independence, and the *Preface to Cromwell* became their rallying cry.

Le Globe, in an article from the pen of M. de Rémusat, kept to its office of mediator. The Toulouse friends of M. Victor Hugo felt that their neo-tragedy was about to disappear in this violent eruption of thorough and unscrupulous art. The death of Talma had been the first shock to them, the *Preface to Cromwell* put the finishing stroke to it. They willingly resigned themselves, and nobly espoused the cause which laid them low. M. Soumet wrote to the author thus:—" I read and re-read incessantly your *Cromwell,* dear and illustrious Victor. It seems to me full of new and daring beauties; and although in your preface you spoke mercilessly of mosses and climbing ivy, I cannot do less than own to your admirable talent, and I shall speak of your work—grand in the style of Michael Angelo—as I formerly spoke of your odes."

XLVIII

DEATHS.

THE year ended sadly. Madame Foucher, who had been ill some time, had thought that perhaps the summer and country air might set her to rights again. But she returned to Paris, given up by the doctors, and soon laid down to rise no more. This excellent woman displayed in all her intolerable sufferings the greatest calmness and angelic goodness. The disease that tormented her would sometimes draw from her a stifled cry, but she would immediately begin to smile. She only busied herself with her husband and her children, especially with a second daughter, whom she had had some years before, and whom on account of her illness she had been obliged to place at school whilst yet quite young. She would worry herself about the dinner, and about the linen, as to whether Paul had what he required, as to whether there was a letter from Alençon, where her son Victor, who was married, occupied the post of substitute to the King's procureur. Nothing could be more touching than to see this martyr to suffering so anxious about the well-being of others.

Death had no terrors for her. The priest she had sent

for found her calm and serene. She might have confessed all she had to confess in public. All her life had
been one long act of devotion. She had possessed that
first of all virtues a large charity for the faults of others.
She who lived entirely in her family, occupied only by her
duties, had always excused the faults of other women;
she could hardly be made to believe in wrong, but when
forced to do so through incontestable evidence, she would
reply, " I don't like people to be severe towards women,
they have so much to suffer."

The priest was a kind of almoner to the family. He
had baptized Victor Hugo's first child. He was a native
of the South, sanguine, irascible, a good fellow, and
rather free in his expressions. When attending the
dying woman he became quite changed, and administered
the offices of the Church with sacerdotal gravity. Although he was much used to death-bed scenes, he could
not help feeling deep emotion when he witnessed the
painful end of a woman with whose whole life he was
acquainted. He left the room bathed in tears.

There was an apparent amelioration in the state of the
sick woman. " I feel better," said she; " I think I am
about to get well again."

That same evening the anguish returned. The next
day but one she gave back to her God one of the purest
souls which had ever lived on earth.

Life is a perpetual alternative of funerals and wed-
dings. At Victor Hugo's wedding, his brother Abel had
taken notice of a young lady, Mademoiselle Julie de
Monferrier. He was not then in a position to entertain

thoughts of marriage; but since that time his affairs having prospered, he had requested her hand, and obtained it. He was married by the same priest who had just buried Madame Foucher.

General Hugo, established temporarily in Paris, was present at the wedding. The reconciliation between father and sons was complete. Abel and Victor had both come round and had recognized their step-mother. Victor had dedicated *Cromwell* to his father, and the General was happy in every way. The Government had at length pardoned his desperate resistance to the stranger. He was no longer obliged to keep out of sight, but was recognized as General of Division. Reinstated in his rank, in his liberty, and in his family circle, he had time to breathe freely, after a life so laborious and so little appreciated. He had already two grandchildren, Leopoldine and Charles. This new marriage seemed to promise others. He was young enough to hope to see his grandchildren grow up; and there was a prospect that they would be brought up to love him.

In order to be nearer to his sons, he took apartments in their neighbourhood. He resided in the Rue Plumet. Victor would go and see him almost every evening. He would spend whole hours with him, wishing to make up for lost time. On the 28th January, 1828, he hurried over his dinner, and took his wife with him. The General was in a gay and chatty mood, and they did not separate till eleven o'clock. His son had returned home and was undressing, when he heard a violent ring at the door. This bell, at an hour when visits are not expected, frightened him. He ran and opened the door, and saw a man who was unknown to him.

" What do you want ? "

" I am sent by the Countess Hugo to tell you that your father is dead."

M. Victor Hugo had but just left his father : he had just seen him full of life. At first he was stunned by the blow, and thought it must be a mistake or a horrible dream. Without knowing what he did, he dressed himself again, and mechanically followed the messenger to the Rue Plumet.

He found his father stretched on the bed, rigid and discoloured, his shirt buttons unfastened, one sleeve raised, and some ligatures on his arm. By his side was a man whom at first he did not recognize. It was a doctor, who lived close by the General. They had gone for the nearest help ; he had arrived, and found the General in a fit of apoplexy. He had begun to bleed him, and had done everything in his power ; but it was all to no purpose.

The General had died a soldier's death. The apoplexy had struck him, when he was standing upright, with the rapidity of a shot.

The doctor who had thus been called in to the father was found to be the same as the one who had attended the son at M. Cordier's school, when suffering from the wound in the knee.

The mourning garments and the crape which had been bought for the mother were not yet worn out, and helped to serve as mourning for the father.

XLIX

AMY ROBSART.

SIX years before, when he was nineteen years of age, at the moment when his father being at Blois and his mother dead, he was alone in the world, his marriage had been postponed on account of poverty. At this time, Victor Hugo sought everywhere for that money which should bring him nearer to happiness, and M. Soumet had proposed that, between them, they should concoct a play from part of Walter Scott's novel, entitled "Kenilworth." M. Soumet was to prepare the plot, Victor Hugo was to write the three first acts, and M. Soumet the two last. Victor Hugo had done his share; but when he had read over his three acts, M. Soumet had not been much pleased with them. He did not approve of a mixture of the tragic and the comic, and he wished to expunge everything that was not grave and serious. Victor Hugo had put forward the example of Shakespeare; but at that time English actors had not caused Shakespeare to be popular in Paris, and M. Soumet had replied, that, however interesting to read, these plays of the English dramatist would not bear representation, that *Hamlet* and *Othello* were rather sublime essays and beautiful monstrosities than real masterpieces, and he insisted that a correct play must be either one thing or the other. It must move the audience either to cry or to laugh. The two coadjutors, not being able to agree on the subject, had parted good friends, each of them had carried away his acts and his independence, and completed his piece as he chose. M. Soumet had written an *Emilia,* which, when acted at the Théâtre Français by Mademoiselle Mars, had had only partial success. M. Victor Hugo had terminated his *Amy Robsart* in his own way, freely intermingling comedy and tragedy. But, at the moment when it became a question as to its being performed, the pension granted him by Louis XVIII. enabled him to dispense with literary speculations, and he had hidden his play away in the bottom of a drawer.

Iu 1828, the younger of his two brothers-in-law, Paul Foucher, •left college. He felt himself drawn towards literature, and particularly towards theatrical literature. But theatrical managers always made him the same reply they invariably did to young men :—" When you have a name." He sought, therefore, the means of acquiring that reputation which alone opens all doors. One day M. Soumet, upon whom he was calling, asked him if he knew *Amy Robsart,* and spoke to him of it as of a kind of singular and curious work, well worth reading.

" I was a little startled by it formerly," said he, " and even now there are. certain bold flights in it which I should never have ventured to take ; but since English dramas have become the rage, I do not see why it should not answer. If I were Victor Hugo I should not throw away a piece in which are some very beautiful scenes. The fifth act, which is almost entirely his own plot, is very original."

Paul Foucher begged his brother-in-law to lend him the play, and was as much astonished as M. Soumet had been that the author would not have it acted. His brother-in-law explained to him that he had written it when he was nineteen years of age, and struggling with poverty, but that it did not become him now to borrow plots from other writers.

" And what shall you do with your play ? "

" I shall burn it."

" Will you give it to me ? "

He assured him that it would be doing him a real kindness, that such a play would gain him admittance amongst theatrical people, and would extemporize him a name.

"Upon my honour," said Victor Hugo, "I do not look on it as on a play of my own composition. Do what you like with it. Walter Scott is as much yours as mine."

Amy Robsart was at once offered to the manager of the Odéon, and was received with acclamations, and distributed amongst the principal actors belonging to the theatre, M. Bocage, M. Provost, Mademoiselle Anaïs, &c. M. Eugène Delacroix undertook to select the proper dresses. It was agreed upon that Victor Hugo's name should never be mentioned in connection with it ; but certain phrases and turns of expression betrayed him, and the delighted manager hastened to spread the news far and wide that the drama was written by the author of *Cromwell*. M. Victor Hugo in vain tried to deny it; the manager perceiving that the name rendered it attraction, continued to proclaim it on the housetops.

The piece was much hissed. "Yesterday was performed at the Odéon," wrote the *Journal des Débats*, the following day, "an historical drama in five acts, entitled *Amy Robsart*; the subject is borrowed from Sir Walter Scott's 'Kenilworth,' and though it had already been performed on three different stages, this play has now been produced for the fourth time without any further improvement than that of being lengthened out beyond measure, and spoilt by a multitude of trivial expressions. Hisses and bursts of laughter did justice to this old novelty."

Victor Hugo, who did not mind giving away what was likely to be successful, would not let it be said that he had given away a failure. He therefore wrote immediately to all the newspapers to say that the parts which had been hissed had proceeded from his pen.

This, as far as the play was concerned, was an involuntary acknowledgment. The young men, who would not have put themselves out of their way for an unacknowledged play, now hastened to see it. When they applauded it the hissing grew worse: the tumult in the pit spread into the Quartier Latin; and the Government interfered, and forbade the play being acted.

L

FRIENDS.

AMONGST the most assiduous friends of the house, two were in the habit of calling almost daily. These were M. Louis Boulanger, an equal admirer of Shakespeare and Rembrandt, and M. Sainte-Beuve, who excelled in conversation as much as he did in his writings. M. Abel Hugo's marriage having disorganized the dinners at Mother Saguet's, the rural pleasures of the summer of 1828 consisted in going to watch the sunset on the plains of Vanvres and of Montrouge. Often they would pause at the *Butte au Moulin.* M. Victor Hugo would stretch himself under one of the enormous sails, and inhale the fresh breeze whilst watching the twilight as it gradually made the horizon less distinct, indulging in reveries which afterwards became the *Soleils Couchants* in the *Feuilles d'Automne.*

They would finish the evening in the Rue Nôtre-Dame des Champs, where M. Victor Hugo, urged by his two friends, repeated the verses he had made during the day. Afterwards he would request the same of M. Sainte-

Beuve, who was obliged to sacrifice himself; but, confused at being brought thus into notice, would desire little Leopoldine and the great fat Charlot to make as much noise as they could whilst he was speaking. But they took care not to obey him, and they would then listen to some beautiful lines from *Joseph Delorme* and from the *Consolations*.

Sometimes the poet of the evening was Alfred de Musset. He would recite *Don Paez, La Camargo,* and *La Ballade à la Lune.* One day that he had read a portion from *Mardoche,* they began to discuss rhymes in general. M. Emile Deschamps said that he should like rhymes in three letters.

" Like these," said M. Victor Hugo :—

> " Ici git le nommé Mardoche
> Qui fut Suisse de Sainte-Eustache,
> Et qui porta la hallebarde.
> Dieu lui fasse miséricorde ! "

> [*Translation.*]
> Here lies the man Mordoche,
> Who was beadle at Saint Eustache,
> And who always bore the halberd.
> God have mercy on his soul !

Victor Hugo often saw M. Gustave Planche, who had been introduced to him by M. Sainte-Beuve as understanding English. A new edition of the "Odes and Ballads," very handsomely got up, was about to appear, with a frontispiece which was a reduction from M. Louis Boulanger's beautiful lithograph of "*La Ronde du*

Sabbat." The engraver, who was to make the reduced
drawing on the stone, understood nothing at all about so
fantastic and diabolical a subject. Being English, and
not understanding a word of French, he begged to have
the ballad translated. M. Sainte-Beuve said that he knew
some one who would be willing to undertake it, and who
would do it in first-rate style, and he brought with him
a tall young man, with a Greek profile, who would have
been handsome, but for his prominent eyes and narrow
skull. It was M. Gustave Planche.

M. Mérimée would sometimes come. One day, when
he was at dinner with them, the cook had quite spoilt
a dish of macaroni. He offered to come and prepare
some, and, accordingly, a few days afterwards, he came,
took off his coat, put on an apron, and made a dish of
macaroni in the Italian style, which was as successful as
his books. He often visited some English ladies, the
Misses Clarke, whose society was *doctrinaire* (free-
thinking), liberal, and classical; he persuaded M. Victor
Hugo to go too, and there he met M. Benjamin Constant,
then an old man, with white hair, careless in his dress,
and possessing a venerable, yet jaded countenance. M.
Fauriel, M. Henri Beyle, &c., were also of the party.

One of the *habitués* of this drawing-room was M.
Eugène Delacroix. This young man, though the leader
of a sect in art, had not the same audacity in words as in
pictures. He tried to disarm his enemies by the originality of his talent, or by giving way in conversation. A
Revolutionist in the studio, he was a Conservative in the
drawing-rooms, disavowed literary innovations and the

literary insurrections, and preferred tragedy to the drama.
The young literary men of the day pardoned this
prudence, which he did not display on canvas, and
which generally turned out differently to what he had expected. One evening, when he had just left the Misses
Clarke, after a discussion with Victor Hugo, in which
he had insisted on the beauty of Voltaire's *Tancrède*,
the eldest of these English ladies, who was of the same
opinion as he was, exclaimed enthusiastically,—

" How charming and sensible M. Delacroix is! What
a pity it is he paints pictures ! "

A certain song condemned M. Béranger to three
months' imprisonment. Victor Hugo went to visit him
in La Force. His cell was always full of visitors. For
the most part they consisted of good citizens, proud to
have the opportunity of approaching the great writer of
popular songs, and of bringing him substantial consolation. Thus the poet was inundated with pâtés, game,
fruit, and wine.

" See how they spoil me," said he to M. Victor Hugo.
" I have positively nothing left to desire but a stomach."

M. Béranger was at that time remarkable for the dress
and manner which have always been peculiar to him. His
hair floated on his shoulders; the collar of his shirt was
turned down ; and he wore a long great-coat, and a singular kind of waistcoat. He was already celebrated
for that exquisite conversation which distinguished him
in later years, veiling an exquisite wit under great good
sense and an appearance of good-nature, which, however,
it was not more safe to trust blindly than it would be to
forget the claw under the velvet paw of a cat.

The claw with him was never far off.

His room overlooked the courtyard of thieves. His friends regretted it very much, and wondered that he could exist in the immediate vicinity of such wretches.

"Lafitte, who called yesterday," he remarked one day to his visitor, "could not get over it, and said he should not be able to hold out an hour. I replied, My dear Lafitte, pick out a hundred men from that courtyard: when I get out, I will attend your first evening party, and select one hundred from your drawing-room,—and then we will weigh them both, and see what they are worth."

When one has passed the Barrière d'Enfer, and the Butte au Moulin, and descended into the Valley of Briére, a little beyond the cottages of Brinvilliers, a gate is reached which opens on to a gravelled walk and shady avenue. At the end of the avenue stands an unpretending-looking house, rather broader than it is long, of irregular construction, and surrounded by a garden, which, having been increased by degrees, has assumed park-like proportions. This habitation, called Les Roches, then belonged to M. Bertin senior, chief editor of the *Journal des Débats*. He spent his summers there, and invited every one who was of any celebrity in the literary world. M. Victor Hugo was asked thither. He was requested to repeat some verses, and recited *La Douleur du Pacha*. Gosselin, the bookseller, who was present, came next day and bought *Les Orientales*.

The poet and the journalist formed a friendship, and in subsequent years, M. Victor Hugo, with his wife and children, spent part of the autumn at Les Roches.

M. Bertin was the patriarch of a united family, consisting of Madame Bertin, who was an excellent and respectable woman, and of two sons, Armand, who, under a rough exterior, was both cordial and timid ; and Edouard, who already occupied a distinguished position as a landscape painter. There was also a daughter, Mademoiselle Louise, who was very intelligent, and possessed the double gift of music and poetry, being capable of writing fine verses, and of composing beautiful music. I ought rather to say, there were two daughters, for Armand was a married man, and his wife, an elegant, graceful, smiling creature, was to them a fourth child, no less dear than the others.

A free hospitality, which just stopped short of extravagance, was the characteristic of the house. Five or six friends, and the principal editors of the journal, were always there. M. Victor Hugo there became especially intimate with M. Jules Janin, whose honest affection has resisted the lapse of time, and has generously redoubled when its object became an exile. Beyond his private circle, M. Bertin seldom welcomed any but men of talent. He might have filled his house with titled or political people, but he had no vanity, and cared but little for social distinction. He had refused all appointments and distinctions, which the power of his journal had been the means of having offered to him. That which he despised for himself did not dazzle him in others. He used to remark, that the only aristocracy consisted in intelligence in men and beauty in women. This hospitable house was never but once closed, and that was to the King. Louis Philippe wishing to make himself agreeable to M. Bertin, sent to tell him that he much wished to see Les Roches. M. Bertin declined the honour, which so many would have coveted.

"The King is very well off at Versailles, and I am very well off at Les Roches," said he to the messenger; "were he to come here, we should both feel uncomfortable."

Once, at Paris, M. Guizot, the Minister, requiring to speak with him on important business, sent in his name just as he was about to sit down to dinner. The Minister was requested either to wait till dinner was over or to call again. It was not the usual hauteur of an editor, wishing to make himself of importance, but simply the habit of seeing in a Minister a man like any other man.

At Les Roches, the whole party met at table, and also after dinner. The rest of the day they spent as they pleased. Everybody occupied himself as he thought fit; some remained in their rooms; others would walk in the park, which was full of fine old oaks, and whose turf, flowers, and summer houses, were very delightful. There was a pond, where swans were sailing about, and which was fed by narrow rivulets, murmuring pleasantly as they went along. There were also peacocks expanding their tails in the sun. The master of the house was to be seen at early dawn, giving the gardeners his orders, or seated on a bench with a book in his hand, sometimes fast asleep.

"Et du fond de leur nid, sous l'orme et sous l'érable,
Les oiseaux admiraient sa tête vénérable.

Et, gais chanteurs tremblants,

Ils guettaient, s'approchaient et souhaitaient dans
    l'ombre
D'avoir, pour augmenter la douceur du nid sombre,
        Un de ses cheveux blancs."

[*Translation.*]

Deep in their nests, 'neath elms and 'neath the shade,
Birds would admire his venerable head,
    With gay yet trembling songs.'
They watched, approached, and perched in the shade,
They longed to acquire for their nests
    One of his white hairs.

At the sound of the dinner-bell, Madame Bertin and
Madame Amand left their needlework, Louise her
piano, Edouard his pencil, and Victor Hugo his pen,
while M. Bertin entered, and placed a rose on the plate
of his neighbour at table. Literature was the chief subject of conversation : they were impassioned, everybody
spoke as he thought. At dessert, Victor Hugo's children
were brought in. The little family was by this time
increased by a second boy, who had been named Victor.
All the three children reaped a rich harvest of caresses
and sweetmeats.

The children were never in a hurry to return to Paris.
They lived in the open air, drinking foaming milk from
white bowls in the dairy, frightening the chickens and the
golden pheasants. These pleasures were only interrupted
by Mademoiselle Louise, who called them to her to tell
them some interesting story. They soon collected round
her. She took Victor on her knee, made Leopoldine and
"Son Charlot" sit by her side, and improvised some tale

which was for them alone, as she allowed no one else
to be within hearing. It was amusing beyond measure
to hear them at night, when their mother was putting
them to bed, endeavouring to retail for her benefit these
marvellous stories.

LI

THE SCAFFOLD.

ONE day in the year 1820, Victor Hugo fell in with Louvel, who was on his way to the scaffold. There was nothing in this wretched murderer of the Duke de Berry that could excite his sympathy, for the man was a great burly fellow, with a flat nose and thin lips, and glassy blue eyes. The author of the ode on the death of the Duke hated him with the ultra-royalism of his childhood. And yet, when he saw this man still living and in health, but who was about to be killed, he could not help pitying him, and he felt his hatred for the assassin changed into pity for the victim. He reflected : it was the first time he had met the question of the punishment of death face to face. He felt surprised that society, in cold blood and without excitement, should commit precisely the same act as that which it punished. From that time he had an idea of writing a book against the guillotine.

At the end of the summer of 1825, as he was on his way one afternoon to the library of the Louvre, he met M. Jules Lefèvre, who took him by the arm and led him to the Quai de la Ferraille. The place was exceedingly crowded, everybody going towards the place of public execution.

"What is going on?" he asked.

"They are about to cut off the thumb and the head of a fellow named John Martin, who has killed his father. I am writing a poem, in which there is a parricide to be executed, and so I want to see this execution, but I'd rather not be alone."

The horror that Victor Hugo experienced at the idea of seeing an execution was the very reason why he forced himself to go. The frightful spectacle would strengthen him in the projected attack on the punishment of death.

At the bridge, the crowd became so dense that it was difficult to get on, but the two friends succeeded in reaching the open square. There, all the houses were full to overflowing. All the inhabitants had invited their friends to this grand fête, and the tables were covered with fruits and wine. Windows had been let for the occasion, at a fabulous price, and young women were to be seen, elbowing each other, and holding on to the window-frames, with wine-glasses in their hands, laughing loudly and ogling the young men. Soon, however, this coquetting was checked by a pleasure of a more lively kind—the cart was approaching with the convict.

The poor wretch was seated with his back to the horse, and also to the executioner and his assistants. His head was covered with a black rag, tied round the neck, and he was dressed only in grey trousers and a white shirt. He was shivering in the rain, which had already begun to fall, and was increasing. The prison chaplain spoke to him, and offered him a crucifix to kiss without removing his veil.

Victor Hugo was so placed as to have a side view of the guillotine. Thus, to his eye, it was merely a red post. A space round the scaffold was kept clear by a large body of soldiers, and when the cart had entered this space, the prisoner got down, assisted by his companions, and then, always supported by them, he went up the steps of the scaffold. The chaplain followed, and afterwards the jailer, who read the sentence with a loud voice. The executioner then lifted the black veil, and the man's face was seen. It was young, scared, and haggard. He next took the right hand of the convict, fastened it to the post with a chain, seized an axe, and raised it in the air. Victor Hugo could not bring himself to look any longer. He turned his head aside, and was not master of himself till the " Ha !" of the crowd informed him that the victim had ceased to suffer.

On another occasion he saw the executioner's cart occupied by a highway robber named Delaporte. This was an old man. His arms were tied behind his back, and his bald head shone in the sun.

There seemed a kind of fatality, and the punishment of death would not let itself be forgotten. He met the cart once more, but this time it contained two murderers. Victor Hugo was struck with the different appearance of these two criminals. One, named Ratta, a fair man, was pale and frightened, and was seen to tremble and shake with fear. The other, Malagutti, a dark man, was strong, and held his head in the air in a careless manner, going to die as he would have gone to dine.

On one occasion, Victor Hugo saw the guillotine as he was crossing in front of the Hôtel de Ville, about two o'clock, one afternoon. The executioner was rehearsing the performance of that evening. The cutting apparatus went stiffly, so he oiled the grooves, and then tried again. This time it was all right. This man who sold himself to kill his fellow-creatures, who followed his bloody trade in open day and in public, chatting with any curious idler who passed, while some wretched fellow-creature was writhing desperately in his prison, mad with rage, or was allowing himself to be tied and prepared for the evening's sacrifice with the listlessness and stupefaction of terror, was for Victor Hugo a hideous object; and the rehearsal was odious as the performance.

The very next day, he set himself to write "Le Dernier Jour d'un Condamné" (The Last Day of a Convict), and he finished it in three weeks. Every evening he read to his friends what he had written during the day. M. Edouard Bertin having been present on one of these evenings, spoke of it to M. Gosselin, who was then printing "Les Orientales," and who came to request the volume in prose, as well as the volume of poetry. The bargain settled, he read the manuscript. At that part of the book where the author, desiring that his convict should remain strictly impersonal, so that the interest should not possibly attach to any particular convict, but to the class generally, assumes the sheets that contained the history of his life to have been lost, M. Gosselin advised him—thinking it would increase the sale of the book—to find the lost leaves. The author replied that he had accepted M. Gosselin as publisher, not as coadjutor. This was the commencement of a coolness that grew up between them.

" Les Orientales" appeared in January, 1829, and " Le Dernier Jour d'un Condamné" three weeks afterwards.

LII

THE CONSEQUENCES OF "THE LAST DAY OF A CONVICT."

VICTOR HUGO was not satisfied with this public protest against capital punishments. For the last thirty-three years, he has never seen a scaffold or a gibbet, without proclaiming the principle of the sacredness of human life.

In 1832, he wrote a long preface to *Le Dernier Jour d'un Condamné,* illustrating by argument the subject that the book had undertaken to present in a story, and appealing to the understanding as he had previously appealed to the heart. In 1854, he wrote *Claude Gueux.*

To present in one view the various efforts made by Victor Hugo, in the cause of the abolition of capital punishments, I will speak here of *Claude Gueux,* and the other writings which may be regarded as a continuation of *Le Dernier Jour.*

Claude Gueux first appeared in the *Revue de Paris,* whose editor, M. Buloz, received on the occasion the following letter :—

" Mr. EDITOR, "Dunkirk, 3rd July, 1834.

"*Claude Gueux*, by Victor Hugo, inserted by you in your journal of the 6th instant, is a noble lesson. Assist me, I entreat you, to take advantage of it.

" Do me the favour to strike off as many copies as there are deputies in France, and forward a copy to each individually, and with the greatest precaution that it shall be duly received.

"I am, &c.

"CHARLES CARLIER (Merchant)."

It was two years since the poor wretch had been executed, whose name Victor Hugo had brought again before the public. Among some papers preserved relating to Claude Gueux, I have found a petition for his pardon accompanied by the following note.

"The person named Gueux (Claude) has been condemned to suffer the penalty of death, for a crime to which the pangs of hunger had impelled him. His affection for his father has interested in his favour all who have had anything to do with him. Unhappily the affair is now at an end: the Cour de Cassation and the Chancellerie have examined into it, and the sentence will be executed, if the King does not grant some commutation of the penalty. The convict is now awaiting the word that shall restore him to life or leave him to die. The mercy of His Majesty, so generally known, is implored by the convict, and even by the jury."

A decision of the Council of Ministers had rejected this appeal.

I find tied up in the same packet the two following letters, the first addressed to M. Delaunay, and the second to M. Hugo :—

" MONSIEUR, " Troyes, 4th June, 1832.

" We did not receive your letter till after the execution of the unhappy Claude. The event took place on Friday, the 1st June, at 10 A.M. Your efforts to assist him have been a great consolation. He did not doubt your kind interest in him, and, when dying, requested us to express to you his gratitude.

" Without being informed of your intentions, we have, however, fulfilled them to the letter.

" The sum you had the kindness to send for the poor prisoner remained in my hands, with his consent, because he was not permitted to keep it himself. At the last moment, we requested to know how he would have it disposed of. One part of it has been given to two prisoners condemned to hard labour for life, and the rest of it one of his sisters has received. We could have desired that something should have been reserved for masses to be said after his death ; but he did not suggest it, and we did not venture to remind him.

" This poor man has suffered much since his conviction, on account of the kind of death to which he was sentenced. We sympathized with him, and it affected him a good deal. We have had the satisfaction of seeing him receive, with proper feelings, the consolations of religion. He terminated his career with an edification and courage which deeply affected those who were present at his last moments.

"We believe that he is happy, and this now is our comfort, and will, I trust, be some satisfaction to you. Permit me, sir, to express my deep gratitude for your great charity towards him. You have done as much good to me as to him.

"I am, &c., "SISTER LOUISE."

"SIR,

"A person who considers himself well-informed has stated to me your intention of publishing a tale on the subject of Claude Gueux.

"I think, sir, it is important you should know that the father of Claude, a very old man, had been sentenced to a punishment which was inflicted in the prison of Clairvaux, and that the son, in order to bring help to him, committed, intentionally, an act whose consequences would bring him within the walls of the same prison.

"On fine days, Claude Gueux would take his old father in his arms and carry him out with the greatest care, that he might enjoy the warmth of the sun.

"I shall be glad if these facts can be of any use to you. Should you need any information that can be found in the records of the court, I shall have the greatest satisfaction in procuring them for you.

"MILLOT,
"Chief Clerk of the Court of Assizes in Troyes."

On Sunday, the 12th May, 1839, at about two o'clock in the afternoon, Victor Hugo, while talking on his balcony in the Place Royale, heard a sound of firing. It was the insurrection of which Barbès and Blanqui were the ring-leaders. The disturbance was easily stopped, and Blanqui escaped, concealing himself in the house of David the sculptor. Barbès, however, was taken, and was tried by the Chamber of Peers. Victor Hugo was present at the trial. The free, open bearing and appearance of youth that characterized the criminal interested him greatly. The next day he was at the opera, where an act of *La Esmeralda* was being performed, and while in the orchestra, listening to *L'Air des Cloches*, a peer of France (M. de Saint-Prièst) came and sat near him. When the act was finished they chatted together. M. de Saint-Prièst remarked:—

"We have just performed a duty, always very painful; we have condemned a poor man to death."

"Barbès is condemned?"

"And he will be executed. The Ministers have made up their minds."

"When?"

"Probably to-morrow morning. You know there is no appeal from the Chamber of Peers."

Victor Hugo quitted the peer, went behind the scenes, and walked up to the manager's private room. The manager was absent, but he found on the table a blotting-case, strewn with pen-and-ink caricatures; there was M. Nourrit with a barrel instead of a stomach; Mademoiselle Falcon with matches for legs; M. Levasseur dressed like a porter, &c. He took from the blotting-case a sheet of paper and wrote these four lines:—

"Par votre ange, envolée ainsi qu'une colombe !
 Par ce royal enfant, doux et frèle roseau !
 Grâce encore une fois ! grâce au nom de la tombe !
 Grâce au nom du berceau !"

[*Translation.*]

By your guardian angel fled away like a dove,
By your royal child, a sweet and frail reed,
Pardon yet once more, pardon in the name of the tomb !
Pardon in the name of the cradle !

These verses he put into one of those common en-
velopes, used to enclose the play-bills, sealed it with a
large red wafer, and went to the Tuilleries. He gave
the letter to the porter, begging him to deliver it
immediately.

The man said it was too late for the King to receive it
before the next morning, but that he should have it early.
But Victor Hugo explained to him that it was a matter
concerning the life of a man who was to be executed that
very next morning, and then the porter, calling his wife
to take care of the entry, went into the palace. Victor
Hugo wished to await his return, and at the end of
twenty minutes he came back again.

"Sir," he said, "the King has read your letter, but
you were quite right to put your name on the envelope.
It seems that M. France d'Houdetot, who is the aide-
de-camp in waiting, knows you—he was going to throw
the letter on the table when he saw your name. Then he
took it in at once, and the usher saw through the glazed-
door that the King read it.

M. Victor Hugo, the next day, was delighted to find
that the execution had not taken place. The King had
generously resisted his Minister. The Ministers, among
whom was General Cubières, who himself was afterwards
condemned by the Chamber of Peers for some other
than a political offence, returned to the charge during
the day; but Louis Philippe held firm, and Victor Hugo
received this reply:—"Sa grâce est accordée: il ne
me reste plus qu'à l'obtenir." (His pardon is granted:
it only remains for me to obtain it).

This proceeding of Victor Hugo's was the cause of the
following two letters being written at a later period:—

"DEAR AND ILLUSTRIOUS CITIZEN,

"The convict of whom you speak in the seventh
volume of 'Les Misérables,' must seem to you an
ungrateful wretch.

"It is now twenty-three years since he was indebted
to you for his life, and he has not yet acknowledged it.

"Pardon him—pardon me.

"In my prison of last February I have often promised
myself that I should rush to your house, if, some day,
liberty should be restored to me.

"Dreams of youth! That day came, but only to
throw me, like a broken straw, in the whirlpool of 1848.

"I can do nothing of that which I have so ardently
longed for.

"And since then—pardon me for saying so, dear
citizen—the majesty of your genius has always checked
the utterance of my thoughts.

"I was proud in my hour of danger to see myself

protected by a spark of your flame. I could not die with you there to defend me.

" Would that I had been able to show myself worthy of the protection afforded me ! But each has his destiny, and all those whom Achilles saved were not heroes.

" An old man now, I have been for the past year in a miserable state of health. I have sometimes thought that my heart or my head would burst. But, in spite of all my sufferings, it is a satisfaction to me to have lived so long, since under the sense of your new kindness, I take heart to thank you for the old one.

" And since I have once spoken, I also thank you a thousand times, in the name of our sacred cause, and in the name of France herself, for the great work you have just completed.

" I say France, for it seems to me that this much-loved country of Joan of Arc and of the Revolution was alone capable of giving birth to your heart and your genius. Happy son ! you have placed on the glorious brow of your parent a new crown of glory !

" Yours, with the deepest affection,

" The Hague, July 10, 1862."   " A. BARBÈS.

_____

" Hauteville House, July 15, 1862.

" MY BROTHER IN EXILE,

" When a man has—as you have—been the champion and martyr of progress; when he has, for the holy cause of democracy and humanity, sacrificed fortune, youth, the prospects of happiness and liberty ; when he has, for the sake of an idea, been subject to every mode of attack, to all forms of trial, to calumny, persecution, the loss of friends, long years of prison, and long years of exile ; when he has allowed his devotion to the good cause to carry him even to the scaffold ; when, I say, a man has done all this, every one is indebted to him, and he can owe nothing to any human being. He who has given his all to human nature, is free with regard to any individual man.

"Thus, it is not possible that you should be ungrateful. Had I not, twenty-three years ago, done that for which you offer your thanks, it is I—as I now clearly see—who would have shown ingratitude to you.

"All that you have done for the people, I recognize as a personal service to myself.

"At the time you allude to, I simply fulfilled a duty— a strict duty. If I was then fortunate enough to pay you a little of the universal debt of mankind towards you, this is nothing compared with the devotion of your whole life, and we all remain your debtors as before.

"My reward, even granting that I deserved reward, was in the action itself; but I accept affectionately the noble acknowledgment you have sent me, and I am deeply touched by your magnanimous gratitude.

"I reply in the feeling of your letter. This spark, passing from your solitude to mine, is a touching event. We shall soon meet, either on this earth or elsewhere.

"V. H."

As a peer of France, Victor Hugo had to give a verdict in two causes where capital punishment would follow conviction.

In 1846 he sat in judgment on Joseph Henry, and in 1847 on Lecomte, both of whom had fired at the King. He voted in favour of perpetual imprisonment in the former case, and the prisoner was condemned to the galleys for life. He advocated the same punishment in the other case, but this prisoner was condemned to death and executed.

In 1848 the question of capital punishments was suddenly brought under consideration in the Assembly. M. Victor Hugo mounted the tribune immediately, and spoke as follows :—

" I regret that this question—perhaps the most important of all questions, should have arisen in the midst of your deliberations almost unexpectedly, and thus have taken by surprise those orators who were not prepared for it.

" For my part, I shall say but little, but what I do say will proceed from a deep conviction of long standing.

" You have just acknowledged the principle that a man's private dwelling should be inviolate :—we ask you now to acknowledge a principle much higher and more sacred still—the inviolability of human life.

" My lords, a constitution and especially a constitution made by France and for France, is of necessity a step in civilization. If not that, it is nothing.

" Consider, then, what is the penalty of death ? It is the especial and eternal mark of barbarism. Wherever the penalty is, death is common, barbarism dominates; wherever the penalty of death is rare, civilization reigns supreme.

" These, my lords, are facts that cannot be denied. The reduction of this penalty is a great and real progress. It is a part of the glory of the eighteenth century to have abolished torture. The nineteenth century will abolish the penalty of death.

" You will not do away with it, perhaps, at once; but be assured, either you or your successors will abolish it.

" At the commencement of the preamble of your constitution you write, ' In the presence of God;' and you begin by depriving Him—this same God—of that right which belongs only to Him, the right of life and death.

" My lords, there are three things that belong to God and that do not belong to man : they are the irrevocable, the irreparable, and the indissoluble. Woe to man if he introduces them into his laws ! Sooner or later they will bend society under their weight. They derange the necessary equilibrium of laws and manners; they abstract from human justice its fair proportions; and the result is— reflect well, my lords, upon the fact—that the law alarms the conscience.

" I mounted the tribune to say one word—in my opinion a decisive word. It is this :—

" After February, the people had a great thought : the day after they had burnt the throne they wished to burn the scaffold.

" Those who influenced the public mind at that time had not, I deeply regret to say, attained the elevation of this thought. They prevented the carrying out of this sublime idea.

" Well, in the first act of the constitution that you vote, you have carried out the first thought of the people —you have overturned the throne. Now carry out the other : overturn the scaffold !

" I vote for the abolition, pure, simple, and definitive, of the penalty of death."

In March, 1849, the advocate of Daix, one of those condemned in the affair of Bréa, came to request Victor Hugo to interfere in favour of his client, who was about to be executed. M. Victor Hugo made application to the President of the Republic, but he did not grant the pardon. I extract the following details from the letters of a sister of Daix, who was an under-nurse at the Hospital of Saint Sulpice :—

" After two years of grief, I am only now able to collect my ideas so far as to inform you that I have preserved the precious remembrance of the efforts you made to obtain from the President of the Republic a commutation of the punishment to which my brother had been sentenced. Fate had decided otherwise. My brother was not a bad man. He was excitable; but this was the result of the state of his head since he had been trepanned in the Hospital of La Charité, and, when excited, he was out of his mind. For this reason I had placed him at the Bicêtre. When the unfortunate Revolution of June broke out, he was out of the hospital. On the Monday, for the first time in my life, I disregarded the orders of the Director that we should not stir from the establishment, and I went to look over the heap of dead, expecting to find him. A yet sadder fate was reserved for him. He remained nine months in prison before his death, and my pen refuses to write the terrible scenes that took place in the forts. But, notwithstanding this, I was struck with admiration at the Fort of Ivry by the conduct of a young officer. An order had been given not to admit the prisoners' families. Some children called out to their fathers, and this officer took the youngest of them from their mothers' arms and said, 'I have received no order with regard to children.'

"God grant that my brother's blood may be the last. The victims, I hope, will suffer no more; but, for the families—alas, what torture! Such is the lot reserved for those who labour for the poor; for I have been attached to the hospital for more than twenty years. My cross was already heavy enough, but now I can only drag it along. I cannot escape from my misery. It only remains for me to visit this sad tomb, where I have not even been able to inscribe his name; but I submit with resignation to the law which forbids it. Pardon me for entering into all these miseries; but you are so good, you sympathize so completely with the wretchedness of families, that you will have pity on a poor woman who ventures to make you share in her legitimate causes of distress, while she requests you to vouchsafe a few words of consolation."

In 1851, M. Victor Hugo's eldest son was summoned before the Court of Assize, for having, in the journal *L'Evènement,* protested against an execution which had been accompanied by horrible circumstances. The father thus wrote to the President of the Court :—

"MR. PRESIDENT,

"My son, Charles Hugo, has been cited to appear on Tuesday, the 10th June next, before the Court of Assize, presided over by you, being accused of disrespect to the laws, in an article he has written on the execution of the person named Moncharmont.

"M. Erdan, the responsible editor of the *Evènement* is cited at the same time. He has selected M. Cremieux as his advocate; but my son desires to be defended by me, and I desire to undertake his defence.

"According to the Article 295 of the Code of Criminal Instruction, I have the honour to request your permission to do so.

"Receive, M. President, the assurance of my distinguished consideration.

"5 *June*, 1851.   "VICTOR HUGO."

"He received this answer:—

"Palais de Justice, 7 June, 1851.

"SIR,

"In reply to your request, I have to inform you that I grant you permission to defend your son.

"The President of the Court of Assize,"
"PARTARRIEU LAFOSSE."

I give here the pleadings, which were not published in the "complete works" of Victor Hugo.

"GENTLEMEN OF THE JURY,

"In what I may call the old European code, there exists a law, which for more than a century all the philosophers, all the great thinkers, all real statesmen, have desired to expunge from the venerable book of

universal legislation.   It is a law which Beccaria declared
to be impious, and which Franklin described as abominable, without either Beccaria or Franklin being proceeded against.   It is a law which, while pressing specially
on that portion of the people still weighed down by
ignorance and misery, is hateful to the Liberal, but not
less hateful to the intelligent Conservative.   It is a law
of which the King Louis Philippe—whom I name only
with the respect due to his age, his misfortunes, and his
tomb in a foreign country—has said : '*I have detested it
all my life.*'   It is a law against which M. de Broglie
has written, against which M. Guizot has written, which
the Chamber of Deputies twenty years ago (in the month
of October, 1830) demanded by acclamation should be
got rid of, and which at the same period the half-savage
parliament of Otaheite erased from its code.   It is a
law which the assembly of Frankfort abolished three
years ago, and which our constitution of 1848 maintained
only with the most painful indecision, and the most
marked repugnance.   To repeal this law, there are at
this moment two propositions before the legislative tribune.
Finally, this penalty of death is a law which Tuscany
no longer retains, which Russia has done away with, and
of which France is tired.   The human conscience recoils
from it, with feelings that daily become more intense.

"Well, gentlemen, it is this law which has brought
the action I am now defending; this law is our adversary.   I am sorry for the Advocate-General, but I perceive this law under his robe.

"I will confess that, for the last twenty years, I have

fancied that the guillotine—to call it by its name—
had shown symptoms of giving way; that it felt itself
reproved, and was preparing to leave us. I have myself
said thus much in pages which I could read to you, but I
prefer quoting a remark by M. Léon Faucher, published
in 1836, in the *Revue de Paris*. He says, 'The scaffold
now no longer appears on the public places, except at
rare intervals, and as a spectacle which justice is ashamed
to offer.'

"And so it is. This guillotine has retired from its
usual quarters; it is not now seen in broad daylight, or
surrounded by a crowd; it does not announce itself in the
streets like other spectacles. It has sought out obscure
corners, it is found only in the gloom, in the barrier of
Saint-Jacques, in deserted places, in solitary spots. It
seemed to me that it was beginning to hide itself, and
I complimented it upon its modesty.

"But, gentlemen, I was mistaken; M. Léon Faucher
was mistaken. It has recovered from this shyness. The
guillotine feels that it is a 'social institution,' as they say
now-a-days. And, who knows? perhaps it also dreams of
a restoration!

"The Barrière Saint-Jacques was its resort when in
disrepute. Perhaps we may look forward to see it some day
soon reappearing in the Place de Grève* in broad daylight, with its vast crowd, with its procession of executioners, with its guard of honour, and its heralds;
perhaps even under the very windows of the Hôtel de

---

* The ordinary place of execution in former times. —(Tr.)

Ville, where once, on a certain 24th of February, it was insolently stigmatized and mutilated!

"Meanwhile, it is holding up its head. It feels that an unsettled state of society, in order to re-establish itself —to use another cant phrase of the day—must return to all the ancient traditions. And it, the guillotine, is an ancient tradition. It protests against these demagogic declaimers—Beccaria, Vico, Filangieri, Montesquieu, Turgot, Franklin; against this Louis Philippe, this Broglie, this Guizot; who dare to affirm that a machine for chopping-off heads is out of place in a society which acknowledges the Gospel as an authority.

"Yes, it is indignant against these anarchical Utopians; and the very day after its most funereal and bloody sacrifices have been performed, it presents itself for admiration, it asks that we should pay respect to it. If this is not done, it declares itself insulted, it brings an action for damages in the civil courts.

"It has had blood, but that is not enough, it is not satisfied; it now claims other penalties and the prison.

Gentlemen of the jury, the day on which the citation was brought to my house, addressed to my son—when, I say, I received this announcement of an action, which seemed to me so utterly unjustifiable, although it is true that we see strange things in these times, and one ought to get accustomed to them,—I will confess to you that I was stupefied.

"I said to myself, 'What! are we come to this?

"'Is it that by successive encroachments on common sense, on reason, on the liberty of thought, and on our natural rights, we are brought to such a pass that we are bound to pay, not only a material respect, which is not refused, but also moral respect to those penal laws which alarm our consciences? These laws, indeed, do more than shock the moral sense, for they are offensive to religion herself: *abhorret a ˋsanguine.* Knowing that they may err, they dare to be irreparable. They dip the finger in human blood to write, Thou shalt not kill. They are impious laws, for they make us suspect human nature when they strike the guilty, and they make us suspect the Deity when they strike the innocent. No, no; ten times no. We cannot yet have arrived at such a pass as not to be allowed to protest against this iniquity.'

" For it is the case, and since I have come to this point, I must inform you, gentlemen of the jury, and you will then understand the depth of my emotion: the real culprit in this matter, if there is a culprit, is not my son. It is I myself.

" I repeat, I am the real culprit. I, who for a quarter of a century, have not ceased to battle against all forms of the irreparable penalty—I, who during all this time, have never ceased to advocate the inviolability of human life.

" This crime, then—the advocacy of the principle of the inviolability of human life—I committed long before my son: I have committed it much more frequently. I denounce myself, M. Advocate-General. I have committed it under the most aggravating circumstances, with premeditation, with contumacy, repeating the crime again and again.

"Yes, I assert it, this remains of barbarous penalties—this old and unintelligent law of retaliation—this law of blood for blood, I have battled against it all my life; all my life, gentlemen of the jury, and so long as there remains one breath in my body, I will continue to battle against it with all my power as an author, and with all my acts and votes as a legislator. And I make this declaration—(*the pleader here stretched out his arm towards the crucifix at the end of the hall above the tribunal*)—before the victim of the penalty of death, whose effigy is now before us, who is now looking down upon us, and who hears what I utter.

"I swear it, I say, before this sacred tree, on which, two thousand years ago and for the instruction of men to the latest generations, the laws, instituted by men, fastened with accursed nails the sacred law of God.

"All that my son has written has been written, I repeat, because I have so taught him from his childhood; because he is my son intellectually and morally, as well as physically; because he follows the example of his father. To follow the example of his father: a strange crime truly, and one for which a man deserves to be punished! It was reserved to those who are the exclusive defenders of the family tie to exhibit to us this novelty.

"Gentlemen, I confess that the accusation I have to meet astonishes me.

"What, then! A law is mischievous; it gives to the crowd spectacles that are immoral, dangerous, degrading, ferocious; it tends to render the people cruel; on certain occasions it is the cause of horrible proceedings; and the horrible proceedings that this law is the cause of, it is forbidden to point out. To point out these consequences is called a failure of respect, and one is liable to be brought to trial for it; to be adjudged to pay a fine of so much, to be imprisoned for such a term. But, if this is the case, let us close the Chambers at once; let us shut up our schools; progress is no longer possible; let us call ourselves Mongols, or belonging to Thibet, for we are no longer a civilized people. Yes, the readiest thing will be to declare ourselves transported to Asia—to say that there was, indeed, once a country called France, but that this country has ceased to exist, and has been replaced by something that is no longer a kingdom it is true, but which certainly is not a republic.

"But let us look a-little further; let us attend to the facts and study the phraseology of the accusation.

"Gentlemen of the jury, in Spain the Inquisition was formerly the law. Well, it must be confessed, people failed in their respect to the Inquisition. In France torture was legal. I am obliged to repeat that there was a failure of respect towards torture. Cutting off the thumb was legal: people have actually found fault—I myself have found fault—with this punishment of mutilation. Branding with a red-hot iron was a legal punishment, and this has been objected to. And now the guillotine is the law. Well, gentlemen, I repeat there is a failure of respect for the punishment of the guillotine.

"Do you know why this is the case, Mr. Advocate-

General? I will tell you. It is because the guillotine is about to be cast into that abyss of execration into which branding, mutilating, torturing, and the Inquisition have been already hurled amidst the applause of the whole human race. It is because, from the bright and noble sanctuary of justice, the sinister presence of the executioner is about to disappear, a presence that has long overshadowed it with horrors.

"And it is because we desire that this should be accomplished that we are accused of overturning society. Ah, yes, it is true, we are dangerous characters, we would suppress the guillotine ! The very idea is monstrous !

" Gentlemen of the jury, you are the sovereign citizens of a free nation, and, without going beyond the proper range of discussion in a question of this kind, I may— I ought, to address you as men having an interest in political affairs. Well, then, think a little ; and since we are passing through a period of revolutions, deduce the consequences of what I am about to say to you. If Louis XVI. had abolished the penalty of death as he abolished torture, his head would not have fallen ; the year '93 would have not had the guillotine ; there would have been one bloody page the less in history, and the 28th January would not have existed as a day of universal mourning.

" Who, if that had been the case, in the face of the public conscience, in the face of the civilized world, would have dared to erect a scaffold for a king of whom it must be said, ' He is the man who has overthrown the scaffold ? '

"The editor of the *Evènement* is accused of failure of respect to the laws; of a want of respect for the penalty of death. Gentlemen, let us lift ourselves a little above the mere controversial question; let us look to the origin of all legislation—the inner conscience of man. When Servan, who, notwithstanding, was an Advocate-General —when this Servan, I say, applied to the criminal laws of his time this memorable stigma, 'Our penal laws afford every chance for the prosecution, none for the defence;' when Voltaire thus described the judges of Calas, 'Ah! don't speak to me of these judges, half apes and half tigers;' when Chateaubriand, in the *Conservateur,* described the law of double voting as 'a foolish and mischievous law;' when Royer-Collard, before the Chamber of Deputies, and in reference to some penal law —I know not what—exclaimed, 'If you pass this law, I swear to disobey it;' when these legislators, these magistrates, these philosophers, these noble spirits, these men, some illustrious, some venerable, speak in this language, what is said of them? Did they fail in respect to the law of their time and place? It may be so. Mr. Advocate-General says it is so; but I am not aware of it. What I do know, however, is, that these expressions were the sacred echoes of the law of laws and of the universal conscience of mankind. Did these men offend justice, the justice of their time, the transitory and fallible justice? I cannot tell; but I know, at least, that they proclaimed the justice which is eternal.

"It is true that now-a-days—so, at least, they have done us the favour to inform us in the bosom of the

National Assembly—they would have brought to justice the atheist Voltaire, the immoral Molière, the indecent La Fontaine, the demagogue Jean Jacques Rousseau. You see, then, what is thought; you hear what is avowed; you recognize our position. Gentlemen of the jury, you will not fail to appreciate all this.

"Gentlemen of the jury, this right of criticizing—and even severely criticizing—the law, especially, and above all, the penal law, which so easily communicates a barbarous impress; this right of criticizing, which is placed side by side with the duty of ameliorating, as the torch by the side of the work that has to be done; this right of the author, not less sacred than the right of the legislator; this necessary and inalienable right, you will, I feel sure, recognize by your verdict; for you will acquit the accused.

"But the public Minister—this is the second argument—asserts that the critique in the *Evènement* has gone too far; that it was too severe. Ah! indeed, gentlemen of the jury, let us look at the facts that formed the foundation of the pretended crime of which the editor is accused; let us look, I say, a little more closely at these frightful facts.

"A man, a convict, a miserable wretch, is dragged one morning to one of our public squares. There he finds a scaffold. He rebels; he resists; he refuses to die. He is quite young still, scarcely twenty-nine. My God! I know well that you will say, 'He is an assassin.' But listen! Two executioners lay hold of him; his hands are tied, his feet are tied, but he beats back the two executioners.

A frightful struggle takes place. The convict entwines his feet in the steps of the gallows, and makes use of the scaffold to save himself from the scaffold. The struggle is prolonged. A sense of horror pervades the crowd. The executioners—perspiration and shame on their brows, pale, gasping, terrified, disheartened — make frantic efforts ; they are desperate with I know not what horrible despair ; depressed under that public feeling of reprobation which ought to exhibit itself in condemnation of the penalty of death, and which does wrong in crushing its passive instrument, the headsman. It is absolutely necessary that the law should prevail, that is the maxim. The man clings to the scaffold, and implores pardon ; his clothes are torn, and his naked shoulders are covered with blood. He still resists. At length, after three-quarters of an hour—three-quarters of an hour—(*the Advocate-General makes here a sign of denial. M. Victor Hugo resumes*) — they cavil about minutes ! thirty-five minutes, if you will, of this monstrous effort ; this spectacle without name ; this agony—an agony, mark, for every person present—an agony for the people as well as for the convict ; after this century of anguish, gentlemen of the jury, they take back the victim to his prison. The people breathe ; the people, possessing the prejudices of old humanity, and merciful because sovereign, the people understand that the man is spared. No, not at all ! The guillotine is conquered for the time, but it remains in its place. It remains there the whole day, in the midst of a frightened population. And in the evening they obtain a reinforcement of executioners ; the man is choked in some manner, till he is no longer anything more than a senseless mass; and when night falls, he is brought again on the public square, weeping, howling, haggard, covered with blood, praying for his life, calling upon his God, calling for his father and his mother! In the presence of death this man had become a child.

"He is hoisted on to the scaffold, and his head falls; and then a thrill is felt passing through all consciences, for never did a legal murder take place with greater indecency and in a more offensive manner. Each felt personally responsible for this dismal event that had just taken place; each felt at the bottom of his heart that which would be experienced if, in the face of all France, and in the open day, civilization were insulted by barbarism.

"It is at such a moment that a cry escapes from the breast of a young man—from his very heart and soul—a cry of pity, a cry of anguish, a cry of horror, a cry of humanity; and this cry you are called on to punish. In the presence of the frightful facts which I have recalled and presented before your eyes, you are to inform the guillotine that it was in the right, and you are to inform pity, holy pity, that it was in the wrong.

"I say that this is not possible, gentlemen of the jury.

"Mr. Advocate-General, I must tell you, without bitterness, that you are engaged in a bad cause. You undertake an unequal struggle with the spirit of civilization, with improved manners, with progress. You have against you the inmost resistance of the human heart. You have against you all those principles, under whose shadow France has for sixty years been advancing herself, and forcing the world to advance. These are the inviolability of human life, brotherhood for the uneducated classes, the dogma of improvement replacing the dogma of vengeance. You have against you everything that enlightens the reason, everything that vibrates in the soul—philosophy as well as religion : on one side, Voltaire; on the other side, Jesus Christ. It is a fine thing, this frightful service that the scaffold pretends to render to society; but society, in reality, has a horror of it, and will none of it. You have done all in your power, the partisans of the penalty of death have done all in their power—and you see that we do not mix them up with society in general—the partisans of capital punishment have, I say, done all they could; but they will not prove the old penalty of retaliation to be innocent and right, they will not wash clean those hideous laws on which the blood of innumerable decapitated heads has been trickling for so many ages.

" Gentlemen, I have finished.

" My son ! thou wilt this day receive a great honour. Thou art judged worthy of fighting, perhaps of suffering, for the sacred cause of truth. From to-day, thou enterest the true manly life of our time, the struggle for the just and the true. Be proud, thou who art now admitted to the ranks of those who battle for the human and democratic idea ! Thou art seated on the bench where Béranger and Lamennais have sat.

" Remain unshaken in thy convictions, and let this be my last word ; if thou hast need of a thought to strengthen thy faith in progress, in the conviction of a future, in thy religion for humanity, in thy execration for the scaffold, in thy horror of irrevocable and irreparable penalties, call to mind that thou art seated on the bench where Lesarques has sat."

M. Charles Hugo was sentenced to six months' imprisonment.

In 1854, M. Victor Hugo, then dwelling in Jersey, learnt that a man was to be hanged in Guernsey. He wrote the two following letters on the subject :—

"TO THE INHABITANTS OF GUERNSEY.

" People of Guernsey,

" It is an outlaw who approaches you.

" It is an outlaw who comes to appeal to you in favour of a convict. A man who is in exile, stretches out the hand to a man who is in the sepulchre. Do not object, but listen to me.

" There is a certain divinity, horrible, tragical, execrable, pagan. This divinity was called Moloch by the Hebrews, and Tentates by the Celts; now it is called *the penalty of death*. In former times, its high priest in the East was the Magus, and in the West the druid; now this high priest is called the executioner. The legal murder has replaced the religious murder. In times gone by, the latter has filled your island with human sacrifices, and it has, everywhere, left monuments ; those melancholy stones on which the rust of centuries has obliterated the stain of blood, and which are found half buried among brambles on the tops of your hills. In this present year, now only commencing, the monstrous idol reappears among you; it calls on you to obey it, it fixes a day for the celebration of its mysteries; and now, as formerly, it demands from you—from you who have read the Gospel, whose eyes are fixed on Calvary—it demands a human sacrifice. Will you grant this demand? Will you become once more pagans during two hours on the 27th January, 1854? Will you become pagans for the purpose of killing a man? pagans for the sake of destroying a human soul? pagans in order to mutilate the destiny of a criminal, by cutting off from him the time for repentance? Will you do this? Would this be progress? Where are men, if human sacrifices are still possible? Is this idol still worshipped in Guernsey, this old idol of the past, which kills, standing in opposition to God who creates? Why have taken away the sacrificing stone if he is to be allowed the scaffold?

"What! To commute a penalty, to leave to a guilty person a chance for remorse and reconciliation, to substitute for a human sacrifice an intelligent expiation, to decline killing a man, is all this so difficult? Is the ship in such danger, that a man must be thrown overboard? Does a repentant criminal weigh so heavily upon society, that he must be cut off—that this creature of God must be thrown into the shadow of the abyss?

" Guernseymen, the penalty of death is daily losing ground, it retreats before the sentiment of humanity. In 1830, the Chamber of Deputies of France demanded its abolition by acclamation. The constitution of Frankfort erased it from the code in 1848. It was suppressed in Rome in 1849. Our constituency in Paris has retained it only by an imperceptible majority. I say, further, Tuscany, which is Catholic, has abolished it. Russia, which is barbarous, has abolished it. Otaheite, which is savage, has abolished it. It seems that the powers of darkness will no longer retain it. Do you desire to retain it—you, the inhabitants of this good land ?

" It depends on you whether the penalty of death be abolished or not in Guernsey. It depends on you whether or not a man shall be " hanged by the neck till he is dead," on the 27th of January next. It depends on you to prevent this frightful spectacle, which would leave a black spot on your beautiful sky.

" Save this life—save this soul—you can do it—it depends on you.

" It may be replied, that after the melancholy way-laying of the 18th October, death and justice are insepa-rable—that the crime of Tapner is very great. I reply, the greater the crime the longer the time needed for repentance.

" What! a woman assassinated, killed in the most cowardly manner, a house pillaged and burnt, a murder accomplished, and around this murder, a crowd of other crimes committed ! Is it that because, on the one side, a crime has been committed—I should rather say, many crimes—demanding a long and solemn reparation; a punishment that shall involve reflection; a ransom to be paid by repentance; the bringing of the criminal to bow himself down under the weight of his crime, and the convict under his punishment—a whole life of pain and purification ; and, because, on the other hand, on the morning of a certain day, and within a few minutes, a gibbet shall have been erected, a cord tightened round the neck of a man, a human soul made to take flight from a miserable body with the howling of a demon; is, therefore, I say, the account settled ? Is this a satisfactory conclusion ?

"Wretched brevity of human justice !

"But, oh, this is the nineteenth century ! We are a modern people ; we are a people thoughtful, serious, free, intelligent, industrious, sovereign; this is the best age of humanity, the period of progress, art, science, love, hope, brotherhood. Scaffolds ! what would you have ? Oh, monstrous machines of death, hideous frameworks of nonentity, apparitions of the past—thou who holdest in thine arms the triangular knife, thou who holdest a skeleton suspended at the end of a cord; by what right do ye reappear in broad daylight, in the middle of the nineteenth century, in full vigour of life ? You are spectres—you are things of the night. Return into the night.

"Is it that the darkness will serve the light ? Depart from us ! To civilize men, to correct the guilty, to enlighten the conscience, to plant the seed of repentance in the sleeplessness of crime, we are worth more than you ; we have thought, instruction, patient education, religious example, intelligence above, trials below, austerity, work, mercy.

"What! From the midst of all that is great, from all
that is true, from all that is fine, from all that is noble,
one sees rise up with obstinate persistence the penalty
of death. What! The sovereign city, the central city of
the human race, the city of the 14th July and the 10th
August, the city where Rousseau and Voltaire sleep, the
metropolis of revolutions, the asylum of the ideal; this
city must also have its places of execution, its Grève, its
Barriére Saint-Jacques, its Roquette! But even this is not
enough of the abominable contradiction. All this mis-
construction is a trifle, and this horror is not sufficient.
Here also, in your archipelago, among these cliffs, trees,
and flowers, under the shadow of the clouds that drift to
us from the pole, the scaffold rises up, and dominates,
and asserts its right and rules. It claims sacrifice also
here, 'mid the noise of the winds, the eternal murmur of
the waves in the solitude of the abyss, in the majesty of
nature. Go, I repeat; disappear from before us! What
is it that thou art about to do, thou the guillotine in the
midst of Paris—thou the gibbet before the expanse of
ocean?

"O population of fishermen, brave and good men of
the sea, do not let this man die! Do not let your charming island be blighted by the shadows of the gibbet!
Into your heroic and uncertain sea adventures do not
introduce this mysterious element of death! Do not
accept the formidable responsibility of this encroachment
of human power over the power Divine! Who knows, who
believes, who has guessed this riddle? There are abysses
in human actions, just as there are gulfs in the waves.

Think on the stormy days, on the wintry nights, on the angry and dark powers which take possession of you at certain times. Think how jagged is the coast of Sark, how perfidious the depths of the Minquiers, how stern the Paternoster Rocks. Do not allow the wind of the sepulchre to puff out your sails. Never forget, O navigators, that there is but one plank between you and eternity; that you are at the mercy of these waves which are unfathomable, and of that destiny of which we are all ignorant; that, perhaps, there is some unknown will at work, even in things that you regard as chance; that you struggle incessantly against the sea, and against time; and that you, men who know so little, and who can do so little, are always in the presence of the infinite and the unknown!

" The infinite and the unknown are the grave.

" Do not dig with your own hands a grave in the midst of you.

" What, then? These voices of the infinite, do they say nothing to you? Do not all mysteries speak to you of one another? Does not the majesty of the ocean proclaim the holiness of the grave? In the tempest, in the storm, during the equinoctial gale, when the night-winds swing the corpse suspended from the gibbet, will it not be a terrible thought,—this skeleton cursing your island before infinite space?

" Will you not reflect, with a shudder, that this same wind, which will come and whistle through your riggings, must have met, on its way, with that cord and that corpse, and that that cord and that corpse have spoken to it?

"No, let there be no more penalties of death. We, great men of the present century, we will no more of them. We will not allow them for the guilty more than for the innocent. I repeat it, crime is redeemed by re-morse, and not by a noose; blood is washed out by tears, and not by more blood. Let us give no occupation to the executioner. Let us always bear this in mind—and may the conscience of the pious and honest judge think with us in the matter!—that, independently of the great crime against the inviolability of human nature, whether in the case of the brigand or the martyred hero, every scaffold has been guilty of crimes. The code of murder is a wretch wearing thy mask, O Justice! killing and committing massacres with impunity. Every scaffold is tarnished by the names of innocent and martyred men. No, let us have no more capital punishment. For us, the guillotine is Lesurques; the wheel, Calas; the stake, Joan of Arc; the torture, Campanella; the block, Thomas More; hemlock is Socrates; and the cross is Jesus Christ.

"Oh, if there be anything august in those paternal teachings, in those doctrines inculcating gentleness and love; if there be any truth in those lips which are per-petually exclaiming 'Religion!' and in those mouths which utter 'Democracy!'—doctrines which the united voices of the old and the new Gospel are planting and extending, in our days, from one end of the world to the other: some in the name of the God-man, others in the name of the people—if these doctrines be just, if these ideas be true, if the living is brother to the living, if the life of

man is holy, if the soul of man is immortal, if God alone
has the right to take away what He alone can give, if the
mother who feels the child stir within her is a sacred
being, if the cradle is a sacred thing, if the tomb is a
sacred thing, O islanders of Guernsey, kill not this man!

"I repeat 'Do not kill him;' for be well assured that
not to prevent death, being able to do so, is to kill.

"Do not be astonished at the earnestness with which I
urge this subject. Allow the exile to plead for the convict. _ Say not, 'What does this stranger want with us?'
Say not to the exile, 'Why do you interfere? The affair
is none of yours!' I interfere where I find misery: it is
my right, because I suffer myself. Misfortune takes pity
on misery, grief leans on despair.

"Besides, this man and I, have we not mutual sorrows? Do we not, each of us, spread out our arms to
catch that which is escaping from us? I an exile, he a
convict, do we not each of us turn our eyes to the light—
he towards life, I towards my country?

"But, what matter? In my eyes the assassin is no
longer an assassin; the incendiary no longer an incendiary; the thief no longer a thief; he becomes a shuddering
being about to die. Misfortune has turned him into my
brother. I defend his cause.

"When adversity tries us, it is sometimes useful to us
beyond the mere trial; and it may happen that our trials,
explained by events whose purpose they serve, take unexpected and consolatory shapes.

"If my voice is heard; if it is not lost as an empty breath
in the noise of wave and storm; if it is not lost in the

stormy atmosphere which separates the two islands [Jersey and Guernsey]; if the grain of pity which I throw into this ocean-breeze shall germinate and fructify in the hearts of men; if it so happen that my words, the obscure words of one who is vanquished, should have the distinguished honour of exciting a movement from whence will emerge a punishment commuted, and a criminal penitent; if it be given to me, a useless and rejected exile, to put myself across a yawning grave to bar the passage of death and to save a human life; if I am the grain of sand which has fallen by accident from the hand of chance, but has weighed down the scale, before evenly balanced, and thus elevates life and puts down death; if my exile has been of use in this way, if that was to be the mysterious object of my banishment from the domestic hearth, and of my presence in these islands; oh, then all is well! I shall then never feel that I have suffered. I shall be grateful, and raise my hands to heaven; and on this occasion, where the will of Providence is so clearly shown, I shall feel that thine, O God, will be the triumph; to have brought a blessing on Guernsey by the agency of France; to have blessed this almost primitive people by the civilization of the world; men who have never killed, by a man who has killed; the law of pity and of life by a murderer, and banishment by an exile.

" Men of Guernsey, it is not I who now speak to you— I, who am but an atom carried away in the night by the winds of adversity! That which is now addressing you is, as I have just said, the whole of civilization; it is this that stretches out its hands towards you. If the exiled

Beccaria were amongst you, he would say, ' *Capital punish-ment is impious.*' If the exiled Franklin were amongst you, he would say, ' *The law which kills is a hurtful law.*' If Filangieri the refugee, Vico the exile, Turgot the ex-pelled, Montesquieu the banished—if these had dwelt among you, they would all say to you, ' *The scaffold is an abomination.*' If Jesus Christ, flying from before Caiaphas, had disembarked on your island, He would have said, ' *Strike not with the sword.*' And should Montesquieu, Turgot, Vico, Beccaria, Franklin, all exclaim ' Mercy !' would you reply ' No ?'

" No ! It is the reply of evil. No ! It is the reply of no-thingness. The man who is free and a believer says ' Yes !' to life, ' Yes !' to pity, ' Yes !' to mercy, and ' Yes !' to pardon. He proves the soul of society by the mercy of the law, and only replies ' No !' when it is a question of opprobrium, despotism, and death."

The Guernsey people petitioned for the life of the con-vict but were refused, and the execution of Tapner drew from Victor Hugo the following letter :—

" To Lord Palmerston, Her Majesty's Principal Secre-tary of State for the Home Department in England.

" My Lord,

" I place before your eyes a series of facts which oc-curred in Jersey within the last few years.

" Fifteen years ago, Caliot, an assassin, was condemned to death and pardoned. Eight years ago, Thomas Nicole, an assassin, was condemned to death and pardoned. Three years ago, in 1851, Jacques Fouquet, an assassin, was

condemned to death and pardoned. For all these criminals the penalty of death was commuted to transporta-
tion. To obtain these pardons at different periods a petition from the inhabitants of the island was sufficient.

"I would add that, in 1851, Edward Carlton was transported for the murder of his wife under horrible circumstances.

"All this occurred in the fifteen years I spent in the
island from whence I write to you.

"Now let us quit Jersey and consider the case of
Guernsey.

"Tapner, an assassin, an incendiary, and a robber, is
condemned to death. At the present day, my lord—and
the facts I have just mentioned would suffice to prove
what I say in every upright and healthy conscience—the
penalty of death is abolished. Tapner being condemned,
a general outcry is heard, petitions multiply, and one,
energetically asserting the inviolability of human life,
is signed by 600 of the most enlightened inhabitants
of the island. It is worthy of notice that not a single
minister of any form of Christian worship has added his
signature to these petitions. These men are probably
ignorant that the cross was a gibbet. The people cry
'Pardon!' but the priest cries 'Death!' Let us pity the
priests, and pass on. The petitions were duly forwarded
to you, my lord, and you granted a respite. In such
cases a respite signifies a commutation of the punishment. The island breathes: the gibbet will not be
erected. Not so: the gibbet is erected. Tapner is
hanged.

"After reflection.

" Why ?

" Why is that refused to Guernsey which has been so frequently granted to Jersey? Why the concession to one island and the refusal to the other? Why is mercy to be granted here and the executioner sent there? Why this difference where the cases were parallel? What was the meaning of this respite, which is now only an aggravation? Is there any mystery connected with it? Of what use is reflection?

" Things have been said, my lord, before which I turn away my head. No, what has been said cannot be.

" Whatever may be the state of the case, you have commanded,—these are the words of the despatch,—'that justice should take its course.' Whatever it may be, all is now at an end. Whatever may happen, Tapner, after three respites and three *reflections,* was yesterday, on the 10th February, hanged; and the following, my lord, is an account of the day's proceedings :—

" There was a garden attached to the prison, and there the scaffold was erected. A breach was made in the wall in order to enable the crowd to pass. At eight o'clock in the morning, the crowd invaded the neighbouring streets, two hundred spectators, ' privileged ones,' being stationed in the garden. The man appeared in the breach. He looked bravely around, and walked with a firm step; he was pale, and a red rim encircled his eyes. The month that had just passed away had added twenty years to his age. This man of thirty years looked at least fifty. ' A white cotton nightcap was pulled over his head, but was raised up so as to show his forehead '—

these are the words of an eye-witness—'he was dressed in the brown great-coat which he generally wore on his trial, and on his feet he had a pair of old slippers;' he walked all round the garden on a walk ready gravelled for the occasion. The constables, the sheriff, the deputy-sheriff, and the Queen's Procureur, surrounded him. His hands were tied, but not securely, as you will see. Nevertheless, according to the English custom, whilst his hands were crossed over his breast by these cords, another cord tied his elbows together behind his back. Beside him the chaplains, who had refused to sign the petition for pardon, were weeping. The gravelled walk led to the ladder. The noose was ready, suspended. Tapner ascended the steps : the executioner was trembling. Tapner placed himself under the running noose, and put his neck through it, and his hands being insecurely tied, as he saw the executioner was unequal to the occasion and went clumsily to work, he himself assisted him. Then, 'as if he foresaw what was about to happen,'—adds the same witness—he said, '*Do tie my hands tighter.*' ' It is of no use ! ' said the executioner. Tapner, standing thus in the running noose, with his feet over the bolt, the executioner pulled down the cap over his eyes, and nothing more was seen of his countenance than his mouth, in the act of praying. After a few seconds, just about the time it would take to turn round, the man of 'great actions' pressed the spring of the trap. A vacant space was then left under the convict's feet, and he fell suddenly into it ; the cord stretched, the body turned, and the man was thought to be dead. 'It was supposed,' said the eye-

witness, 'that Tapner had been killed outright by breaking his neck.' He fell from a height of four feet, and
with his full weight, he being a tall man. My informant
adds, ' This notion, which was a great relief to all present,
was hardly felt for as much as two minutes.' On a sudden, this man, who was not yet a corpse, but was already
a spectre, was seen to move; his legs were raised and
lowered, one after the other, as if they were feeling for a
footing in the empty space beneath him. What was now
seen was becoming truly horrible. The man's hands,
which had nearly become untied, spread apart and joined
themselves together again, 'as if to ask for assistance.'
The cord which tied the elbows together had been broken
in the shock of the fall. During the convulsions that
took place, the cord by which he was suspended began to
oscillate. The elbows of the wretched man presently
grazed against the edge of the trap, and his hands clung
to it; his right knee then leant against it; his body half
raised itself; and the hanged man leant over the crowd.
He fell back again, and this scene was twice repeated.
He then raised his cap, and the crowd could see his face.
This had now lasted too long, and it became necessary to
put a stop to it. The executioner, who had descended,
mounted the platform again, and—I still quote the words
of the eye-witness—'made the dying man quit his hold.'
The executioner and the spectre struggled for a moment,
and the executioner gained the mastery. Then this man,
a convict himself, precipitated himself into the hole where
Tapner was hanging, clasped his two knees, and hung
from his feet. The cord still swung for a moment, carry-

ing the dying man and the executioner—the crime and the law—backwards and forwards. At length, the executioner let go his hold, and all was over. The man was dead.

" You see, my lord, things went off very well. It was a very complete affair. If they wished for a shriek of horror, they certainly had it.

" The town being built like an amphitheatre, the people could witness the scene from their houses. Everybody was anxiously looking into the garden.

" The crowd were exclaiming, ' Shame! shame!' Some women fainted.

" Whilst all this was going on, Fouquet, who had been respited in 1851, has since repented. The executioner turned Tapner into a corpse; mercy has made Fouquet a man once more.

" A last detail.

" In the interval between Tapner's falling into the hole, occasioned by removing the trap-door, and the moment when the executioner, feeling that the last death struggle was over, dropped from the feet of the corpse, twelve minutes intervened. Let it be calculated what this amounts to, if indeed there be any who know by what dial the hours of agony may be reckoned.

" It was in this way, my lord, that Tapner died.

" The theory of example is satisfied. The philosopher alone is sad, and asks if this is justice, ' taking its course.'

" We must assume that philosophy is wrong. The death was frightful, but the crime was a hideous one.

Society is bound to defend itself, is it not true? Where should we be if, &c., &c., &c.? The boldness of malefactors would be unlimited. Nothing but atrocities and crimes of violence would be heard of. It is necessary to repress all this. In fine, it is your opinion, my lord, that the Tapners should be hanged.

" Let the will of the statesman be done!

" Listen, my lord, it is horrible. We inhabit—you and I—the infinitely small. I am but an exile, and you are only a Minister. I am ashes, and you are dust. Being both atoms, we may speak together. From one nothingness to another, home truths may be told. Well, be it known to you, whatever be the actual splendours of your political position, my lord, this rope tied round a man's throat, that trap-door which opens under his feet, that hope one entertains that he will break his neck in falling, that face which turns blue under the lugubrious veil of the gibbet, those bloodshot eyes which start from their sockets, that tongue which is thrust out of his mouth, that groan of anguish which the noose stifles, that distracted soul which struggles in its prison-house, the skull, without being able to escape; those convulsed knees, seeking some place against which they may press; those hands bound, and mutely appealing for help; and that other man, that dark shadow, who throws himself on this shuddering and palpitating mass of humanity, who clings to the wretch's knees, and who hangs himself to the hanging man; all this, my lord, is frightful. You said, let justice 'take its course.' You gave these orders as they are wont to be given, and these repetitions but little affect you. To hang a man is to you very much like drinking a glass of water. You did not recognize the enormity of the act. It is one of the occurrences of daily life to a great statesman—nothing more. My lord, keep your thoughtless acts for the earth; do not offer them to eternity. Believe me, do not trifle with depths like these; do not throw anything of yourself into them. It is an act of imprudence. With regard to these depths, I am nearer them than you are. I see them. Take care, *Exul sicut mortuus.* I speak to you from within the tomb.

"Bah! what matters it? A man hanged, and then a rope to be taken away, a scaffold to be unnailed, a corpse to be buried; what does it all amount to? We will fire a gun off; there will be a little smoke in the east, and nothing more will be said about it. Guernsey— Tapner—we must have a microscope to see little things like these. But that rope, that scaffold, that corpse, that wretched gibbet, hardly seen, that misery, these are immensity. It is a social question, much higher than any political question. It is yet more, it is something that no longer exists on earth. What is really of no importance is your firing of guns, your politics, your smoke. The assassin, who, between sunrise and sunset, has been assassinated, this is the frightful thing; a soul which takes its flight, holding a piece of the rope torn from the gibbet, this is really formidable. Statesmen, between the signing of two protocols, between two meals, between two smiles, you carelessly press with your white-gloved thumb the spring of the gallows, and the trap gives way under the feet of the hanging man. Do you know what that trap is? It is eternity which is dawning, it is the unfathomable and the unknown; it is the great shadow which opens unexpectedly and terribly upon your littleness.

"Go on. It is well. Let us see men of the old school at work. As the past will not pass away, let us look back at it. Let us see all its members in succession. At Tunis, we have impaling; under the Czar, the knout; under the Pope, garrotting; in France, the guillotine; in England, the gibbet; in Asia and America, the slave-market. Ah! all this will fade away. We anarchists, we demagogues, we bloodthirsty men, we declare unto you, unto you, the Conservatives, that human liberty is august, human intelligence is holy, human life is sacred, and the human soul is Divine. After this, will you still hang?

"Take care. Futurity draws near. You believe that which is dead to be living, and that which is living you believe to be dead. The old society still holds its position; but I tell you, that is dead. You have deceived yourselves. You have placed your hand on the spectre in the night, and you have made it your bride. You turn your backs on life, and presently it will rise from behind you. When we pronounce those words, Progress, Revolution, Liberty, Humanity, you smile, unhappy men! and you show us the night, in which we are, and in which you are. Truly, do you know what the night means? Learn its meaning, for ere long, ideas will emerge from it, vast and radiating. Yesterday democracy was France, to-morrow it will be Europe. The present eclipse masks the mysterious aggrandisement of the planet.

> "I remain, &c.,
>
> > "VICTOR HUGO.
>
> "Marine Terrace, 11th February, 1854."

Three years before this, M. Victor Hugo had tried to save John Brown. On the 2nd December, 1859, he published the following :—

"A WORD CONCERNING JOHN BROWN.

"When we think of the United States of America, a majestic figure arises in our minds. It is the figure of Washington.

"Now, in this land of Washington, see what is taking place at this moment.

"There are slaves in the Southern States, a fact which offends, as the most monstrous contradiction, the logical and pure conscience of the Northern States. A white man, a free man, John Brown, sought to deliver these slaves, these negroes. Certainly, if insurrection can ever be a sacred duty, it must be so when it is an insurrection against slavery. John Brown wished to commence his pious undertaking, by delivering the Virginian slaves. Himself a Puritan, a religious man, austere, full of the Gospel, which says *Christus nos liberavit*, he stirred up in the hearts of these men, these brothers, the cry of freedom. The slaves, enervated by servitude, did not respond to the appeal. Slavery produces deafness of soul. John Brown, left to himself, fought the battle; with a handful of heroic men he entered into the contest. He was pierced with balls, his two young sons, holy martyrs, fell dead at his side, and he was taken prisoner. This is what is called the affair of Harper's Ferry.

"John Brown, having been captured, has just been tried, with four of his men, Stephens, Copp, Green, and Coplands.

"What was this trial? Let us explain it in a few words.

"John Brown, stretched on his bed of straw, with six wounds yet unhealed: one from a gunshot in his arm, one in his loins, two in his breast; scarcely hearing, bleeding through his mattress, the shadowy forms of his two sons hovering around him; the four men who were accused with him wounded and walking painfully by his side, Stephens having received four sword-cuts—such were the prisoners. 'Justice' was in a hurry; she had other business on hand. An attorney, named Hunter, desired to hasten matters; a judge, named Parker, consented; all discussion was shortened; almost all delay refused; the documents produced were false or mutilated; the witnesses for the defence were sent out of the way; the defence was interrupted; two cannons, loaded with grape-shot, were stationed in the court of tribunal; the order was given to the jailors to shoot the accused if any attempt was made to rescue them; there were forty minutes of deliberation, and then three human beings were condemned to death. And all this did not occur in Turkey, but in America.

"But these things are not committed with impunity in

the face of the civilized world.   The universal conscience
of mankind is an eye that never sleeps.   Let the judges
of Charlestown, let Hunter and Parker, let the jury who
possess slaves, and the whole of the population of Virginia
think of this—they are seen.   There is One watching
them.   Europe, at this moment, is watching what is going
on in America.

"John Brown, condemned to die, was to be hanged on
the 2nd December (this very day).

"But news arrives as I write: a respite is accorded;
he will die on the 16th.

"The interval is short.   Is there yet time that a cry
for mercy may reach from us to America?

"It matters not.   It is our duty to make the attempt.

"A second respite may, perhaps, be granted.   America
is a noble land.   Human feelings are quickly stirred up
in a free country.   We still hope that Brown may be
spared.

"Were it otherwise, if John Brown is to die on the
16th of December on the scaffold, how terrible an event!

"Brown's executioner—let us speak the truth boldly
(for kings are disappearing from the earth to make way
for nations, and to nations we must speak the truth)—
Brown's executioner would neither be the Attorney Hunter,
nor the Judge Parker, nor the Governor Wyse, nor the
State of Virginia; it would be, though one shudders to
think it and still more to say it, the great American
Republic itself.

"Before such a catastrophe, the more one loves this
Republic, the more one venerates it, the more one admires

it, the more is the heart pained. A single State ought not to have the power allowed it of dishonouring all the others, and here federal intervention is evidently due. If it were not so, when a crime is committed that might be prevented, union is complicity. However indignant the generous Northern States may be, the Southern States associate them in the opprobrium of murder. All we, whoever we may be, whose common country is the symbol of democracy, we feel injured, and, so to speak, compromised, if the scaffold is erected on the 16th December. From that day the august federation of the New World will, in the pages of incorruptible history, add to all its holy responsibilities a bloody responsibility, and the splendid union of this glorious Republic will be burdened for ever with the running noose of John Brown's gallows.

" That tie would be death itself.

" When one reflects on what Brown, the liberator and Christ's faithful soldier, attempted, and when one knows that he is about to die, his throat cut by the American Republic, this attempt at crime assumes the gigantic proportions of the nation by whom it is committed. When, therefore, we consider that this nation is the glory of the whole earth, that, like France, England, and Germany, it is one of the organs of civilization, that it has even gone beyond Europe in certain sublime strokes of bold progress, that it is at the summit of the whole world, that it wears on its brow the star of liberty, we are tempted to affirm that John Brown will not die ; for we shrink back horrified at the idea of so great a crime being committed by so great a nation !

"In a political point of view, the murder of Brown would be an irreparable fault. It would make in the Union a rent, at first concealed, but which would end by splitting it asunder. Brown's death might consolidate slavery in Virginia, but it is certain that it would disquiet the whole of the American democracy. You save your dignity, but you destroy your glory.

"Looking at it in a moral point of view, it appears to one that a portion of human life would be eclipsed, that proper ideas as to justice and injustice would be obscured, on that day when the attempt to deliver the enslaved was assassinated by liberty.

"As for me, who am but an atom, but who, like other men, have in me a human conscience, I kneel, with tears, before the great star-spangled banner of the New World, and I entreat, with clasped hands and with filial and profound respect, that this illustrious Republic of America —this sister to the French Republic—will consider the well-being of the universal moral law, will save John Brown, will destroy the threatening scaffold of the 16th December, and will not permit that beneath its eyes, and —I add with shuddering—almost by its own fault, a fratricide more terrible than that of Abel by his brother Cain should occur.

"Yes, let America know it and believe in it, there is something more alarming still than Cain killing Abel: it is Washington killing Spartacus."

During the year just concluded [1861], a Belgian jury having pronounced on one single occasion nine sentences of death, some person, astonished, no doubt, that the pertinacious foe of the penalty of death did not take up the affair, ventured to assume his name, and the Belgian journals published some verses, signed "Victor Hugo," imploring pardon of the King for the nine convicts. These verses provoked the following letter :—

" To the Editor of the *Indépendance Belge.*

" Hauteville House, Guernsey,
21 January, 1862.

" Sir,

" I live in solitude, and, especially during the last two months, pressing occupations absorb my time to such an extent that I have not been aware of what was passing in the world.

" This day a friend has brought me several journals containing some excellent verses, imploring the pardon of nine criminals, sentenced to death. My name is appended to these verses.

" They are not written by me.

" Whoever the author may be, I thank him; for when it is a question of saving life, I am quite willing that my name should be used, and even abused. I would add, that in such a cause it cannot be abused, for here most certainly the end justifies the means.

" But allow the author to permit me to restore to him the credit of his verses, which I repeat, seem to me very fine; and to this first acknowledgment I would add a second—it is that of making me acquainted with this bad affair of Charleroi.

"I regard these verses as an appeal addressed to me, as a way of calling on me to lift up my voice, by bringing into notice the efforts I have made under analogous circumstances, and I thank him for this generous act.

"I answer his appeal. I unite my efforts to his in the endeavour to spare to Belgium this fall of nine heads on the scaffold. He addresses the King—I address the nation.

"This affair of Hainault is for Belgium, in respect to progress, one of those occasions from which the people emerge either lowered or elevated.

"I entreat the Belgian nation to be great. It clearly depends on itself whether this hideous guillotine, constructed for nine victims, shall or shall not appear in the public square. No Government resists the pressure of public opinion in the direction of mercy. No Government can desire the scaffold. It must originate with the people. It has been said, 'What the people will, God wills.' It depends on you, Belgians, to have it said, 'What God wills the people will.'

"We are now passing the dark hour of the nineteenth century. During the last ten years there has been an apparent retrogression of civilization. Venice enslaved, Hungary garotted, Poland tortured, everywhere the penalty of death. The monarchies have their Haynau, the republics their Talaferro. The penalty of death is raised to the dignity of an *ultima ratio*. Races, colours, parties throw it at the heads of each other, and make use of it as a reply. The whites employ it against the negroes; the negroes in melancholy reprisals sharpen its edge to use it against the whites. The Spanish Government shoots the Republicans, and the Italian Government the Royalists. Rome executes an innocent person. The author of the murder discovers himself and implores justice. It is in vain—the deed is done, and the executioner's work cannot be undone. Europe now believes in the penalty of death, and remains obstinate. America suffers a civil war because of it. The scaffold is the friend of slavery. The shadow of a gibbet projects itself over the fratricidal war of the United States. Never was there so complete a parallelism and understanding between America and Europe, as on this point. They are divided on all questions, except this one—to kill! It is concerning the penalty of death that the two worlds, the Eastern and the Western, agree. The penalty of death reigns triumphant—a species of right divine of the axe is admitted by the Roman Catholics of the Gospel and the Virginian Protestants of the Bible. Penn constructed, by thought and a bond of union, a triumphal arch between the two worlds. On this triumphal arch must now be placed the scaffold.

" The situation of affairs being thus, the opportunity is admirable for Belgium.

" A people that possesses liberty must also possess a definite will. The tribune free, the press free; here is the organization of opinion complete. Let public opinion speak then, for this is the decisive moment. In the circumstances in which we now are, it is possible for Belgium, this small people, to place itself, if it will, at the head of civilization. This noble Belgium, which like France is a part of ancient Gaul, may manifest its nationality by a striking exception, as being the one human society whose hands are not dyed with blood, among all the numerous Governments of cut-throats.

" The opportunity, I repeat, is admirable, for it is clear that if there is no scaffold for the criminals of Hainault there will be none hereafter for anybody, and the guillotine will not be able to take root in the free soil of Belgium. Your public squares will not be exposed to this sinister apparition. By the irresistible logic of events, the penalty of death, virtually abolished amongst you to-day, will be legally abolished to-morrow.

It would be a noble thing that a small people should give a lesson to the great, and by this fact alone should become greater than they. It would be a fine thing that, in the face of the abominable growth of darkness, in the presence of a growing barbarism, Belgium, taking the place of a great Power in civilization, should communicate to the human race by one act the full glare of light; proclaiming, under conditions best adapted for bringing out the greatness of a principle, not on the occasion of some religious or revolutionary schism, not in the case of a political offender, but on account of nine wretches unworthy of all other pity than philosophical pity, the great principle of the inviolability of human life. And thus would they succeed in driving back definitively into the night this monstrous penalty of death, whose glory it is to have instituted a double crucifixion, that of Jesus

Christ in the old world, and that of John Brown in the new.

" Let generous Belgium think of this, for it is to her that the scaffold of Charleroi would do the greatest injury. When philosophy and history put a civilization into one scale of the balance, decapitated heads weigh on the other side.

" In writing thus, I fulfil a duty. Assist me, sir, and give me your publicity for this great and supreme interest.

" Accept, &c.

" VICTOR HUGO."

Two of the convicts were executed, the punishment of the rest being commuted to imprisonment for life with hard labour.

At the end of 1862, the Republic of Geneva revised its constitution. The principal question to be decided by the constituents was that of the abolition of the punishment of death. A member of the Church of Geneva, M. Aug. Bost, author of several remarkable works, wrote to Victor Hugo, requesting his influence in the discussion. I extract from his letter these pressing lines :—

" The Genevese constituency has voted the retention of the punishment of death by forty-three votes against five or six; but the question will shortly be brought forward again in a fresh debate. What strength it would be for us, what new force, if by a few words you would interfere, for this is not a cantonal or federal question, but a social and humanitarian question where all interventions are legitimate. For great questions, great men are needed. Our discussions will require to be enlightened by genius, and the support that would come to us from you, towards whom so many eyes are turned, could not fail to be a great help to us all."

M. Victor Hugo answered immediately :—

> "Hauteville House, Guernsey,
> "November 17, 1862.
>
> " SIR,
>
> " All that you do is well done. Your efforts are noble. Your writings are excellent. You need help, you apply to me for it; I thank you. You call me, and I at once reply. What is it? I am here.
>
> " Geneva is on the eve of a crisis such as in nations, as in individuals, mark the changes caused by age. You are about to revise your constitution. You govern yourselves, you are your own masters, you are free men, you are a republic. You are about to do an important act, to rearrange your social compact, to examine into your progress and civilization, to understand each other better on questions of common interest; deliberation is about to commence, and amongst other questions, the gravest of all, the inviolability of human life, comes under consideration.
>
> " It is on the subject of the penalty of death that I am about to speak.
>
> " Alas, the gloomy rock of Sisyphus! When will it cease rolling up and falling back again upon human society, that block of hatred, tyranny, and obscurity, of ignorance and injustice, that is called the penal code?

When will the word 'Instruction' be substituted for the words 'Penalty of Death'? When will it be understood that a guilty man is an ignorant man? The principle of retaliation, an eye for an eye, a tooth for a tooth, evil for evil, this is much like our own code. When will Vengeance renounce that old effort which she is always making, and give us a change by calling herself Revenge? Does she think to deceive us? Not more so than felony when it calls itself a reason of state. Not more so than fratricide when it puts on epaulettes and calls itself war. De Maistre vainly glosses over Draco : sanguinary rhetoric loses its time, and cannot succeed in disguising the deformity of the act it tries to conceal. Sophists are useless disguisers ; injustice causes injustice ; that which is horrible remains so. Certain words are masks, but from under them the gloomy light of evil may be seen.

"When will the law and right agree? When will human justice take example from divine justice? When will those who read the Bible understand why God spared Cain? When will those who read the Gospel understand the meaning of the cross on which Christ was crucified? When will people incline their ears to listen to the great living voice, which from the depths of the unknown, exclaims through the darkness, ' Do not kill'? When will those who are here below, the judge, the priest, the populace, the king, perceive that above them there is a greater power than they? Republics with slaves—monarchies dependent on soldiers—societies provided with executioners; everywhere strength, nowhere the right. Oh, the melancholy masters of the world ! Worms of infirmity, boa-constrictors of pride !

"An opportunity occurs when progress may advance a step. Geneva is about to deliberate on the penalty of death. To this circumstance I owe your letter, sir. You ask me to step in, to take part in the discussion, to say but one word. I fear you think too much of the efficacy of a poor word from me, isolated as I am. Who am I ? What can I do? For many years now (as far back as from 1828) I have been struggling with the weak strength of a man against that colossal thing, both contradictory and atrocious, the penalty of death ; a system, with enough of justice in it to satisfy the multitude, and sufficient iniquity to overwhelm the thinker. Others have done more and have done better than I have. The penalty of death has given way a little : but this is all. It grew ashamed of itself in Paris before so much light. The guillotine has lost its boldness, but it has not abdicated : banished from the Grève, it has reappeared in the Barrière Saint-Jacques ; dismissed from the Barrière Saint-Jacques, it has reappeared in the Roquette. It keeps in the background, but is still to be found.

"As you ask for my help, sir, I owe to you. But do not deceive yourselves about my share in the success should you succeed. For thirty-five years, I repeat it, I have been trying to raise obstacles against murder in the public highways. I have incessantly denounced this beaten track of the lower law against the higher. I have pushed to rebellion the universal conscience of mankind. I have attacked both by logic and by appealing to pity, this most supreme logic. I have combated, both in its totality and in detail, against that blind and immoderate penalty which kills. Sometimes I have considered the general subject, trying to reach and to wound the fact in its inmost principles, and trying to overthrow, once for all, not a single scaffold, but scaffolds in general. Sometimes I have taken up a particular case, my aim then being simply to save the life of a man. I have occasionally succeeded, but more frequently have failed. Many noble spirits have devoted themselves to the same task, and hardly ten months ago, the generous Belgian press coming to my aid with energy, on the occasion of my intervention in favour of the Charleroi convicts, succeeded in saving seven victims out of nine.

" The writers of the eighteenth century caused torture to be abolished : the writers of the nineteenth will, I cannot doubt, cause the abolition of the penalty of death. They have already in France obtained the suppression of mutilation and branding. They have got rid of civil death, and have suggested the admirable expedient of ' attenuating circumstances.'

" ' It is to execrable books such as " The Last Day of a Convict," said the Deputy Salverte, ' that we owe the detestable introduction of attenuating circumstances.' This is, in fact, the commencement of the abolition ; for these attenuating circumstances once admitted into the practice of the law is the thin edge of the wedge fixed in the plank. Let us seize the divine hammer ; let us strike on the wedge without ceasing ; let us strike the great strokes of truth, and we shall shiver the block into atoms.

"Slowly, I grant; no doubt, we must take time. But do not let us be discouraged. Our efforts, even in particular cases, are not always useless. I have just reminded you of the case of Charleroi; I now tell you of another. Eight years ago in Guernsey (in 1854), a man named Tapner was condemned to the gallows. I stepped in: a petition for pardon was signed by six hundred of the principal people of the island, but the man was hanged. Now, listen! Some of the European newspapers, containing a letter I wrote to the Guernsey people, with the object of preventing this death, reached America in time to be republished usefully by the American journals. A man at Quebec, named Julien, was about to be hanged; the people of Canada considered with reason that the letter, which I had written to the people of Guernsey, was equally addressed to themselves, and, by a happy chance, this letter was the means of saving, not, indeed, Tapner, for whom it was written, but Julien, whom it had nothing to do with. I quote these facts, and why? Because they show the use of perseverance. Alas! the axe is persevering also.

"The statistics of the guillotine and the gibbet preserve a hideous parallelism, and the number of legal deaths has not fallen off in any country. During the last ten years the sense of moral duties having become weakened, the penalty of death has even come into favour again, and there is a move in the opposite direction. You, a small

community, even in your town of Geneva, have witnessed
the erection of two guillotines in eighteen months.   In
fact, as you have killed Vary, why not kill Eley?   In
Spain they garotte; in Russia they kill by the rod; at
Rome, as the Church loathes the sight of blood, the convict is knocked on the head—*ammazzato*; in England,
where a woman reigns, a woman has just been hanged.

"This does not prevent the old penal code from loudly
exclaiming and protesting that it is calumniated, and pre-
tending to be innocent.   People make it a subject of
common conversation.   Oh, it is awful!   It had always
been gentle and merciful.   The laws are apparently severe,
but they are rarely carried into execution.   What! the
law send Jean Valjean to the hulks because he stole a
loaf?   That is too bad!   It is true enough that in 1816,
it sentenced hungry rioters of the department of the
Seine to hard labour for life; it is true that, in 1846 . . .
Alas! those who deny that Jean Valjean was sent to the
galleys, forget the guillotine of Buzançais.

" Hunger has always been looked upon suspiciously by
the law.

"I spoke just now of the torture being abolished.
Well, in 1849, torture still existed.   Where?   In China?
No, in Switzerland.   In your country, sir, in October,
1849, at Zug, a judge of instruction, who wished that
the robbery of a cheese (an eatable: hunger again!)
should be confessed by a girl called Matilda Wildenberg,
squeezed her thumbs in a vice, and by aid of a pulley,
hoisted the unfortunate creature up to the ceiling by a
cord attached to this vice.   When thus suspended by her

thumbs, she was flogged by the executioner's assistant. In 1862, in Guernsey, where I live, the penalty of the lash is in full force. Last summer a man of fifty years of age was scourged, by order of the Court. This man's name was Torode, and he also had become a thief through starvation.

"No, do not let us weary. Let us move heaven and earth that the laws may become more merciful. Let us diminish the penalty and increase the instruction. From the step already taken, let us judge of those it will be advisable to take. How much good the admission of attenuating circumstances is capable of doing! It would have prevented that which I am about to relate.

"At Paris, in 1818 or 1819, on a summer's day, towards twelve o'clock at noon, I was passing by the square of the Palais de Justice. A crowd was assembled there around a post. I drew near. To this post was tied a young female, with a collar round her neck and a writing over her head. A chafing-dish, full of burning coals, was on the ground in front of her; an iron instrument, with a wooden handle, was placed in the live embers, and was being heated there. The crowd looked perfectly satisfied. This woman was guilty of what the law calls *domestic theft*. As the clock struck noon, behind that woman, and without being seen by her, a man stepped up to the post. I had noticed that the jacket worn by this woman had an opening behind, kept together by strings; the man quickly untied these, drew aside the jacket, exposed the woman's back as far as her waist, seized the iron which was in the chafing-dish, and applied it, leaning heavily on the bare shoulder. Both the iron and the wrist of the executioner disappeared in a thick white smoke. This is now more than forty years ago, but there still rings in my ears the horrible shriek of this wretched creature. To me, she had been a thief, but was now a martyr. I was then sixteen years of age, and I left the place determined to combat to the last days of my life these cruel deeds of the law.

" Of all bad actions, the penalty of death is the worst. And what has one not seen, even in our own century, proceeding from the ordinary tribunals, and common crimes ? On the 20th April, 1849, a servant, Sarah Thomas, a girl of seventeen years of age, was executed at Bristol, for having in a moment of passion killed her mistress, who had beaten her with a log of wood. The poor convict refused to be executed ; seven men had to drag her to the scaffold, and she was hanged, resisting to the last. At the moment when they adjusted the noose round her neck she was asked if she had anything to say to her father. She interrupted the very death-rattle to say, ' *Yes, yes, tell him that I love him !*' At the commencement of the century, in the reign of George the the Third, in London, three ragged children were condemned to death for theft. The eldest of them—the ' Newgate Calendar ' proves the fact—was not fourteen years of age. The three children were hanged.

" What ideas, then, do men entertain of murder ? Is it that when I wear an ordinary coat, I may not kill ; but when I put on a robe, I may ? Like Richelieu's cassock, the toga covers all. Public vengeance ! ah, I pray you, do not revenge me; it is murder—it is murder I tell you. Except in the case of legitimate self-defence, taken in its strictest sense (for if you have once wounded your adversary, and he has fallen, you are in duty bound to assist him), can homicide ever be permitted ? can that which is forbidden to the individual, be allowed to a member of individuals ? The executioner is a sinister kind of assassin ; the official assassin, the licensed assassin ; kept, hired, required on certain days, working publicly, killing in the full light of day, having for machines ' the weapons of justice;' the recognized State assassin, the official assassin, the assassin who has a recognized legal position, the assassin in the name of society; he has my warrant and yours, too, to kill. He either strangles or cuts the throat, and then taps, in a friendly way, on the shoulder of society, and says, I have done your work, pay me. He is the assassin *cum privilegio legis*, the assassin whose assassination is decreed by the legislator, deliberated on by the jury, ordered by the judge, consented to by the priest, guarded by the soldier, contemplated by the populace. He is the assassin, who sometimes has the assassinated person on his side, for I myself have discussed the subject with a convict named Marquis, who was in theory a partisan of the penalty of death. So also, two years before a celebrated lawsuit, I had discussed the subject with a magistrate named Teste, who was a partisan of ignominious punishment. Let civilization consider the matter : it is answerable for the executioner. Ah ! you so detest assassination, that you would kill the assassin ; I so detest murder, that I would prevent you from becoming a murderer. All against one, social power condensed into the guillotine, collective strength employed in causing death. What can there be more odious! One man killed by another man is shocking to the idea, but one man killed by society is to create a wholesome feeling of dread. What has become of your consciences, and what are your views as to good and evil? He is a criminal, say you. What are you?

"Must I repeat it, again and again? This man, in order to know himself thoroughly, and amend his life, and also in order to extricate himself from the overwhelming responsibility which weighs down his soul, needs every moment of that life which remains to him. You give him but a few minutes; and why? How dare you take on yourselves this formidable abbreviation of the varied phenomena of repentance? Do you know what an account you will have to give of this responsible being condemned to all eternity through your agency, who falls back upon you, and becomes your responsibility? You do more than kill a man, you destroy a conscience.

"By what right do you constitute God a Judge before the time He has allotted? What right have you to shorten that time? Is it that His justice is only a step beyond yours? Is there an inclined plane from your bar to His? Is it that after M. Troplong comes God? You must accept one or other alternative: either you are a believer or you are not. If you are a believer, how can you venture to launch an immortal creature into eternity? If you are not, how dare you condemn a fellow-creature to nonentity?

"A criminal lawyer exists who has made this distinc-

tion :—'It is wrong to say *execution ;* one ought rather
to say *expiation.* Society does not kill; it curtails.' We
are not lawyers; we do not understand such niceties as
these.

"People talk of justice. Justice! Oh, that idea, the
personification of everything that is august and venerable; that perfect balance, that uprightness, which belongs to the depths of our nature; that mysterious
scruple derived from the ideal; that sovereign rectitude,
combined with a tremulous sense of the vastness of
infinity, which opens before us; that chaste modesty of
inaccessible impartiality; that weighing, in which things
enter that are imponderable; that respect, paid to every
minutest matter; that perfection of wisdom, combined
with pity; that examination of human affairs with the eye
of God; that severe goodness, the luminous resultant of
the universal conscience; that abstraction of the absolute,
making itself a reality of the earth; that vision of right;
that spark of eternity, made manifest to man! Justice
indeed! That sacred intuition of truth, which determines,
by its presence only, the relative quantities of good and
evil, and which, when it enlightens man, converts him for
the moment into a god; that finite thing, whose law it is
to possess a relation to infinity; that celestial entity, of
which Paganism made a divinity, and Christianity an
archangel; that gigantic figure whose feet rest on the
human heart, and whose wings are among the stars; that
Jungfrau of human virtues; that summit of the soul;
that virgin—O God, eternal God, is it possible to
imagine this Justice, standing supported by the guil-

lotine ? Can one imagine this being, buckling the straps
on the legs of the victim, or untying, with its fingers of
light, the cord that keeps up the axe ?   Can we imagine
it rendering sacred, and at the same time degrading, its
terrible valet, the executioner ?   Can one imagine it
spread out and fastened in the infamous framework of
the pillory ? Can one imagine it packed up in the
travelling-bag of Calcraft, with various articles of dress,
with the cord used for one victim yesterday, and that
destined to send another victim to eternity to-morrow ?

" So long as the penalty of death exists, one should
shudder on entering a court of assize, and the darkness
of night will prevail there.

" Last January, in Belgium, when the Charleroi affair
was under discussion (a discussion, indeed, which seemed
to prove, by the evidence of a person called Rabet, that
Goethals and Coecke, the two persons who had been guillotined in the preceding year, were possibly innocent :
fearful possibility !) ; during this discussion, and in the
face of so many crimes, proceeding from the brutalities of
ignorance, an advocate thought to show the necessity of
gratuitous and obligatory instruction. The Procureur-
Général interrupted him, and rallied him on the subject.
'Advocate,' said he ; 'this is not the Legislative Assembly.' 'No, Mr. Procureur-Général ; this is the grave.'

" The penalty of death has two kinds of partisans,
those who explain it, and those who apply it ; in other
words, those who devote themselves to the theory and
those who attend to the practice. Now, the practice and
the theory do not agree, and argue strangely together.
In order to abolish the penalty of death, it is only

necessary to open the question between theory and practice. For example: both insist on the penalty being carried into execution. Why do they do so? Is it for the sake of example? Theory says yes; Practice says no. For she conceals the scaffold as well as she can; she destroys Montfaucon; suppresses the public crier; avoids market-days; she erects her machinery at dead of night; and, finally, she sacrifices her victim at early dawn. In certain countries, in America and Prussia, they hang and decapitate privately.

"And, again, is it because the penalty is just? 'Yes,' says Theory; 'the man was guilty, he is punished.' 'No,' says Practice; 'The man must be punished—that is quite right. He is punished therefore—he is dead. But what of that woman? She is his widow. And what of her children? They are orphans. Death has left them behind; but the widow and orphans are punished, though innocent. Where, then, is the justice to be found?'

"But if the penalty of death cannot be called just, is it of any use? 'Yes,' says Theory. 'The carcase will do us no more harm.' 'No,' says Practice, 'for this carcase bequeathes to you a family, a fatherless family, a family wanting bread; and in consequence of this, in order to gain her livelihood, the widow becomes a prostitute and the orphans learn to steal in order to get food to eat.'

"Dumolard, a thief from the age of five years, was the orphan child of a man who had been guillotined; and some months ago I was abused for having ventured to say that this was an 'attenuating circumstance.' You see plainly,

however, that the penalty of death is neither good for
example, nor is it just, nor is it useful. What is it, then?
It exists, *sum qui sum*. Its reason lies in itself. But why
so? The guillotine on account of the guillotine, that is,
art on account of art.

" Let us recapitulate.

" All the great questions of the day, without a single
exception, bear upon this subject of the penalty of death.
The social question, the moral question, the philosophic
question, the religious question, are all alike in this respect. This last, however, more especially because it is
in itself quite unfathomable, requires to be taken into
consideration.

" You, then, who insist on death, have you deeply reflected on it? Have you pondered on this abrupt change
from a human life into eternity, an unlooked-for and sudden fall from a height into an abyss happening unexpectedly and as a surprise to mystery? You station a priest
there, but he trembles as much as the victim. He, too, is
ignorant on the subject. You veil the blackness of the
deed in obscurity.

" Have you, then, never hovered over the unknown? If
not, how can you venture to launch into it any human
being whatsoever? As soon as a scaffold is seen on the
pavement of our towns, in the very gloom which surrounds
so terrible an object a shudder is experienced, which pervades every one in the Place de Grève, and never stops
till it has reached heaven. Night wonders at this encroachment. A capital execution consists in the hand of
society holding a man over the abyss and letting him
drop into it. The man falls. The thinker to whom cer-

tain phenomena of the unknown world are perceptible, feels a tremor in the darkness. O men, what have you done? Who can understand the shudderings of the world of shadows? Whither flees that human soul? what know you of its future?

"There is near Paris a hideous field, Clamart. It is the place of accursed graves, it is the rendezvous of those who have been executed—there is not a skeleton there with its head on—and human society sleeps tranquilly by the side of all this. That there are upon the earth receptacles of those dead who have been killed by the hand of God need not surprise us, for God knows the reason of His works. But can one think without horror of this—a receptacle of those dead who have been put to death by man himself?

"No, let us never tire of repeating this:—No more scaffolds : let legal death be henceforth at an end !

"It is by a certain mysterious respect for life that one recognizes a thinking man.

"I know what will be said: the philosophers are dreamers. What would they have? Truly, they desire to abolish the penalty of death—they call the punishment of death a mourning for humanity. A mourning ! Let them go, then, for a while, and watch the crowd laughing round the scaffold—let them enter a little into the reality of the case. When they talk of mourning, we are obliged to laugh. These good people are in the clouds. They cry out about savageness and barbarity because one hangs a man, or cuts off a head or two now and then. See these dreamers ! No punishment of death ! What are they thinking of? One cannot imagine anything more extravagant. What! no more scaffold, and, at the same time, perhaps, no more war—no more killing anybody. I ask you for a moment—is that common sense? Who will deliver us from these philosophers? When will they have done with systems, theories, impossibilities, and follies? Follies, indeed! and in whose name, I should like to know?—in the name of progress—an empty word? In the name of the ideal—a mere sound? No more executioners! Where shall we be? A society without death in its code. What a chimera! Life, what a Utopia! Who are all these reformers? They are poets! Preserve us from poets! What the human race wants is not Homer—it is M. Fulchiron.

"It would be a fine thing to see a society started, and a civilization carried on by Æschylus, Sophocles, Isaiah, Job, Pythagoras, Pindar, Plautus, Lucretius, Virgil, Juvenal, Dante, Cervantes, Shakespeare, Milton, Corneille, Moliere, and Voltaire. It would make one's sides split with laughter. Serious men would burst. All the gravest men would shrug their shoulders, John Bull as well as Prudhomme. And besides, it would be a chaos; ask among all classes—among the stockbrokers as well as the lawyers.

"However that may be, sir, you will have to discuss once more this vast question of legal murder. Courage —don't let it go—let people talk, and they will be surprised at the result.

"'There is no such thing as a small people.' I made this remark a few months ago to Belgium, in reference to the convicts of Charleroi—let me repeat it to Switzer-

land to-day.The greatness of a people is not more affected
by the number of the inhabitants than the greatness of
an individual man is measured by his tallness.   The only
measure is the amount of intelligence and the amount of
virtue.   Whoever presents a great example is great.
Small nations will become a great people when—existing
by the side of countries thickly peopled, and of vast ter-
ritorial extent, who shut themselves up in fanaticism and
prejudice, in hatred and war, and slavery and death—
they gently, but firmly, exhibit brotherhood, hating the
sword, demolishing the scaffold, glorifying progress, and
smiling serene as the heavens.   Words are vain if ideas
do not correspond.   It is not enough to be a republic—
liberty is also necessary.   It is not enough to be a democracy—humanity is also necessary.   A people should be
as a man ; and to be a man, there must be a soul.   At
the moment when Europe recedes it would be a grand
thing that Geneva should advance.   Let Switzerland, and
your noble little Republic especially, consider how admirable would be your position—a republic existing in the
face of monarchies, able to do without the penalty of
death.   It would be a noble thing to revive thus under
a new form the old instructive antagonism of Geneva to
Rome, and offer to the regard and meditation of the whole
civilized world, on the one side, Rome, with its popedom,
which condemns to temporal death and eternal dam-
nation, and on the other side Geneva, with its evangelism,
which pardons.

"O people of Geneva, your city is situated on a lake in
the Garden of Eden ; you live in a blessed place ; all that

is most noble in creation surrounds you; the habitual contemplation of the beautiful reveals the truth, and imposes duties on you. Your civilization ought to be in harmony with nature. Take counsel of all these merciful marvels. Believe in your sky so bright; and as goodness descends from the sky, abolish the scaffold. Be not ungrateful. Let it not be said that, in gratitude, and, as it were, in exchange, for this admirable corner of the earth, where God has shown to man the sacred splendour of the Alps, the Arve, and the Rhone, the blue lake, and Mont Blanc in the glory of sunlight, man has offered to the Deity the spectacle of the guillotine!" . . .

When this letter arrived the work of the constituent committee was completed, and they had decided to retain the punishment of death. But M. Victor Hugo did not give up the question; and not having been able to address the committee, he addressed the people. He wrote again to M. Bost :—

"Hauteville House, Nov. 29, 1862.

"Sir,—The letter which I had the honour to forward you on the 17th Nov., reached you, I think, on the 19th or 20th. The very day after I had dictated this letter, the affair of Gardin came before the Court of Assize and the Somme. This affair has not only brought to light certain frightful consequences of the penalty of death, but has also rendered evident the urgency of an important revision of the penal code. Monstrous facts have a way of their own in demonstrating the necessity of reforms.

"To-day—the 20th Nov.—I read in *La Presse* these lines from Berne:—

"'You have reproduced the letter addressed by Victor Hugo to M. Bost, of Geneva, on the subject of capital punishment. The publication of this letter is rather late, as a fortnight has elapsed since the Genevese constituency terminated its labours. The constitution it has elaborated does not satisfy the wishes of the poet, since it does not abolish the penalty of death, except in the case of political crimes.'

"No, it is not too late.

"In writing, I addressed myself less to the constituent committee, which prepares, than to the people, who decide.

"In a few days (on the 7th Dec.) the project of the constitution will be submitted to the people. There is, therefore, still time.

"A constitution which, in the nineteenth century, assigns the punishment of death for any crime or offence whatever, is not worthy of a republic. A republic is essentially civilization ; and the people of Geneva, in re-jecting—as it is its right and its duty to do—the project which is about to be submitted to it, will perform an act which is doubly grand, as having at the same time the imprint of sovereignty and of justice.

"You may perhaps think it well to publish this letter.

"I offer, sir, &c."

The people rejected the project of a constitution.

Some days afterwards M. Victor Hugo received this letter :—

" Geneva, December 11, 1862.

" We have triumphed : the constitution of the Conservatives is rejected. Your letter has produced an immense effect—all the journals have published it : the Catholics have objected to it. M. Bost has printed a thousand separate copies, and the Radical Committee 4000 copies. The Radicals, M. James Fazy at their head, have made of your letter a weapon of war, and the Independents have also pronounced in your favour for the abolition. Your preponderance has been complete. Some Radicals were not very decided before. It was a Radical, M. Heroi, who has the credit of having used his influence against Vary and D'Elcy, who were executed, and the Grand Council, which refused the pardons in both cases, is altogether Radical.

" But, on the whole, the Radicals are people of progress, and now that they are once engaged in opposition to the penalty of death they will not recede. Here the abolition of the scaffold is considered certain, and the credit of this matter is due to you. I hope we may arrive at that other great step in progress, the separation of Church and State.

" I am but a very obscure individual, sir, but I am happy. I felicitate you, and I felicitate my fellow-countrymen. The immense effect of your letter does us credit. The country of M. de Sellon cannot be insensible to the voice of Victor Hugo.

" Excuse this letter written in haste, and believe me to be, &c.

"A. GAYET (DE BONNEVILLE)."

LIII.

A READING.

M. Victor Hugo had two subjects for a drama fresh in his mind ; he hesitated whether he should first undertake *Marion de Lorme* or *Hernani :* he decided on *Marion de Lorme*, and began to write it on the 1st June. On the 20th June, at break of day, he commenced the fourth act, worked at it with great zest, spent his night at it, and wrote the last verse at sunrise the next morning. The whole act, therefore, had been written between sunrise and sunrise. On the 24th June the play was finished.

The friends to whom M. Victor Hugo read, by degrees, all that he had written, advised him to have a more public reading of it. He had already rather enlarged his circle of hearers in the case of *Cromwell*, but he hesitated at the idea of increasing it still more. When, however, it was rumoured that he would perhaps give a reading, he was inundated with solicitations and entreaties which he did not feel at liberty to refuse.

He read, then, one evening in July, *Marion de Lorme*, originally called *Un Duel sous Richelieu*, before a nu-

merous assembly, in which were particularly to be noticed,
M. de Balzac, Eugène Delacroix, Alfred de Musset,
Alexandre Dumas, and Alfred de Vigny. There were
also M. Sainte-Beuve, M. Villemain, M. Mériméc, M.
Armaud, and M. Edouard Bertin, M. Louis Boulanger,
M. Frederic Soulié, M. Taylor, M. Soumet, the Deschamps, the Deverias, M. Charles Magnin, Madame
Tastu, &c. The success was decided. It was rather a
subject of astonishment to the audience that M. Victor
Hugo had been able to write a drama fit for acting. The
excessive development of *Cromwell* had given rise to fears
that he would be unable to reduce his ideas within the
limits of a play short enough for representation ; *Marion
de Lorme* allayed these fears, and placed him at once and
decidedly amongst dramatic authors.

Congratulations at an end, the auditors dispersed. M.
de Merimée, who had lingered to the last, objected to
the dénouément. Didier, in the original play, died without forgiving Marion. It appeared to him that this cruel
death would leave too painful an impression on the
audience ; Didier would have attracted more sympathy if,
at the last moment, his sternness had become softened.

The next day, at nine o'clock in the morning, M.
Taylor called in the Rue Nôtre-Dame des Champs.

" I could not speak to you yesterday in such a crowd,"
said he to M. Victor Hugo, " but I suppose it is quite
understood that you will let me have *Marion de Lorme*
for the Theâtre Français. I am the very first person
who ever asked you for a play, therefore to me your first

play belongs. Besides, Mademoiselle Mars alone could act Marion de Lorme. Is it understood?"

"Yes," replied M. Victor Hugo.

That same evening M. Victor Hugo received a letter from M. Jouslin de Lasalle, manager of the Theatre of the Porte Saint-Martin, offering his theatre. M. Frederick Lemaître was to be Didier, Madame Dorval was to be Marion, and M. Gobert, M. Lockroy, M. Provost, and M. Jemma, &c., were to take the other parts.

The next morning the servant ushered into the author's private room a gentleman, in a black coat and white trousers, wearing an order, whose pale countenance contrasted with a pair of large clever-looking eyes and enormous whiskers. This gentleman's name was Harel, and he was the manager of the Odéon.

"Sir," said he, "people are everywhere speaking of a drama which you read the evening before last. I come early in the morning in order to be the first person to request it of you."

"You are the third," said M. Victor Hugo.

When he heard that the drama was promised to the Théâtre Français, the manager of the Odéon persisted in his request. The Théâtre Français was not the right place for an unconventional and new style of performance. The people who frequented it were old, accustomed to routine, and averse to novelty; the audience at the Odéon consisted of the rising generation: the generous and intelligent hands of the students went there to fight for a literary revolution. It was necessary for M. Victor

Hugo and for theatrical liberty that he should come off victorious in his first battle with the old system. At the Odéon the part of *Marion* should be acted by Mademoiselle Georges, &c.

M. Victor Hugo replied, that it was all very true, but that he had given a promise, and that he was to-morrow to read it to the committee.

"They require you to read it, then!" exclaimed M. Harel. "I, on the contrary, have no need to know what the play is about."

And seeing the manuscript on the table, he took a pen and wrote hastily on its outside,—

"Received at the Théâtre de l'Odeón on the 14th July, 1829.

"HAREL."

"Come," said he, "it is the anniversary of the taking of the Bastille. Well, I take my Bastille."

He placed the manuscript quite coolly under his arm, and was about to carry it off. M. Victor Hugo had some difficulty in making him give it back.

At the Théâtre Français the reading was as well received as at the Rue Nôtre-Dame des Champs.

"There is no need to put it to the vote," said M. Taylor. "M. Hugo does not offer his play, we request him to let us have it."

It was in the middle of summer, and nothing hurried the rehearsals. M. Taylor began by sending the manuscript to receive the legal permission from the censors. He rather dreaded the fourth act, and had

advised the author to weaken some passages in it, but
M. Victor Hugo had insisted that the act should remain
as it was. As the commissioner had feared, the report
of the censors tended towards prohibition.

The Minister of the Interior was M. de Martignac.
Being himself something of a literary man, he was considered to be a protector of literature, and it was he, it
was rumoured, who had insisted that, in spite of being
objected to by the censors, M. Casimir Delavigne's
Marino Faliero was to be acted. M. Victor Hugo called
on him.

M. de Martignac had two different expressions of
countenance. His face as a man was amiable and cour-
teous, but his ministerial expression was cold and
formal. He received M. Victor Hugo with his official
expression. M. de Martignac was, where theatrical
matters were concerned, in favour of the old divisions
of style, tragedy on one hand, and comedy or vaudeville on the other. In the present century he had
his own special Racine, M. Casimir Delavigne, and
his own Molière, M. Scribe, who had been his coadjutor.
In his eyes M. Victor Hugo was an innovator, who upset
all dramatic customs, and *Marion de Lorme* appeared to
him dangerous, both in his capacity as a literary critic
and a politician. He treated the author, therefore, with
all the arrogance of his ministerial position, and of his
vaudevilles. The censurers had spoken against his fourth
act; he had read the play, and considered they had
only spoken moderately of it. Not only was a king's
ancestor turned into ridicule, but even the king himself.

In Louis XIII., who was described as a hunter, and represented as governed by a priest, everybody would see an allusion to Charles X.

M. Victor Hugo exclaimed against this. He had made no allusions when describing Louis XIII.; it was Louis XIII. he had wished to describe, and no one else. He had given no one a right to accuse him of hypocrisy, and it was not in his nature to insult a living king, by his manner of speaking concerning one who was dead.

"I believe you," said the Minister. "I am convinced that it is not Charles X. whom you have introduced into your drama; but still it would be taken for granted that Charles X. was really intended. We are living in troublous times, the throne is attacked on all sides, the violence of parties is every day redoubled; this is no time to expose the royal personage to laughter and public insults. It is too well known since *Le Mariage de Figaro* how powerful a play may become. As it happens, the subject is about to be discussed this very day in council. But I warn you, that I shall give my vote against it, and that if it depends on me your play will not be acted."

M. Victor Hugo, chafed at the refusal, and, above all, at the Minister's stiffness of manner, immediately requested an audience of the King. The next day he received an answer from the Duke d'Aumont to the effect, that that very day the King would grant a private audience to the Baron Victor Hugo. He had never assumed his title, and this was the first time he was called by it.

He was to be at Saint-Cloud by twelve o'clock. The worst of it was, that he could not be admitted unless he wore the usual formal costume, and he did not own one. His brother Abel, who was present, offered to go and find one, and succeeded in doing so. At that moment they were bringing back from the theatre the fourth act royally copied on fine paper.

At twelve o'clock, M. Victor Hugo was introduced by the usher then on duty into a room, where from fifteen to twenty persons were waiting, all in full dress. There was also one lady. The gentlemen were standing, etiquette not allowing any but ladies to sit down in the palace, even if the King were not present. The lady who was seated, was Madame du Cayla, whom M. Victor Hugo had before seen at his brother's wedding. Whilst he was chatting with her an usher came, requesting her to wait a few minutes: the mass was about to end, and the King would be coming out of chapel.

Almost immediately afterwards the Duke d'Angoulème made his appearance, preceded and followed by the Body Guard, wearing the collar of the order of Saint-Esprit, and on his breast the crosses of the Legion of Honour and of Saint-Louis. He carried his hat under his arm, and his prayer-book in his hand. He walked heavily, in a mincing way, bowing low from right to left. He crossed the drawing-room without noticing any one.

A moment afterwards the same usher who had come to speak to Madame du Cayla came back and called her. She rose, walked unconcernedly through the ranks of assembled gentlemen, and entered the King's presence. M. Victor Hugo felt that before his turn came he would have some time to spare, and he went to a window to amuse himself by looking at the scenery. He had not stood there more than ten minutes when he heard himself called. This sudden reception astonished him ; he was naturally timid, and felt much more awkward than Madame du Cayla did at all the looks which were fastened on him, and he entered the presence of the King with a very red face.

The warm reception the King gave him soon set him at his ease. Charles X. told him that he knew him by reputation, and that he would be happy to do anything in his power to oblige him. M. Victor Hugo explained to him that which brought him there.

"Ah, yes, I know," said the King. "It was mentioned to me yesterday. It seems to me," said he, smiling, " that you rather ill-treat my old ancestor, Louis XIII. M. de Martignac says that there is a terrible act in your play."

" Perhaps your Majesty would not agree with your Minister, if you would take the trouble to enlighten yourself on the subject. I have brought the fourth act with me."

"Only the fourth act ?" said the King, graciously. " Certainly I shall read it. You ought to have brought me the entire play."

Between the King and the poet there then ensued a long conversation, which M. Victor Hugo has related in *Les Rayons et les Ombres*. On taking leave of the King, he solicited a prompt decision; the Comédie Française, in which the King took a lively interest, was suffering from every day of delay.

"Don't be afraid," said Charles X. "I shall make haste for the sake of the Comédie Française, as well as for yours. I admire your talent very much, M. Hugo; I only recognize two poets, you and Désangiers."

"I have every confidence in the King," said M. Victor Hugo, "but not so much in the Minister."

"Oh, if M. de Martignac causes you any anxiety . . ."

The King stopped short. The next day M. de Martignac was no longer Minister.

Some days afterwards, M. Victor Hugo was asked to call on the new Minister of the Interior, M. de la Bourdonnaye. The King had read the act, and was sorry not to be able to give his sanction to its representation. The Government was ready to do anything to make amends to the author. M. Victor Hugo thanked the Minister, but would accept nothing.

The next day, when he was chatting with M. Sainte-Beuve, a letter was brought him with the Minister of the Interior's seal affixed to it. M. de la Bourdonnaye announced to him in it that the King granted him a fresh pension of 4000 francs. The man who had brought the letter asked if there was any answer?

"Yes," said M. Victor Hugo.

He sat down and wrote a letter which he handed to M. Sainte-Beuve before sealing it.

"I was sure of it," said M. Sainte-Beuve.

In this letter he refused the pension.

M. Sainte-Beuve saw no reason for hushing up the matter. The journals were full of it. " M. Victor Hugo's conduct," said the *Journal des Débats,* " will cause no astonishment to any who know him, but it is right that the public should know how much the young poet is entitled to their esteem." The *Constitutionnel* wrote thus :—" Youth is less easily corrupted than the Ministers think."

LIV

HERNANI.

M. Victor Hugo was not one of those whom a trifle could easily discourage: he fully understood that the fact of *Marion de Lorme* being forbidden would help his approaching drama. Next week he was dining at M. Nodier's with Baron Taylor, who was just about to set off on a journey.

"When shall you be back again?" said M. Victor Hugo.

"At the end of the month."

"That gives us rather more than three weeks. Well, then, summon the committee for the 1st October, and I will read something or other."

On the 1st October he read *Hernani*.

The play was received with acclamations, and the parts immediately distributed. Mademoiselle Mars had Doña Sol; M. Firmin had Hernani; M. Joanny had Don Ruy Gomez; and M. Michelot had Don Carlos. Very minor parts were both accepted and even requested by actors of great merit, such as M. Regnier, Sampson, &c.; the few

verses repeated by Jaquez, the page, were allotted to
Mademoiselle Despréaux (who afterwards became Madame
Allan).

The first rehearsals went on very well: M. Michelot,
without caring much for new literature, was a man of the
world and of agreeable manners. M. Firmin had much
sympathy with the drama. M. Joanny, who had white
hair like Don Ruy Gomez, was an old soldier who had
lost two fingers whilst fighting under the orders of
General Hugo. He showed the author his mutilated
hand, and said to him with that peculiar emphasis which
was natural to him, "I shall glory in having served under
the father in my youth and the son in my old age."

The new style had been already tried at the Théâtre
Français, and had succeeded there. The *Henri III.* of
Alexandre Dumas had just been acted there. Till then
little known, and not having any part to excite opposition,
it had taken the classical school by surprise. Thus unexpectedly attacked, classics had not been able to resist.
The public, left to itself, and tired at heart of always
hearing the same kind of tragedy and the same kind of
comedy acted over and over again, each worse than the
last, had given itself up to the unlooked-for charm of
this sprightly, youthful drama, so touchingly interesting.
It had been a triumph without a struggle, a festival, a
joy, a public rejoicing.

Mademoiselle Mars was the first to check this excitement.

Mademoiselle Mars was then fifty years of age, and it
was only natural she should prefer the plays she had acted

in her youth, and others resembling them. She was quite opposed to the reconstruction of the drama. She had principally undertaken the part in order that it should not be performed by any one else. *Henri III.* had proved that a drama could succeed. *Hernani* had made a great impression during the reading, and she did not like the idea of giving up to a rival the possible applause and attention it might attract. But she rehearsed Doña Sol in a sulky manner, and with the distant and surprised manner of a person who had lowered herself in passing from *La Fille d'Honneur* and *Valérie* to *Hernani*. Thirty-five years of success had given her such an importance in the theatre that she was all-powerful, and she made authors feel her importance. I copy from the lively Memoirs of Alexandre Dumas an episode from the rehearsal of *Hernani*.

"Things were conducted somewhat in this way:—In the midst of the rehearsal, Mademoiselle Mars would suddenly stop short.

" 'Excuse me, my dear friends,' she would say to Firmin, to Michelet, and to Joanny, ' I must speak a word to the author.'

" The author to whom she spoke made a sign of assent, but remained in his place and did not speak.

" Mademoiselle Mars would advance towards the hand-rail, shade her eyes with her hands, and although she perfectly well knew at what part of the orchestra the author was to be found, she seemed to search for him.

" This was a little by-play of hers.

" 'M. Hugo,' she would ask, ' is M. Hugo there?'

" 'I am here, madame,' replied M. Hugo, rising.

" 'Ah! very well! Thank you. . . . Tell me, M. Hugo. . . .'

" 'Madame!'

" 'I have to repeat this line,—

" 'Vous êtes mon lion superbe et généreux!'

" 'Yes, madame. Hernani says to you,—

" 'Hélas! j'aime pourtant d'une amour bien profonde!—
Ne pleure pas, mourons plutôt!—Que n'ai-je un monde!
Je te le donnerais! Je suis bien malheureux!'

" 'And you reply—

" 'Vous êtes mon lion superbe et généreux!'

" 'Do you really like that, M. Hugo?'

" 'What?'

" '*Vous êtes mon lion.*'

" 'I have written it so, madame, and therefore I thought it to be correct.'

" 'So you stick to your *lion*?'

" 'I neither stick to it nor the contrary, madame. Find me something better, and I will alter it.'

" 'It is not for me to do that. I am not the author.'

" 'Well, madame, since that is the case, let us leave it as it is.'

" 'Really, it seems to me so droll to call M. Firmin my *lion*!'

" Yes, that is because, in acting the part of Doña Sol,

you desire to remain Mademoiselle Mars. If you were really the pupil of Don Ruy Gomez de Sylva, that is, a noble Castilian of the sixteenth century, you would not see M. Firmin in Hernani, but one of those terrible chiefs of bandits who made Charles the Fifth tremble in his capital. . You would then understand that such a woman might call such a man *"mon lion,"* and the phrase would seem to you less droll.'

" ' Well, since you stick to your *lion,* we'll say no more about it. I am here to speak what is written : in the manuscript I find *"mon lion."* I shall of course say *" mon lion."* Dear, dear, it's exactly the same thing to me ! Come, Firmin.

     " ' Vous êtes mon lion superbe et généreux ! '

" But next day, when they reached the same place in the rehearsal, Mademoiselle Mars stopped. As before, she put her hand before her eyes. As before she pretended to look for the author.

" ' M. Hugo," said she, in her dry voice—her own voice, and not that of Célimène — ' is M. Hugo there ? '

" ' I am here, madame,' replied Hugo, with his invariable placidity.

" ' Ah ! so much the better. I'm glad you are there.'

" ' Madame, I had the honour of paying you my respects before the rehearsal commenced.'

" ' True. Well, have you thought better of it ? '

" ' Of what, madame ? '

" ' Of what I told you yesterday.'

" ' Yesterday, you did me the honour to tell me a great many things.'

" ' Yes, you are right . . . But I wish to speak of this famous line.'

" ' Which line ? '

" ' Good gracious, you very well know which.'

" ' I assure you, madame, I have not an idea : you make so many good and wise observations, that I mix them up one with the other.'

" ' I speak of the line about *the lion* . . .'

" ' Ah, yes, " *Vous êtes mon lion !* " I remember.'

" ' Well, have you found another line ? '

" ' I frankly own I have not looked for one.'

" ' Don't you think that a dangerous line ? '

" ' I don't know what you understand by dangerous, madame.'

" ' I mean likely to be hissed.'

" ' I never presumed that I should not be hissed.'

" ' Yes, that's all very well, but the less the better.'

" ' Then you think the line about the *lion* will be hissed ? '

" ' I am sure of it.'

" ' Then, madame, the reason will be that you will not repeat it with your usual talent.'

" ' I shall say it as well as I can ; nevertheless, I should prefer . . .'

" ' What ? '

" ' Saying something else.'

" ' What ? '

"'Saying something else, I tell you.'

"'What?'

"'Saying . . .' and Mademoiselle Mars appeared to be thinking what word she should substitute, when for three days she had had it on the tip of her tongue, 'saying, for instance, heu . . . heu . . . heu . . .

"'Vous êtes, monseigneur, superbe et généreux!'

"'Is not *monseigneur* as good as *mon lion?*'

"'Yes, madame, only *mon lion* raises the style of verse, and *monseigneur* lowers it. I had rather be hissed for a good verse, than applauded for a bad one.'

"'Very well, very well, don't let us get into a passion! . . . Your *good verse* shall remain unaltered! Come, Firmin, my friend, let us go on! . . .

"'Vous êtes mon lion superbe et généreux!'"

However indifferent M. Victor Hugo might be to these little impertinencies, a time came when he would bear them no longer. Towards the close of one of the rehearsals, he told Mademoiselle Mars that he wished to speak to her. They adjourned to the little greenroom.

"Madame," said M. Victor Hugo, "I beg you will give me back your part."

Mademoiselle Mars turned pale. For the first time in her life she was asked to give up a part. Until then she had always been entreated to undertake them, and was in the habit of refusing. She felt the loss of prestige that might result from such an act. She owned herself in the wrong, and promised not to do so again.

She certainly never was impertinent again, but she was dumb. She protested against it by an icy demeanour.

Her example chilled the others. Except M. Joanny, who kept up his sympathies with the play—at least, apparently so—the author found himself daily more and more isolated. Besides all this, an opposition was raging outside the theatre, which reacted on the interior.

The tragic and comic actors put up very indifferently with this new-comer, who threatened their doctrines and their interests. They combined beforehand against this annihilator of a style of literature which must be good because it was their own. They would listen at the doors, and excite indiscretions; they picked up here and there several verses which they disfigured, related scenes and caricatured them, invented others at pleasure, and caused much laughter in private drawing-rooms at this would-be *chef-d'œuvre*. An author of the Théâtre Français was discovered hidden in the dark during a rehearsal. Others would come to M. Victor Hugo's house, represent themselves as great admirers, and almost dragging them from him, would become possessed of one or two scenes, and these they would hawk about in a mutilated form.

A certain tragedian, an academician and one of the censors, was one of the most active of these; and one of his hearers, indignant at such conduct, sent a notice of the fact to the journals. The censor wrote thus to M. Victor Hugo:—

" . . . . What say your spies (he called the others spies), and the journals who support you? That I have revealed the secret of the drama, that I have quoted your verses, in order to caricature them? Well, then, even if it were so, in what am I to blame? If I praised you when you deserved praise, may I not blame you when you

deserve blame? Are your works sacred? Must we
admire them in silence? You cannot think so, you cannot have such ridiculous self-love. You know that he
who has so frankly applauded your first odes, is at liberty
to condemn with the same frankness your new dramas.
I have blamed, it is true, the style of *Hernani*. . . ."

The majority of the journals found fault with the play.
The ministerial journals looked on M. Victor Hugo as a
deserter, ever since his " Ode à la Colonne," and could not
forgive his having refused the pension. The liberal political journals had as their literary editors the very authors
whom the drama had just thrown out of fashion. The
Constitutionnel, especially, which, some weeks before, had
praised the incorruptibility of the man, was now the most
violent adversary of the poet.

One of the theatres went so far as to parody the play
before it was acted. When reviewing the plays of the
year, the Théâtre des Vaudevilles exhibited the picture
scene to the laughter of the public. Don Ruy Gomez
was represented as a bear-leader.

There was another source of anxiety. The manuscript
forwarded to the censors had not yet been returned. M.
Victor Hugo applied, and was told that the commission
had read the play, and had authorized its performance a
fortnight before, and that the Minister was keeping it
back. M. de la Bourdonnaye sent back the play to the
theatre, "pointing out a few alterations which had been
deemed necessary." These changes altered the principal
scenes; the author resisted; they did not wish to re-enact
the case of *Marion de Lorme*, and they allowed him to

keep the text as it was, but he had to fight for the passages one by one. I find one letter where three words are permitted :—

"Sir,—I am happy to be able to inform you, that His Excellency, taking into consideration your remarks, which I hastened to put before him, has consented to replace certain passages which had been suppressed in *Hernani*. You are, therefore, at liberty to allow the following expressions addressed to Don Carlos, to remain in the authorized manuscript,

'*Lâche, insensé, mauvais roi!*'

"I remain, sir, &c.,

"Trouvé,

"Master of Requests,

"Chief of the Bureau des Théâtres."

But the Minister would not give his consent to this verse :—

"Crois tu, donc, que les rois à moi me sont sacrés?"

Hernani was obliged to say :—

"Crois tu, donc, que pour nous il soit des noms sacrés?"

The winter of 1829 and 1830 was one of the most severe on record. The Seine was frozen from the 20th December to the end of February. M. Victor Hugo would go to the theatre wearing list shoes, in order to avoid breaking his legs, as he was crossing the bridges. A foot-warmer was brought him. The actors shivered, their verses froze upon their lips, and they made haste to jabber over their parts, in order to go and warm themselves at the stove. All this did not help on the work, and all the ill feelings and ill wishes had time to become organized.

At length the play was fit for acting. It would be cruelly attacked, and would require to be warmly defended. The *claqueurs* belonging to the theatre had too long applauded M. Casimir Delavigne not to admire him, and would be a formidable opponent of the insurrection against the system that had made his fortune. The Commissaire Royal proposed that they should avail themselves of the *claqueurs* of the Gymnase, who were under personal obligations to him, and of whom he thought he could make sure. It is true that these persons were in the habit of applauding M. Scribe.

" Select some one," said the Commissioner.

" I shall make no selection."

" What! There will be no systematic applause ?"

" There will be no systematic applause."

When this news reached the theatre, everybody asked M. Victor Hugo if he was mad. No play could succeed without a *claqueur*. His play was more threatened than most others, and if not warmly supported, it would not be allowed to be acted out. He replied that, in the first place, paid applause was repugnant to his feelings; that besides this, the defenders of the old style would have but little to say in favour of the opposite system; that neither M. Delavigne's nor M. Scribe's *claqueurs* were his; that to a new style a new audience was necessary; that his audience ought to bear some kind of resemblance to his drama; that as he desired freedom for art, there ought also to be a free pit; that he would invite young men, poets, painters, sculptors, musicians, printers, &c. He was unanimously declared to be in the wrong, and they did what they could to change his resolution; but he insisted on it, and they gave up to him, leaving the responsibility of the representation to him.

Curiosity was excited, and the demand for places was enormous. The author was constantly receiving letters in this style :—

"I am about to proffer a request, sir, which will perhaps appear indiscreet, and which I fear still more may perhaps be too late. Madame B. Constant and I partake of the anxious desire, common to all France, to see *Hernani*. Is there any possibility of obtaining a box, or, at least, two seats in a box? Or if this be quite out of the question, could we possibly be present at a rehearsal? Should it be possible for us to obtain the box, or the two seats, be so kind as to inform me how I can secure them, and forward the price; and should it not be possible, what I must do in order to be admitted to the rehearsal. I hope you will only see in my importunity the very natural result of the anxiety we, as well as the public in general, experience.

"Believe how much I value your remarkable talent, also in my sincere attachment, and in my cordial esteem.

"Benjamin Constant."

———

"January 12th, 1830.

' "A mistake, the particulars of which I need not

trouble you about, prevents my obtaining certain seats on which I had reckoned in the box M. Fitz-James obtained from you. Would it be possible for you to retrieve a misfortune which to me would be real, namely, that of not being one of the first to admire and applaud *Hernani?* If I cannot secure a whole box, I should require three places, or at least three seats together. At any rate, sir, I will do everything in my power to be present at your triumph.

" Accept the sincere expression of my esteem and admiration.

" LIZINKA DE MIRBEL."

———

" SIR,—I have vainly tried to secure a box for the first representation of *Hernani.* I have been informed, sir, that you would be so kind as to obtain one for me. I should be very grateful if you would do so, and thank you for your kindness beforehand. I should like, if possible, that it should contain six places, and as near the ground-floor as possible.

Accept, &c.,

" A. THIERS.

" 13th February, 1830."

———

"The whole world comes to me for boxes and stalls. I can only speak to you of the requests made to me by the *intellectual notorieties,* as the *Globe* would say. Madame Recamier asks me, if through my interposition, &c. See what you can do. You know she has some influence in certain circles. I said that it was impossible to obtain a box. She then asked me if it was possible to obtain two *bonnets d'evêque*. Where does virtue hide itself?

" Ever yours,

" Mérimée."

During the week which preceded the performance, the journals had a great deal to say about the drama, and excited their readers to the highest pitch. Some were in favour of it, but most of them against it. The ministerial papers tried to tame down the great excitement. The *Quotidienne* wrote thus :—

"To-morrow, it is announced that the first performance of *Hernani* will take place. We do not know if those people who, before seeing and hearing, have declared themselves against the play, have made a league to cause its downfall; but certain it is, that the author's friends will do their best to ensure the success of the drama. It may easily be believed that they look on this affair as a question of life or death to the romantic school. Whatever the case may be, the *Journal des Débats*, impressed with the importance of the great question at issue, puts aside to-day its own cares, and abandoning for a moment the idea of self-defence, hastens to accept with resignation the reprimand of the *Globe*, in order to reserve to itself a place which it devotes to the cause of *Hernani*. 'Of that *Hernani*,' it observes, 'which is the cause of so much excitement, so much hatred, and so much ill-will, and which runs the chance of being chosen as the field of battle by so many opposite interests.' We, who are very far from wishing *Hernani* to be chosen as the field of battle, and who do not believe it the intention of the author that it should be, consider that its advocates are guilty of imprudence in striving to give to a mere literary subject a kind of political importance. The gentlemen of the *Débats* have managed to drag forward both M. de Martignac and M. de la Bourdannaye—both the late and the present Minister—who certainly have never thought either of prohibiting, attacking, or modifying M. Hugo's drama. Whatever importance *Hernani* may have for the literary republic, there is no occasion for the French Monarchy to feel any anxiety about it."

Every friend the author possessed, and every well-wisher to the new style of dramatic art, had come to offer their services. M. Louis Boulanger, M. Théophile Gautier, who was yet but a child, but who had already a man's talent, M. Gérard de Nerval, M. Vivier, M. Ernest de Saxe-Cobourg, illegitimate son of the reigning Duke, the Deverias, Auguste de Chatillon, Français, Célestin Nantueil, Edouard Thierny, Pétrus Borel, and his two brothers; Achille Roche, who would have become famous as a painter had he not been drowned in the Tiber; all these came forward at the very beginning. These beat the *rappel* in literature, in music, in the studios of artists, sculptors, and architects. They returned with lists of names that they had collected, and each entreated that he might bring his tribe to the combat. I have found again a list of the tribes of Gautier, Gérard, Pétrus Borel, &c. I read on the list the following names:—Balzac, Berlioz, Cabat, Augustus MacKeat, Préault, Jehan du Seigneur, Joseph Bouchardy, Philadelphe O'Neddy, Gigoux, Laviron, Amédée Pommier, Lemot, Piccini, Ferdinand Langlé, Tolbecque, Tilmant, Kreutzer, &c. These names are marked with collective appel ations; the architectural atelier of Gournaud, thirteen places; the architectural atelier of Labrousse, five; the architectural atelier of Duban, twelve, &c.

Victor Hugo bought several quires of red paper, and cut it into little squares, on which he printed with a stamp, the Spanish word *hierro* (iron), and these he distributed to the leaders of the tribes. The theatre gave up to him the orchestra of musicians, the second galleries, and the whole of the pit, with the exception of fifty seats.

In order to combine their strategical plans, and arrange an order of battle, the young men begged to be allowed to take possession of their seats in the theatre before the public were admitted. It was granted them on the condition, that they should enter before people began to form themselves into a line. They allowed them till three o'clock. It would have been better, had they allowed them to enter as the *claqueurs* did, by the little door in the dark passage, which is now suppressed. But the authorities who, it seems, did not wish to hide them, assigned to them the door in the Rue de Valois, which was the royal entrance. For fear of arriving too late, the young battalions arrived too soon, the door was not yet open; and from one o'clock, the innumerable passers-by in the Rue Richelieu, witnessed the accumulation of a band of wild and queer-looking beings, bearded, hairy, dresssed in every imaginable style, except in that of the rest of the world, with Spanish cloaks, waistcoats of the Robespierre cut, flat caps à la Henri III., displaying the tastes of every century, and of every country, both on their shoulders, and on their heads, in the very middle of Paris, in broad day. Quiet citizens paused, stupefied and indignant. M. Théophile Gautier made himself especially remarkable, wearing a waistcoat of scarlet satin, and having his long thick hair falling down his back.

The door not being opened, the tribes became trouble-some to the passers-by; this was a source of utter indif-ference to them, but they nearly lost all patience at the following occurrence. Classic art could not quietly allow of these hordes of barbarians, who were about to invade its asylum. Its followers picked up all the sweepings and other filth of the theatre, and threw them from the roofs on the besiegers. M. de Balzac received for his share the stump of a cabbage. The first impulse was to get angry. This was perhaps what classic art had hoped for : the tumult that would have arisen would have brought the police to the spot, and they would have taken up the authors of the disturbance, the disturbers very naturally being those who had been pelted. The young men felt that the merest pretext would have been taken advantage of, and determined not to give it.

The door was opened at three o'clock, and then closed again. Once in the interior of the theatre, they organized themselves. But being settled in their places by half-past three, it became a question what they should do till seven. They talked and they sang, but conversation and singing flagged in time. Luckily, they had arrived too soon to have dined beforehand, and had brought sausages, ham, bread, &c. They dined, then; the benches were made use of as tables, and pocket handkerchiefs as table napkins. As there was nothing else to do, they were so long in dining, that the public made their entrance whilst they were still at table. On seeing the house thus turned into a restaurant, the box-keepers thought they must be dreaming, and at the same time their olfactory nerves were offended by the garlic in the sausages.

When M. Victor Hugo reached the theatre, he found the employés smiling, and the Commissaire Royal quite upset.

" What's the matter ? " said he.

"The matter is, that your drama is done for, and that your friends are the cause of it."

M. Victor Hugo, when told of the affair, said it was not the fault of his friends, but of those who had shut them up for four hours. At any rate, Mademoiselle Mars knew nothing about it; for the Baron Taylor had had the precaution to keep the thing secret. The author entered her private box.

" Well," said she to him directly she saw him, " you have nice friends ! You know what they have done ! "

All M. Taylor's care had not prevented the enemies of the play from telling her all about it. She was furious.

" I have performed before many an audience," said she, " but I shall owe it to you that I have acted before this kind of people."

M. Victor Hugo could but repeat what he had already said to the Commissaire Royal, and went into the green-room. Actors, figurantes, machinists, managers, had all passed from coldness to absolute hostility. Only M. Joanny, who looked superb in his costume of Ruy Gomez, said to him,—

"Take courage. As for me, I never felt in a better mood."

M. Victor Hugo looked through the aperture in the curtain. From top to bottom, nothing was to be seen but silk, jewellery, flowers, and bare shoulders. Amidst all this splendour, two sombre masses, in the pit and in the galleries, shook their flowing manes.

The three strokes were struck. The author saw the curtain rise, with the sensation only known to those who are obliged to depend on an accident for present success, and perhaps for their whole future.

The little scene between Don Carlos and Josefa passed off satisfactorily; then Doña Sol entered. The young men, who were but little used to theatrical customs, and who were, besides, not over enthusiastic about Mademoiselle Mars, omitted to receive her in her usual way, and her own party, who were vexed with her for acting in a drama, did not make amends for this want of respect. So unusual a silence somewhat disconcerted her.

M. Firmin, who was too old for Hernani, but who was always young in animation and verve, recited these lines very well :—

> " O l'insensé vieillard, qui, la tête inclinée,
> Pour achever sa route . . . .
> Vieillard, va-t'en donner mesure au fossoyeur ! "

The orchestra, the pit, and the second gallery warmly

applauded; but it was not responded to in other parts of the house.

At the second act, when it came to the dialogue between Don Carlos and Hernani:—

> —— " Mon maître,
> Je vous tiens de ce jour sujet rebelle et traître . . .
> Je vous fais mettre au ban de l'empire.
> —— A ton gré.
> J'ai le reste du monde où je te braverai.
> Il est plus d'un asile où ta puissance tombe.
>
> Et quand j'aurai le monde ?
> —— Alors j'aurai la tombe.

some of the boxes united in the applause. At each scene which passed without opposition, the actors and the people about the theatre became more and more friendly. After the second act they smiled, and some of them really admired the play.

But the most dangerous part was not yet passed. This was the scene of the pictures, which had already been held up to ridicule by the parody at the " Vaudeville." The third act began well. The verses of Don Ruy Gomez to Doña Sol,—

> " Quand passes un jeune pâtre," &c.

said by M. Joanny with a melancholy boldness, touched the women's hearts, and even some of them applauded. M. Ernest de Saxe-Coburg called out, " Vivent les femmes ! " (The ladies for ever.)

M. Joanny had a sort of proud awkwardness and a

familiar kind of nobleness of manner which suited the character admirably. He started on the file of portraits in a grand manner, and was followed by the public without interruption, until the sixth. They then, however, began to object, and murmurs were heard. After the two next there was hissing. Then came the verse,—

" J'en passe, et des meilleurs,"

which saved everything. The last portrait was received with acclamations, and the applause redoubled when Don Ruy prefers giving up his life and his betrothed rather than the guest whom he knows to be his rival. From that moment no one in the green-room had any further doubt about the success of the piece.

The success was secured by the monologue of Charles V. in the fourth act; that tremendous monologue was interrupted at almost every verse by bravos, and ended in interminable rounds of applause.

These shouts were still going on, when some one came to tell the author that he was wanted. He went out and saw a little man with a round belly and staring eyes.

" My name's Mame," said the little man. " I'm the partner of M. Baudoin, the publisher : but we can't talk here : will you spare me a minute outside the house ? "

When they were in the street, " Now, then," he said. " M. Baudoin and I were at the performance, and we should like to publish *Hernani*—will you sell it ? "

" What do you offer ? "

" Six thousand francs" (£240).

" We will talk about it when the performance is over."

"I beg your pardon," said the publisher, "but I make a great point of settling the matter at once."

"Why? You don't know what you are buying. The success may be less complete."

"Ah, that's true, but it may be much greater. At the second act I thought of offering 2000 francs; at the third act I got up to 4000; I now, at the fourth act, offer 6000; and after the fifth I am afraid I should have to offer 10,000."

"Well," said M. Victor Hugo, laughing, "since you have so much fear about the play, you shall have it. Come to-morrow morning, and we will settle the matter."

"If it's the same thing to you, I should prefer settling it at once. I have got the 6000 francs in my pocket."

"I've no objection, but how can it be managed? we are in the street."

"Here's a tobacco shop."

The publisher entered with the author, bought a sheet of stamped paper, and asked for a pen and ink. The treaty was written and signed on the counter, and the author received the money, which was by no means unacceptable, as he had not more than fifty francs in his possession.

He went back into the theatre as fast as possible, and saw, by the universal attention paid, that the success had not diminished. The fourth act was now over—Michelot, Joanny, and Firmin were radiant; their three parts had largely contributed to the success, for during the four first acts Doña Sol is a secondary character. M. Hugo thought it necessary to go and see Mademoiselle Mars.

He found her sour and dry. At first she pretended

not to see him. She continued quarrelling with her
dresser. "What's the matter with you to-day ? I shall
never be ready. Here, give me my white—it is an hour
since I asked you for it. The place will never be clear—
one does not know where one is with all these visits ! Ah,
you're there, M. Hugo."

And then, all the time occupied in covering her
shoulders and neck with the white preparation, she went
on,—

"So your piece is going on very well—at least for you
and your gentlemen friends."

"We have now reached your act, madame."

"Yes, I begin when the play is just over. By the way,
I have not given much trouble to your friends. Do you
know, it is the first time in my life that I have not been
applauded on entering ?"

"But now you will be applauded at the conclusion !"

"Well," she said, assuming the air of a victim resigned to her fate, "from the moment that I accepted such
a part, I ought to have looked for this kind of success."

When she appeared in her white satin robe, a crown of
white roses on her brow, her brilliant teeth, and her
figure which always looked as if she were just eighteen,
she produced all the effect of youth and beauty. The
whole scene was charming. The terrace on which the
masks were chatting, the palace lighted up, the gardens
with the glittering fountains, the movements of the *fête*,
the music accompanying the dances, and then the silence,
and the bride and bridegroom left alone,—all this had prepared the house and produced a favourable impression ;

and when Mademoiselle Mars repeated these lines, which lent themselves admirably to her musical voice, she had no reason to envy the gentlemen :—

> " La lune tout à l'heure à l'horizon montait,
> Tandis que tu parlais, sa lumière qui tremble
> Et ta voix, toutes deux m'allaient au cœur ensemble ;
> Je me sentais joyeuse et calme, ô mon amant,
> Et j'aurais bien voulu mourir en ce moment."

The whole of the fifth act justified the precipitation of the publisher, M. Mame. When M. Joanny took off the mask, under which Don Ruy Gomez has appeared at the wedding, the spectral face which he presented produced an impression of terror, and throughout the house there was a sepulchral rigidity which was felt as a chill. Mademoiselle Mars demanded of him the life of Hernani with an energy of which no one would have thought Célimène capable. She was positively violent while threatening Don Ruy :—

> " Il vaudrait mieux pour vous aller aux tigres même
> Arracher leurs petits, qu'à moi celui que j'aime . . .
> Voyez-vous ce poignard ? Ah ! vieillard insensé,
> Craignez-vous pas le fer quand l'œil a menacé ?
> Prenez garde, don Ruy !—Je suis de la famille,
> Mon oncle !"

The last scene was a complete intoxication. A shower of bouquets fell at the feet of Mademoiselle Mars. The name of the author was shouted even by the boxes. Only five or six remained silent ; not one objected.

M. Victor Hugo went to pay to the great actress the compliments she merited. Her room was crowded, but this time she did not complain of the crowd. She was radiant; her part was superb; the play was a master-piece.

"What," she said, "you won't embrace your Doña Sol."

And Doña Sol offered the cheek of Madamoiselle Mars to the author.

M. Victor Hugo found at the door of the theatre a crowd of friends who were waiting to accompany him home. On arriving at the house, he found his saloon quite full. The street in which he lived was astonished to find itself so noisy at one o'clock in the morning. M. Achille Deveria declared that he would not sleep on such a night, and he went home to make a sketch of the last scene.

Next morning when he awoke, he found the following letter :—

"I was present, sir, at the first representation of *Hernani.* You know how much I admire you. My vanity attaches itself to your lyre, and you know the reason. I am going—you are coming. I recommend myself to the remembrance of your muse. A pious glory ought to pray for the dead.

"CHATEAUBRIAND.

"29th February, 1830."

The first performance had taken place on a Saturday. On the Monday, the day of the second performance, the newspapers appeared. With the exception of the *Journal des Débats,* all were hostile. They objected to the drama and to the audience; the author had brought with him

spectators worthy of his play, a sort of bandit tribe, un-
cultivated and ragged, picked up from no one knows
where, who had turned a respectable theatre into a filthy
cavern; they had sung songs, according to the Liberal
journals, obscene; according to the Royalists, blasphem-
ous: the temple was profaned for ever, and Melpomene
was in a pitiable state.

The Commissaire Royal hastened to see the author.
He was very uneasy. It was evident that this unanimity
of the newspapers would be likely to excite and reproduce
the opposition that had been overcome the day before,
and there would be a battle that night. As M. Victor
Hugo did not like *claqueurs,* it was necessary that his
friends should return to applaud the second representation as they had done the first. There was no need to
look after them: the heads of the tribe would no sooner
have read the papers, than they would return of their
own accord. They well understood that the struggle had
not yet come to an end, and that it would be warm work
that evening; they were delighted at it, they considered
they had won the day too easily the first night, and they
would only have been half pleased to win without having
fought.

The Rue de Valois was crowded towards midday by
loungers, who hoped to see the strange bands mentioned
in the newspapers. But the managers of the theatre no
longer insisted on their entering by the king's door, nor
that they should be shut up for four hours. The young
men entered, a short time before the office was opened, by
the little door in the passage. There were, therefore,

ncither songs, nor sausages flavoured with garlic, nor the other things. There was nothing remarkable but the eccentricity of dress, which, however, was quite enough to horrify the boxes. Everybody was pointing out M. Théophile Gautier, whose flaring waistcoat shone out brightly that evening over a pair of trousers of pale grey, ornamented at the sides with a band of black velvet. His hair fell down in large locks from under a flat, broad-brimmed hat. The perfect calmness of his regular features and pale countenance, and the coolness with which he looked up at the honest people in the boxes, plainly showed the amount of abomination and desolation into which the theatre had fallen.

At the moment that the curtain was about to rise a circumstance happened, which has since been repeated at every play of M. Victor Hugo's: a swarm of little white papers fell from the heights to the dress circle and balcon, and also to the orchestra. These little papers stuck to people's coats, to their noses, to ladies' curls, and even fell into the bosoms of the dresses. Everyone in the theatre began shaking and plucking themselves. This was a new grievance against *Hernani*. Who was concerned in this affair? Was it an enemy? Was it some implacable hater of the middle classes, who desired to irritate them, first, for the sake of doing so, and next, in order to excite them to the battle, as the picador excites the bull? This riddle was never solved.

It was felt from the very first that a storm was brewing. It burst forth in the first act. That line,—

" Nous sommes trois chez vous ; c'est trop de deux, madame,"

was welcomed with bursts of laughter from the whole of
the principal gallery and the orchestra stalls. The laughter
redoubled at the line,—

"Oui, de ta suite, ô roi! de ta suite!—J'en suis."

It was a piece of good luck for the boxes that, instead
of saying the line as it was written, M. Firmin said :—

"Oui, de ta suite, ô roi! De ta suite j'en suis."

This *"De ta suite j'en suis!"* was a joke which lasted,
which was prolonged long after that evening came to an
end: for months the classical party never met without
saying to each other : *"De ta suite j'en suis!"* and this
produced a few moments of gentle hilarity.

It may easily be imagined that these bursts of laughter
were warmly met by the young men. Sneering and applause were intermingled, and the skirmish began. At
the second act occurs this passage,—

"Quelle heure est il?
Minuit."

That a King should ask what o'clock it is, and in order
to ask the question, should say, *"Quelle heure est il?"*
and then that he should add, in rhythmical measure, that
it was midnight, when it would have been so easy to
answer,—

"Du haut de ma demeure,
Seigneur, l'horloge enfin sonne la douzième heure,"

all this appeared, naturally enough, to be quite intolerable, and the laughter passed into hissing. The
young men got rather angry, and imposed silence so

resolutely that the scene between Hernani and the King was listened to without trouble, and succeeded even better than on the first occasion. M. Joanny, who was very firm when opposed, saved the cause of the portrait scene by reciting it boldly; he had an irresistible gesture when he offered his hand to the King.

> " 'Jai promis l'une ou l'autre :
> N'est il pas vrai, vous tous?   Je donne celle-ci."

On the other hand, the monologue of Charles the Fifth, so much applauded on the Saturday, was made great fun of.

> . . . . " Eteins toi, cœur jeune et plein de flamme,
> Laisse régner l'esprit, que longtemps tu troublas.
> Tes amours désonnais, tes maîtresses, hélas !
> C'est l'Allemagne, c'est la Flandre, c'est l'Espagne."

Here the laughter redoubled.

> " Mais tu l'as, le plus douce et le plus beau collier,
> Celui que je n'ai pas, qui manque au rang suprême ;
> Les deux bras d'une femme aimée et qui vous aime ! "

At this point the laughter pealed forth.

The masked-ball and the dancing-tunes of the fifth act pleased the *beau monde* for a short time, but when Doña Sol, after wishing to fly from the music, expresses a wish to hear a song in the night, and Hernani says to her,—

> . . . . . . " Capricieuse !"

the word seemed very ridiculous, and the sneers recommenced and continued to the end.

The newspapers next day spoke of the sneers, but forgot to add that they had been stifled by applause. They had done justice to this scandalous drama, now the whole thing was at an end, and no one would think anything more about it. Thank God! not even curiosity had been excited by it; at the second performance the theatre was half empty, &c.

It was true that there had been some vacant places, principally two of the centre boxes, which had caused some astonishment to the crowd who were much distressed for room in other parts of the theatre. This was also a source of astonishment to the author, too, who knew that every box had been hired. He was anxious to know who those people were who had paid in order not to come, and he found out that they were the brother and friend of an author attached to the theatre, and at that time a person of great name.

The third performance was even more noisy than the second. The opposition party contented themselves indeed, with sneering, only they sneered oftener than ever. The author still had all his friends at hand, who responded to every hoot by a vigorous and enthusiastic reply.

But after three representations, M. Victor Hugo had to fall back upon the usual custom for authors, and would only have a few places to give away. The actors entreated to return to the *claqueur* system, but these people could not feel very warmly disposed towards a play from which they had been excluded. The Commissaire Royal, devoted to the new style of art, took upon himself to present the author with 100 seats to give away.

100 seats against 1500: the battle was now about to be fought under these circumstances. The opposing journals said, that now *the real public* would be able to penetrate into the theatre and take its revenge on outraged art.

Then began the real struggle. At every performance there was a tremendous uproar. The boxes sneered, the stalls hissed; it was the fashion with people to quit their drawing-rooms and go and have a "laugh at *Hernani*." Everyone protested in his own way, and according to his own nature. Some who could not sit out such a play would turn their backs to the stage; others, being unable to hear it, would exclaim, "No more of this!" and would leave in the middle of an act and bang their box-door violently. Peaceful people were content to show their want of interest in "this drama," by unfolding and beginning to read their newspapers. But the real partisans of the good old style never went away, never read, never turned their backs. Their eyes and their ears were all devoted to the play, they watched every word, hooting, hissing, preventing people from hearing, and putting the actors out of countenance. The hundred—lost in the crowd—never gave way; their twenty years of age and their convictions supplied the thunder to this hurricane.

They held their own against the multitude, defended the scenes line for line, would not allow a hemistich to be lost; they would stamp, roar, insult those who hissed. M. Ernest de Saxe-Coburg respected neither age nor sex. A young lady was indulging in fits of laughter during the portrait scene, and he said to her,—

"Madame, you do wrong to laugh. You show your teeth!"

To old men, with venerable bald heads, who were hissing in the stalls, he would exclaim,—

"To the guillotine, the knees!"

The author, whose success was thus questioned, no longer encountered in the green-room all those respectful salutations which had been lavished on the first night. The masterpiece had fallen back into the "drama"—a bastard mixture of comedy and tragedy—a something or other. The actors were deserting to the enemy: one of the best of them would wink at the hissers, as much as to say,—"You are right; I am obliged to act this against my will." M. Joanny himself was baffled. Mademoiselle Mars held out to the last. She was no more spared than the rest; and the innovator was the cause of her being hissed for the first time. She bitterly reproached him for it, and never now praised his play; but she was as stedfast on the stage as she was disagreeable in her private room. She teazed the author when they were alone; but in public she carried out his ideas.

That which upheld the drama, notwithstanding the vehemence of the enemy and the discouragement of the actors, was the money it brought in. People came to hiss, but they came nevertheless. Hatred went so far as to deny the amount of the receipts even in the theatre itself. A comedian, who was acting a minor part, and was himself a dramatic author in the style of Colin d'Harleville and Andrieuse, replied one day, when asked why, if the play was so bad it attracted so many people, that it attracted no one, that all the seats were given away, that the theatre was full, but that the till was empty.

"Look here," said he, "to-night the theatre is full; well, I bet that the receipts . . . ."

"Amount to four thousand five hundred and fifty-seven francs seventy-eight centimes," said M. Victor Hugo, who was passing at the time, and who had in his hand the cashier's memorandum.

The attack on the play had its caprices. Sometimes it hit one part, sometimes another. A scene which had been overwhelmed the night before was suddenly left quite quiet; and, on the contrary, a scene which one might have thought unattackable was broken to pieces by interruptions. In the interval between the acts, on the evening of the third performance, the author and Mademoiselle Mars who (for a wonder) was amiable on that occasion, amused themselves by trying to recollect which of the verses had not been hissed. They did not hit upon a single one.

"There's the whole of my part," said Madame Thénard, who was present.

She had a line and a quarter to repeat in the fifth act:

"Mon cher comte,
Vous savez, avec tous, que mon mari les compte."

"Your lines were not hissed?" said the author. "Well, they will be."

It happened that same night that they were hissed.

The struggle fatigued the actors more and more, and they had at last began to wish for failure in the receipts, that the performances might be stopped. Some of them hoped they should not have to wait so long, that the young men, tired of hostilities, would give up, and that at length hatred having gained the mastery would cause the curtain to fall before the catastrophe. This was what the author expected. Madame Hugo's first question to her husband when he returned from the theatre was, "Did they keep on till the end?" And this life of anxiety and violent emotion became so painful that she almost hoped he would reply no.

But the young men, themselves, would not listen to such a thing. Their devotion never flagged, and they quarrelled amongst themselves as to who should have one of the hundred seats. The following letter will give some idea of the liveliness and spirit of the defence: —

"Four of my janissaries offer me their assistance. I lay them at your feet, and request from you four places for this evening if it is not too late, or for Wednesday if there are no longer any tickets to be disposed of.

"I can warrant my men. These are the kind of men who would cut off men's heads in order to get at their wigs. For my part, I encourage them in persisting in such noble sentiments, and I never let them go without blessing them in a paternal manner.

"They kneel down. I spread out my hands and say to them,—'Come to me, right-thinking men, and may God assist you! It is a good cause. Do your duty.' They rise, and I always take care to add, 'Come now, my children, let us take care of Victor Hugo; for though Providence means very well, it has so much to do that our friend must need reckons upon us first. Go, and prove yourselves worthy of him whom you serve. Amen.'

"Yours devotedly, in heart and soul,

"*Monday Night.*"   "CHARLET.

M. Victor Hugo was in the habit of receiving letters in another style. One ended thus:—"If you don't withdraw your dirty play within the next twenty-four hours, we'll take away your appetite for dinner." Two young men who were present when he received this letter took the matter seriously. They waited for the author after every performance, and would accompany him from the door of the theatre to the Rue Nôtre-dame des Champs, which was not a little out of their way, for they lived in the Boulevard Montmartre. They continued this even to the very last of the performances.

But while these literary disturbances were going on, there were also political ones. *Hernani* and the address of the *two hundred and twenty-one* were equally the subject of general conversation. An editor of the *Courier Français*, a friend of M. Victor Hugo's, notwithstanding his newspaper, said to him,—

"There are two men much hated in France, M. de Polignac and you."

The quarrel reached the provinces. At Toulouse, a young man named Batlam fought a duel about *Hernani,* and was killed. At Vannes, a corporal of dragoons died, leaving an instruction in his will—" I wish to have it engraved on my tombstone, ' *Here lies one who believed in Victor Hugo.'* "

Mademoiselle Mars being absent on leave, the performances were interrupted at the forty-fifth representation.

When it was performed on one occasion eight years afterwards, and when nothing but applause was to be heard, two spectators were discussing the play as they descended the staircase of the theatre at the conclusion of the performances.

" It is not at all extraordinary," said one of them, who no doubt had been one of the hissers at the early performances, " he has changed every line."

" You are mistaken," answered the other; " it is not the drama which has changed, but the public! "

LV

NÔTRE-DAME DE PARIS.

A FORTNIGHT before the close of the theatrical season, the landlady of the house in which M. Victor Hugo occupied the first floor, came up from the ground floor, on which she lived herself, and entered the room with a distressed countenance.

"My little lady," said she to Madame Hugo, "you are very amiable, and your husband is an excellent person; but you are not sufficiently quiet lodgers for me. I left business in order to live in peace at home. I bought this house on purpose in a quiet street; and for three months there is here, entirely on your account, a perpetual rush of people all day and all night—a fearful kick-up on the stairs, and a regular earthquake over my head. At one o'clock in the morning I am awoke all of a sudden, and I am always fancying that the ceiling will give way and fall on my bed. We can no longer live under the same roof."

"In other words, you give us notice to quit?"

"I am really distressed to do so. I shall regret you

very much. You are a nice couple, and love your children. But you never get any rest yourself. How much I pity you, my poor lady! Your husband has a very arduous profession."

Hernani having had this odd kind of success—that of turning the author out of his house—the family crossed the Seine, and established themselves in the Rue Jean Goujon. There a fresh worry awaited them.

Amongst the crowds of people whom the landlady had not been able to put up with, it happened that, on the day after the performance, Gosselin, the publisher, came to buy the manuscript. He had not seen M. Victor Hugo, who had gone to the theatre. Madame Hugo, who knew very little of him, had not noticed him in the crowd, and had not spoken to him. Some one having asked who would publish the drama, she had related the rapid arrangement made the night before. M. Gosselin had gone out directly, doubly enraged, and had written to tell M. Victor Hugo that he was at liberty to sell his plays to whoever he pleased; but that Madame Hugo had no right to treat uncourteously a man who was both a juryman and an elector.

He had his revenge in his own hands. When selling the *Dernier Jour d'un Condamné*, M. Victor Hugo had also sold him a novel which he was thinking of writing, and which should be called *Nôtre-Dame de Paris*. He had engaged to have it ready in April, 1829. Being quite absorbed by the theatre, he had been unable to give his attention to any other subject. A year had passed after the proper time had expired without his having

written a single line. The publisher, who till then had
not hurried him, requested at once and immediately the
execution of the treaty.

It was quite impossible to deliver up a novel which
was not even begun. The publisher demanded damages.
M. Bertin had to interfere to settle the affair. The
author was allowed five months to write *Nôtre-Dame de
Paris*. If it was not ready by the 1st December he was
to pay one thousand francs for every week's delay.

He was therefore obliged to set to work at *Nôtre-Dame
de Paris*, whilst quite upset by the feverish encounters
relating to *Hernani*, and whilst still in all the disorder of
a moving that had been forced upon him.

In the first place, he established himself in his new
abode. One day, when he was hanging up in his study
a bookcase, composed of four shelves fastened together by
cords, a matter that he got on with rather badly, the
Prince de Craon introduced to him a fair young man
with an agreeable countenance, where at first one saw
nothing but gentleness, but where, after a little observation, it was equally easy to read great shrewdness. This
young man had been to see *Hernani*, and had wished to
compliment the author on it. He was enchanted to see
that the theatre was about to assert its liberty — he
wished for liberty in all places. His name was
Montalembert.

As soon as M. Victor Hugo was comfortably installed
he set to work. He began to write on the morning of
the 27th July. M. Gustave Planche had called during
the day, and had invited little Léopoldine to come and eat

ice in the Palais-Royal; his carriage was in waiting below, and the pleasure of a drive induced the child to say "Yes." They set off, but could not go far; they met great crowds of people, in such a state of excitement, that M. Planche was alarmed on account of the child and brought her home.

The next day the Champs Elysées were a bivouac. They were not a fashionable resort in those days, nor built over as they are now. There were only a few houses, in the midst of large tracts of ground, occupied by the proprietors of kitchen-gardens. These were very far off from any part of the town, and it was difficult to get out to buy provisions because of the troops. One was a prisoner in one's own house; and as no letters nor newspapers were received no news was to be had. The echoes of the artillery waggons were heard as they rolled along by the Quai; there was also the noise of guns, and the sound of the tocsin. One of M. Victor Hugo's fellow-lodgers, General Cavaignac, who was uncle to the Cavaignac afterwards head of the executive power of the Republic, informed him that the house being detached and built of stone, it would certainly be occupied by the troops if a contest took place in that direction, and in that case they would be besieged.

A heat of 90° was very trying to the soldiers, and their foreheads being bathed in perspiration, they would knock at the door and ask for a glass of water. One of them, when giving back the glass, fell down fainting.

A slight engagement took place so near them that

balls whistled through the garden. A short time afterwards, the children found under their windows, in a field
of potatoes, which stretched along by the side of the
house, a man, dressed in a blouse, lying on his face, immovable, hidden under the leafy shelter of the vegetables.
They thought he was dead, but seeing that there were no
traces of blood about him they imagined that, perhaps,
he was an insurgent, who was awaiting nightfall, in
order to make his escape from the troops, or perhaps that
he was only some poor devil alarmed at the firing. He
did not move all day. He certainly must have been
hungry. They only had a four-pound loaf in the house,
and it would be difficult to get another, but the children
cut a large slice from it and threw it out of window. The
next morning the man and the bread had disappeared.

They continued blockaded and without news. The
only means of obtaining news was by going in search of
it. M. Victor Hugo went out with M. de Mortemart-
Boiste, another lodger in the same house. On entering
the avenue in the Champs Elysées they found a battery
of cannons, and were only allowed to pass after being
questioned. The military display was formidable enough.
The soldiers, who were constructing redoubts, were sawing
the trees up in order to construct *chevaux de frise*.

Near the square of Marigny, a youth of fourteen or
fifteen years of age was tied to a tree, looking quite pale.
M. de Mortemart asked why he was tied up.

"That he may not escape before he has been shot,"
replied a soldier.

" Shot ! " said M. Victor Hugo ; " why, he's a mere child."

" A child who has killed a man. He has brought down our captain, but he shall pay for it."

At that moment a picquet of cavalry made their appearance on their way from the Barrière de l'Etoile. M. Victor Hugo recognized General Girardin and went to him.

" What on earth are you doing here ? " said the General.

" I live here."

" Well, I advise you to move. I am just come from Saint-Cloud, and they are going to fire red-hot balls."

M. Victor Hugo showed the General the boy who was fastened to the tree, and he had him unfastened and conducted to the next station.

The next day the Revolutionists gained the mastery, and the Champs Elysées became free again.

These great disturbances made a powerful impression on intelligent minds. M. Victor Hugo, who had but just headed his own insurrection and constructed his own barricades at the theatre, quite understood that all kinds of progress are related to each other, and that in order not to be inconsistent we must accept in politics that which we desire in literature. He set to work at writing, and jotted down his ideas just as they arose in his mind as to the events of every day. At a later period he published in the *Littératures et Philosophies Melées*, a " Journal of a Revolutionist in 1830."

Whilst singing the victory of the people, he still felt sympathy with, and inclined to comfort, the fallen King:—

Oh ! laissez-moi pleurer sur cette race morte
Que rapporta l'exil et que l'exil remporte,
Vent fatal qui trois fois déjà les enleva !
Reconduisons au moins ces vieux rois de nos pères.
Rends, drapeau de Fleurus, les honneurs militaires
     A l'oriflamme qui s'en va !

Je ne leur dirai point de mot qui les déchire.
Qu'ils ne se plaignent pas des adieux de ma lyre !
Pas d'outrage au vieillard qui s'exile à pas lents !
C'est une piété d'épargner les ruines.
Je n'enfoncerai pas la couronne d'épines
Que la main du malheur met sur des cheveux blancs.

D'ailleurs, infortunés ! ma voix achève à peine
L'hymne de leurs douleurs dont s'allonge la chaîne.
L'exil et les tombeaux dans mes chants sont bénis ;
Et tandis que d'un règne on saluera l'aurore,
Ma poésie en deuil ira longtemps encore
     De Sainte-Hélène à Saint-Denis !

[Translation.]

Oh, let me weep at ease for this dead race,
Which exile gave us back, and claims once more !
Oh, fatal wind which three times bore them off !
At least, let us lead back these old kings of our fathers.
Give back, O flag of Fleurus, all military honours
     To the departing oriflamme.

I will not rend their hearts with sad adieux,
They shall not blame the farewells of my lyre ;
No insult to the aged man who sadly chooses exile ;
It is a godly work to spare a ruin.
I shall not rudely press the crown of thorns
Placed by misfortune's hand on silvery hair.

Besides, O sorrowing ones! my song is yet unsung,
Hymns telling of their grief which deeper grows,
The grave and exile in my songs are blest.
And whilst they welcome the new-comer's reign,
My poetry in mourning garb will rove
　From Saint Helena e'en to Saint Denis.

The *Globe*, which published this ode, headed it with the following remarks (19th August) :—

" Poetry has hastened to celebrate the grandeur of late events, which were, indeed, well adapted to inspire all who have a heart and a voice. M. Victor Hugo now steps forward with his almost military boldness, his patriotic love for France, when free and glorious, and his lively sympathy with youth, one of whose most striking leaders he is. But at the same time, in accordance with his original opinions and the warm affections of his youth, which he has consecrated in more than one memorable ode, the poet's heart was closely bound up in the past, which is now gone for ever, and was anxious to bid it a sad farewell whilst detaching himself from it. He has known how to conciliate, in a perfect manner, the outbursts of his patriotism with the decency due to misfortune. He is a citizen of young France, without having to blush at the remembrance of the former France; his heart was touched, but his reason has not wavered. *Mens immota manet, lacrymæ volvuntur inanes.* Already, in his ' Ode à la Colonne,' M. Hugo had shown that he fully entered into the glories of his country. His conduct, on more occasions than one, has also shown that he was accustomed to the practice of liberty. His talent will live and increase with liberty, and from this time a boundless career opens before him. Whilst Chateaubriand, an old man, nobly gives up public life, sacrificing the remainder of his existence to the evenness of a well-spent life, it is well that the younger man, who began by fighting under the same banner, should continue to go on in spite of certain recollections, and that he should bear, without fatigue, the various doctrines of his country. Each is thus doing what he ought, and France, whilst honouring the sacrifice of the one, will accept the labour of the other."

One afternoon, in September, M. de Lamennais called on M. Victor Hugo, whom he found busy writing.

"You are at work, and I fear I disturb you?"

"I am hard at work, but you don't disturb me."

"What were you writing?"

"Something you would not like."

"Tell me, nevertheless."

M. Victor Hugo handed him a sheet, on which M. de Lamennais read as follows:—

"The Republic, which is not yet fully fledged, but which will be universal in all Europe in a century, consists in society being the sovereign of society, instituting a national guard, in order to protect itself; instituting a jury, in order to judge itself; instituting communes, for the purposes of administration; and, in order to govern itself, instituting an electoral college.

"The four members composing the monarchy, namely, the army, the magistracy, the administration, and the peerage are, in the eyes of the Republic, only four trouble-some excrescences, which will soon rot away and die."

"Exactly so," said M. de Lamennais; "I felt quite sure that a mind such as yours could not remain contented with Royalism. There is but one word too many: '*La République n'est pas mûre*' (the Republic is not yet ripe). You speak of it as in the future. I consider it belongs to the present."

M. de Lamennais, not believing any longer in absolutism, ceased to have confidence in the monarchy. His straightforward nature declined all intermediate terms and postponements. M. Victor Hugo, who saw in the Republic a definite form of society, only believed it feasible after due preparation; he wished that one should arrive at universal suffrage by universal instruction. The mixed royalty of Louis Philippe seemed to him a useful transition.

"Nôtre-Dame de Paris" had been much neglected during this political eruption. Besides this, an accident had resulted from the situation in which the author's house had been placed. He wrote thus to M. Gosselin :—

"The dangerous position of my house in the Champs Elysées, on the 29th July, had made me resolve to take my most valuable goods and my manuscripts to the house of my brother-in-law, who lives in the Rue du Cherche-Midi, and whose neighbourhood, in consequence, was but little threatened. During this operation, which was very hastily accomplished, a memorandum book was lost, quite full of notes, which had cost me more than two months' research, and which were indispensable to the completion

of ' Nôtre-Dame de Paris.'   This memorandum book has
not yet been found, and I now fear that all my researches
will be in vain.   I hasten to acquaint you with the fact.
Is not this one of the important and unforeseen circumstances which had been anticipated as possible to occur
when we drew up our agreement of the 5th June?
Nevertheless, if fresh events do not occur to prevent my
continuing my book, I hope, by dint of hard work, to be
able to give you up the manuscript when the proper
time comes.   I own, however, that a delay of two
months, granted to me by you in consideration of this
accidental circumstance, would be pleasing to me, as much
in your interests as in mine, and that I should consider
this proceeding on your part as completely making up for
anything I may have thought I had reason to complain of
in your former dealings with me.   It appears to me, that
it might also be in your interest that the manuscript
should not be given up to you so soon after the Revolution
as the 1st December.   It is doubtful whether literature
will then have re-assumed that amount of importance
which it possessed two months ago, and I think that
a delay in the work would be as good for you as for
me."

The publisher entered into these reasons, and the date
was postponed till the 1st February, 1831, which gave
M. Victor Hugo five months and a half.

But no further delay was to be looked for ; it was
necessary to be ready by that time.   He bought a bottle
of ink and a thick piece of grey worsted knitting, which
enveloped him from the neck to the heels ; he locked up

his clothes, in order not to be tempted to go out, and set to work at his novel, as if in a prison. He was very melancholy.

From that time he never left the writing-table, except to eat and to sleep. His only amusement was an hour's chat after dinner with some friends, who would call on him, and to whom he sometimes read the pages he had written during the day. He read aloud thus the chapter headed "Les Cloches," to M. Pierre Leroux, who thought this kind of literature very useless.

After the first few chapters, his melancholy disappeared; his sadness left him, and his work took possession of him; he neither felt fatigue, nor the wintry cold which had come upon them. In December, he would sit at work with open windows.

He never doffed his bear-skin but on one occasion. On the morning of the 20th December, the Prince de Craon came to offer to conduct him to the trial of Charles the Tenth's Ministers. In order that this holiday should not be a long one, he did not even release his clothes from their prison, and wore his costume of the National Guards.

This was the stormy sitting. Towards four o'clock, whilst M. Cremieux was pleading in favour of M. de Guernon-Ranville, a great noise was heard outside. It was a mass of people hurrying to the Chamber of Peers. The National Guards, who filled the streets of Tournon and Vaugirard, were powerless to keep back the avalanche. The court was likely to be invaded. The crowd were exclaiming *"A bas Polignac! A bas Peyronnet! A mort les Ministres !* M. de Chantelauze, and M. de Guernon-Ranville, were so much terrified as to excite pity. M. de Polignac seemed as if he could not understand what was going on. M. de Peyronnet, who was standing with his head raised and his arms crossed, was the only one who defied death.

The sitting was suspended. The Prince de Craon and M. Victor Hugo set out to see what was going on. The National Guard, pressed against the walls of the palace, could hardly be said to defend it any longer. The multitude were pushing each other against the walls, climbing on the ledges, and scrambling up to the windows. Hatred was depicted in every face, every voice; anger was heard in all the cries; prisoners, judges, National Guards, everybody was insulted. General Lafayette, accompanied by M. Ferdinand de Lasteyrie, was trying to harangue the malcontents, but the people had had haranguing enough, and enough of Lafayette too. Urchins were seizing the General by the legs, hoisting him into the air, and handing him one to another, loudly exclaiming, in an indescribable tone, "Here is General Lafayette! who'll have him?" A detachment of the line made an opening and rescued him. When the way was free, M. Victor Hugo and the Prince approached the General, who took them by the arm.

"I no longer recognize my Parisians," said he to them, never imagining that perhaps the people of Paris no longer recognized their Lafayette. He then added, "The people themselves are excusable, but these Royalists! . . ."

And pointing out a balcony in the style of Louis XV., in the Rue de Tournon, he said,—

"I sent to ask M.—— to let me stand on his balcony and harangue the people. He replied, that his door should never be opened to General Lafayette. Out of revenge to the Revolution, they would allow their friends to be massacred."

M. Victor Hugo was about to re-enter the Chamber, but the sitting was not renewed. He therefore returned to Rue Jean Goujon, reinstated himself in his knitted garment, and continued his work.

On the night of the 7th January, a vivid light caused him suddenly to raise his eyes towards his window, which always stood open. The light was caused by an aurora borealis.

On the 14th January, the book was finished. The bottle of ink, which M. Victor Hugo had bought the first day, was also at an end; he concluded the last line and the last drop at the same moment, which made him think of changing the title of the work, and calling it "The Contents of a Bottle of Ink." Some years afterwards, Alphonse Karr, who thought the idea charming, begged it of him, since he had not made use of it, and published under this title several novels, amongst others, that master-piece of wit and emotion *"Généviève."*

Whilst he was writing *Nôtre-Dame de Paris,* M. Victor Hugo, of whom M. Gosslin begged some hints respecting his book, in order to advertise it, wrote to him thus:—

" . . . It is a representation of Paris in the fifteenth

century, and of the fifteenth century in its relation to
Paris. Louis XI. appears in one chapter. He decides
the dénouement. The book has no historical pretensions, unless they be those of painting with some care
and accuracy, but entirely by sketches and incidentally,
the state of morals, creeds, laws, arts, and even civilization, in the fifteenth century. This is, however, not the
most important part of the work. If it has a merit, it is
in its being purely a work of imagination, caprice, and
fancy."

After the conclusion of *Nôtre-Dame de Paris*, M.
Victor Hugo felt disinclined for work, and melancholy;
he had become accustomed to live with the creatures of
his imagination, and he felt, on parting with them, the
same sadness he would have experienced in parting with
old friends. He quitted his book with as much difficulty
as he had experienced on commencing it.

M. Gosselin gave his wife the manuscript to read; she
was an agreeable and talented person, who had translated
the novels of Walter Scott. She considered the book
horribly dull, and her husband had no scruple in saying
that he had done a bad stroke of business, and that it
would be a lesson to him never again to buy books
without first reading them.

The novel appeared on the 13th February, the day on
which the Archbishop's palace was pillaged. The author,
who was a witness of the popular fury, saw the books of
the library thrown into the water, and amongst others
one which had been of use to him in writing his novel.
This book, which was called *The Black Book*, be-

cause it was bound in black shagreen, was a unique copy, and contained the charter of the cloister of Nôtre-Dame.

The majority of the journals were, as usual, hostile. M. Alfred de Musset, in the *Temps*, remarked, without seeming greatly to regret it, that the book had been un- lucky in appearing on a day of riot, and that it had been drowned with the archiepiscopal library. The *Avenir* was one of the most charitable of the journals; it was edited by M. Lamennais, M. Montalembert, and M. Lacordaire, who each wrote an article upon the new book.

I find the following note :—

"MY DEAR HUGO,

"I send you a strong-backed, broad-shouldered man. Load him fearlessly. He will bring me back *Nôtre-Dame de Paris*, which I feel impatient to become acquainted with, because every one is speaking to me about it, and also because you wrote it.

"I give you due notice, however, that I am an enemy to the descriptive style. I know beforehand that of a certain part of your book I shall be a very bad judge. But towards all the rest of your work I am inclined to be that which I feel I am with respect to all your pro- ductions,

"Yours with all my heart, and for ever,

"BÉRANGER.

"*29th March.*"

————

Here is a still more curious letter from the author of the *Mystères de Paris.*

" I have procured *Nôtre-Dame;* I was one of the first
who did so, I assure you.   If the useless admiration
of a barbarian like myself had the power to express and
interpret itself in a manner worthy of the book which has
inspired it, I should tell you, sir, that you are a great
spendthrift; that your critics resemble those poor people
on the fifth story, who, whilst gazing on the prodigalities
of the great nobleman, would say to each other, with
anger in their hearts, ' I could live during my whole life
on the money spent in a single day.'

" And, in fact, the only thing they have been able to
say against your book is that there is too much of it.
This is an amusing animadversion in the present day, is
it not ?

" But from time immemorial men of extraordinary
genius have excited a base and narrow jealousy, and a
whole heap of dirty and lying criticisms.   What would
you have ?   Glory must be paid for.

" I would say, also, that apart from all the poetry,
all the richness of thought and dramatic power, there is
one thing which has struck me very much.   It is that
Quasimodo, combining beauty of soul and devotion to
others ; Frollo, who combines, in like manner, learning,
science, and intellectual power ; and Châteaupers, who
possesses physical beauty :—that you should have had the
admirable idea of placing these three types of our nature
face to face with a young and artless girl, almost a savage
in the midst of civilization, in order to make her take her
choice; and that she does make a choice so thoroughly
in the manner a woman would.

" . . . I only wished to recall myself to your kind and amiable remembrance. I called on you to tell you all I had written, and a great deal more; for you received me with so much kindness, and so much courtesy that I felt at my ease with you, although no one feels more than I do the influence of superiority.

"Accept the assurance of my devotion and sincere admiration.

"EUGENE SUE."

Madame Gosselin's opinion, and the hostility of most of the newspapers, did not prevent *Nôtre-Dame de Paris* from being extraordinarily successful. The editions were multiplied, and the publishers, with M. Gosselin at their head, came incessantly to ask for other novels from the author. He had none to give them; then they begged at least for a title, for something which should resemble the shadow of a promise. Thus for whole years M. Renduel's catalogues announced the *Fils de la Bossue*, and *La Quiquengrogne*. In reference to this subject I read in a letter of M. Victor Hugo's,—

"*La Quiquengrogne* is the popular name of one of the towers of Bourbon l'Aschembault. This novel is intended to complete the account of my views concerning the art of the Middle Ages, of which *Nôtre-Dame de Paris* furnished the first part. *Nôtre-Dame de Paris* is the cathedral. *La Quiquengrogne* will be the dungeon. In *Nôtre-Dame* I have more especially depicted the sacerdotal Middle Ages; in the *Quiquengrogne* I shall portray the feudal Middle Ages. All this, of course, will be according to my own views of the matter, which, be they correct or incorrect, are entirely my own. *Le Fils de la Bossue* will appear after the *Quiquengrogne,* and will be in one volume only."

These two novels, announced thirty years ago, were never written; the first novel of M. Victor Hugo's after *Nôtre-Dame de Paris,* was to be *Les Misérables.*

LVI

MARION DE LORME.

THE Revolution of July had naturally suppressed the censure; and all the prohibited plays had been immediately thrown upon the theatres. The Comédie-Française had directly thought of *Marion de Lorme.* In the beginning of the month of March, Mademoiselle Mars had called on the author with M. Armand and M. Firmin; the right time had come, especially for the fourth act, which, having been personally interdicted by Charles X., was sure to cause a political reaction. The author had replied that it was the certainty of that success which prevented him from allowing it to be acted. Although, since he had arrived at the age of manhood, he had acquired and become devoted to all the ideas of progress, improvement, and liberty; although he had given proof of this so recently as the previous year in reference to this very *Marion de Lorme;* he remembered that his first opinions, or rather his first illusions, had been Royalist and Vendean. He did not choose that some day he might be reproached with the past, a past no doubt of error, but also of conviction, of conscience, of disinterestedness, as he hoped the whole of his remaining life would be. He desired that in the midst of this intoxicating Revolution of July his voice might unite with those who applauded the people, not with those who cursed the King.

It is well known with what rapidity the aspect of things changes in revolutionary times. In the spring of 1831 the King whom they attacked was no longer Charles X.; it was already Louis Philippe. M. Victor Hugo did not now object to the representation of his drama, which could not be considered in the light of an offence against a king who was forgotten.

But he felt disinclined to return to the Théâtre Français. The hostility he had there met with from the audience, from the employés, and even from the actors, made him feel somewhat coolly towards it. M. Taylor alone had been friendly to him; but the power of the Commissaire Royal was limited; they had to deal with a divided authority, and with concealed malice. It was not easy to say who was the proper person to apply to, or whom to refer to. The author of *Hernani* felt a great wish to deal with a manager who was powerful and responsible; he preferred the theatre of La Porte Saint-Martin, which M. Crosnier, who had succeeded M. Jouslin de Lasalle, had come to offer him.

When Mademoiselle Mars first heard of this, she hastened to the author, this time amiable and beseeching. The piece was hers, she had acted in it, the valour and perseverance she had shown in Doña Sol, which was only the fourth character in *Hernani*, plainly foretold what she would do for Marion de Lorme, who was the principal character of the piece. Notwithstanding her entreaties, she had to leave without obtaining a single promise. The next day, as M. Victor Hugo was sitting at home alone, and at work, he heard the bell ring, but did not disturb himself. The bell continued ringing; still he did not stir, but as the sound continued, he felt curious to know who it was, and went to see. Before he answered the door he thought he would just look out of window, and he recognized Mademoiselle Mars's carriage. He had considered the subject since the day before, and had resolved upon the Théâtre de Saint-Martin ; he felt that it would be less disagreeable to Mademoiselle Mars to be able to say that she had found no one at home, than to admit that she had met with a second refusal, so he did not open the door at all.

That evening he signed a treaty with M. Crosnier, in which I notice these two articles :—

" M. Victor Hugo undertakes to give yearly to the theatre of the Porte Saint-Martin, two works of such importance that each will, by itself, take the whole evening to act, at least, for the first representations.

" Should an official censure or any officious interference of any kind, caused by the directors or exercised by the censors *ad hoc*, become established by Government, the present treaty would only be valid on condition that M. Crosnier should announce on the bill that that writing of M. Hugo's, which he is about to have represented, has not been submitted to censure. In case of refusal on the part of M. Crosnier, the present treaty would be cancelled entirely."

At the theatre of the Porte Saint-Martin, they were rehearsing the *Antony* of M. Alexandre Dumas. This beautiful drama was performed some days after with a success as striking as it was legitimate, and the name of Alexandre Dumas celebrated since the appearance of *Henri III.*, was now established. The only inconvenience of this success was, that it separated the young men, who, until then, had always fought under the same standard, and who, together, had opened the attack in the case of *Henri III.*, and given the assault in that of *Hernani.* They now divided themselves into two parties. There was Victor Hugo's party and Alexandre Dumas's party: they no longer joined forces against the enemy, but skirmished with each other.

The day after *Antony, Marion de Lorme* was distributed. Marion could only fall to Madame Dorval. M. Frederick Lemaitre had left the theatre; the part of Didier was given to M. Bocage, who was but half pleased with it. He would rather have played Louis XIII., and the more so that there was a certain resemblance between the part of Didier and Antony, which part he was then acting. Both were bastards and misanthropic characters, and it would be the same actor over again in the same character. But as he was the only fit person, the author had to take him.

Louis XIII., a character that had been a trouble at the Théâtre-Français, very nearly hindered the cast at the Porte Saint-Martin. The author had given it to a M. G——; the manager begged that he would take it from him. He had a personal quarrel with M. G——, which could not be settled: it related to a *Napoleon,* which he had induced him to act after the Revolution of July. M. G——, who was rather like the Emperor, and very well knew how to assume his appearance, had had unbounded success in it. At the time that the largest receipts were being made, he one day came into the manager's private room, and told him that he should not perform that evening. "Are you ill?" "No." "Then, why will you not perform?" "Because I won't. And I warn you that I shall not perform either to-morrow or the succeeding days. I break my engagement." The manager reminded him that he could not break it under a penalty of 10,000 francs. "Here is the money." This was a terrible blow to M. Crosnier, as the success of the play was centred in the actor. He had, therefore, endeavoured to make some arrangement, and M. G—— had consented to go on acting, provided he had a share in the receipts. The manager had been obliged to put up with it, but he had since paid him out by always choosing very minor parts for him. "I was in his hands," said he, "but now he is in mine. This money, badly earned, was quickly spent, and he can no longer pay me what he owes me. He belongs to me. He has had no further parts allotted to him, nor shall he have any. I will destroy him. When he leaves my theatre no one will accept of him, even as a supernumerary." M. Victor Hugo, seeing that the actor had been in the wrong, took the part from him.

The actor thus treated, hastened to his house the next day. He owned that he had been in the wrong, but it appeared to him that, as he was the cause of the success of the piece, he ought to get some of the profits. He had a wife and children, and he owed money: to crown all, the 40,000 francs that he had gained had not prevented M. Crosnier from pocketing 200,000. Nevertheless, he acknowledged his fault and repented of it, and had he the 40,000 francs now to spare, he would willingly have given them back. They had been of very little use to him, for his creditors had swallowed them all up. He had already been well punished; his career was ruined. Louis XIII. would save him, but if it was taken from him he knew not what would become of himself and family. M. Victor Hugo was touched, and gave him back his part. The manager exclaimed against it, but had to give in to the wishes of the author, but he bore him a grudge in consequence.

Madame Dorval was as charming during the rehearsals as Mademoiselle Mars had been sulky. All the people belonging to the theatre were most sympathizing and devoted to the cause.

One day, at the close of the fifth act, Madame Dorval touched the author's arm.

" M. Hugo," said she, with her peculiarly bewitching smile, " your Didier is a bad man. I do everything in my power for him, and he dies without even giving me a good word. Tell him he is wrong not to forgive me."

The piece of advice given by M. Merimée to the author on the night of the first reading of the play, caused him to reflect. On his return home he sauntered round the Champs Elysées and determined that, at the very last moment, he would make the inflexible Didier give way!

The ardour of the young men was not equal to that which they had felt for *Hernani.* The excessive political excitement had the effect of diverting attention from literature; some of them would now only fight for M. Alexandre Dumas, and the rest were not sufficient in number to keep up the piece by their own unaided efforts; the pit, therefore, was left to the *claqueurs.* The dress rehearsal was incomplete, and a failure. The manager was not present, which gave rise to reports which interested the actors far more than their parts. The first performance was to take place the next evening. The author arrived at the theatre at noon. He found M. Bocage there, who said to him,—

"You are aware that we are sold?"

"What do you mean by sold?"

"Sold in every way. Crosnier has sold the theatre; this was the reason he did not come yesterday. We are now without a manager. He has doubtless sold it to some-body, to somebody who will only take possession to-morrow. To-day things may take their own course. No-body commands and nobody obeys."

The theatre was altogether upset. The new manage-ment, on which every person holding a position was de-pendent, was of far more importance to the employés and the actors than the new play. The author went home to dinner and returned just as they were about to begin. Madame Dorval was looking through the hole in the cur-tain. She turned round quite furious.

"Ah, well, it will be a fine audience! But can you imagine a man such a fool as to enter into possession of a theatre the day after the first performance of a play? Much Crosnier cares whether the piece succeeds or not: he only thinks of this evening's profits; he has the whole house! I can read it in the faces of the people sitting in the stalls; those persons bought their tickets at twenty francs apiece on the boulevards, and we are expected to pay for them. See if it is not as I say!"

"Madame," said the author, "anger gives you animation, and you will act admirably!"

But this compliment did not pacify her, and she persisted in abusing both the old manager and the manager-elect in such very energetic terms that I really cannot repeat them.

M. Victor Hugo, hardened by what had taken place with *Hernani*, witnessed the raising of the curtain with as much tranquillity as if it had been the composition of another.

The first act was a success. The second was received somewhat coldly. In the third act, Madame Dorval, whom the character of Chimène did not suit, repeated the *Cid's* verses badly, and there was no applause for anybody but Le Gracieux, who was very amusingly represented by M. Sevres. The whole act was a failure. The drama picked up a bit at the fourth act. Madame Dorval was very melting when entreating the King to grant a pardon to Didier; the speech of the Marquis de Nangis brought down the whole house; the scene between Louis XIII. and Angely was exceedingly well performed by M. G——

and M. Provost, and had a great effect. At the fifth act
a lively opposition disturbed the scene between Didier
and Saverny. Didier made people laugh, and Saverny
made them hiss. But Madame Dorval entered, and so
acted, with such spirit, grief, and truth, that the men all
applauded and all the women wept. No words can describe the way in which she said,—

> " Ecoute,
> Ne me réfuse pas,—tu sais ce qu'il m'en coute !—
> Frappe-moi, laisse-moi, dans l'opprobre où je suis,
> Repousse-moi du pied, marche sur moi ;—mais fuis ! "

M. Bocage, who until then had been rather dull and
sad, was admirable also when he pardoned Marion :—

> "Eh bien, non ! non ! mon cœur se brise ! c'est horrible !
> Non, je l'ai trop aimée ! il est bien impossible
> De la quitter ainsi !—Non ! c'est trop malaisé
> De garder un front dur quand le cœur est brisé !
> Viens ! oh ! viens dans mes bras ! "

When the curtain fell there was a volley of hisses.
But the applause was decidedly predominant, and the
author's name was very warmly received.

M. Crosnier came up to congratulate the author, and
mentioned the hissing with all the unconcern of a man
whom it now interested no longer.

" It will do nicely," said he. " I only advise you to
cut off a great many heads."

As the author did not understand what he meant, he
explained to him that he had noticed that the word *head*
was repeated too often.

The fact that *Marion de Lorme* had been written first,
which was clearly proved by the two readings, one at the

Rue Nôtre-Dame des Champs and the other at the Théâtre Français, did not hinder several journals from asserting that Didier was a plagiarism of Antony. M. Bocage having had a slight illness, the play was interrupted at the fourth representation. Two disturbances, that of the *Chapeliers* and that of *La Pologne*, obliged them to close the theatre. It was the height of summer too, and the first representation took place on the 11th of August. All these causes injured the receipts, which were inferior to those from *Hernani*.

Although the performances of *Marion de Lorme* were less tumultuous than those of *Hernani* had been, they were also very much disturbed. The drama was but ill defended. The heroic bands of the Théâtre Français never returned; the new manager, who only looked in at the theatre every now and then, was represented by his stage manager, who was an author of *vaudevilles*.

In contradistinction to Mademoiselle Mars, Madame Dorval treated the author better in the green-room than when acting. This ceaseless struggle fatigued her, and she lost the spirit of her part. Her talent, moreover, required such an audience as she had had at the first performance of the play, and she was no longer herself before a less literary audience, or when the audience gradually became smaller as the play continued to be acted.

The author never had reason to repent of having upheld M. G——, whose gratitude and zeal never flagged for one moment.

LVII

THE CHOLERA.

AMONGST those who had fought for *Hernani* and remained faithful to *Marion de Lorme*, none had been more
ardent than M. Ernest de Saxe-Coburg. He was a fine
young fellow, whose intelligent face would not anywhere
have been passed by unnoticed. His mother was a
Greek, of a classical and statuesque style of beauty; he
resembled her, though with an admixture of the Saxon
race, for he had fair hair and blue eyes. He resided in
Paris with his mother, on a pension granted them by the
Duke. He lived alone and in a manner incognito, but
where art was concerned he was expansive and noisy.
On his return from these performances, in which he had
battled so bravely, he would scribble the author's name
on the walls. He was constantly in the Rue Nôtre-Dame
des Champs, and when Victor Hugo removed to the Rue
Jean Goujon, M. Ernest had determined not to be parted
from him, and he also removed to apartments in the same
street.

In March, 1832, some days elapsed without their

seeing him. This caused some surprise, and they went to look after him. He was ill, and the doctor told Victor Hugo that it was pleurisy, but that he would answer for his recovery if his mother could only be induced to attend to the prescriptions.

This poor woman, who had a blind adoration for her son, fancied that the doctor would leave him to die of hunger, and persisted in making him eat, giving that strength to the illness that she thought she was giving to the invalid.

M. Victor Hugo spoke to the mother about it, and she consented to obey rules, but did not keep her promise.

One night, M. Victor Hugo was suddenly awakened by a white spectre, kneeling at the foot of his bed, and pulling him by the arm, crying and sobbing. It was the poor mother, who, half naked and with her hair loose, was entreating him to come to the help of her son.

"Quick! You alone can save him! Come at once! at once!"

M. Victor Hugo got up. But a servant, who felt very anxious, had followed her mistress, and said to Madame Hugo, "He is dead!"

A heart-rending scene took place in the chamber of death. The unhappy woman, who had but this one child in the world to love, would not believe that he was dead. He was but cold!—and she threw herself on his bed, encircling him in her arms in order to impart warmth to the corpse. She frantically kissed his marble face, which was already cold. Suddenly she felt within herself that it was all over, she raised herself, and haggard and wild as she was, though still beautiful, she exclaimed, "He is dead!"

M. Victor Hugo spent the night by the side of the mother and the corpse. The doctor, whom they had immediately sent for, was surprised at this sudden death. He made some inquiries, and learnt that the sick man had taken food that very night.

In order that the mother might have something left to her of her dead son, M. Victor Hugo brought M. Louis Boulanger to the house, who took a beautiful portrait of the dead man. M. Victor Hugo undertook to see to the funeral, the expenses of which were, however, afterwards defrayed by the father. I have found the following letter on the subject :—

"Sir,   "Coburg, 30th March, 1832.

"I have just received your letter, which contains news that afflicts me greatly. I can hardly believe it, and am deeply affected by this event, as unfortunate as it was unexpected. I am not less affected at all you tell me concerning the last moments of my dear and excellent Ernest, but am still too much overcome to express to you all I feel.

"An unlucky fate had placed him in a false position. Removed from me, I have never been able to show him how deep was my attachment for him. I have never had any other interests than those concerning his welfare. That which you relate to me of his last moments proves in a touching manner that he did not misunderstand me.

" You will oblige me very much by sending me the portrait you mention, also the plan of the monument that is being prepared for my poor boy, together with an account of the expenses incurred. The reimbursement of the 2000 francs that you have been kind enough to advance should already have reached you.

" Accept, sir, the assurances of my lively gratitude for the proofs of friendship which you have given during this fatal illness to my dear Ernest; also, for the kindness you have shown his most unfortunate mother.

" I am, with the highest esteem,
" Yours devotedly,
" ERNEST DE SAXE-COBURG."

It was long before Victor Hugo forgot this sudden death and the despairing mother. He did not like remaining alone at night, he required movement and life.

The year dawned inauspiciously to all parties; the cholera was on its way. It was coming with rapid strides; its march was traced day by day, and it would reach France in the spring. It was punctual to the time appointed.

Its second victim in Paris was a porter living in the Rue Jean Goujon. The next day a score of persons were attacked; the day after the victims might be counted by hundreds.

When the epidemic was at its height, little Charles was brought home from school, pale and suffering. He had been vomiting. The servant said he had been poisoned. He had drunk some water at school, and as they were in the habit of poisoning the casks of the water-carriers, &c. This was the popular explanation of this unknown scourge. The family doctor, M. Louis, said it could only be indigestion, that it would be better to put the child to bed, and he left, promising to return soon. When in bed the child felt better, his vomiting ceased, they grew less anxious, and left him to go to sleep. On a sudden they heard a noise in the dining-room, and on hastening to the spot they found the child lying on his face beneath a marble fountain, of which he had turned the tap, and he was drinking eagerly. They wished to carry him away, but he fought against this, crying out, " Let me drink, I must drink." M. Louis, who had just entered the room, then said, " It is the cholera."

A few minutes afterwards the poor dear child became as rigid and cold as a corpse. The eye had sunk into its socket, the cheeks were hollow and livid, the fingers black and wrinkled. Among other measures recommended by the doctor, was that of continued friction with hot flannels moistened with spirits of wine. His father allowed no one to do this but himself; all night long he went backwards and forwards between the bed and the fire-place, heating the flannels, and violently rubbing the delicate skin of the child, who never ceased vomiting and asking for drink. The flesh became excoriated and bled. The sick child hardly felt it. Once only he said, " Don't touch me like that, you hurt me !" He kept on saying, " I am thirsty," but his bleeding skin remained cold.

Towards morning heat and sensation returned, and his face got back its colour. Three days afterwards joy had revisited the house on the restoration of the sick child, and Charles might truly say that he was "in a twofold sense, his pertinacious father's son."

About this time, M. Hugo received a visit from a young man, who spoke with a Southern accent. He had a black beard and hair, a sunburnt countenance, and an intelligent eye. This person related to him the following circumstance :—

His name was Granier de Cassagnac. He was from Toulouse, where he had distinguished himself, and where he was first nominated Professor of Literature to the Faculty. He was living there on his own exertions, delivering his lectures twice a-week, and employing the rest of his time in managing a Liberal journal which he had instituted. On one occasion, he received a letter signed Victor Hugo, thanking him for having quoted *Nôtre-Dame de Paris* and *Hernani* in his lectures, and congratulating him on his talent, both as a writer and as a speaker. It had rather astonished the young journalist professor that the writer begged for a reply, not directed to M. Victor Hugo's house, but to a friend's, whose address was given. No matter, delighted at being put into communication with one he so greatly admired, he had replied to the letter, and a correspondence had ensued, which became more and more frequent and friendly.

One of the subjects on which the letters most frequently touched was the regret the writer entertained,

that a man of such worth should be shut up in the provinces. He was earnestly advised to quit Toulouse and
come to Paris, but he had replied that at Toulouse he
had his professor's chair and his newspaper, and that
at Paris he had nothing. To which it was one day
urged, that he would no longer require either his newspaper or his chair, for that in Paris a situation worth
5500 francs in the secretary's office of the Minister of
Justice had been obtained for him. He had, prudently
enough, postponed the resignation of the post he then
held until he had secured his nomination : it had been
sent to him, officially sealed with the Minister's seal.
He then sold his newspaper, tendered his resignation
of his chair, and hastened to the great capital. As soon
as he had arrived, he had called at the office of the
Minister, where he had been laughed at, and where
he discovered that he had been the dupe of a long
mystification.

M. Victor Hugo, who read a few articles by this
young man in his journal the *Patriote,* and who considered them very remarkable, would not allow his name
to remain coupled with a perfidious trick played to a
talented man. He gave M. Granier de Cassagnac a
letter for M. Bertin. One of the editors of the *Journal
des Débats*, M. de Bourqueney, was about to leave on
receiving some diplomatic appointment, and M. de Cassagnac took his place.

LVIII.

" LE ROI S'AMUSE."

On the 1st June, M. Victor Hugo commenced *Le Roi s'Amuse*. Too much nightwork, and having looked too much at the setting sun, had given him a chronic irritation of the eyelids, and he had been ordered to wear green spectacles, to take a good deal of exercise, and to live in the open air as much as possible. He was living close to the gardens of the Tuilleries, and had discovered on the terrace which skirts the water a solitary corner where he could work whilst he was walking about.

On the 5th June he was just finishing the first act, and was writing the speech of Saint-Vallier, when he was turned out of the gardens because the gates were about to be closed. There was an insurrection; he went towards the spot where the fighting was going on, and as he was passing through the Passage du Saumon the gates were suddenly shut, and balls whistled from one entrance quite through to the other. There was no shop to be found in which he could take refuge, as the doors had all been closed before the gates were shut. All he could do was to shelter himself between two of the slender

columns in the passage. The shots continued for a
quarter of an hour, and, as the troops did not succeed
in dislodging the insurgents, they changed their position.
The combat took place in another neighbourhood, and
the gates were thrown open again.

The next day M. Victor Hugo was dining with' M.
Emile Deschamps. One of the guests, M. Jules de
Rességuier, was relating the heroic defence of the cloister
of Saint Merry, which deeply affected the future author
of *L'Epopée Rue Saint-Denis.*

Le Roi s'Amuse being finished, M. Victor Hugo immediately wrote *Lucrèce Borgia,* which he at first entitled *Le Souper à Ferrare.*

Baron Taylor, hearing that M. Victor Hugo had two
completed dramas, hastened to the spot. Surely there
would be one for the Théâtre Français ! M. Victor Hugo
must have felt that he had done wrong in giving *Marion
de Lorme* to the Porte Saint-Martin. *Hernani* had
caused quite a sensation; *Marion de Lorme,* which was
quite equal to *Hernani,* was far from having had so great
a success. The Théâtre Français was the real literary
theatre; verses especially were an impossibility on the
Boulevards, &c.; M. Victor Hugo allowed himself to
be persuaded, and gave them *Le Roi s'Amuse.*

Triboulet was allotted to M. Ligier; Saint-Vallier to
M. Joanny; Blanche to Mademoiselle Anaïs; Maguelonne to Mademoiselle Dupont; Saltabadil to M. Beauvallet; Francis I. to M. Perrier, contrary to the advice of
the Commissaire Royal, who recommended M. Menjaud,
and who was right.

The rehearsals then began. Unfortunately it was now

the month of September, and M. Victor Hugo had accustomed himself to spend that month in pleasant retirement at Les Roches. He would not deprive himself of his holiday, and allowed them to rehearse without him. Whilst the drama was thus taking its chance, the author was spending the last few days of summer in playing with his children beneath the green trees, and in working hard with Mademoiselle Louise Bertin at the manufacture of little birds, boats, and wonderful coaches, which he gilt, and which celebrated artists did not think it beneath them to paint, when they came on a visit to M. Edouard Bertin. It was a great pleasure to see the children when these fine carriages were given them, and when they were told that they were their very own, and that they might take them back with them to Paris. *Le Roi s'Amuse*, however, was not entirely neglected. M. Ingres was at that time taking M. Bertin's portrait; he came daily from Paris, and when he had to be back early he would sometimes carry off M. Victor Hugo with him, setting him down at the Théâtre Français.

October brought our author back to town, but the rehearsals were then complicated by another accident: he was about to leave the Rue Jean Goujon, in order to settle in the Place Royale, to which neighbourhood he was drawn by the fact that M. Charles Nodier would be in his immediate vicinity. The removal was hardly less an amusement than the visit to the country had been.

The theatres at that time were in the department of the Minister of Public Works. The Minister, M. d'Argout, sent to request that the author would communicate the contents of his manuscript to him. The author refused.

The Minister then begged that at least he would come and talk over the play with him. This did not commit him to anything, and the author allowed himself to be taken to the Minister's office by M. Merimée, who was at the head of the cabinet. M. d'Argout who was *blasé*, and easy-going, received him good-naturedly.

"Come, M. Hugo, speak to me in confidence. I am no puritan, as you know; but I am told that your drama contains insinuations against the King."

M. Victor Hugo replied to M. d'Argout, that which he had already replied to M. de Martignac, that he made no insinuations; that in depicting Francis I. it was Francis I. that he had meant; that no doubt, if any one was determined to do it, it would be possible to discover a sort of resemblance between Louis XIII. and Charles X.; but that it was quite impossible to imagine any resemblance between Francis I. and Louis Philippe.

The Minister then changed the subject, and told him that it was said that Francis I. was very much abused in the play; and that the monarchical principle would suffer from this attack on one of the most popular Kings of France. The author replied, that the interests of history were to be considered before those of royalty. M. d'Argout asked him whether he could not manage to modify certain details, but could get nothing out of him, and did not trouble himself further. He would have preferred there being nothing against Francis I. in the play, but since M. Victor Hugo gave him his word of honour that there was nothing in it against Louis Philippe, that was quite sufficient for him.

As at the Porte Saint-Martin, the *claqueurs* occupied

their usual seats. The young men, nevertheless, were more numerous than at *Marion de Lorme*. The faithful, with M. Théophile Gautier and M. Célestin Nanteuil at their head, amounted to 150, who dispersed themselves about the orchestra, stalls, and the second tier of boxes. They entered by the passage shortly before the rest of the audience. Political fermentation, which was kept up by the riots, had affected these young heads, and they greeted the entrance of the public by singing *La Marseillaise* and *La Carmagnole* at the pitch of their voices.

Just as the performances were about to begin, the news reached the theatre that the King had been fired at by an assassin. The conversation naturally turned on this subject, which interested everybody, and the curtain rose whilst the whole audience was thus preoccupied. Thus, the first act, which was, besides, very indifferently acted, went off in a manner which was chilly in the extreme. The scene of Saint-Vallier slightly modified this Siberian reception.

M. Beauvallet, who was first-rate in Saltabadil, kept up the interest in the first part of the second act, which was less important, when his first part was performed. M. Samson (Clément Marot) omitted these two lines,—

"Vous pouvez crier haut et marcher d'un pas lourd,
  Le bandeau que voilà le rend aveugle et sourd;"

so that it was not explained why Triboulet did not perceive that the ladder was propped up against his own wall, and also that he should not hear the shrieks of his daughter. Besides this, the carrying off of Mademoiselle Blanche was clumsily managed, and Mademoiselle Anaïs was removed with her feet higher than her head,

and this awkwardness made the play appear so defective,
that the second act finished amid a volley of hisses.

At the third act, the King entered, "clothed in a magnificent morning gown." They had copied the costume
of the performer on the double bass, in the well-known
picture of the "Wedding at Cana," by Paolo Veronese.
The boxes considered it unseemly that a King should
make his appearance in a dressing-gown, and Paolo
Veronese was hooted at.

Things improved a little at the moment when Triboulet
demands his daughter from the gentleman. The paternal
anguish of the buffoon gained the ascendency for a time
over the opposition party, but they afterwards revenged
themselves thoroughly at the very beginning of the first
line in the next act.

> " Et tu l'aimes?
> Toujours! "

These five words struck the audience as so comic, that
a hearty burst of laughter pervaded the whole house, in-
termixed with hisses. From that time, the hubbub never
ceased. It was in vain that Mademoiselle Dupont did
her best; in vain M. Beauvallet was admirable in his
costume, his manner, his sarcastic comedy, and fierce
recklessness. Saltabadil and Maguelonne were hissed at
every line.

Until then the combat had remained undecided. The
claqueurs, who bore malice about Hernani were but feeble
in their applause; but the hundred and fifty young men
fought vigorously. An accident in the getting up of

the piece was of service to the enemy. Whilst Triboulet is yet treading on the corpse of his daughter, which, owing to the darkness of night and the man's dress he fancies is that of the King, the King comes from the tavern singing the burden of a song and frightens the buffoon. The door, however, through which M. Perrier ought to have gone out was found to be locked and the effect was spoiled; the actor re-appeared at the extremity of the theatre, and no one knew from whence he came. This was the *coup de grace :* the audience had had enough of such a drama, in which the supernumeraries did not know how to carry off women, and in which the doors were not opened when they ought to be, and the conclusion was but a continued struggle where the applause was not indeed absent, but in which it was overwhelmed.

When the curtain dropped, M. Ligier approached the author.

" Shall I mention your name ? " said he.

Though a question, this was evidently meant as a suggestion.

" Sir," answered M. Victor Hugo, somewhat coldly, " I have rather a higher opinion of my play now that it is a failure."

The enemy, as in the case of *Marion de Lorme,* allowed the author to be named without further remark.

M. Victor Hugo went into Mademoiselle Anaïs's private box. M. Paul Delaroche, who did not know him, entered it almost at the same moment, rubbing his hands and exclaiming, " What a failure ! but then what a play ! Why would they act such pieces ? At least, they should

in future get rid of that Victor Hugo !" Mademoiselle
Anaïs was making signs to him which he could not
understand. He had never seen anything so wretched.
In *Hernani* a few good lines were to be found here and
there, but in *Le Roi s'Amuse* not a single one. The
actress was obliged to tell him that M. Victor Hugo was
present. M. Delaroche, who piqued himself on being
a perfect man of the world, became whiter than his cravat,
and tried to make up for his thoughtlessness. He had
been able to hear so little in consequence of the noise :
besides his opinion could only be taken as that of an
artist who never pretended to understand literary matters.
M. Victor Hugo's real enemies were his friends, who compromised his success by wishing to force the piece on the
house ; they were heard to sing the *Marseillaise :* had it
not been for them every one would have applauded.
Even in the midst of all the hubbub, he had noticed some
superb scenes. M. Victor Hugo stopped him just as
Le Roi s'Amuse was about to become a masterpiece.

The author went back home, unescorted now. He
retraced his steps to the Place Royale through a pelting
rain, and found his wife alone. Before going to bed he
cast a glance round the drawing-room, and threw some
water on a burning log which was not quite extinguished.

The next day he received the following note :—

"It is now half-past ten o'clock, and I have just received an *order* to suspend the performance of *Le Roi
s'Amuse*. M. Taylor has communicated this order from
the Minister.

"13*th November*."   "JOUSLIN DE LASALLE.

The former manager of the Porte Saint-Martin was now the stage manager of the Théâtre Français.

The reason given for this suspension was, that the play was an offence against public morality. The fact was, that a certain number of authors of the classical school, several of whom were members of the Chamber of Deputies, had set out in search of M. Argout, and had informed him that a play, the subject of which was the assassination of a king, was not to be tolerated the very day after the King had himself escaped assassination; that *Le Roi s'Amuse* was an apology for regicides; that the author's friends had sung *La Carmagnole,* and outrageously applauded the particular line which was so evidently intended for the King :—

> " Vos mères aux laquais se sont prostituées ! "

One friend only came to see M. Hugo on that day. It was M. Théophile Gautier.

The Ministers deliberated on the subject, and the play which had only been suspended in the morning was prohibited by night.

The author took no steps about it. He did not call on the Ministers but he went to the judges. He inquired of the Tribunal of Commerce whether, in spite of the Charter which abolished censure and confiscation, a Minister had any right to censure and confiscate a play. The Tribunal of Commerce replied in the affirmative.

M. Victor Hugo's advocate was M. Odillon Barrot, who advised him to address the court himself. As he had never before spoken in public, and did not know how he might go through it, he wrote down his speech. Several

copics of it were required for the journals; some young
men offered to help him with these, and M. Théophile
Gautier was the first to do so. They spent part of the
night before the cause was heard in making these copies.
The speech was a long one, and the dictation was not
over before two o'clock in the morning. It was then too
late to go home; for these formidable singers of the
Carmagnole had a wholesome dread of their own porters.
M. Victor Hugo's study was a capacious one, and by
the help of the sofa and a few mattrasses they improvised a dormitory.

On his way to the court, M. Victor Hugo fell in with
M. de Montalembert, who was also on his way thither.
They entered together. The hall of the tribunal was full
to overflowing with a sympathizing crowd. M. Victor
Hugo's discourse was applauded more than once, and the
president was several times obliged to call the public to
order. When M. Victor Hugo had done speaking he
was surrounded and congratulated. M. de Montalembert
told him that he was as great an orator as he was a writer,
and that should the doors of the theatre be closed to him
the tribunal was still available.

The Revolution of July had deprived M. Victor Hugo
of the pension of a thousand francs that Louis XVIII.
had granted out of his privy purse, and that Charles X.
had continued to allow him; but he still received the
two thousand francs allowed him by the Home Minister.
The ministerial journals taxed him with it. He immediately wrote to M. d'Argout as follows:—

"SIR,

"Ten years ago, in 1823, Louis XVIII., who was a literary monarch, granted, of his own accord, two literary pensions, to be paid out of the funds of the Minister of the Interior. These pensions were of two thousand francs each, and one of them was in favour of my noble friend, M. de Lamartine, the other being to me. It may be supposed that I recall this fact with great satisfaction.

"In 1829, at the time when the censure of the Polignac Ministry stopped the performance of *Marion de Lorme*, Charles X., wishing to make me amends for it, commanded that the pension of two thousand francs, which I was in the habit of receiving, should be increased to six thousand. I refused to accept this increase, which appeared to me in the shape of a bribe. My letter to M. de Labourdonnaye, your predecessor, is still to be seen in the Minister's portfolio.

"Until now, I have never considered this pension in any other light than as a recognition—exaggerated, if you will—of my literary efforts; as a legitimate indemnity for the numerous and exceptional taxes which, in France, fall so heavily on my profession; and, perhaps, during the last three years, as the interest of a capital of 47,000 francs, the sum which the two works which I have been allowed to see performed have, up to this time, yielded, in the form of the tax on hospitals. The various Ministries of the Restoration have, probably, seen the matter in the same light.

"But now that the Government appears to regard what are called literary pensions as proceeding from itself, and not from the country, and as this kind of grant takes from an author's independence; now that this strange pretension of the Government serves as the basis to the somewhat shameful attacks of certain journals, the management of which is, unfortunately, though no doubt incorrectly, imagined to be in your hands; as it is also of importance to me to maintain my relations with the Government in a higher region than that in which this kind of warfare goes on; without discussing whether your pretensions relating to this indemnity have the smallest foundation, I hasten to inform you that I entirely relinquish it.

"You may make yourself quite easy on the subject. I need not state that this incident, of very little interest in itself, is to me a reason that my opposition to the arbitrary act which has suppressed the performance of *La Roi s'Amuse* should maintain, more than ever, a character of dignity, reserve, and moderation.

"I remain, &c.,

"VICTOR HUGO.

"*Paris, 23rd December, 1832.*"

M. d'Argout replied that the pension was a debt due from the country, and that it should be reserved for M. Victor Hugo, in spite of his letter. It is needless to add, that M. Victor Hugo never made his appearance to claim a single farthing of it. Two years afterwards, a poor young girl, who was a poetess, Eliza Mercœur by name, being utterly unprovided for, he inquired of the Home Minister, then M. Thiers, whether it would be possible to allow Mademoiselle Mercœur this pension, which was then unclaimed. M. Thiers replied that the pension had been made use of, and that he was sorry to be unable to assist Mademoiselle Mercœur.

Amongst the letters received by M. Victor Hugo, relative to this drama and its suit, I notice the following :—

"Sir,   "*London, 3rd January,* 1833.

"I have received two copies of *Le Roi s'Amuse,* and on New Year's Eve we read it. Yesterday, after dinner, we were obliged to read it again. We cannot conceive why its performance was prohibited in Paris; ill-will may object to everything, and we have reason to believe that the Parisians are right in being annoyed that they are to be prevented from amusing themselves with *Le Roi s'Amuse,* which has greatly interested us. Our party only consisted of eighteen people; but I can assure you that your success was complete, so much so, that I made a boast of your friendship for me; to-day, I think myself obliged to own it, in order that you should justify my small vanity. Allow me to congratulate you. This work has interested me more than any I have read for a long time. None of the characters, it is true, excite so lively and perfect an admiration, as the heroes of works of the classical school. Here there is no absolute perfection; but in that leaden body of Triboulet how much pure gold may be found! What truth, nature, and depth in that malediction of Saint-Vallier! It is the voice of the living God pursuing powerful, yet degraded, man! I must conclude. I have neither time, talent, nor wish to sit in judgment on your play. I say to you what Molière's servant was in the habit of saying to him: 'It interests me, read on.' Your preface betokens a man of feeling and a true citizen. You have acquired the esteem of all who feel keenly and patriotically. I regret that your father, my friend Hugo, cannot be a witness of your efforts, and of that success which will surely follow after so many reverses.

"'Un Jeune Patriot' has printed a biography, which had appeared some years ago, relating to a writing of one of your brothers, M. Abel Hugo. I thought it my duty to reply to his kindness in sending it me by a letter, of which I enclose a copy. I have taken advantage of this opportunity to make manifest both my sentiments and my opinions; and I own that I was tempted to write the last few lines in the hopes of convincing honourable men like yourself.

"That which you say of Napoleon, when replying at the tribunal, seemed to require that I should state at present that which I hope one day to be able to prove, namely, that his despotism was only a dictatorship, which took its rise from the war, and would have ceased with it. Pitt, alone, desired war perpetually; and the event of the Restoration proved that, as representing the interests of the oligarchy and of the absolutism of the reigning houses of Europe, Pitt was in the right. The whole question between Napoleon and Pitt consists in this:—Which of them desired war?

"I have sufficient documents to prove that Napoleon always desired peace, and Pitt war. Both had reason on their side, as the leaders of the interests which they represented—those of ancient and modern Europe. The civilization of which you speak so properly in your preface was that which Napoleon desired; in order to attain to a peace with the great maritime Powers that should have been firmly consolidated, was necessary for that *Non lo conobbe il mondo mentre l'ebbe—conobb'il io!*

"If the approaching opening of Parliament could induce you to come and spend a few days here, how happy I should be to talk at length and openly with you; how useful it would be, in inducing the better knowledge of one of the greatest of historical characters, were I able to deposit in your keeping positive information, which, if shown in its true light, would make Frenchmen love him as much as I do! The sword with which M. de Chateaubriand always depicts him, was in his eyes but an arm of justice, and to the eyes of others, a shield with which he defended his country; he was obliged to attack others in order to defend himself.

"I have, before now, and since my nephew's death, asked many people to see you on my account. No one, that I know of, has as yet performed the commission I gave him. I have no time to allow my letter to be copied. Believe in the true esteem and in the lively sympathy I entertain for the son of my friend General Hugo.

"JOSEPH."

LIX

LUCREZIA BORGIA.

THE violent opposition with which all M. Victor Hugo's plays had been received, had somewhat discouraged the managers of theatres. Nobody came to him for *Le Souper à Ferrare*. The success his speech had obtained at the Tribunal, proved that he was living still. At the end of December, M. Harel, then director of the Theatre of the Porte Saint-Martin, was announced. M. Harel's eyes, silvery hair, and trinkets, all glittered.

"I have just been reading *Le Roi s'Amuse*," he exclaimed, before taking a seat. "It is superb! It needed the Théâtre Français to make such a thing as that fail. I am come to beg for *Le Souper à Ferrare*."

He then sat down, opened his snuff-box, and took a pinch noisily. He had M. Frédérick Lemâitre, Mademoiselle Georges, and a premium to offer. M. Victor Hugo knew that the theatre was almost entirely governed by Mademoiselle Georges, and would enter into no agreement until he had read his play in her presence. M. Harel, who was in a great hurry, begged that the reading might take place that very evening. It was held at the house of the actress. Mademoiselle Georges was delighted with her part, and M. Harel expressed unbounded admiration. In the very first act he applauded, blew his nose, took snuff by the handful, and shrieked out. The drama was in every way suited to him. First, he saw in it a first-rate part for Mademoiselle Georges, then a good bit of business for his theatre. Besides all this, he was very intelligent and very enthusiastic, and he was as much pleased in his capacity of man of letters, as in that of manager.

"It's too good," he said, "to be only called *Le Souper à Ferrare*. The title is neither important enough, nor grand enough. Were I you, I should call it simply and gravely *Lucrezia Borgia*."

M. Victor Hugo saw through the manager's motive, which was to please Mademoiselle Georges, by calling the piece by the name of the character she was to represent. The advice, though far from disinterested, was good, and the author accepted and acted upon it.

The next day, after the play had been read to the actors, M. Victor Hugo gave M. Frédérick Lemâitre his choice between Alphonse d'Este and Gennaro. M. Frédérick replied "that Alphonse d'Este was a brilliant and sure part, that all its effects being concentrated in one single act, it would carry the actor through safely, and that anyone could succeed in it." On the contrary, Gennaro's was a difficult part to act, the last scene was a dangerous one, and there was a terrible speech in it, "*Ah! vous êtes ma tante*," &c., and that in consequence of this, he chose Gennaro.

M. Victor Hugo wished M. Serres to take Gubetta, as

he had done very well in L'Angely. The manager
advised otherwise, and secured Gubetta for M. Provost.

At one rehearsal, the manager came to the author with
an embarrassed air, holding close to his nose a pinch
of snuff, which he seemed in doubt about taking.

"Monsieur Hugo, there is one favour I rather shrink
from asking of you. You are in the habit of giving the
orchestra up to the young men of your acquaintance. I
should like to seat them elsewhere; and have you any
idea who I should put in the orchestra? The musicians
themselves."

"With all my heart!" said the author.

"Really? You don't mind there being a little music
here and there? You allow me to have music at the
goings out and comings in, and in those situations where
it is required?"

"I ask it of you as a favour."

"Bravo!" said the manager, finally taking his pinch of
snuff. "There's a man for you! Can you conceive, now,
that Casimir Delavigne never would allow of any music
in *Marino Faliero!* He said it was all very well for melo-
dramas, but that it was not the custom at the Théâtre
Français. His tragedy would have been compromised, if
it had been seen in company with a violin. At least,
your literature is not a haughty prude!"

M. Meyerbeer and M. Berlioz offered, in a friendly way,
to compose the music for the song which was to be sung
at the supper of the Princess Negroni.

"Ah, just so!" said M. Harel. "Great musicians
who will compose music worth listening to, and which

Q 3

will take people's attention off the drama. I intend to have a tune which will grovel on its belly beneath the words. Let Piccini settle the music."

M. Piccini was the leader of the orchestra at the theatre. He selected a beautiful melody, suited to the words, but as for the chorus, he found nothing to satisfy him. He told the author how puzzled he felt.

"Nothing so easy," replied M. Victor Hugo. "You have but to follow the words. Listen."

And he began repeating the lines, accenting them with a sort of rhythmical chant. Never having been able to manage a single correct note in his life, he beat time on the prompter's table.

"I've got it," said the leader of the orchestra, who picked out the air from the taps on the table, and jotted them down on the spot.

It was time now to think about the stage arrangements. The day when they were deciding about the supper scene, the manager, seeing the author come in, ran up to him.

"Would you like to see the 'Cadran-Bleu?'"

He led him up to the orchestra. The decorations were decidedly a failure. Sideboards were set up between the windows, and on them were placed candelabra and pyramids of fruits, looking precisely like the shop window of a fashionable *restaurant*, and all this instead of the dazzling but gloomy hall imagined by the author, and intended to give the idea of a glittering tomb. In order that his ideas on the subject might be understood, he turned himself into a scene-painter, just as he had done into a musician, and he himself designed the kind of hall he required.

They went quickly through the rehearsals. M. Harel never allowed them to rehearse twice, book in hand. Mademoiselle Georges, who was delighted with her part, was as quickly ready as could be desired: she had, besides, none of the susceptibilities or pretensions of Mademoiselle Mars, and never took upon herself to give literary instruction to M. Victor Hugo. M. Frédérick Lemâitre, who had less need of advice than anyone else, was the most willing to take it from the author. His secondary part did not put him out of conceit with the play; he acted in it with his whole heart. He would assist his fellow-actors thus:—"That's not the way; here, say it more like this!" and would give the exact intonation. Sometimes, in order to show them what he meant, he acted their scene for them, and caused people to feel regret that he could not perform every character.

Until then, all M. Victor Hugo's dramas had been in verse. The young men inquired whether they ought to applaud the prose parts. They hesitated about it. A deputation of them, one of whom was M. Théophile Gautier, came to ask the author to be kind enough to read them some of the scenes from *Lucrezia Borgia* without telling him why. The reading satisfied the deputation, who declared that prose such as that was equal to any verse, and that they might manage safely enough.

The opposition journals denounced the play beforehand as the height of obscenity, stating that there was a frightful orgie in it. *Lucrezia Borgia* would share the

same fate as *Le Roi s'Amuse*, it would only be performed
once, &c.　Every one in Paris wished to see this single
representation, and the author received more letters about
it than he did about *Hernani*.　I take one from the pile
before me :—

"It is a long time since I had the pleasure of seeing
M. Victor Hugo, although I have much wished to congratulate him on his admirable theatrical defence.　One of
our friends was also commissioned to learn whether it was
possible to obtain a box for the first representation of his
new play.　The Princess de Belgiojoso had already tried
to secure one, but was too late, and she was told that the
author's protection was necessary in order to obtain it.
M. Victor Hugo will allow me to address him personally,
and, at the same time, permit me to take this opportunity
of renewing to him the assurance of my sincere attachment.

" 29th January, 1833."　　　　　　　　" LAFAYETTE."

Lucrezia Borgia, not occupying three hours in the
acting, would not satisfy the appetite of the public of the
Boulevards.　M. Harel caused it to be preceded by a
vaudeville, called *Un Souper chez Louis XV.*, on the
first night.　The author reached the theatre as the
vaudeville was about to begin.　He went to Mademoiselle
Georges' dressing-room.　She was dressing, and at the
same time chatting with M. Alexandre Dumas, M. Jules
Janin, M. Frédérick Soulié, &c.

" I have plenty of time, have I not?" said she to
M. Harel, who was leaving it.

" More than three-quarters of an hour. The little play has only just commenced."

She made no haste, she was radiant in beauty and confidence. All of a sudden a terrible hubbub was heard, and M. Harel returned in a state of great alarm.

" Be quick, dress yourself, you must be on the stage in ten minutes."

People had come to see *Lucrezia Borgia,* and they would not allow the *Souper chez Louis XV.* to be performed. They had had to drop the curtain after the first scene, and the impatient audience were calling out " *Lucrezia Borgia ! Lucrezia Borgia !* "

The manager rushed out of the box exclaiming, " Ring the bell for the curtain to rise."

The decorations of the first act were charming. In the first scene, when Gubetta says that both brothers loved the same woman, and that this woman was their sister, a violent hissing was heard.

" What ! They are hissing ! " said M. Harel, who was quite upset. " What does that mean ? "

" It means," replied M. Victor Hugo, " that the play was written by me."

But in the scene with Gennaro, Mademoiselle Georges read the letter with so touching an accent that the whole body was in arms. The insults from the young lords, which immediately followed upon it, proved irresistible. At every epithet lavished on the poisoner, the emotion increased, and the scene finished with a perfect fury of applause.

When, at the commencement of the second part of the

first act, Gennaro hears that his scarf had been sent to him by Lucrezia Borgia, and throws it from him in disgust, the scarf caught on the sword and on an ornament, which M. Frédérick had thought he ought to wear, and people began to sneer. Everything is a subject of triumph to great artists. M. Frédérick drew his sword, cut off the scarf and ornament, and crushed them beneath his foot, with an air and gesture so perfectly adapted to the part he was acting, that he drew down thunders of applause from all parts of the house.

The author, wishing to go to his wife's box, begged that the door of communication with the body of the theatre might be opened for him.

"Here is my key," said the manager. "I never part with it. But now you may be said to be master here."

In the interval between the acts M. Alexandre Dumas came to pay Madame Hugo a visit: he was transported with admiration and delight; this great success made him as happy as if it were his own; he wrung Madame Hugo's hands weeping for joy.

The author had never seen the decorations of the second act. When they were arranged he saw that the private door, through which Lucrezia Borgia was about to help Gennaro to escape, was bedizened with all sorts of ridiculous ornaments.

"That door is an absurdity," said he.

"Yes; that's true," said the manager. "They are told to make a private door, and they make you one prominent enough to put your eyes out."

"Is M. Séchan in the theatre?"

They went in search of M. Séchan, but they could not find him. The minutes fled by, and the pause between the acts had already lasted too long.

" Is there any paint at hand ? " said M. Victor Hugo.

" Yes; the painters have been at work all day, and have not taken away their things."

" Go and fetch me the pots and brushes."

They brought what he wanted, and the author commenced repainting his decorations. The hangings of the room were red, with golden lines. He covered with red all the ornaments of the door, and continued the golden lines over it so that it was not more seen than the rest of the hangings.

The act in which the Duke d'Este appears was a complete success from beginning to end. It was acted very fairly by M. Delafosse, and admirably by M. Frédérick Lemaître, who was, at the same time, simple and grand. As for Mademoiselle Georges, her powerful, though somewhat hard talent, exhibited a quality of feminine and almost feline flexibility, which had not till then been thought possible.

The public was completely secured. There was no interval between the two parts of the second act; some of the spectators, who thought that they should find time to go out, seeing the curtain rise returned hastily and disturbed the first scene. The public, however, would not lose a word of it, and insisted on its being re-commenced.

The supper scene went off very well. The young lords were crowned with flowers, notwithstanding M.

Harel, who insisted on it that this was only suitable for women. The public, in this matter, agreed with the author. Gennaro, gloomy, under the weight of his crown, immovable and cold as a statue, became immediately a source of anxiety to the audience. The interest of the piece, however, carried through everything : there was a truce in the literary war ; both the classical and the romantic school desired above all to know what was about to happen. Nobody troubled themselves about tragedy and the drama : it was no longer a question as to author, actor, or the stage. A son was about to be poisoned by his mother who adored him ; no one even applauded now ; when, suddenly, in the midst of peals of laughter and joyful songs, the mournful chaunting of monks was heard, and there was a universal shudder. In order that the chaunting should be quite correct they had selected, instead of supernumeraries, some genuine choristers belonging to the parish. The entrance of the monks, the contrasts between their cowls and the wreaths of flowers, the five coffins, the appearance of Lucrezia Borgia to the young men, the more terrible apparition of Gennaro to his mother, the last scene, everything was enthusiasm and transport : orchestra, galleries, boxes, everybody rose and applauded, both by hands and voice ; the stage was strewn with bouquets ; the name of the ' author did not suffice to the public, who must see the author himself. He was already in Mademoiselle Georges' dressing-room. M. Harel entered, quite scared, with disordered hair, and his dress more in disorder than usual.

" M. Hugo, save my life ! They insist on seeing you ;

they demand it of you; they are striding over the orchestra, and forcing their way into the theatre. You positively must make your appearance, or they will break everything they can lay hands on."

"M. Harel, I give to the public my thoughts, but I do not give them my person."

"But what can I say to them?"

"Tell them I have left."

M. Harel looked at his torn great-coat, which was white with the plaster on the walls, brushed one of his sleeves which had somewhat too thick a coat of it, buttoned the only two buttons left, ran his fingers through his hair, and said,—

"Now I am clean, I can show myself."

I have not spoken of the way in which the acting had been performed. The actors had so thoroughly identified themselves with their parts, that they had been forgotten in them. Mademoiselle Georges, titanesque, sinister, implacable in her vengeance, had been poignant in her expiation. M. Lemaître had electrified the audience, when he suddenly startles Lucrezia Borgia, whilst counting the coffins, "There must be a sixth, madame!" During the whole of the last scene he had acted with a depth and appreciation of his part which were admirable. He was one of the great elements of this great success. He never thought the worse of his part because it was only the third in importance; his only complaint was expressed in a reply to one of his friends, who remarked, "You acted superbly!"

"Yes," said he, "I was superb in abnegation."

M. Victor Hugo was awaited at the theatre door; the horses of the fiacre in which he and his wife and daughter were to be driven home were unharnessed; but he escaped by the other door and returned home on foot, escorted by the crowd till he reached the arcades of the Place Royale. Old friends who had abandoned him re-appeared that evening; unknown people begged to shake hands with the conqueror; the ovation which had com-menced under the lamps was continued under the stars.

M. Victor Hugo was awakened next morning by M. Harel brimming over with joy; his theatre was trans-formed; the Porte Saint-Martin was now the real Théâtre Français; he would only have art, and high art; he hoped that from henceforth the author of *Lucrezia Borgia* would never go elsewhere, and would enter into the same treaty with him that he had done with M. Crosnier. M. Victor Hugo, who had seen the manager's countenance fall at the hissing in the first act, would not bind himself to anything. M. Harel persisted in his demands that he would at least promise him another play. The author neither consented nor refused.

They suppressed the vaudeville, and *Lucrezia Borgia* was alone performed. The façade of the theatre was illumined every evening, and two municipal guards on horseback kept the crowd of carriages in order. The second and third performances were as successful as the first. M. Delafosse, who was consumptive, was replaced by M. Lockroy on the evening of the fourth representa-tion. M. Lockroy had left the theatre some time back, and his return added to the success of the piece. The

newspapers were disarmed, and were almost all in favour
of the play. The most enthusiastic article was that of
M. Jules Janin, in the *Journal des Débats*. Parodies were
acted in all the small theatres, and amongst others, that
of *L'Ogresse Borgia*; masks representing the principal
people in the drama circulated on the boulevards on
Shrove Tuesday, and halted under Mademoiselle Georges'
windows, exclaiming, "The Poisoner!" All this redoubled the general curiosity, and the receipts rapidly
accumulated. The following letter is a curious one, as it
authenticates the success, and mentions what were the
gross receipts at the theatre before railways had multiplied tenfold the fluctuating population of Paris :—

> "*Paris, 3rd November*, 1841.
"Sir,
> "The greatest monetary success obtained under
my administration is that of *Lucrezia Borgia*.
"The receipts of the three first performances present
a total of 84,769 francs.
"No other work has, under any management for more
than eight years, equalled or even approached this sum.
> "I remain, with sincere esteem,
> > "Sir,
> > > "Your very humble servant,
> > > > "Harel."

Lucrezia Borgia did not, however, entirely escape
hissing. The journals of the classical school, at first
taken by surprise and drawn along by the stream, soon

recovered themselves, and their approbation cooled down. M. Armand Carrel attacked the author in the *National*. He had a fresh grievance against him. Just at the time of the first performance he had been wounded in a duel, on account of the Duchess de Berri's pregnancy, which was denied by the Royalists, and asserted by him. The cause of the duel, the celebrity of the journalist, and his wound, had made this event the talk of Paris; the state of the sick man's health was announced every morning: people went to his house in crowds to write down their names; even Royalists would do so, and amongst others, M. de Chateaubriand. *Lucrezia Borgia* however, caused a diversion. This cause did not weaken the expression of opinion of the wounded journalist, who was always decidedly classical.

The example set by M. Armand Carrel was followed, at first in the journals, and afterwards by people in the body of the theatre; and every evening, from that time, there were a few hisses heard, on such occasions as when the mother pours out poison for her son, on the entrance of the monks, at the exclamation of *"Ah! vous êtes ma tante!"* &c.; but M. Victor Hugo's dramas were used to worse receptions than these, and *Lucrezia Borgia* troubled itself very little about the matter.

Many different causes conspired to foment a misunderstanding between the author and the manager. One evening, on his way to the theatre, M. Victor Hugo saw that the play-bill announced a change of performance. *Lucrezia Borgia* was still drawing large houses, and he had not been told anything about it. He entered

Mademoiselle Georges'. room, which might be considered as the real manager's office, and asked what the bill meant? M. Harel replied that it meant that he, being the manager, had a right to select the pieces which should be performed. The author asked what they had taken that day?

"2500 francs."

"And how much do you hope to make to-morrow by the change?"

"500 francs."

"Then, why do you interrupt me?"

"Because I choose to do so."

"So be it," said the author. "But bear in mind that you have performed the last piece you will ever get from me."

"The last but one," said M. Harel. "You forget that you promised me your next play."

"I never made you any promise."

The dispute became a warm one. The manager declared that the day after the first performance, and also several times in Mademoiselle Georges' room, a play had been promised him. The author replied that, both in Mademoiselle Georges' room and in his own, he had always said the same thing, namely, that he did not refuse, but that he should wait till he had written his play before he promised it.

"I assert," said M. Harel, "that you did promise it to me."

"And I," said M. Victor Hugo, "assert the contrary."

"Therefore you give me the lie."

" You may take it as you please."

On his return home M. Victor Hugo found the following letter :—

" Your persistence in refusing to keep the promise which you have given me frequently and before witnesses, and your declaring that *I may take it as I please*, I regard as a cause of offence.

" I therefore request satisfaction.

" Let me know when and where you will meet me.

"30th April, Evening."   " HAREL."

The next day, M. Victor Hugo rose early to look out for seconds. As he turned round the boulevard he saw coming towards him a National Guard, whom he did not at first recognize, but who turned out to be M. Harel.

" Monsieur Hugo," said the manager, " I wrote you a very foolish letter. Killing you would be an unlikely way of getting a play out of you, and it would not be a very great glory to you to have killed M. Harel. We had better be friends again. I am the offended party, nevertheless, I make the apology. Will you forgive me, and let me have your piece ? As a matter of course, *Lucrezia* will be performed this evening."

The author would not bear malice, and this time he promised him the piece.

" Faith," said M. Harel, " you are probably the first author to whom a manager has said, ' *Your play or your life !* '"

LX.

MARIE TUDOR.

At the end of August, M. Victor Hugo informed the manager of the Porte Saint-Martin that the promised drama was ready. M. Harel and Mademoiselle Georges were enchanted with *Marie Tudor,* as they had been with *Lucrezia Borgia*; and M. Harel begged harder than ever to have more plays from the author. M. Victor Hugo declined; but the manager contrived to make him promise one. The treaty concerning *Marie Tudor,* signed in a moment of mutual good understanding, did not allude to the getting-up of the piece. The director wrote to the author as follows :—

" .... It is a fine work, a very fine work. Its great success is more than probable. But, precisely because I rely on the intrinsic merits of the piece, do I intend to avoid, if you do not come to my assistance, incurring foolish expenses, which to my mind are also useless ones. The *Chambre Ardente,* by authors who certainly have not your reputation, was a success, although not a penny was spent on decorations. It will be the same with *Marie*

d'Angleterre, which will have every success without my
running the risk of ruining myself, or, at least, of seriously
inconveniencing myself, as I should do by useless expenses. These expenses, as I know you desire they
should be incurred, I should have undertaken at your
desire and at your responsibility. Am I unreasonable in
this matter? I think not; but, since you see things in
another light, let us say no more about it. To-morrow
the rehearsal will take place, and you will have a great
success entirely by the help of your great talent."

M. Victor Hugo was in the hands of the manager.
He therefore gave way; but undertook, in a fresh agreement, to write a third drama for the Porte Saint-Martin.
It was to be in prose, and of the usual length of pieces
in five acts. On this condition, M. Harel undertook, on
his part, to "follow exactly, both in the decorations of
the fourth part of *Marie d'Angleterre* and in the other
details consequent on the getting-up of the piece, every
indication given him by M. Victor Hugo." This article
did not appear sufficient for the author, who added the
following words:—"It is agreed upon and understood
that the getting-up of the piece shall be carried out,
both in respect to decoration and to costumes, with the
utmost possible brilliancy." M. Harel added everything
the author pleased, and gave splendid orders for the costumes and decorations. The expenses would no longer
ruin him now that he would have to incur them twice
over.

As in the preceding years, M. Victor Hugo spent the
autumn at Les Roches, but he came up daily for the re-

hcarsals. M. Bertin, who was driving him home one day, showed him some proofs which he was bringing away from the *Journal des Débats*. It was a fly-sheet of M. Granier de Cassagnac, very inimical to M. Alexandre Dumas, and very glowing towards M. Victor Hugo. As it was well known that M. Granier had obtained his situation in the *Débats* through the influence of M. Victor Hugo, it might have given rise to the idea that M. Victor Hugo had prompted the article, and that M. Bertin wished to speak to him on the subject before publishing it. M. Victor Hugo thanked M. Bertin; but told him that M. Alexandre Dumas was his friend and companion-in-arms, and quite recently, during the performance of *Lucrezia Borgia*, he had found him exceedingly cordial, and that he should feel most uncomfortable at being supposed to injure him even in the slightest matter. M. Bertin promised that the article should not appear. The following week M. Bertin, on opening the *Journal des Débats*, which the postman had just left at Les Roches, made an exclamation. The article was there. He ordered his carriage, and set off for Paris. M. Becquet, who undertook the management of the newspaper in his absence, not having copy at hand, had inquired if there was anything composed. He was told that he would find on the table an article by M. Granier de Cassagnac; but that M. Bertin, the last time he had come, had said it was not to appear until further notice. He did not think it was meant to forbid its insertion; and, not having anything else to put in, he had looked over a passage which struck him as very well written, and had therefore inserted it.

"The fact is," said M. Bertin, who was very much displeased, "that you only read the abuse of Alexandre Dumas; if you had read the part in which Victor Hugo is praised, you would have thrown it into the waste-paper basket."

The article was signed G. C. Some people thought they were fancy initials, and that it was written by Victor Hugo himself—many even said as much. The moderate party recognized it as having proceeded from the pen of M. Granier de Cassagnac, and said that Victor Hugo had only suggested it. M. Bertin stated the exact truth in *Les Débats,* and also related M. Victor Hugo's strong wish that the article should not appear. But it was too useful a calumny to be allowed to drop just as another drama by Victor Hugo was about to be acted; and the falsehood was upheld and circulated by all the enemies of *Lucrezia Borgia.*

M. Harel bethought himself that the moment was inopportune for Victor Hugo, and favourable for the other. He had therefore no scruples in deserting *Marie Tudor,* and in going over to Alexandre Dumas, to whom he offered his theatre. He returned with two dramas —*Angèle* and *La Vénitienne*—and the only thing now was to get rid of M. Victor Hugo as quickly as possible. Mademoiselle Georges still clung somewhat tenderly to her part. Marie Tudor was as good as Lucrezia Borgia; but a very effective part was allotted to her in *La Véni-*

tienne, which comforted her under her loss; so she consented to the sacrifice. The thing was settled simply enough. A few days previous to the performance, at the bottom of the bill, there appeared the following words :—

Immediately,
MARIE TUDOR.
Shortly,
ANGÈLE.

In this way the public knew all about it beforehand. M. Victor Hugo was displeased, and *Angèle* disappeared from the bill; but the first blow had been struck. Although hostility was no longer openly proclaimed, still it was none the less deep for that. Every day there were quarrels in the green-room, because the author had distributed the parts, and the manager considered that they were not done justice to. One of the parts was that of the Jew, performed by M. Chilly, whom M. Harel considered too young. M. Victor Hugo, who was much pleased with M. Chilly, and who also happened to know a circumstance which reflected great credit on him, insisted on his keeping the part. M. Harel had no better success with the others.

Meanwhile, all kinds of rumours against the play were being spread about. The friends of the author grew anxious. One of the best and most intelligent wrote to him as follows :—

" I hear on all sides, my dear Victor, that your play is more than ever a tissue of horrors—that your Mary is a blood-thirsty creature, that the executioner is perpetually on the stage, and several other reproaches, all equally well founded. I should have liked to have come to Paris myself, in order to have a chat with you on the subject; but I shall only be able to get there next Wednesday morning. I have every reason to believe that your enemies are more than ever disposed to do all in their power to prevent your success; and that the presence of the executioner on the stage is the watchword given to the ill-disposed. Is the arrival of the executioner in the second act, and his presence in the procession in the fourth, really necessary to your drama? Would it be less effective without him? And would it not be more prudent to give up the point out of consideration to the susceptibilities of a part of the audience? As for me, after all 1 have heard said in the last two days, I think it my duty as a friend to persist in doing my utmost to persuade you to do so. I am aware that the executioner has been introduced upon the stage by others besides yourself without any complaints from the public; but latterly people have thought very much on the subject, and even now dwell on it more than you can conceive; and I am very much mistaken if that particular scene between the queen and the executioner in the second act does not expose your play to great danger. I am so annoyed by the idea, that I thought I ought to communicate to you. If, nevertheless, you think otherwise, I need not tell you that I should be only too happy to be found in the wrong.

" Yours, with all my heart,

" E. B."

On the eve of the first performance, M. Victor Hugo, on leaving the theatre, was followed as far as the portico by M. Harel.

"M. Hugo," said the manager, "you have quite resolved on not changing the parts?"

"It would be rather late to make any change, considering that to-morrow the play will be performed."

"I have made every one learn double parts. Do you consent?"

"No."

"Well, then, your play will be a failure."

"You mean that you intend that it shall be so?"

"You may interpret my words as you please."

"Well, then, M. Harel, if my play fails, I shall take care that your theatre does so too."

These were the last words interchanged between the author and the manager previous to the battle.

M. Harel was to have sent the author 250 tickets—he sent but fifty. M. Victor declined them all, and only accepted a private box for his wife. Some of the author's friends, much annoyed at not having seats secured to them, applied to M. Alexandre Dumas, who with his usual disinterestedness, gave them an entrance.

When Victor Hugo arrived at the theatre on the evening of the performance, he did not go as usual to Mademoiselle Georges' apartment, but immediately proceeded to the green-room. One of his friends found him there, and showed him, from the prompter's box, several copies of the *Journal des Débats*, which were being circulated in the orchestra and galleries; these were the numbers containing the article written by M. Granier de Cassagnac.

Whilst he was looking at this, a messenger was sent to tell him that Mademoiselle Georges wished to speak to him. He did not hurry away, but remained chatting with his friend. The three blows were struck; and then the author set out in search of the actress. She received him coldly, told him that he came too late, that now the curtain was raised, and that she had nothing more to say to him.

The first act, in which Mademoiselle Georges performed, was but little applauded. M. Frédérick, whom the author had selected to act Gilbert, was not at the theatre at that time, so the part had been allotted to M. Bocage, and finally, after one of the skirmishes attendant on these stormy rehearsals, to M. Lockroy, who, though a man of talent, had none of M. Bocage's authority, and certainly in that particular fell very far short of Frédérick Lemaître. M. Chilly proved that the manager was in the wrong, by performing the Jew in a first-rate manner.

Mademoiselle Georges was dazzling. Half-reclining on a couch, dressed in scarlet velvet, and crowned with diamonds, hers was a really regal style of beauty. The insult addressed to Fabiani she spoke with a great appearance of truth, and a superb familiarity. Everything went on well till the executioner made his appearance. The author had made no alteration, and his appearance was evidently the signal for the attack to begin.

The whole of the third part, and especially the scene between Gilbert and Jane, was received with perpetual sneers. The procession to the execution, in the last act, was, however, most effective, and the executioner, who had been hissed in the second act, was applauded in the fourth. But the hisses soon gained the ascendancy. Even Mademoiselle Georges herself was not spared; her imprecation against London was stormily received; the great final scene between the two women was hissed from beginning to end. Notwithstanding this, there was a strong feeling on the other side, and a very considerable proportion of the audience had protested against this attack. The author's friends asserted that, although a few stray hisses had certainly been heard to proceed from the boxes and stalls, the disturbance and hissing had principally sprung from the pit, which had been given up to the *claqueurs*, that is to say, which was influenced by the manager. In fact, the evening was in no way decisive. There was a great difference between this play and *Le Roi s'amuse*, the latter having been undoubtedly hissed and crushed by the public; this was a combat, but not a defeat.

One difference between this and *Le Roi s'amuse* was, that for the first time the author's name was received with hisses.

M. Victor Hugo hastened into Mademoiselle Georges' box, as he was curious to see how she bore those hisses, which were meant for her. She was furious.

" There was a queer set in the house," said she.

" In the house ?" was all that he replied.

M. Harel entered at that moment, and the actress

loudly reproached him for having allowed her to be hissed. M. Hugo left them to fight it out together.

The actress who performed the character of Jane being seriously unwell, they were obliged to announce no performance for the next day. The journals were very hostile. After the fourth performance, *Angéle* was again announced on the bill. Notwithstanding this, the receipts, although inferior to those of *Lucrezia Borgia,* were so good that the manager was obliged to withdraw the announcement once more, and *Marie Tudor* was performed so often as to be more than an ordinary success.

M. Hugo and the Porte Saint-Martin could have no further dealings with each other. Even M. Harel acknowledged the fact, and the treaty which had been signed in favour of a third drama was cancelled by mutual consent.

LXI

ANGELO.

In the early part of the year 1834, M. Victor Hugo wrote *L'Etude sur Mirabeau,* which was a decidedly revolutionary work. His ideas had expanded since writing his first odes, which were so blindly Royalist. He felt the necessity of inquiring into the road over which he had travelled, of glancing back at the various halting-places, of comparing the present with the past, and of rendering an account of himself. As he was quite sure that he had never listened to any voice save that of his conscience, and had nothing either to deny or to hide, he made this examination of his conscience a public one, and published it in his *Littérature et Philosophie Mêlées.*

The failure of *Le Roi s'amuse* had not prevented the Théâtre Français from asking him for another play, since *Lucrezia Borgia* had been so wonderfully successful. M. Jouslin de Lasalle having returned in February, 1835, M. Victor Hugo replied that he was then putting the finishing touches to a drama which required two first-rate actresses. The Théâtre Français had already Mademoiselle Mars; and Madame Dorval, who was not engaged, might be had, but it was necessary to ascertain whether Mademoiselle Mars would consent to act with Madame Dorval. As for the latter, she did not mind with whom she acted.

The author read *Angelo* to Mademoiselle Mars. The actress then lived in the Rue de la Tour des Dames, in a house which was reached by an avenue and by stairs in the form of an amphitheatre. M. Hugo was shown into a drawing-room, furnished according to the taste of the Empire. The more modern taste was represented by a picture-clock, the picture being a village church, of which the steeple clock was real, and chimed the hours. These chimes mixed themselves up with the reading of *Angelo*.

Victor Hugo had not seen Mademoiselle Mars since he had refused her *Marion de Lorme*. She was very good-natured, listened attentively to the play, told him that he was very much improved in his reading, and praised the drama in terms which she had not been in the habit of using to the author of *Hernani*.

"Most decidedly, I will act in it," said she, "and in company with your Madame Dorval! Both the parts are very fine. Come, be quick; which is meant for me?"

"Whichever you please."

Catarina, who was depicted as a chaste married woman, was very suitable to the honest and decent tastes of Mademoiselle Mars; but La Tisbé, a passionate and undisciplined prostitute, seemed made on purpose for Madame Dorval whose tastes were roving and free.

Mademoiselle Mars selected La Tisbé as a matter of course.

The drama in its original state was in five acts. The death of Homodéi, instead of being a mere description, was acted. Rodolfo was about to punish the spy in a room occupied by bandits, a kind of boozing-ken, where wine and blood were intermingled. After the reading to the committee, M. Taylor and M. Jouslin de Lasalle came in search of the author; the act in which the bandits were introduced made them feel anxious. The failure of *Le Roi s'amuse* had been partly owing to the drinking scene of Saetabadil; the filthy den of Homodéi would cause *Angelo* to be a failure. It was not a necessity in the drama. The death of Homodéi might be related in a few words; and they obtained from the author the suppression of the act.

The rehearsals were remarkable as bringing together two celebrated actresses. Mademoiselle Mars treated Madame Dorval with the haughty aristocracy of a performer on the staff of the Théâtre Français, who had been forced into contact with one who had emerged from the Boulevards. She felt, nevertheless, that she had in her a formidable rival. She was both humiliated and alarmed at it; and her manner was a curious mixture of contempt and hatred. As for Madame Dorval, she was yielding and caressing. She would reply to coarse speeches by flattering words; she was quite willing to own that she had been very bold in venturing to place her melodramatic foot on the noble boards of the Théâtre

Français. She became quite humble and small, but had every intention of making up for it in public.

She would go though the rehearsals, speaking below her breath; she threw no effect into her acting, and was dull, extinguished, and nowhere. Mademoiselle Mars took heart, and was congratulating herself on the good arrangement she had made in selecting the part least suited to her; but how very much more ill-suited Catarina was to Madame Dorval! A woman who had no restraint or decorum about her, was to represent a character full of purity and dignity! It would be a lucky chance if she did not get hissed. But at one rehearsal Madame Dorval forgot herself, and acted in such a style that Mademoiselle Mars lost all hope. She could not contain herself; and in the third act interrupted Catarina's outbreak of passion against Angelo and La Tisbé thus:—

" Tell me, Monsieur Hugo, what kind of expression I ought to wear whilst madame is abusing me in this agreeable manner. Don't you think that the unpleasant things she says to me are rather drawn out ? "

" They are not longer than those which you say to her in the preceding act, madame."

" As for me," said Madame Dorval, " I don't think madame spends too much time in abusing me. When there are such fine speeches in a play, I am as fond of hearing them as of saying them."

Mademoiselle Mars said no more about it. But the next day she found out that she had many useless things to say; that she could not manage all those fine phrases, and that her part must be very much abridged. The author declined clipping any part of it, and Madame Dorval was allowed to repeat her whole part.

Madame Dorval having once betrayed herself, always now did her best. Catarina, who had been poisoned by her husband, adjourned to her oratory, there to die. Madame Dorval was so touching and true in this scene, that a few of the spectators who were present applauded.

At the conclusion of the act Mademoiselle Mars came up to the author, and said, trying to force a smile :—

" You never take my advice. Nevertheless, I am come to give it you again. Were I you I should kill Catarina in another way. Always poison ! You introduce it into *Hernani,* into *Lucrezia Borgia,* and now again into *Angelo.* Really, it is overdoing the thing. In the first place, it is very disagreeable to witness those contortions. It was all very well in *Hernani,* being the first time."

" It was not the first time, madame; I did not invent poison. I only make use of it as Corneille did in *Rodogune,* or as Shakespeare did in *Romeo and Juliet,* which did not prevent his again making use of it in *Hamlet.* It had been employed many times before *Hernani* appeared, and it will be often made use of after *Angelo* is forgotten, by myself the first."

Seeing that nothing was to be done in this way, the actress proceeded to open war; and at the next rehearsal, just as Madame Dorval was advancing with faltering steps towards the oratory, Mademoiselle Mars, who was quite at the other side of the stage, came across, and positively stationed herself in such a position as to hide Catarina from the spectators.

This was going too far. The author stepped in, and reminded the actress that her place was on the other side of the stage. She replied that she felt more comfortable where she was. M. Victor Hugo informed her that he was of a contrary opinion, and that the author was the best judge of what was suitable to the piece. She observed that the actress was the best judge of what was suitable to the actress. It was lost time speaking to her; she absolutely refused to stir. He then lost all patience, just as he had done in *Hernani*. He declared that he had often known envy, but that this was the first time he had ever seen it unblushingly avowed; that women who exposed their persons appeared to him as emblems of modesty by the side of this exposure of self-love. And for what? What did Mademoiselle Mars hope to gain by it? She could easily have crushed poor beginners of no reputation, and as yet unknown; but did she for a moment imagine she was likely to destroy Madame Dorval, her equal in talent and success? And as she shuddered at these words, he repeated them:—"Your equal, I tell you, in talent and in success! And if my words offend you, you are at liberty to give me back the part. As it is, it is useless to go on with the rehearsals. Either the play shall be acted as I wish, or it shall not be acted at all!"

Having said this, he closed the proceedings, and left the theatre.

In the evening M. Harel was announced. He had

heard of the commotion at the Théâtre Français. He had behaved very ill to M. Victor Hugo, he acknowledged it; he had been well punished for it; his theatre had been going down in the world ever since; he repented, owned his fault, and had but himself to blame. If M. Hugo would forgive the offence and let him have *Angelo,* he would engage Madame Dorval, whom the Théâtre Français would be only too glad to get rid of, and he still had Mademoiselle Georges—she would act Tisbé in quite a different style to Mademoiselle Mars. The author replied that, as yet he did not know whether Mademoiselle Mars would persist in her refusal, but that even were he to deprive the Théâtre Français of *Angelo,* he should not think of allowing the Porte Saint-Martin to have it.

"I am very sorry for you if you really require my assistance. But I always say what I mean. You told me that *Marie Tudor* would be a failure, and you kept your promise; I told you that your theatre would be a failure, and I shall keep mine!"

Many times after that day M. Harel trod the stairs of the author of *Marie Tudor.* He begged him, implored him, offered him every conceivable advantage. M. Victor Hugo would always receive him politely, and enter into conversation with him, but when he begged for a play he invariably refused him. It is well known that M. Harel became a bankrupt.

During the evening Victor Hugo received a letter from Madame Dorval:—

"If Mademoiselle Mars will not consent to your wish let her do as she pleases. My success does not depend on this exit only, but on all those adorable things she cannot take from me. Tell me if it was only your own work you were defending? I thought at the time, and I have since thought, that you also wished to protect me, and I feel proud and happy at the idea. But do not get out of patience with Mademoiselle Mars; you are always forming resolutions which make me tremble. If I had to give up this part, which is the only link which unites me to the theatre, I should be very unhappy."

The manager was no less a suppliant.

"On my arrival I find that you have again encountered difficulties as to the places in which the actors must be stationed on the stage, and that you will not return to witness the rehearsals of your own play unless Mademoiselle Mars does as you wish. I think you are in the right in demanding obedience to your rules. But is it quite indispensable to the success of the piece that the position should be the very one you select? Could it not be managed so as not to injure you and to satisfy every one? It appears to me that every one taking up a position a little more to the front, or, rather, more on one side, cannot mar the success of a piece like yours. I am sure you will agree with me, that, after much study, much expense incurred, and a very difficult result partly obtained, it would be cruel to stop short just as the play is about to be acted. Do be persuaded; come to the rehearsal to-morrow, and we will settle the matter. Just fancy in what a plight I should find myself, and do for a poor manager that which you would not do for yourself. I rely on you for to-morrow, and pray come in a conciliatory mood."

M. Victor Hugo went to the rehearsal the next day. Just as Catarina was about to die, Mademoiselle Mars went of her own accord to the spot he had selected for her. She was very much softened. After the rehearsal she begged he would come and look at her dresses. He did so, very willingly. He had formerly brought her some very beautiful drawings of M. Louis Boulanger, in the style of the pictures and engravings of that day, in order to facilitate the arrangement of her costume as Doña Sol. She had thought them hideous, and had told him to take away those daubs. She had dressed up Doña Sol in a head-dress which had been the astonishment of all the painters, and very numerous they were, who had been present at the performance of *Hernani*. Doña Sol's head-dress reappeared on the head of La Tisbé with embellishments which left one undecided as to whether it was intended for a turban or for a carriage-wheel.

"Ah!" said the author, in consternation, "do you mean to wear that again?"

"Yes, the head-dress becomes me! it makes me look young! You have seen my portrait by Gérard as a Muscovite? I wore that head-dress."

M. Hugo hazarded the remark that La Tisbé was not a Muscovite but an Italian, but he did not say much about it, being unwilling to quarrel afresh on a mere question of dress.

On the eve of the performance he took care to see the bill of the play. Just as he had foreseen, the name of Mademoiselle Mars had a line to itself, and that of Madame Dorval appeared in quite a subordinate place, even after those of the supernumaries.

"There is some mistake here!" he said.

"Where?" said the stage-manager.

"Madame will tell you!"

Mademoiselle Mars was present; M. Victor Hugo handed her the bill.

"Oh, I never meddle with the bill!" said she, turning from him abruptly and leaving the room.

The manager remarked that the line to itself was a privilege belonging to Mademoiselle Mars; that all except herself were on an equality, and their names were put down in order of seniority; and that, as Madame Dorval was the last new-comer, she must be the last on the list. M. Victor Hugo replied that Madame Dorval who had been specially engaged for this drama, was not on the footing of the rest, and that as they could make an exception in favour of one person they might easily make one in her favour. Madame Dorval, therefore, also had a line to herself.

Mademoiselle Mars was in a very bad humour whilst dressing for the performance.

"Excuse my not talking," said she to the author. "But you are the cause of my being hurried, as you introduce me at the first scene. You are aware that this is the first time I have acted on the rising of the curtain."

Our hero went to Madame Dorval's room in search of

kinder greetings. She threw her arms round his neck, told him she had never had such a fine part, that she doted on it and on Tisbé too, and on the whole play, and she called on her husband, who was present, to say if it was not so. "Is it not so, Merle?" M. Merle acquiesced, less coldly than usual; he was by nature very indifferent to what was going on, and feared to be thought vulgar if he was as demonstrative as his wife.

In the body of the theatre were stationed two distinct kinds of public, the admirers of Mademoiselle Mars, and those of Madame Dorval; the one grave, affected, starched, biting their lips;—those rich or titled people, whom artists call the *bourgeois;* and the other set earnest, young, lively, noisy and disorderly spectators, whom the world calls *bohêmes.*

The appearance of Mademoiselle Mars was warmly welcomed both by *bourgeois* and by *claqueurs.* The *bohêmes* kept silence. The first act interested and delighted everybody. M. Beauvallet was a taking Angelo. Mademoiselle Mars recited, without feeling it is true, but still with a very well-acted tenderness, the speech of the mother saved from the gallows. The *key* scene was one more like those to which she was accustomed. She enunciated sharply every word of it, and was applauded in it from beginning to end. During the whole act there was not a single moment of opposition.

It was now the turn of Madame Dorval. When she made her appearance the *bohêmes* tried to get her up an " *entrée,*" but they were kept down by the bourgeois and also to a certain extent by the *claqueurs.* The great actress felt that it was to be success or death, and performed her part not with her ordinary but with her extraordinary talent. She was so real, so youthful in her passions, and so chaste in her renunciation, that even the *bourgeois* were carried away by it, and almost began to suspect that there was a vast difference between an acquired and a spontaneous talent.

Mademoiselle Mars was in the green-room awaiting her turn.

"Well," said she to the author, " I hope your actress has been sufficiently applauded."

" To which of the two do you allude ?" politely asked he.

" Oh, to the one to whom you allotted the best character."

M. Victor Hugo was about to reply that she had chosen her own part herself, but he at that moment perceived in the hand of Tisbé the lamp with which she enters into the chamber of Catarina. It was a tragic and mythological-looking lamp, evidently picked up amongst the ruins of Herculaneum. He took no notice of it, in order not to irritate the actress just as her principal scene was about to take place, but he could not hold his tongue when he saw her crowned with the eternal head-dress. He reminded her that in order to save Catarina she told Angelo that she was wearing the cloak of a man, and that she also wore a hat, and the spectators would be likely to inquire how Angelo could possibly mistake a turban for a hat.

" Pooh ! " said she, " do you think people notice such trifles as those ? "

And Tisbé went into Catarina's chamber, holding in her hand an antique lamp, and wearing a Russian cap. She was right; the audience appeared to take no notice of the fact.

Mademoiselle Mars had none of the vehemence and passion which were necessary in the character of Tisbé. She was but mediocre in it. Madame Dorval in a few words ensured success for herself. Mademoiselle Mars, who was decidedly her inferior in the scene of the insult, regained her superiority in the scene of the sacrifice, and refuted Angelo's suspicions with such melancholy noble-ness that soon the equality of the two rivals was pro-claimed.

At the third act, by one of those strange fatalities in performances which put to rout the surest previsions, Madame Dorval acted badly that very scene in which she had excelled at the rehearsals. She was wanting in authority in her revolt against her husband; her exit, so much dreaded by Mademoiselle Mars, was applauded, but without enthusiasm. The great success of the act was for M. Beauvallet, who, standing erect in his close-cut scarlet coat, with bare neck and closely-clipped hair, looked sternness itself, and as inflexible as marble.

The last act was very nearly compromised by an acci-dent in the getting-up. It had been foreseen that if the cold air from the side scenes suddenly came in contact with the heated air of the crowded body of the theatre, it would agitate the curtains of the bed in which Catarina, who is supposed to be dead and buried in the palace vaults, lies concealed. They had provided against this inconvenience by sewing bars of iron to the curtains and hanging weights from them. But the draught of air was such that the weights were of no use. Two mechanics were obliged to lie down on their faces under the bed and keep down the curtains; but, in spite of this, the wind made it tremble in their grasp, and every now and then they were seen by the audience, who quite enjoyed the fun. Mademoiselle Mars got uncomfortable, and performed her part awkwardly, and the play would have come to an unlucky end had it not been for Madame Dorval, who gracefully awoke, full of surprise, and acted so charmingly that success was restored. When Rodolfo took her in his arms, she had all the lightness of a shadow returning to life, and all the poetry of Eurydice brought back to earth.

The drama ended at *"Par moi, pour toi."* Mademoiselle Mars had won over the author to cut out the rest, saying that the play really ended there, that the audience now knew all about it and would not listen to the concluding sentences; but Mademoiselle Rachel, who acted Tisbé in 1850, repeated the whole of the part, and the last phrases were listened to and applauded.

Taking everything into consideration, *Angelo* was successful. It continued to be so during the succeeding performances. Mademoiselle Mars had resigned herself to Madame Dorval's success, and was satisfied with her own. The author had but one more quarrel with her, and that was on a matter apart from theatrical interests.

Just then the trial of M. de Laroncière was proceeding in reference to the affair of Mademoiselle Morel. The court held night sittings because Mademoiselle Morel, who was ill and light-headed, was only sane at midnight. M. Victor Hugo attended one of these nocturnal audiences. He saw the accused, a young man of middle height, with a dark complexion and a chiselled and refined-looking face. He had not so good a view of the accuser; she made her appearance at the solemn hour, her face covered by a thick veil which she wore over a straw bonnet. She gave her testimony in a clear and distinct manner. M. de Laroncière rose, and most respectfully and, at the same time, with the most penetrating glance, asked her if she was quite sure of the infamous deed which she attributed to him, whether she was not making a mistake in identity, if she was not still under the influence of some fatal vision, or whether, without his knowledge, he might not have done something against her for which she was desirous of revenge. She drily made answer that she had spoken the truth. M. de Laroncière sat down again quite annihilated.

Victor Hugo had been struck by the dignified attitude and appearance of sincerity in the accused; he was already quite inclined to believe in his innocence since hearing the act of accusation against him. The next day he happened to be in Mademoiselle Mars's room; every one was talking about the trial, and they, too, were conversing on the subject. M. Victor Hugo observed that he believed in the innocence of the accused.

On hearing this Mademoiselle Mars rose from her seat, pale and trembling, as if she had just been insulted. M. Victor Hugo could not at first understand it, but he afterwards heard that the actress was intimate with an uncle of Mademoiselle Morel, and that she looked on her as a kind of niece. Being ignorant at the time of the state of the case, he maintained his opinion, but Mademoiselle Mars became so indignant that she fell ill, and was for some days unable to act.

LXII.

LA ESMERALDA.

The exceptional success of *Nôtre-Dame de Paris* had brought on M. Victor Hugo numerous requests from several musicians, and amongst others, from one very celebrated one, M. Meyerbeer, who, indeed, had desired that the novel should be an opera. He had always declined. But M. Bertin requested it of him on behalf of his daughter, and he did for friendship what he had never done for money.

When the music was composed, there was a preparatory performance. The evening party was preceded by a dinner party, at which were present Victor Hugo, Eugène Delacroix, Rossini, Berlioz, Antony Deschamps, &c. It was observable that throughout the dinner, Rossini persisted in addressing M. Delacroix as M. Delaroche. M. Bourqueney, Mr. Lesourd, M. Alfred de Wailly, Antony Deschamps, and one of M. Bertin's nieces, sang selections from the opera, which were loudly praised. Rossini had a delightful voice, and was very good-natured in singing when asked. They begged him

to favour them with a song; but he refused. M. and
Madame Bertin pressed him to do so; several pretty
women almost went on their knees to him; he replied
that he had a cold, and could not get out a single note.
He almost immediately left the room, and hardly had
he reached the ante-chamber, when he struck up an air
from one of his operas in a clear and ringing voice.

The rehearsals of *La Esmeralda* took place in the
summer of 1836. The author of the words was not
present, as he was travelling in Brittany. On his return,
he was astonished at the meanness of the getting-up of
the piece. The Paris of former days lent itself to decorations and costumes; now, there was nothing rich or
picturesque. The rags of the Cour des Miracles, which
might have been characteristic and novel at the opera,
were all manufactured of new cloth, so that great lords
resembled poor men, and vagrants had all the appearance
of respectable citizens. Victor Hugo had given them an
idea of decoration, which would, probably, have had
great effect. It was for the scene in which Quasimodo
carries off Esmeralda from storey to storey, to the top of
the tower; in order to make Quasimodo seem to ascend,
it was only necessary to make the cathedral descend. In
his absence, the thing had been declared an impossibility. This decoration, which was considered impossible at the Opera, was afterwards carried out at the
Ambigu.

The opera, in which M. Nourrit, M. Levasseur,
M. Massol, and Mademoiselle Falcon all sang, was
applauded by those who were present at its first per-

formance, but there was a general gloom felt at the time, occasioned by the news of the death of Charles X.

The newspapers were extremely violent against the music. Party spirit was mixed up with it, and the unpopularity of the father's journal was exhibited by abusing the daughter. After this, the public began hissing. The opposition increased each night; and on the eighth, the curtain fell before the close of the performances. All that M. Duponchel, the manager, could do—and he owed his licence to M. Bertin—was, to perform, now and then, before the ballet, a single act, in which the author had combined the principal effects of the whole drama.

The novel is founded on the word *ananké*. The opera finishes by the word *fatalité*. There was fatality in the failure of a work which had M. Nourrit and Mademoiselle Falcon for singers; a woman of great talent for the composer; Victor Hugo for the writer of the libretto; and *Nôtre-Dame* for the subject. A fatality clung to the actors. Mademoiselle Falcon lost her voice; M. Nourrit went to Italy to kill himself; a ship called the *Esmeralda* was lost in crossing from England to Ireland, and every soul perished; the Duke of Orleans gave the name of *Esmeralda* to a very valuable mare, and during a steeple-chase she ran against a horse at full gallop, and broke her head.

LXIII

THE BROTHER'S DEATH.

In 1837, M. Victor Hugo lost his brother Eugène. I have previously related that the poor fellow had become insane on the very night of his brother's marriage, and that General Hugo, who would not come to the wedding, came to Paris to see his sick son. After trying to take care of him at home, his father had been obliged to place him under the care of M. Esquirol, whose asylum bore a very high reputation. The principal doctor of the establishment, M. Royer-Collard, had paid particular attention to his case; the violent paroxysms had left him, and when his father or his brothers visited him, he would chat with them most affectionately, and even reasonably, except on one subject. He considered that he was shut up in a prison for having conspired against the Duchess de Berri. The General thought the best means of undeceiving him would be to set him at liberty; he had asked the doctor whether he should not be doing right in taking him home. M. Royer-Collard saw no objection to it in the present tranquil state of the convalescent, and the General had him carried off to Blois.

He allowed himself to be removed, without expressing either regret or satisfaction; indeed, when he left the asylum, his attitude and his physiognomy expressed torpor. The robust and valiant young man who had thrown himself so completely into the struggles of a literary existence, was now as gentle, and, in this state, unimpassioned, as a lamb. He remained thus at Blois, gentle, docile, and sensible; only obstinate in one particular, and that was in insisting on exposing himself to the sun, with his head uncovered, just as, when a child, he had insisted on taking off his stockings in the snow on the Mont Cenis. One day, however, while at dinner, he threw himself suddenly on his step-mother, armed with a knife, and endeavoured to kill her.

The General brought him back to Paris, and tried the Maison Saint-Maurice at Charenton, which was a military establishment. The medical establishment having to deal with officers, treated them in military style. The energetic methods adopted reduced the violence of the attack; but Eugène believe more firmly than ever that he was in a state prison. He would protest against his incarceration without having gone through a trial, he would try to escape, and was once stopped as he was trying to throw himself out of a window.

When he heard the shrieks of lunatics, he thought that they were people being assassinated, and he would beg his father and his brothers to take him away. Seeing that they gave him no assistance in his efforts at escape, he gradually began to feel a coolness towards them. He remained attached to his brother Victor for some little time longer; he took an interest in literature, and wished to read *Hernani*. But the governor having shown this brother over the establishment, and having accompanied him everywhere with the usual polite attention shown to a distinguished visitor, the poor invalid considered that his brother was too friendly with his enemies, and would neither see him nor any one else again. They were obliged to give up visiting him as it only exasperated him.

Contrary to custom, his health partook of the weakness of his brain, his strong constitution became enfeebled; he was a long while in wasting away, for his youth and vigour bore him up, but he lingered only till February, 1837.

Thus died the companion of Victor Hugo's childhood and youth. The two brothers, so closely united, had been apparently adapted to the same kind of life, they had had the same amusements as children. They had been taught by the same masters; they had the same poetical aspirations, and the same instinct of higher aspirations: they had never been parted a single day until their mother's death. Fate then suddenly separated them. To one was allotted an existence of excitement and publicity, while the other was doomed to darkness and isolation.

LXIV

THE FÊTE AT VERSAILLES.

In the summer of 1837, Louis Philippe desired to celebrate at Versailles the marriage of the Duke of Orleans. Victor Hugo was invited. The day before, Alexandre Dumas called on him in a state of great irritation. There were to be some promotions in the Légion d'Honneur; and the King having noticed his name on one of the lists presented to him had drawn a line through it. This offence had justified him in returning the invitation that had been sent him. M. Victor Hugo said that he should not go either, and wrote to inform the Duke of Orleans of the reason of his refusal.

That evening one of the secretaries of the Prince hastened to the Rue Royale. The Duke of Orleans, on receiving M. Hugo's letter, had immediately set out in search of the King, and had spoken urgently to him on the subject, begging him to restore the name of M. Alexandre Dumas to the list. The secretary had not yet started on his way home, when M. Dumas returned, full of joy.

He had just heard from the Duke of Orleans that the cross was obtained, and that he was at liberty to wear it from that moment. Every difficulty having been met, M. Victor Hugo promised the messenger that he would go to Versailles. He inquired whether any particular style of dress was to be worn, and was told that anything would do except plain clothes.

The *fête* was to take place the next day. There was but little time left to procure a suitable costume. But M. Victor Hugo had formerly belonged to the Garde Nationale in 1830, and had been promoted to some rank in it. I no longer recollect what it was, but he found this uniform where it had been put away. M. Alexandre Dumas and he examined the uniform throughout, from the epaulettes to the belt: it was still very presentable. Both would appear in uniform, and they would be doubly brothers from being dressed alike.

The *fête* commenced by a general inspection of the interior of the palace. Although the crowd was so great, they wandered at ease through those vast royal apartments, and also through the interminable galleries. There were to be seen everything which literature, painting, sculpture, music, science, or politics had rendered illustrious. One of the first persons the two National Guards encountered was M. de Balzac, dressed as a marquis. The dress was probably a hired one, and was certainly made for some one else.

After a tolerably long walk, M. Victor Hugo seated himself with M. Alexandre Dumas, M. Eugène Delacroix, and three or four other friends who had joined the group. Their conversation was interrupted by the entry of the King and royal family. The Duke of Orleans was walking arm-in-arm with his wife. The King, who was by nature very amiable, and who was particularly happy just then, made some very polite speeches to his guests, and especially to M. Hugo, who fancied he perceived that the King was pleased rather than not at his costume of the National Guard. When the compliments came to a conclusion, he asked him what he thought of Versailles, on which M. Victor Hugo courteously replied, that the age of Louis XIV. had provided a beautiful work, and that the King had set it in a magnificent binding.

The Duchess of Orleans advanced towards Victor Hugo and told him that she was happy to see him; that there were two people with whom she wished to become acquainted—M. Cousin and himself; that she had often spoken of him to Monsieur de Goethe; that she had read all his works; that she knew his poems by heart; that her favourite one of all was "Chants du Crépuscule," commencing thus :—

> "C'était une humble église au cintre surbaissé,
> L'église où nous entrâmes."

She then added, "I have visited *your* Nôtre-Dame."
At four o'clock an usher came up with the announcement, "*Le Roi est servi.*" At six o'clock they rose from table. Then there was a crowd and a medley. The play began directly after dinner; everybody wished to be so placed as to see, not the stage, but the royal box, or

rather, perhaps, some wished to be so seated that they could be seen by its owners. They hurried, they pushed, they elbowed each other, they trod on each other's feet, they tore each other's clothes. This furious assault was put a stop to when they reached a great glass door, which remained closed whilst the King and his family were seating themselves. In a quarter of an hour's time it opened, and then began the real elbowing. They still had to traverse the long gallery, the waxed floor of which shone so brightly and looked so transparent, that people might have attempted to swim in it; it was as slippery as ice; it was a regular breakneck affair, especially for old people. Marshals, knights, dignitaries, venerable persons, decorated with their various orders, pressed on all sides, and jostled over this dangerous surface, lost their equilibrium, and measured their lengths on the ground. Nearly twenty fell down. M. Victor Hugo helped to raise several of them; but seeing M. d'Argout stretched on the floor, he recollected that it was he who had forbidden the performance of *Le Roi s'amuse,* and he left him where he was.

The theatre in the palace is large and handsome. The decorations are of the most charming rococo style, producing a really grand effect, with a kind of coquetry that is very pleasing. It had been regilt for the occasion, and the number of lustres and candelabra had been much increased. Mademoiselle Mars and the *élite* of the troop from the Théâtre Français acted *Le Misanthrope* that evening; but the performance fell flat. The liveliness of a theatre consists in the swarms of people who attend it. The

Theatre Royal, which was intended for a privileged and restricted audience, had only two rows of boxes, separated by thick columns; so that when full it looks empty. No cohesion or communication between the spectators took place, none of those electric currents were felt which make all hearts beat in unison. Another reason for the general dullness was, that the only female guests were the wives of the ministers and ambassadors. Therefore, lively and clear colours of silks, the flowers in the hair, the glittering jewellery on arms and neck, the white shoulders, the airy motion of fans, all these were absent from the scene. To crown all, people feared to applaud unless the King gave the signal, and this he seldom did. After the performance, generals and high functionaries were heard to say:—"That is the *Misanthrope*, is it? I had often heard the play spoken of, and I fancied it was amusing."

The evening finished by a torchlight procession in the picture galleries. Whenever the King pointed out any picture to a guest, a servant, entirely dressed in red, turned the reflection of a lamp, which he held in his hand, so that it exactly fell on the canvas. At eleven o'clock the fête came to an end, and every one set out in search of his own carriage, which it was difficult to find in the midst of the confusion. Alexandre Dumas and Victor Hugo did not find theirs till one o'clock in the morning, and only reached Paris at daybreak.

M. Victor Hugo, who still was only a Chevalier of the Legion of Honour, was promoted to the rank of an Officer, the grade which he still retains.

On the 27th June, 1837, M. Victor Hugo published *Les Voix Intérieures*. That day, two footmen, wearing the livery of the Duke of Orleans, were seen approaching the Place Royale, accompanied by some porters, carrying a large picture. This picture was painted by M. Saint-Evre, and its subject was Inez de Castro. It had been considered the gem of an exhibition. On the gilding of the frame was inscribed, "*Le Duc et la Duchesse d'Orléans à M. Victor Hugo, 27 Juin, 1837.*"

LXV.

RUY BLAS.

M. ALEXANDRE DUMAS, also, was not long before he had reason to complain of M. Harel, and this without quitting the Porte Saint-Martin. He was, moreover, on bad terms with the Comédie Française. One day, he called on Victor Hugo, and mentioned a conversation he had with the Duke of Orleans. The Prince, having asked him why he now never wrote anything for the theatre, he had replied that modern literature owned no theatre; that it had never been in its right place in the Théâtre Français; that sometimes it had been tolerated there, but never cordially welcomed; that its proper position would have been the Porte Saint-Martin; but that the behaviour of the manager had driven away every man of talent or even of self-respect, and that it had become a mere exhibition of strolling menageries. He added, that, what with the Théâtre Français, which was devoted to the dead, and the Porte Saint-Martin, which had delivered itself over to the brute creation, modern dramatic art was completely turned out of doors. He said that he alone did not complain; but that all authors of dramas felt as he did, Victor Hugo being at their head. His plays, indeed, were only to be found here and there, although he would have written two a-year had there been a theatre where they could be acted.

The Duke of Orleans had replied that that state of things could not possibly last, that contemporaneous art had a right to a theatre, and that he should mention it to M. Guizot.

"Now, then," said Alexandre Dumas, "it will be necessary that you should see Guizot. I have persuaded the Prince; do you persuade his Minister."

"A theatre is all very well," said M. Hugo, "but one must have a manager."

Alexandre Dumas knew no one on whom he could rely.

"Do you know of any one yourself?" asked he of Victor Hugo.

"I do and I don't. I receive a theatrical newspaper which entirely enters into my views, and which upholds us both, evidently conscientiously and without any idea of ultimate advantage; for the worthy fellow who manages this paper never even comes to be thanked for his pains, and I don't remember to have seen him more than four times. I trust in him, then, positively because I don't know him. They tell me his hopes are centred on becoming the manager of a theatre. I am alluding to the director of the *Vert-Vert*."

"Anténor Joly?" said M. Alexandre Dumas. "Why, he has not a penny."

"Give him a licence, and he will soon find the money."

M. Alexandre Dumas raised some objections, but being very easily influenced soon gave way. When he was gone Victor Hugo began to consider that they had been somewhat hasty in disposing of a theatre which had no existence. Princes, who receive petitions from almost every quarter, are polite in their replies, and people sometimes consider this politeness as equivalent to a promise. Most likely the Duke of Orleans had forgotten all about that morning's conversation. M. Victor Hugo did not call on M. Guizot, and forgot all about it himself.

Some time afterwards a mutual friend told him that M. Guizot was astonished at not seeing him, and that he wished to speak to him. He called on him the next day.

"How now?" said M. Guizot, as he entered the room, "so you will have nothing to say to your theatre?"

M. Guizot told him openly and very cordially that he was quite right to have asked for a theatre; that never was there a more legitimate request; that a new style of art required a new style of theatre; that the Comédie-Française, which was the seat of tradition and conservatism, was not the proper arena for original literature of the present day; that the Government was only doing its duty in creating a theatre for those who had created a department of art.

"And now," said M. Guizot, "let us regulate the terms on which the licence is to be held."

The Minister and the author agreed upon the subject, and M. Guizot wrote with his own hand the conditions on which the theatre was to be held. They were very liberal but exclusively literary. M. Hugo, however, requested that the right to perform music should be included; he remembered the effect produced in *Lucrezia Borgia* in the scene where the drinking-song is interrupted by the notes of a psalm; he had visions of linking songs and words still more closely together: he wished that a complete union of the different styles of art was a possible thing, from the symphonies in the *Tempest* to the choruses of *Prometheus*. M. Guizot granted all he asked.

"And now," said he, "all we require is the signature of the Minister of the Interior; but I have already spoken to him on the subject, and he agrees with me. Go and see him to-morrow, and he will give you your licence."

"My licence?" asked Victor Hugo.

"Why not? We give you the theatre."

"I cannot accept it. My business is with art, and I can't manage the business part of the subject. I will have no privileges granted to me either as manager or author. I do not ask for a theatre for myself, but for the rising generation, which is not provided with one."

"So be it," said M. Guizot; "but in order to give away a theatre we must find some one to whom to give it. Have you a manager?"

"Yes, M. Anténor Joly."

"I don't know him, but if you are responsible for

him that is sufficient. Take him to see M. Gasparin to-morrow."

M. Victor Hugo on his return home wrote a few lines to M. Anténor Joly, who hastened to call on him the next morning.

" I have a bit of news for you," said he to him, " you are the proprietor of a theatre."

M. Joly's gratitude equalled his astonishment. His dreams were fulfilled! M. Victor Hugo stopped him short in his thanks by telling him that they were both expected at the office of the Minister of the Interior. M. Anténor Joly had a cab standing at the door; both got into it, and were soon seated in M. Gasparin's private room.

While the licence was being fetched from the office, Victor Hugo repeated to M. de Gasparin all he had said to M. Guizot.

"It is well understood that the theatre is for the benefit of literature—not for my benefit. M. Anténor Joly will apply to me for plays if it suits him, but he is as much at liberty not to ask me for them as I am to refuse them. He will be a manager like any one else, and I shall be an author like any one else. He only undertakes to do one thing, and that is to make of his theatre the theatre of living literature."

They came from the offices to say that the licence was not ready, and could not be ready in less than an hour. It was agreed that M. Anténor Joly should return in the course of the day.

As he was going out, the manager-elect said to M. Victor Hugo,—

"As you tell me that I am at liberty to apply to whomsoever I please, I apply to you for my opening picee."

Victor Hugo replied that it would be time enough to think about the opening of the theatre when a proper building should have been found; and M. Anténor Joly left him to go in search of money, a piece of ground, and actors.

All this took place in October, 1836. Five or six month elapsed before M. Victor Hugo received any news of M. Joly. One day M. Gasparin was announced, who opened the conversation by saying, "I thought you required a theatre for literature." And he showed him on the margin of the licence, which was not yet signed, a memorandum, requesting permission to represent comic operas. M. Victor Hugo replied that there must be some mistake, that he had begged that music should be permitted, but merely to assist and to be in subordination to the drama, not as its mistress. The Minister then said that he also was surprised at the memorandum, and that he should consider about it.

M. Victor Hugo was now a full year without hearing anything of the subject. In June, 1838, M. Anténor Joly reappeared. It had taken him twenty-two months to find the money. He had been offered assistance, but on condition that the person who made the offer should be co-manager. This would not have mattered, if this person had not been a writer of vaudevilles, who had grown rich as an undertaker, and whose ideal was the comic opera. This was the person who had begged for the authorization which the Minister had at first refused to grant, but M. Anténor Joly not having succeeded in finding any one else, had been obliged to put up with this partner and his exactions, and had, by earnest entreaty, obtained from the Minister the right to perform operas. But it would be a dead letter ; the partner himself quite understood that a theatre for dramas was expected, and that he must positively commence by a drama ; this point once gained, and the drama properly installed, he, Anténor Joly, would be on the spot to uphold it. The important thing was to get possession of the theatre, and everything depended on the opening drama. M. Victor Hugo's name was absolutely necessary, &c.

M. Victor Hugo, to whom M. Anténor Joly introduced his partner the next day, promised to let them have a play, and began to write *Ruy Blas*, the subject of which had been running in his head for some time. His first idea had been that the play should commence with the third act. Enter Ruy Blas, Prime Minister, Duke of Olmedo, all-powerful, and beloved by the Queen ; a footman appears, gives his orders to this all-powerful being ; desires him to close the window, and to pick up his handkerchief. Everything would have been explained afterwards. On due reflection, the author preferred beginning at the beginning ; to produce his effect by degrees rather than at once, and at first exhibit the minister as a minister, and the footman as a footman.

He wrote the first line on the 4th July, and the last on the 11th August. Of all his dramas this one took the longest to write. The last act, similar to the fourth of *Marion de Lorme*, was written in one day; but the fourth act of *Marion de Lorme* is much longer than the fifth of *Ruy Blas*.

Whilst M. Hugo was writing *Ruy Blas*, M. Joly would often call on him, to consult him on the site to be selected for the new theatre, and would bring architects to see him, &c. M. Victor Hugo was in favour of a plot of ground, which happened to be free, near the Porte Saint-Denis, and he wished the theatre to be called *Théâtre de la Porte Saint-Denis*. The affair never came to any-thing, to his great disgust; and the two managers were reduced to the Théâtre Ventadour, which was in a bad situation, in a court-yard, through which no one passed. All that could be done for it was to change its name, and to call this tomb *Théâtre de la Renaissance*.

M. Anténor Joly came one morning with a small rough model of a new style of theatre. According to him, the foot-lights were unmeaning; this row of lamps coming out of the ground was an absurdity; in reality light was always from above not from below the object; these foot-lights were a contradiction, and made the actors cease to be human beings. The model was on a new system. The lamps, concealed in the slips, would illuminate the stage like the sun from above, and would give to the stage the effect of being actually a street, a wood, or a room.

Victor Hugo objected to the removal of the foot-lights;

he replied that this crude reality of the representation
would interfere with the poetic reality of the piece; that
the drama was not real life, but life transformed by art;
that it was, therefore, right that the actors should be
altered in appearance; that they were so already with
their powder and rouge; that they were still more so by
the foot-lights, and that this line of fire which divided
the body of the theatre from the stage was the natural
frontier between the real and the ideal.

Before promising *Ruy Blas*, the author had made inquiries as to the performers. They had shown him a
list of actors of vaudevilles and provincials. He had
asked for M. Frédérick Lemaître. This had been, in
fact, his only condition. He had required from this
theatre, which he had given away for nothing, and for
which M. Anténor Joly was once offered the sum of
60,000 francs, the same agreement as that he had made
with the Théâtre Français, and the Porte Saint-Martin.

M. Frédérick Lemaître was starring in the provinces; but a line from M. Anténor Joly brought him
back post haste. As the theatre had to be entirely rebuilt in the interior, and was in the hands of the work-
men, the author, in order to avoid having to read to the
accompaniment of blows of the hammer, had the actors
at his own house. M. Frédérick was enchanted with the
three first acts, anxious at the fourth, sombre at the fifth,
and finally made his escape without saying a word.

It was impossible to rehearse at the theatre. M. Anténor Joly had obtained leave to do so in the hall of the
Conservatoire. There the author distributed the parts

the next day. M. Frédérick Lemaître received his with
a resigned look; but he had barely glanced over it, when
he exclaimed with a cry of surprise and delight :—

"Then I am to act Ruy Blas?"

He thought he was to be Don César. As it always
happens after any great success, his wonderful creation
of Robert Macaire was perpetually thrown at him.
People never ceased telling him that now he could only
act in that; that he was now quite incapable of taking
a serious part. When he saw how Don César gradually
developed in the fourth act, he had said to himself that
M. Victor Hugo felt as others did, and had allotted to
him the comic character. The part was a fine one, but
still it was a ragamuffin. Instead of being merely disen-
cumbered by Ruy Blas of the rags he wore as Robert
Macaire, he was about to be renewed and regenerated.
He thanked M. Victor Hugo warmly for delivering him
at length from irony and derision, and for reconciling
him with passion and poetry.

Literature was not allowed the use of the "Conservatoire" for long, and *Ruy Blas* was entreated to take
its departure. Its only refuge was the "Renaissance,"
which was now more than ever a prey to the masons,
smiths, carpenters, gilders, and upholsterers. In the
midst of this hubbub the last rehearsals took place.
One day, at the commencement of the third act, as M.
Victor Hugo considered that two of the actors stationed
themselves awkwardly, he got up, in order to settle their
positions himself. Hardly had he risen for the purpose,
when a great bar of iron fell from the arch directly on to

the chair in which he had been sitting. Had it not been for the ungracefulness of his actors he would have been killed on the spot.

The drama ran as great risks as the author. M. Anténor Joly had not fought against musical encroachment to the extent of his promises. At the same time that they were getting up *Ruy Blas* they were rehearsing a comic opera; and the co-director, who was in reality the ruling spirit, since he was the monied man of the two, very seldom attended the rehearsals of *Ruy Blas*, but was very punctual in his attendance at the rehearsals of *L'Eau Merveilleuse*.

The musical mania of the true direction was revealed in everything. Once on his arrival, M. Victor Hugo saw some carpenters and upholsterers busily occupied in dividing the benches of the pit into stalls. M. Anténor Joly explained to him that the theatre, considering how badly situated it was, could not reckon upon the audience who were in the habit of frequenting the theatres on the Boulevards; that his connection would lie amongst fashionable people and rich citizens; that it was therefore necessary to build a theatre suitable for them. Victor Hugo replied, that fashionable people might occupy the orchestra and balcony-stalls if they pleased, and also the private boxes, but that he intended that the general public should be allowed to sit in its accustomed places, namely, the pit and the galleries; that he considered them as the real, living, impressionable public, without literary prejudices, and just what was wanted for free art; that perhaps they were not the audience who gene-

rally attended operas, but that they were the audience fit
for the drama; that spectators of this kind were not
accustomed to be shut off and left isolated in their stalls;
that he never felt more full of ardour, intelligence, and
satisfaction then when he was pushed about by, and
mixed up with, the rest of the audience; and that if he
was to be deprived of his pit, he would deprive them of
his play. The benches were therefore not divided into
stalls.

There was now no reckoning on the young men who
had been present at *Hernani*. Some had become celebrated, and age had come upon all. Amongst the
strange crew of 1830, some were now masters, and
were interested in their own works; others, not having
been able to make a living out of art, had given up all
idea of it, and now, as merchants, manufacturers, married
men, were doing penance for their former sins of enthusiasm and literature. Even those who were still pursuing
literature as their career in life, had deserted the *bohêmes*
and enrolled themselves amongst the *bourgeoisie*—had
cut their hair close—had taken to coats and hats of the
shapes worn by other people—had wives or mistresses
whom they could neither take seats for in the pit nor yet
in the galleries. These now considered outrageous applause as a mark of bad taste; and would sometimes clap
with the tips of their gloved fingers.

A new generation was rising. Some years before, a
young man, about sixteen years of age, who was finishing his studies at the Collège Charlemagne, near the
Place Royale, had called on M. Victor Hugo. This was

M. Auguste Vacquerie. He had shortly after returned, accompanied by one of his school-fellows, M. Paul Meurice. Both afterwards became and remained the truest and most intimate friends M. Victor Hugo ever had. M. Auguste Vacquerie travelled eighty leagues to be present at the representation of *Ruy Blas*.

On the night of the first performance, the body of the theatre was still incomplete; the doors of the boxes, hastily run together, grated on their hinges, and would not shut; the stoves gave out no heat, and the November cold chilled the spectators. Women were obliged to put on their cloaks, furs, and bonnets, and men their great-coats. It was remarked that the Duke of Orleans was polite enough to wear nothing but his dress-coat during the whole of the evening. The play soon thawed the spectators. The three first acts, which were well—very well performed by M. Frédérick, took possession of the whole audience. The fourth, which was acted by M. Saint-Firmin, went off less successfully, although he put into it both intelligence and spirit; but at the fifth act, M. Frédérick Lemâitre rivalled the greatest comedians, and success was more decided than ever. The way in which he tore off his livery, drew the bolt, and struck his sword on the table, the way in which he said to Don Sallustre—

> " Tenez,
> Pour un homme d'esprit, vraiment vous m'étonnez!"

the way in which he came back to entreat the Queen's pardon, and finally drank off the poison, everything had so much greatness, truth, depth, and splendour, that

the poet had the rare joy of seeing the ideal of which he
had dreamt become a living soul.

It is worthy of notice, that the pit and the stalls were
less enthusiastic in their applause than the private boxes.
The success, on this occasion, came rather from the
public.   The author had several friends in the body
of the theatre, some of whom were known to him,
others not.

But the success of the drama was nothing in comparison to that of the comic opera which was performed
the next night.   In honour of it, the doors consented to
shut, the hinges to keep silence, the stoves to throw out
heat, and the pit to applaud.   *L'Eau Merveilleuse* succeeded frantically.

The press was for the most part in favour of *Ruy Blas*.
People came to see it rather perhaps for its own merits,
than drawn thither by the music.   After the second
time of acting, there was always a hiss heard when Ruy
Blas picks up the handkerchief of Don Sallustre, and
several marks of disapprobation were heard during the
fourth act.   The hisses increased at the succeeding
representations, and the fourth act was daily more and
more attacked.   The actors would say that it was owing
to the music, which wished to crush the drama in order
to have the theatre to itself.   M. Frédérick, who left the
stage after the third act, pointed out to the author an
individual, who was seated in the pit, whom he asserted
he had witnessed in the act of hissing.   This was the
claqueur of *L'Eau Merveilleuse*. The next time there was
a performance, the *claqueur* was seated in the same spot,

although his attendance was only compulsory at the opera. M. Victor Hugo, who wished to disburden his mind of the affair, adjourned to the body of the theatre, at the third act. As usual, the scene between Ruy Blas and Don Sallustre met with resistance. Just as Ruy Blas was about to pick up the handkerchief, M. Victor Hugo saw the *claqueur* put a little instrument to his mouth, and a shrill hiss resounded. The author was not the only witness of the act. M. Frédérick, who had to say to Don Sallustre,—

> "Sauvons ce peuple! Osons être grands, et frappons!
> Otons l'ombre à l'intrigue et le masque" . . .

did not address himself to Don Sallustre at the close of the lines, but advanced towards the foot-lamps, looked the *claqueur* full in the face, and said to him,—

> . . . "Aux fripons!"

Ruy Blas was performed fifty times. The hissing continued up to the last, and the fourth act never failed to be brilliantly successful.

M. Victor Hugo was about to sell the manuscript to his own publisher, M. Renduel, when another publisher, M. Delloye, came to beg for it, and also for the publication of his complete works, for eleven years, in behalf of a society, whose manager he was. M. Delloye offered 200,000 francs; he added 40,000, and M. Hugo, on his part, added two unpublished volumes.

LXVI

LES BURGRAVES.

ONE of these volumes was a new collection in verse, *Les Rayons et les Ombres.* If my book professed to deal in criticism, there would here be a great gap, for I hardly speak of the lyrical works of the great author. I do not, however, give any opinion as to his works. I merely relate them, and the reader may have remarked how scrupulously I have abstained from all opinion and all eulogy. In this biography, which is purely and simply that of the creations of Victor Hugo, I am obliged to dwell at greatest length on those which possess the greatest number of incidents, and the principal incidents are connected with the theatre, because that was his real difficulty, and it was there that his great struggles have taken place. As a lyric poet, he was accepted from the very first, and the early success has increased from volume to volume. *Les Orientales, Les Feuilles d'Automne, Les Chants du Crépuscule, Les Voix Intérieures, Les Rayons et les Ombres,* and *Les Contemplations,* have had, no doubt, detractors, but these have been a minority.

Besides this, those who oppose books have not the power of those who object to plays; they do not possess the dreaded whistle, by means of which three or four enemies are able to make themselves heard through the applause of a whole house, disconcerting the actors, interrupting the emotion, deforming the piece; they cannot bring down the curtain before the end of the play. The book, if attacked, contradicted, or insulted, still remains. The sympathetic reader is not troubled by the ill-natured reader. Furious articles only make the book more read, and editions multiply under invectives.

I have nothing important to say about *Les Rayons et les Ombres*, nor on *Le Rhin*, and I pass at once to *Les Burgraves*, whose rehearsals form the last episode in the theatrical life of Victor Hugo.

Les Burgraves was written in October, 1842, and read at the Comédie Française, 20th November. The author this time had no fault to find with the theatre, the actors, the manager. M. Buloz, the secretary, M. Verteuil, and indeed everybody, gave him every assistance with the best possible feeling. But he met with a serious hostility in a part of the public.

Politics meddled with it. I have said that M. Victor Hugo had seen in the new kingdom the result of a compromise between the monarchic tradition and the revolutionary right; a useful transition from legitimate royalty to popular sovereignty. Already a republican in theory, he had no actual objection to Louis Philippe. Provided that the monarchy consented to progress, he would willingly postpone the republic.

He was not even one of the regular constitutional opposition. The following letter, written to M. Thiers, in July, 1833, expresses the state of mind in which he remained :—

"Sir,

"It is not on any personal matter that I address you, it is in the interest of another—I may say in your own interest; for I believe it to be the greatest service to a Minister of State to point out to him an opportunity of employing his power to advantage.

"The matter indeed is simple and easy to arrange. It is this :—

"M. Anthony Thouret, formerly editor in chief of the journal *La Revolution de* 1830, has still at this moment to endure twenty-one months of imprisonment, on account of an offence against the laws of the press. He is at La Force. I have just seen him, and I assure you that in simple truth, and without any exaggeration, he is ill-treated, deprived of everything, and suffering under the prison regulations to which he is subjected, in common with the thieves and those sentenced to the galleys. But that which most severely tries M. Thouret is, that he is not allowed to see his family, who inhabit Douai. He is shut out from the three dearest and most sacred members of his family, his mother, his wife, and his child. There is a prison at Douai, and he has written to the Keeper of the Seals to be transferred thither. The Keeper of the Seals has sent him to you. His request is before you. It is not a favour that he solicits. He asks neither a diminution nor commutation of the penalty. He asks only that he be sometimes permitted to see and to embrace his old mother, who is 73 years of age, his young wife, and his sick little child. You will not refuse him this.

" I, who address you, sir, do not, at the present time, thank God, take any definite political part. I regard them as all acting with impartiality, full of affection for France, and anxious for progress. I applaud sometimes those in power, sometimes the opposition, according as those in power or in opposition seem to me to act best for the country. I repeat, I am of no party, and I ardently desire that things may end by our all understanding each other. Meanwhile, I think that the best advice I can give to those in power is, that they treat well both those who have ceased to be and those who have not yet been in office.

" Receive, &c.,

" V. H."

Le Roi s'amuse, prohibited four months after this letter was written, had given the author a moment of anger, but he had soon resumed his usual calmness and indulgent feelings. In January, 1834 (*Etude sur Mirabeau*), he repeated:—"At the present time every kind of criticism is possible, but a wise man should have a considerate regard for the whole epoch. He ought to hope, to trust, to wait. He should make allowances for men of theory, in consideration of the slowness with which ideas are propagated; for practical men, because of that narrow and useful love of things as they are, with-

out which society becomes disorganized by successive ex-
periments.   He should also make allowance for passions,
because of their frequent, though generous, departure from
the established line; and for interests, as being obliged to
calculate on tying men down to their duties for want of
faith in them.   He should make allowance for governments, which must grope about in the dark after what is
good; for oppositions, who must ever keep the goad in
their hands, and must point out the furrow to the ox.
He must give credit to the moderate party for the way in
which they smooth over transitions; to the extreme
parties for the activity with which they advance the cir-
culation of ideas, which are the very life-blood of civilization; to lovers of the past for the care which they
bestow on roots in which there is still life; to people
zealous for the future, for their love of those beautiful
flowers which will some day produce fine fruits; to
mature men for their moderation, to young men for their
patience; to these for what they do, to those for what
they desire to do; to all the difficulty of everything."

Four years after (June, 1837), in his preface to *Les
Voix Intérieures*, he still had the same aim in view. "To
agree with all parties in what is liberal and generous,
but with none in what is illiberal and mischievous."   In
1840, in the preface to *Les Rayons et les Ombres*, he still
assigned the poet this ideal: "No engagement, no chain.
Liberty should pervade both his ideas and his actions.
He should be free in his good-will towards those who
are really working, free in his aversion towards those
who are hurtful, free in his love towards those who serve,

free in his pity towards those who suffer. He should be at liberty to bar the road to all lies, from whatever place or whatever party they emanate; free to harness himself to drag out of the mire principles buried there by private interests, free to alleviate all misery, free to kneel down in adoration before every act of self-devotion. There would be no hatred towards the King mixed up with his affection for the people."

The form of government appeared to him, besides, a secondary affair; he would dive to the bottom of things; he was a "socialist" before the word was ever thought of. "If, in that council of intelligences, where everything that affects the general interest of civilization in the nineteenth century is written or spoken upon, it should be his turn to speak, he would confine himself strictly to the order of the day, and only demand one thing to begin with, namely, the substitution of questions ·involving social interests for mere political discussions" (Preface to *Littérature et Philosophie Mélées*, April, 1834).

The parties themselves paid more attention to political than to social questions. The abolition of the penalty of death, universal peace, gratuitous instruction, the rights of the child, the rights of women, &c., appeared in the eyes of those most advanced as mere chimeras of poets. Neither would they accept that benevolent neutrality which included anybody and everybody. He who did not support them was their enemy. The Republicans especially, of whom there were then very few, were notorious for that intolerance and violence which indeed seem necessary for oppressed minorities. In the heat of the

argument they were incapable of seeing that M. Victor
Hugo, who was a "socialist" since 1828 (*Le Dernier
Jour d'un Condamné*), was further advanced in democracy
than they themselves, and that they were attacking one
of their own party.   The *National* stopped short at the
programme of M. Armand Carrel: progress in politics,
recoil in literature.   He hated the drama, and could only
be said to admire the tragedy of the "Great Reign."

The moment was propitious for tragedy.   A very
talented actress, Mademoiselle Rachel, was reviving a
taste for Corneille and Racine.   Whilst they were rehearsing *Les Burgraves*, a young man arrived from the
provinces with a tragedy, which not only had the merit
of being a tragedy but a republican tragedy.   The
subject was the expulsion of the Tarquins and the establishment of a republic in Rome.   They got hold of
the play and of its author.   *Lucrèce* had public readings
in different saloons; joy was at its full height; they
already possessed Mademoiselle Rachel and were about
to secure M. Ponsard; the tragedy was complete.   Louis
XIV. had come to life again; all this was done in the
name of the Republic.

The public allowed themselves to be persuaded.   For
five-and-twenty years it had always had the same name
ringing in its ears; it had grown tired of all this, and
gladly welcomed a new name.

M. Edouard Thierry, then the writer of feuilletons in a
newspaper which has since disappeared, *Le Messager*,
gave a very good explanation, in an article entitled
Aristide, of that ostracism with which Paris, in imitation

of Athens, punishes people whose renown lasts too long.

Everything, therefore, was against M. Hugo and in favour of M. Ponsard. Even the very actors of the drama went over to the side of tragedy. Madame Dorval and M. Bocage took the principal characters in *Lucrèce.*

Added to this was the fact that *Les Burgraves* was somewhat difficult to perform; those epic figures, taller than nature, would have required exceptional actors. M. Beauvallet, M. Geffroy, and M. Ligier, represented Job, Otbert, and Barbarossa, most cleverly and conscientiously. Mademoiselle Denain was charming and touching in Regina. But the height of the characters was overpowering. Mademoiselle Rachel, who had been present at the reading to the committee (the committee was then composed of all the company, both ladies and gentlemen), and who had expressed much approval of the play, had not asked for the character of Guanhumara, and M. Victor Hugo had not offered it to her. Guanhumara's age had frightened him, although she was still young enough to fear no wrinkles. M. Victor Hugo had tried to bring in Mademoiselle Georges, who was most anxious for it, and who would have been the real Guanhumara, but he had met with an unconquerable resistance from the company. They had three reasons against Mademoiselle Georges: these were, the little affair in Russia at the time of the Empire, her reputation for despotism at the Théâtre de la Porte Saint-Martin, and the despotism of Mademoiselle Rachel, who allowed no rival in tragedy. The author had then asked for Madame

Dorval, who remembering the annoyances she had had to put up with at the Théâtre Français had bargained for being her own mistress there, and only consented to act if admitted as one of the company.   The rest had refused to admit Madame Dorval to this position, and had conferred it on Madame Mélingue who acted Guanhumara very fairly.

The first performance succeeded but poorly.   Opposition declared itself at the second.   Sneers and hissing, although they never reached the pitch they had arrived at in *Hernani*, interrupted the piece nightly.   Disputes and collisions took place.   The actors and theatrical managers, however, bravely carried on the performances up to the very last.

The majority of newspapers were against the *Burgraves*.   M. Edouard Thierry warmly defended it.   M. Théophile Gautier wrote two enthusiastic articles on it in *La Presse*.

M. Victor Hugo after writing *Les Burgraves*, finally abandoned the theatre, although he possessed a drama, which he had concluded as long ago as in 1838, and which was called *Les Jumeaux*.   He no longer chose to expose the fruits of his brain to the insult and anonymous fault-finding, which had pursued him during a career of twenty years.   In addition to this he stood less in need of the theatre now, as he was about to make himself heard in the tribune.

LXVII.

THE ACADEMY.

I HAVE terminated the history of that part of the life of Victor Hugo which may be regarded as exclusively literary, or rather perhaps, I should say, specially literary; for, as we have seen, he had been mixed up with politics from his childhood. In the preface to *Marion de Lorme* he had said of himself that, "he was thrown into the literary world at sixteen years of age by his political passions." From his first odes, dictated by the exaggerated Royalism of his mother, all his works have been more or less mixed up with public events; even *Les Orientales*, which appeared to be the most indifferent to them and the most completely taken up by art, was a poem adapted to a particular period, and had reference to the independence of Greece.

He had been abandoning by degrees the realm of egoistic art. To those who reproached him for forgetting nature, the waters, the woods, and the stars, for the streets, and the calmness of the heavens for the chaos of party, he replied (April, 1839) :—

" Je vous aime, ô sainte nature !
    Je voudrais m'absorber en vous ;
    Mais, dans ce siècle d'aventure,
    Chacun, hélas ! se doit à tous.

    .   .   .   .   .   .

    Dieu le veut, dans les temps contraires,
    Chacun travaille et chacun sert.
    Malheur à qui dit à ses frères :
    Je retourne dans le désert !
    Malheur à qui prend ses sandales
    Quand les haines et les scandales
    Tourmentent le peuple agité !
    Honte au penseur qui se mutile,
    Et s'en va, chanteur inutile,
    Par la porte de la cité ! "

[*Translation.*]

You I love, O holy Nature !
Absorbed in you I fain would be ;
But in this century of adventure,
Servant to all we needs must be.

.   .   .   .

God wills that those who live in adverse times,
Should each a servant and a workman be ;
Sorrow to him who says to fellow-men,
I to my desert solitude will flee !
Sorrow to him who sandals to his feet
Girds on when angry hate and scandal foul
The people can torment and agitate !
Shame to the thinker, who can mutilate
Himself, and through the city's open gate,
With song depart, a vain and useless soul !

The indirect and tardy effects of literature soon ceased

to be sufficient for Victor Hugo; he was anxious to unite with it the immediate action of politics, and complete the writer by the orator.

He could conscientiously acknowledge Louis Philippe. He had more than paid his debt to the fallen monarchy. He did not consider himself to have done enough, because he refused the compensation offered to him when *Marion de Lorme* was prohibited; nor because the day after the Revolution he declined the reactionary success that had been offered him; nor yet for having, during the full effervescence of popular feeling (10 August, 1830), published the lines already quoted,—

> " Oh, laissez-moi pleurer sur cette race morte ! "
>
> . . . . .

On all occasions he had remembered that it was more than ever a time to pronounce the name of Bourbon with precaution, gravity, and respect, now that the old man who had been king had no crown but his white hairs (Preface to *Marion de Lorme*, November, 1831). A year afterwards, when the Duchess de Berri had been treasonably given up, he had vented all his indignation on " the man who had sold a woman."

> " Rien ne te disait donc dans l'âme, ô misérable !
> Que la proscription est toujours vénérable,
> Qu'on ne bat pas le sein qui nous donna son lait,
> Qu'une fille des rois dont on fut le valet
> Ne se met point en vente au fond d'un antre infâme,
> Et que n'étant plus reine elle était encor femme ! "

[Translation.]

Did nothing within you whisper, wretched man,
That venerable is the exiled one ?
That none should strike the breast that gave them suck?
That a king's daughter, whose valet you were,
Sells not herself within a cave of shame,
But if no longer queen, is woman still ?

When Charles X. died in exile (November, 1836), the
last adieu was said by no one with more emotion than by
the author of *Marion de Lorme* :—

"Et moi, je ne veux pas, harpe qu'il a connue,
  Qu'on mette mon roi mort dans une bière nue !
  Tandis qu'au loin la foule emplit l'air de ses cris,
  L'auguste Piété, servante des proscrits,
  Qui les ensevelit dans sa plus blanche toile,
  N'aura pas, dans la nuit que son regard étoile,
  Demandé vainement à ma pensée en deuil
  Un lambeau de velours pour couvrir ce cercueil ! "

[Translation.]

It shall not be, O harp he loved to hear,
That they should place my king on empty bier,
Whilst the crowd's shrieks from far off rend the air !
Imperial Piety, serving outlawed man,
Who wraps him in her purest, whitest sheet,
Shall not, at night, made starlight by her glance,
Have asked in vain of my sad, mourning heart,
A trifling velvet pall his coffin to conceal.

Victor Hugo was then free from the last tie that
bound him to the fallen monarchy, for the recollection of
the pension was balanced by the confiscation of a drama.
He was his own master to follow his convictions, which

indeed, had separated him from the Bourbons before their fall.

There were two tribunes, that of the Chamber of Deputies and that of the Chamber of Peers. Deputy he could not be, the electoral law of that day admitting only those who were richer than he was. *Nôtre Dame de Paris*, and *Les Feuilles d'Automne*, were not equivalent to land or a house. There was indeed a means of evading the law, commonly enough adopted by those whose friends possessed landed or house property—the friend might lend you a house. But even if Victor Hugo had borrowed a house of a friend, the qualified electors had little sympathy with literary men. Writers to them were dreamers, well enough adapted to amuse them in the intervals of serious business, when the mill had stopped or the groceries were not asked for, but from the very moment any one became a thinker, and above all a poet, he was radically incapable of having any common sense or of understanding anything whatever of practical matters. I do not know how it was that Lamartine managed to get elected; but he was already one poet too many, and they certainly would not have admitted a couple.

The Chamber of Peers was still open. But in order to be nominated, it was necessary to have attained to one of certain dignities from which the King selected. One of these only was accessible to M. Hugo—the Academy. He offered himself as a candidate in 1836; the Academy preferred M. Dupaty. He offered himself again in 1839; the Academy prefered M. Molé. He offered himself a third time in 1840, and this time the Academy preferred M. Flourens. In 1841, on knocking a fourth time at the door, it was at length opened to him.

His foot was then on the lowest step of the ladder, by which the tribune was to be reached. From that date commenced a new existence, which will be the object of a new publication. ⤴

THE END.

www.ingramcontent.com/pod-product-compliance
Lightning Source LLC
Chambersburg PA
CBHW021328110726
47900CB00005B/1390